The Snattered Eagle

Colin Payne

THE SHATTERED EAGLE

COLIN PAYNE

For June, Thomas, Sophie, William and Alice,
For their understanding, patience and support.
Love you all
X

THE SHATTERED EAGLE

COLIN PAYNE

Copyright © 2012 Colin Payne
All rights reserved.

First Published 2012
This edition 2014
Lord Doggett Publishing.

All characters in this publication are fictitious and any resemblance to persons living or dead is purely coincidental.

ISBN-10:1481192280
ISBN-13:978-1481192286

For more information please visit:
www.facebook.com/groups/theshatteredeagle

THE SHATTERED EAGLE

-ONE-
Two Years Ago...

There was really so much to do, with so little time available with which to do it, where had it all gone? Anna DuPont thought, as she busied herself around the house. It appeared life had become so hectic of late, the Trust was taking up more and more of her time as she strived to find suitable placements for the boys, yet she just couldn't ease up, couldn't allow herself that much needed rest. Public support had never been so buoyant, donors were despite the economic situation still extremely generous, the cause was becoming the must support charity in French high society, boasting the President himself among its patrons. The funds were pouring in, but the issue was that finding homes, genuinely suitable homes, for ex-Somali Child Soldiers wasn't so easy.

She knew herself the pitfalls, what could go wrong, of course she did, since she and Henri had adopted Alaine just over three years back it had become a genuine struggle with diminishing rewards. To her eternal relief *Ecole de l'Afrique* had been a God send, it allowed the boys not just a chance to spend time with peers, but the school did so much work in undoing the harm inflicted at such an early age. Amongst some of the finest education that France had to offer was also its most cutting edge thinking in tackling Post Traumatic Stress in minors, and it boasted first class Mental Health doctors on hand to ease the poor boys back into normality. The residential aspect also allowed the host families time, with the boys only returning home during the school vacations. It was this return for the five week summer holiday that Anna was preparing for.

As she busied herself with the housework she pondered how the transition to a normal life had been a far from simple one for Alaine, and it had been even harder for them.

He had come to them through Kenya, where he had been arrested at the age of 14 as part of a gang that attempted to kidnap a wealthy American tourist, Marcia Arbetter, from a Kenyan Safari Lodge. Fortunately for Alaine, Marcia was a supporter of *Compassion San Frontieres*, the charity that Anna was a director of.

After discovering Alaine's history, the incredibly magnanimous Marcia contacted Anna at her Paris office, concerned for the boy's plight. A combination of Marcia's forgiveness, Henri DuPont's standing within the French Government, *Compassion San Frontieres* reputation in Africa, and what can only be described as a massive bribe, saw Alaine flown to France via a French military transport plane. The rest of his gang were not so fortunate, with two being shot dead during the operation that saw Marcia regain her freedom, one imprisoned for 15 years - he had the bad luck of being over 18, and the charred remains of the last of them being discovered in a remote village near the Somali border after vigilantes prevented his flight home and beat him almost to death before placing a bald *Goodyear* tyre around his neck and igniting it.

Anna had to immediately find Alaine a home, which transpired to be her own, before even meeting him. There had been an unavoidable need for everything to be in place before the Kenyans would grant his exit, and she was desperate for it all not to fail, to save this boy that Marcia had deemed so worthy of her support. She knew it was a rushed decision, taken in haste, she was used to making quick choices, averting crisis and finding swift resolutions, it was what she was so good at, but even by her standards this one had admittedly been rash. At the time Henri had been far from supportive of her actions, in fact he was furious with her, whilst he backed her 100% in her work, he never thought she would be bringing this work home in such a pro-active fashion. But Anna had made her decision.

The following years were troubled, Alaine seldom communicated with his adoptive family, his relationship with Henri was built on mutual distrust and dislike, although Henri would always try and hide just how much he resented his unwanted ward. Anna, as much as she tried, could not break through Alaine's defences, she was a great believer in love curing everything, but in reality knew she didn't and probably never would actually love this boy. Clearly Alaine picked up on this, as he in turn was hostile when at home, offering nothing that could be seen as any positivity for them to latch onto. His school reports indicated that he was actually a reasonable pupil, though quiet and withdrawn, he got on with his work diligently, achieving good grades. He didn't mix with the other boys much, displaying a need for solitude, enjoying his own space and company. But when at the DuPont's he was nothing but aloof and hostile, apparently resentful and reluctant to offer any indication what so ever that he wanted to be part of a family, nor gratitude for the escape from hell they had given him.

Henri and Anna had come to an agreement that once he reached eighteen they would continue to support him financially, but they would move him out of the family home. It wasn't that Anna had given up on him, it was just the reality that time was running out, he wasn't a small child that could be moulded and influenced, nurtured by pro-social modelling and tenderness, he was an extremely damaged young man, who had issues she now accepted they could never resolve.

Anna finished vacuum cleaning Alaine's room, it smelt fresh, the windows and shutters had been cast open and the sea breeze gently made itself known. The pale grey wall paper worked better than she had expected, she had chosen well, matching perfectly the new curtains and bedding. The large flat screen TV was placed on the wall, and an *I-pod* and speaker system set up on a shelf, all of which had been donated by *Compassion San Frontieres*, who certainly knew how to spend their funds.

She paused for a moment as she glanced at her reflection in the large TV Screen, she looked tired, weary, her workload and its attendant stress showing all too clearly. She still considered herself an attractive woman, in her early forties, her dark hair neatly cut short, and a figure not too dissimilar to the one she possessed twenty years earlier, but it was plain to see for all the good she was doing for others, she wasn't reaping any physical rewards herself.

She felt that usual feeling of guilt that she wasn't looking forward to Alaine's return, she so wanted their relationship to mirror some of *Compassion San Frontieres* great success stories, to be held up as the shining example of what could be achieved, but she accepted it wasn't to be. She would do all she could to help him in life, ensure it was without unnecessary problems and hardships, but she could never be anything resembling a mother, something she was now accepting she would never be to anyone.

She packed the vacuum cleaner away, grabbed her car keys and left the house, Henri was in Iraq, many miles away, as he invariably was for most of the time now, the Ministry appeared to be becoming more and more demanding of him, she knew he was good at his job, but surely he wasn't that indispensable that the Republic couldn't be involved in a war without him having to go out and mop up the mess afterwards.

What about her, didn't she need him?

Not just for practical purposes, but for company, support, understanding, and helping to tackle the

THE SHATTERED EAGLE

impenetrable wall called Alaine. But then Henri was coming home in two days, a fortnight's leave, two weeks of normality, two weeks of quality time, two weeks of not sleeping alone. Just two more days, then he would be back.

She walked out through the double doors that led from the large impressive white timber clad house, just yards from the Brittany beach she so adored, and the bright sun immediately bathed her in its comforting warmth. Climbing into her dark blue *Mercedes SLR* convertible she looked back at the home she had spent so long preparing for Alaine's return and wondered just how much of her labours would be appreciated? Pressing her finger against the small button on the dash board the roof tucked itself away behind her, once more she luxuriated in the sun's rays, it felt good, a much needed blast of vitamin D and natural serotonin. As she put her sunglasses on she closely examined her image in the driver's mirror, yes that was better, the smoked glass screens between her eyes and her reflection once more knocking those tired looking twenty years off, and the crow's feet and puffy bags were hidden from view. Immediately she began to feel happier, she needed to accentuate the positives, maybe once Henri returned they would go into Paris, stop over for the night at a nice hotel, go out dancing, or go to a fine restaurant, she was sure Alaine wouldn't complain at the prospect of not spending a weekend with them, and Henri probably needed a welcome break even more than she did.

***

The light flashed through the overhanging branches as she drove to the railway station with the radio at full blast, on Friday afternoons there was always good music on *Radio Norde*, putting everyone in the mood for the coming weekend. As Nena sang about her 'Ninety Nine Red Balloons' she pressed her foot harder on the accelerator, his train was due to arrive in just 15 minutes, perhaps she should have given it a bit more time, allowed herself those extra few minutes to get there without rush, but somehow she enjoyed that little bit of extra pressure, and as the trees and fields flashed by at ninety kilometres per hour, and the *Mercedes's* engine purred in response to the pressure she applied to the accelerator, she felt just that bit more alive.

A combination of luck with the traffic and liberal abuse of the speed limits fortunately saw her beat the Paris train to the platform. Anna parked up just outside the station, luckily Claveville isn't the busiest stop on the line, and as the train pulled in only Alaine alighted.

She put on her broadest smile as she saw him, and it was partly genuine, despite what she guessed would be coming, but alas there was no running into each other's arms, no warm embraces, although he did at least manage to wanly smile, or was it just a sneer, when she approached him planting a kiss on each of his cheeks. As always Anna started afresh with him, as if today was the day things would fall in place, everything would somehow miraculously change.

THE SHATTERED EAGLE

"Hello darling, you look so well, so grown up, you really are the proper young man."

She brushed her hand across his cheek feeling the first stages of a beard coming through, but Alaine just flinched as way of a response, only the slightest bit, almost imperceptibly, but she knew her contact wasn't welcome.

"You really must tell me all about school, Professor Dreyfus says you are doing so well, and that he expects good things of you, you make me and Henri so proud."

She was of course lying, she was pleased he was supposedly doing so well, although she saw little evidence of it, but pride would have been a gross exaggeration. Still the object of her mock pride said nothing, just shuffling over to the car and throwing his bag onto the floor by the boot. For a brief moment Anna looked down at it, was it worth making a scene over? Was it a battle worthy of a fight so early into his return? Of course it was, but instead she popped the boot open and placed the bag inside, whilst Alaine was already sitting in the passenger seat.

"We've had your room decorated whilst you've been away, it looks lovely, and the Trust have given you a new TV, and other fantastic gifts as well, I think you're going to love it," Anna said as she climbed in next to him, gunning up the engine. "You really are quite a lucky young man."

She could see though that Alaine may well grow to love it, but that wasn't going to prevent him from maintaining his silence, he didn't even acknowledge her, just stared straight ahead as she pulled away from the station, back towards home.

The journey seemed to take an age, any attempt to engage her passenger in conversation was met with nothing but at best a grunt, before finally Anna surrendered to the silence.

"Look Alaine if you really don't want to talk you don't have to, we can talk later, whatever you want. I appreciate you must be tired," she offered as some form of compromise.

But again silence. She didn't feel in the mood for music either, the Friday feeling well and truly dispelled.

When they did get home Alaine went straight up to his room, again without conversation, whilst Anna slumped into an arm chair in the living room, burying her head in her hands, she wondered why she bothered. Why she bothered to persist with him, how Henri was right all along, a fourteen year old disturbed African war child was never going to be a replacement for her own unobtainable baby, especially a disturbed African war child that appeared to now hate her.

She pondered as to whether to call up the stairs to see if he wanted anything to eat or drink, isn't that what a good mother would do? But then again no, leave him, she really couldn't be bothered at this time, the ingratitude of it all annoyed her immensely, she didn't want continuous thanks, praise, fawning gratitude, but she had saved him from a terrible life, if not an even more horrendous death,

THE SHATTERED EAGLE

just some sort of recognition of this from him wouldn't hurt him, would it?

Curling her legs up onto the chair she stared out into the garden, it looked so lovely this time of year, old Monsieur Geesten does a wonderful job, despite him being, what Henri reckons to be, at least 90 years old. She looked out at the rose beds, now in full bloom, meticulously dead-headed and pruned, so only the most fresh vibrant flowers prevailed, the old man is a master, and the hedges, sheer beauty, surely they wouldn't be out of place at Versailles, maybe whilst questioning peoples gratitude, she should show more appreciation of him, he wouldn't accept more money she was sure of that, but perhaps buy him a gift, some form of recognition of just how highly he is regarded, she'd talk about it with Henri when he returned. Then her train of thought was disrupted as she heard music coming from upstairs, very loud music, even from that distance.

At least it appeared Alaine now appreciated something she had arranged for him, was utilising the sound system, even if she was sure there would be no thank you. It was terribly loud, she ought to tell him to turn it down, but then again there's no one within a kilometre to worry about, perhaps it may improve his mood a little. But urghh, it sounded so awfully dreadful, a terrible din. She had got one of the other boys on the programme to load the *i-pod* with music, perhaps she should have given him some parameters, no American rap, especially rap featuring such vile profanities, it was echoing around the house, it really was much too loud.

Too loud for her to hear Alaine come up behind her.

An arm came around her neck, what was that! She felt a wave of horrific panic, her blouse was ripped open, the upper buttons literally flying off, she recoiled around attempting to stand free of the chair, but he pulled her back into it, his forearm around her throat as he pushed his hand into her bra, roughly mauling one of her breasts.

Anna screamed, but no one would hear, even if anyone was near enough all they would hear was the god awful racket being perpetuated by Dr Dre.

Bitches ain't shit but hoes and tricks

He was hurting her, groping, grabbing, scratching, she struggled, both to fight him offg and to breathe, but both were in vain.

"Alaine, no! Please no!" although what should have been screams were little more than raspy gasps.

Lick on these nuts and suck my dick

"No, Alaine! Please stop! Please!" But by now she was making no sounds at all, her voice lost to her.

Still he said nothing, the only sound emanating from him being his frenzied breathing, as he forced himself upon his philanthropic guardian. Anna was kicking and screaming, her hand flailing, her nails ripping into her adopted rapists forehead, gouging vainly in an effort to break free, but he wasn't letting go, as he swung around to face her, his hand now no longer on her breast but on her throat, the other hand in the form of a fist smashing into her nose, she knew she wasn't getting free, for all her fight he was stronger, ruthlessly more powerful, she had no idea what was possessing him, what was driving him, but she knew for sure that this was him doing this to her.

Blinded with pain and by her own blood, her nose broken and smashed, she could feel the fight evaporating, gone, replaced with a hopeless inevitability.

Another punch to the already wrecked nose, her nostrils and throat now full of her own blood, still spluttering to breathe, struggling to get air.

Get the fuck out after you're done.

She closed her eyes tight, whatever was going to happen was now going to happen.

God forgive him.

The gravel crunched under the tyres as Henri DuPont pulled up outside his house around lunch time the following day, he managed to get a flight back a day early but hadn't told Anna, he wanted to surprise her, like one of the grand gestures she used to be so fond of in the days before he became a slave to the Ministry, and she became so involved in that damn charity. He smiled when he saw her car parked on the drive, he was worried she wouldn't be there, that his Machiavellian scheming would have been in vain, but no she was at home.

He picked the two small gift boxes from the passenger seat, one contained a pair of diamond ear rings for his wife, the other a *Tag Huere* wrist watch he had picked up from the airport for Alaine, though this was more for

Anna's benefit, he wanted her to see how reasonable he could be, even to someone who was so unreasonable to him.

He let himself in the front door, the house was still, all quiet.

Should he call out to her?

No, that isn't a grand gesture, maybe she's out, gone for a walk to the village, perhaps even persuaded Alaine to join her, she had been saying on the phone just a couple of days back how she planned to try and get him to do more, integrate him into the family, attempt to make him feel included.

Yeah good luck with that, he had thought at the time, although that was so Anna, so very Anna, he never ceased to be impressed by her persistence, patience, and kindness, although sometimes he wondered whether all three of these attributes were always used for the best purposes.

If she was in she clearly hadn't heard him arrive, even though it appeared all the windows were open in the house, taking his mobile phone from his pocket he dialled the number he had dialled so many times before, as he did so he went into the kitchen and hid behind the door. The telephone in the spacious hall began to ring, but Anna never came to answer to it.

Where was she?

He tried again, still hiding away behind the door, then with a resigned shrug of his shoulders he went to the fridge and took out a can of *Coke*, he hadn't realised just how thirsty he was, pulling the top and taking a couple of much needed deep swigs.

Walking around the kitchen he took his tie off, running his finger around his collar to pull it from his neck where the sweat had stuck the cotton to his skin, he wondered if he would have enough time for a shower before Anna returned from wherever she was. It was good to be home, the kitchen was his favourite part of the house, he had fitted it out himself, although in all honestly it was Anna who had chosen everything, designed it all so perfectly, but there was something magical about that view, that view over the well-tended garden, then across the beach and the Atlantic beyond. He pulled a baguette from the bread basket, and set it upon the board on the island in the middle of 'his' kitchen, fetched some butter and cheese from the fridge, and set about making himself a sandwich, grand gestures were one thing but he hadn't eaten for almost 24 hours. Huh, no bread knife in the block by the board, he walked over to the sink but it was empty, not to worry he'd saw through the bread with a non-serrated knife, he just wanted to eat.

After a little consideration he decided to put the shower on hold, he didn't want to miss her when she returned, he'd park his car in the garage so she wouldn't see it, and he'd wait in the garden for her. Whilst chewing on his breakfast - lunch - dinner he went to the freezer, with his free hand he placed a silver ice bucket under the ice dispenser and half-filled it, before selecting a bottle of wine from the glass fronted refrigerator which was stacked with nothing but fine whites.

Perhaps he would have a shower after all, he'd be really quick, then he could throw on a tee-shirt and some shorts, he needed to get out of those clothes, get something fresh on. He again pulled his phone out, and dialled Anna's mobile, he'd find out where she was first, make out he was phoning from Baghdad. He heard ringing coming from the living room, that was strange she normally took it everywhere she went, still she must have forgot it she had so much on her mind of late, only last week she had told him how she left her bike in the village after forgetting she had cycled to the shop, not even realising until she had walked home, he'd take a chance on that shower anyway, he felt filthy, sticky and needed to cool down.

He skipped up the stairs, the thought of seeing Anna again in his mind, he'd first go and get out of those clothes.

As he opened the bedroom door he struggled to take it in, he immediately knew something was wrong, drawers were pulled open, contents tossed all over the place, Anna's jewellery boxes were scattered across the floor, he saw her purse, turned inside out on the bed, then he noticed bloody hand prints on the furniture, on the jewellery boxes, "Anna, Anna!"

Henri ran from the room, calling her name.

"Anna, where are you?"

He felt panic, terror take a grip, where was she? What has happened? He ran down the stairs.

THE SHATTERED EAGLE

"Anna!"

The phone! When he had dialled, it was ringing in the living room wasn't it, he burst through the double doors that lead there from the hall, and screamed.

"No, No, No, oh Anna!"

He collapsed besides the bloodied and mutilated corpse, of what was his beloved wife, naked bar an *Ecole de l'Afrique* school tie binding her hands. Deep puncture wounds piercing her face, neck, chest and torso, there were dozens of them. Her body was destroyed, blood splatters were on walls metres away. Henri had seen corpses before, mangled and decimated bodies from his time in the army, but none he could recall must have suffered as cruelly as his Anna had.

Kneeling before her he began to sob uncontrollably, "Oh my darling, my darling...."

Reaching down he undid the tie to take her lifeless left hand in his, her ring finger had been hacked off. Oh God! Her face, her lovely face was destroyed, her nose smashed out of shape, cuts contorting her once beautiful features to such an extent it was hard to make out where her mouth even was, large flaps of skin jutted out at unnatural angles, one eye stared out, whilst the other was invisible, lost behind so much swelling and blood, this was Anna, his Anna.

Smeared into the blood between her hideously mutilated breasts and genitalia were the words 'Mama Whore', Henri turned his head to one side and vomited, bringing up his undigested lunch and carbonated drink.

He slumped to the floor lying parallel to her, lying in his own vomit and her congealed blood which was pooled all around her. This was his world destroyed. He reached into his pocket and once again dialled his mobile, "Hello, Police…"

When the Police arrived they found him still there, shocked and dazed lying next to the wife who had been dead for over 24 hours. Anna DuPont, who had dedicated her life to tirelessly helping others far less fortunate than herself, was now a crime statistic, a Police case, a victim, of a truly hideous crime. Henri had no doubt who had done this to her, there was no doubt at all.

-TWO-
Burying Anna DuPont

The rain showed no respect as it poured down from the dark clouds over Claveville, pattering upon the sea of black umbrellas spread out like giant crow's wings over the mourners beneath. As the priest spoke Henri looked down at his highly polished shoes, the wet brown sodden mud lapping up over the soles, caking the shiny uppers. In front of the large alabaster monolith the priest said the final farewells to Anna as she was lowered into the darkness of the ground. The President and his wife watched on, as did the high ranking and socially elite from all over France, Henri was amazed at how many of them he had no idea who they were, but then his wife knew, or had known, so many people. He felt a pang of shame at not becoming more involved in her life, allowing his work to deprive them of those shared moments 'normal' couples enjoyed, but then even when he had been at home, Anna wasn't, was it wrong of him to resent those she helped so much?

As earth was tossed upon the casket containing his murdered spouse the priest's words were lost as his mind kept flitting back to that scene, the day he found her, almost totally naked, bloodied and torn beyond recognition, what she must have experienced, her final thoughts, the sheer terror and blind panic she must have gone through as that animal feasted upon her, destroyed her. He winced and attempted to focus back to what was being said, don't let those images in, don't let them play on the mind he told himself, after all he was trained at keeping such thoughts at bay, controlling his feelings, not letting emotions rule, but then no one could have been trained for this.

The whole affair had shocked a nation. Anna DuPont who had done nothing but good for so many, so brutally slain, by the one she had assisted most. The press had labelled it the 'Death of an Angel', and elevated Anna to iconic status, not since the untimely exits for Princess' Grace and Diana had France been so moved by a loss.

The President had delivered a heartfelt eulogy at the church, sincere and genuine, of how he shared, as did all the Republic, Henri's loss, of how the world had lost a pure and loving soul, which it so badly needed. He talked of Anna's work, the work she carried through, even into her home life, recalling her kindness, warmth and compassion. That she had devoted so much in order to help those cast aside by society with race, creed, and colour offering no barriers to her wonderful generosity and truly loving spirit.

A string of other dignitaries echoed the President's words, as a country wept for Anna DuPont.

THE SHATTERED EAGLE

***

As the assembled mourners relocated to the stately environs of Chateau Normandie to dry off and sample the fine cuisine on offer, four men drifted away to a side lounge. They were seated around a low oak side table, in dark brown deep buttoned leather chairs. A tall man in a dark blue military uniform, medals festooned across his chest, sat opposite Henri DuPont, he had in one hand a large glass of cognac, he was in his mid-forties, with weathered and tanned facial features, and close cropped dark hair. He spoke in solemn hushed tones.

"Henri on behalf of all three of us, can I express my deepest commiserations for your loss. This is indeed something none of us ever foresaw, or imagined possible. You know that you have our full support, now as ever, and we are here for you."

Henri who was dressed in the same dark blue dress uniform, as were the other two, nodded, "Thank you Harold, thank you Gentlemen, I appreciate that. Rest assured I will be requiring that support, and very soon. These are extremely difficult times for me, and I am truly grateful to have you here around me today. Your support and comradeship is most welcome. As you know, he took more than my wife from me. He took something that belongs to us all."

"Henri", an older man, probably in his early sixties, who was sitting to Henri's left spoke up, "there is much to discuss but this is not the time for such matters. There is much to put right, much we have to do, but Henri my friend, that is not for you to worry about, not now. You should mourn your loss, as we will, have no fear what was taken will be returned. He who took it will be found. We have already put in place appropriate measures, this treacherous dog has nowhere to go, there will be no place for him to hide. Please Henri, let us three worry about such matters, please do not concern yourself with things like that now, not with Anna so recently taken from you."

"You are good friends, I am grateful". Henri replied.

The fourth man, of similar age to Henri turned to him, "Not just friends Henri, never just friends, we are the Legion, the last four, we are brothers."

He then stood and raised his cognac glass.

"To Anna DuPont."

The others followed suit.

"We will reconvene soon, now let's not keep Henri from his family and kin any longer."

All three men embraced Henri and kissed him on each cheek, before exiting the room. Henri sat down, alone again in his chair, and drained the last of the brandy from his glass, they were indeed the Legion, the Brotherhood, but how much were they still his friends?

-THREE-
The Day Gary Decided He Wanted To Walk From The Station To Work.

Looking at his watch Gary smiled as the train appeared, slowly arcing around the corner as it shuddered to a halt. The 7.32 from Leighton Buzzard to London Euston was dead on time, it usually was despite the misconception that the trains always ran late, promptness wasn't *London Midland's* problem. Oh no, the amount of bodies on their rolling stock was. This morning, like all mornings, he knew he wouldn't get a seat, he had already accepted this fact, even though he paid the best part of £400 a month, it was £400 for the privilege of standing the 40 or so miles. There was a choice, there was the earlier train, the 7.18, everyone was guaranteed a seat on that one, but there was a higher price to pay for that luxury, Cheddington, Tring, Berkhamsted, Hemel Hempstead, Apsley, King's Langley and Watford Junction. Yes he would have a seat, travel in relative comfort, but would have double the time to 'enjoy' it, as opposed to standing as the train whistled through the arse ends of Beds, Bucks and Herts.

So the 7.32 it was, as it was every week day of his working life, because the less time he spent on a train the better as far as he was concerned. As it drew to a halt they came into view through the thick glass windows, the heaving mass of business suits, mobile phones, personal stereos and over applied perfume crammed within. He jostled with the other human cattle on the platform knowing that in the morning no one ever got off at Leighton Buzzard, it's a place people leave and return to for the purpose of sleep, affordable living, and a chance to get out of bloody London, so he just squeezed in, joining the residents of the Home Counties commuter belt, apologising and excusing himself as he tried to find a spot where his arse wasn't going to be in someone's face or his groin rammed into someone else's ear, he hated this journey with a passion.

And the 'itch' began to make itself known, as an instant reaction he started to scratch the back of his hand, he knew he needed to leave it alone, just ignore it but he couldn't, alternating from one to the other, as the 'itch' had no favourites nor preferences, oh no, it was happy to drive him berserk on either hand. He looked down at the hands, his hands, scratched and sore, small scabs littering both of them between wrists and knuckles, was it eczema, or merely another manifestation of his out of control stress? He had lived with it for months now, the only consolation being that the itchy days were preferable to the long relentless nights, those awful bloody nights, where the 'itch' would become tired of so cruelly tormenting hands and instead decides to cause merry hell by manifesting itself all over his legs, leaving him to tear at his calves and knees, shredding his thighs, knowing that scratching was totally pointless, but helpless to resist, only exasperating those long painfully sore sleep-free nights. He should really go to the doctor, but then he knew what the GP would tell him, it's not eczema, and he didn't need informing that he was stressed, he sure as hell knew that already, no he'd just keep scratching.

He looked around the carriage at the soulless expressions on now vaguely familiar faces as people put a copy of the morning's *Metro* between them and their travelling companions, obeying the golden rule of keeping one to one's impenetrable self. Gary could clearly see there was nowhere for him to sit, or at least not without breaking the cardinal rule, and asking someone to move over. Like some commuting anthropologist he observed those in the seats adjacent to him, each claiming their space by careful positioning of elbows and knees. He could only marvel at the dexterity of some of the more seasoned pros, the blatant disregard for the comfort of their neighbours. Just to the right, by the window, the rotund accountant, although there was no definite confirmation of this profession, he just looked like an accountant, elbows four inches clear of his side, legs slightly apart with his knees marking his territory, safe in the knowledge that no one liked to rub knees on a hot train, clearly claiming his space from the skinny black kid in the seat next to him, who had the misfortune to be sandwiched with a young female student, probably studying psychology, although once again only Gary's presumption. She had wisely kept a bag between her and the hapless crushed lad in the middle, thus ensuring her borders were secure and it was him in discomfort not her.

Hold on, he thought - because on these journeys Gary thought a lot - a quick reappraisal of the space hogging girl, he now had her down as a local Authority employee, probably Camden Council, a Health and Safety junior manager, or perhaps Diversity, but certainly no longer a student.

Oh bollocks. He was still scratching at his hands, subconsciously tearing and sawing into his own skin, STOP! It's never a good look in a public place, he imagined it made him look like some Dickensian character, a portly modern day Scrooge, wringing his hands and sneering as Tiny Tom, or whatever his name was, suffered the cruelty of an eviction on his malicious say so, with Garyneza Scrooge returning home to greedily count huge piles of gold coins piled up around him.

Must stop scratching - must stop scratching - must stop scratching, he was saying the words to himself in time with the sound of the wheels speeding along the track. But then again, could it be scabies, no not scabies, that sounds gross!

THE SHATTERED EAGLE

He thought back to the article he had read in *The Guardian*, about how it was returning, becoming prevalent, brought over from Eastern Europe by migrant workers, jeez, he really didn't want scabies! God he hated this journey, but not as much as he hated the 'itch'.

With the scan of the rest of the carriage complete he decided it was time to drift into one of those time passing self-induced trances, of course reminding himself to look to the right just after Watford Junction, and to snap out of it going through Wembley, there's something about football stadiums that demand attention, even on a daily basis.

As the train trundled through Tring he thought of little Amy, just finished her first year at middle school, the daily swing between loving and hating her class mates, and just as unpredictably loving and hating him and Fran, and the dip in her behaviour at home over the past few weeks, nothing serious of course, they didn't do serious issues when it comes to the kids, but enough to make the difference between a quiet evening and one hollering up the stairs every fifteen minutes as she fought with Josh over almost anything and everything. Josh, a year older, the poor bugger, he only ever wants the quiet life, the easy route, to be alone in his bedroom playing *Fifa* two thousand and whatever it is, but instead ends up at war with Amy. Oh she'd grow out of it, he just wished it was a bit quicker.

He swayed with the motion of the carriage as it hurtled over a set of points, his mind switching to the coming weekend, as it always switched between a multitude of topics on this damn journey. They had been invited to Sheila and Clive's for dinner, those were words no sane rational person would ever want to hear. Damn he didn't want to go, he really didn't want to go, in fact scabies would be preferable, or at least it was a close run thing. He knew it would be like some seventies wife swapping party, only without the bonus of actual wife swapping. Who under the age of sixty five drinks sherry in this day and age? Fran had nothing in common with Sheila except growing up together, it amazed him how they had remained such good friends all that time despite their lives going off in such different directions. Fran always complained to him, but never Sheila, how the friendship was so one sided, how Sheila only phoned when she wanted to sound off, how she never listened to anything Fran had to say, always returning the conversation to the Incredibly Crazy World of Sheila Henderson.

Why did Fran do this to him?

Why couldn't she just lie, invent some prior engagement, feign a child's illness, tell them they couldn't go as the 'itch' had hit terminal proportions and he'd scratched himself into a coma, just say anything other than yes. In fact never mind the coma, just tell them he'd actually got scabies, he was pretty sure that would do it!

Still, Fran wanted to go and he was all too aware of past bail outs on stuff she wanted to do, how she always accommodated the things he wanted, there was no way out, he would have to grin and bear this one, it's only fair.

THE SHATTERED EAGLE

He then remembered the last soirée around their place, it was like something out of 'Abigail's Party', Clive and his cheap awful cigars talking over everyone like he was the only person in the room who could possibly have anything vaguely interesting to pitch in. Sheila's insistence, whenever Clive took a breath of more than two seconds, which wasn't often, going on about their stunted rat of a dog, but then he smiled as he remembered how Fran got the giggles, over pretty much nothing in particular, and decided the best way to try and avoid laughing out loud in her hosts faces was to squeeze his testicles as hard as she could under the table, which on reflection did actually work. Recalling it he smiled inanely to himself, Jeez it had made him horny, which had only increased the desire to flee the evening from hell and had given him the hope, the vain hope as it transpired, that there may have been a decent chance of going home with some oral shenanigans on the cards, or a spot of al-fresco fornication, as it was a well-recognised fact, surely, that surreptitious ball squeezing in company, no matter what the cause should always be deemed a good thing. Then he was back to the reality of the up and coming night at their place, maybe he should suggest a bit of specialist coitus to Fran in advance, give him something to look forward to, as all he could think of now was how if he was going to break his diet, the world's slowest and longest diet at that, he at least wanted to do it scoffing a decent Indian or perhaps a goliath of a pizza, not congealed Beef Bourguignon or some other atrocity from a 1989 'Cooking with Deliha' book. No, he was not looking forward to it at all, the only blessing being that it shouldn't go on too late, and with the chance of outside sex almost certainly already discounted, they would probably be home in time for the 'Football League Show', maybe even the end of 'Match of the Day' if things went well.

Anyway, he thought, another day to get through at work before the pleasure of the weekend. So much to do, and so little enthusiasm to do it, perhaps today he should just do that thing where he pretended to be working, but instead type out a list of countries he had visited, or record his Top Ten Films, or Songs, or perhaps make a list of all the bands he had seen, he could do it on a spread sheet, cross reference it with CDs he had by them, but then did he include stuff he had downloaded?

Hmm tough one that, strictly speaking he owned it, but then not physically, nothing really tangible. But all the stuff he did now actually have on disc or vinyl, well most of it was just shite, over ten years old, or not worth remembering, who listens to the Soup Dragons, Carter the Unstoppable Sex Machine, or House of Love nowadays?

Then again the House of Love!

Bloody Hell, he made a mental note to transfer their CDs to *i-Tunes* when he got home, where did his mind dig them up from?

Hemel Hempstead flashed by, he hadn't even noticed Berkhamsted, he idly gazed down at the fat accountant, noting a stain that looked like the contents of his morning boiled egg rubbed into his jacket lapel, and his unkempt hair, was that hair wax or just natural grease?

The scruffy selfish bloke had claimed even more of the space from the lad next door, who had as a result shuffled up a bit and now had the Camden Council Diversity Manager's bag pressed hard against his arm, with the bag in turn jammed into her own side, she didn't look so comfortable now.

How bad does he want that seat?

He thought how if he was that kid he would just stand, or better still drop his guts, it was no more than they deserved, crushing him like that.

Opposite a wall of *Metro*'s and *FT*'s continued to prevent his analysis of those hidden behind them, although he could see what looked like a pretty fine comb over hopelessly attempting to conceal a shiny pate. Not that he was terribly bothered who was behind the newspapers, over five years of doing this journey and he still didn't talk to any of them, as indeed they hardly talked to each other.

He imagined what the Fat Accountant did, presumably accounting, sometimes he marvelled at his own stupidity, but who for? A fiftyish fat bloke in a shit suit, grotty hair, and a carrier bag, albeit a *Waitrose* 'Bag for Life', as a briefcase? He didn't look happy, content with life, in fact he looked a sad lonely lump, but there again he was not the one scratching his hand thinking of ways to avoid getting through his day and dreading the weekend.

And what about the skinny black kid?

College, *McDonalds*, tourist? Jeans, tee-shirt and the obligatory baseball cap, he had a small holdall rammed behind his legs, perhaps he was travelling, who knows, why was he even thinking about it?

Arghhhh! This journey is so boring!

And there again a change of gears in his head.

Transfer a CD to *i-Tunes*. Where's the romance in that? What happened to lovingly making tapes, hours spent sitting next to the stereo, precisely lowering that arm into the vinyl no man's land between tracks, as simultaneously pressing 'Play' and 'Record' whilst surrounded by stacks of singles and LPs all awaiting their turn to contribute to the meisterwork of the freshly unwrapped C90.

Where had his love of music gone?

It was all too easy now, nothing special, you hear a song you like, you download it there and then. That's rubbish.

No thrill of the chase or joy of the hunt anymore, no trawling through rack after rack at *Our Price* or the monthly visit to *Rough Trade* armed with a wish list and the best part of a week's wages. He remembered back to how Fran had converted him to CDs, sold on the misconception that they presented crystal clear sound, were small, and well errr, compact, and could double as silver jam pots if you so desired, well according to 'Tomorrow's World' they could. He had embraced this new wonder technology whole heartedly, a conversion that coincided with a period in life when money was plentiful, hence fevered buying, replacing his now discarded vinyl at a rapid rate of knots, as well as snapping up any new

THE SHATTERED EAGLE

music he could lay his hands on in this new wonderful medium.

This was probably the start of the long decline, where it started to get too easy. He thought back to another article he had recently read in some Sunday Supplement, 'The Rebirth of Vinyl!' How all self-respecting music fans should re-embrace 12" slabs of plastic, it's the sound you see, analogue, organic and pure. This had struck a chord, he wondered at the idea that people out there had stereo systems that cost thousands, had maintained mountains of vinyl LPs, which he was unaware were still even being produced, and in some cases had rooms specifically devoted to the playing of them.

Oh how he wanted a room he could luxuriate in, cigar in one hand, brandy in the other, listening to the 'Queen is Dead', 'The Stone Roses', 'Highland Hard Rain', or some other long pined after classic, just as they were intended to be listened to.

That really is living the dream. Even if he had never smoked and hated brandy, that's still the life.

First Apsley, then King's Langley flash by, he must remember to look right, after the Junction, he needed the daily glimpse of the Vicarage Road Stadium, no working day was complete without it.

Oh why did he do it, why do this damn awful soul sapping journey every day, why not take the hit and work for someone locally, sure the money would be missed, but there's more to life than that. Then again there isn't is there, the Debt Management Plan needs servicing, another three years to go, ride it Westlake, you're stuck, and you're theirs. Never mind stereos, he hadn't even got a fridge/freezer that worked, minus four is definitely not a healthy temperature to keep frozen food at.

Bollocks, the train whizzed past Carpenters Park Station, he had missed the football ground. He remembered his Dad telling him the houses in Carpenters Park were only built temporarily after the war to house bombed out Londoners, and had a life span of just 10 years, here they were seventy years later, clad in a variety of stone, PVC and peeling paint, maybe they weren't that bad, he supposed they must have been quite well built to still be standing, but the place still looked tatty, though nothing compared to the homes on display as you got nearer to Euston, those God awful flats that look like they are about to topple over at any moment, only held up by razor wire and graffiti.

At last Wembley, bloody beautiful he could only marvel at it, craning to look past Fat Bloke, Skinny Black Kid and Camden Council Diversity Manager, Fat Bloke threw a glance back, Gary diverted his gaze, don't make eye contact on a train, did Fat Bloke think he was staring, damn missed that last glimpse of Wembley before the *Royal Mail* Depot blotted it out, never mind he would catch it on the way back, and every working day for the next 13 years... Was it so wrong to wish your life away, roll on sixty!

THE SHATTERED EAGLE

And that's it Wembley past, the next thing of interest, bar the shabby rear of the Roundhouse, and the earlier mentioned atrocious flats, is Euston. He had already decided that he would walk from the station today, he had had enough of cramped over-crowded trains, really couldn't face the Underground, plus the sun was out, make the most of it. He could feel horrible warm dampness in his pits, already sweat patches were forming, it was definitely too hot for real work, the 'do bugger all Friday' plan was a damn good one, one worth sticking with.

And there's the 'Euston 1 Mile' sign, quick Westlake, he thought, if you're walking to work this morning get to that exit.

He always liked the 'quick getaway' no matter where he went, football, gigs, Sheila and Clive's, especially Sheila and Clive's, or a train journey, first away misses the rush, so once again he shuffled, excusing himself and apologising as he made his way towards the door, as he went he noticed Skinny Black Kid force himself up like a popping champagne cork freeing himself from the grip of his two chair hungry fellow travellers, who instantly filled the void left to prevent anyone else sitting there.

Gary got to his position by the doors just as the train stopped, perfect timing, they opened as if on some personal sensor, well after that usual momentary delay, designed solely by beeping noise manufacturers to justify their beeping noise devices.

They're under starters orders, and they're off!

He went with the flow, they were all rushing towards the ticket barrier, Skinny Black Kid passed by, in a bit of a hurry, probably just keen to feel blood flowing through his legs again, what with being crushed for the best part of half an hour. But Gary noticed he didn't have his holdall with him, quickening his pace he called after him, "Excuse me son…"

The air was sucked clean from his lungs, as if some giant vacuum had created a seal around his lips, he was flying in some surreal slow motion backwards arc, blown clean off of his feet, straight into an advertising board. As he smashed into the plywood hoarding, which in turn was in the process of shattering into splinters and matchwood, he could see lumps of steel, wood and God knows what else in the air around him.

His ears were ringing, a horrible high pitched squeal obliterating all other sound, he couldn't see anything other than dust and smoke yet was aware of the chaos all around, but had no idea why it was happening, what the hell was this about?

Wiping the sweat from his eyes he looked down at his hands, oh Jesus Christ, they were covered in blood, not the tiny bobbles and scratches of overzealous scratching, but lots of the stuff, smeared from knuckle to wrist.

He shook his head, why? Why do that? To see if it's still attached? To clear his ears? Because he could? What was happening to him?

THE SHATTERED EAGLE

Attempting to scramble back to his feet he just crumpled back onto the floor, he needed to move, had to get away. Again what the hell was happening?

He could only watch as people were appearing through the clouds of dust, stumbling around like grey ghosts, the morning of the Living Dead at London Euston Station. One poor soul appeared naked, just coated in an overall of blood, crawling on all fours. He couldn't even tell if it was a man or woman, adult or child, just a wretched soul torn apart like horrendous human road kill.

Just to his left a man was silently screaming, although he was sure if he could have heard, it would have been anything but silent, the poor bastard wandered around, a forearm dangling from a thread-like strip of sinew, hanging at a ninety degree angle like a grotesque scene from a macabre mime act.

It was nightmare, but he knew there would be no awakening, because he was all too awake. Then he saw the woman not four feet away staring motionless at what appeared to be her intestines spilling from her tattered yellow summer dress, she looked puzzled, confused, lost. They made eye contact, for about two seconds only, but that was enough, he wanted to help her, but that was really a lie, he didn't want to be there at all, he wanted to be able to be somewhere else, somewhere so very far away from this bloody mess.

He felt he should at least attempt to assist, but really he just wanted someone to help him, sort out his problems at that very moment in time. What could he possibly offer her anyway, he didn't know the Heinrich Manoeuvre, had never attempted the kiss of life, and was all fingers and thumbs when putting on a sticky plaster, what chance did he have of reuniting her and her innards without as much as an emergency sewing kit?

His nostrils were full of the stench of chaos, the aroma of death, a dozen different smells competing to bombard his mind with just what a messed up situation he was in. He looked at her again, the girl in the yellow dress, but now she was slumped forward, motionless, her chin resting on her chest, her dead brain staring through dead eyes, at her dead mangled body.

His head was swirling, as he again attempted to get back onto his feet, his mind unable to deal with what it was being expected to process. This time though his legs allowed him to stand, he stumbled a bit, but slowly regained control of his limbs, then, like someone had pulled cotton wool from his ears, he could hear, the mayhem now had a soundtrack and it had become all the more alarming due to it, screams and shouts, pleas for assistance, people were running in all directions, those to escape the nightmare and those to assist.

Already sirens could be heard, help was on its way.

Stumbling and struggling to stay upright he inched forward, unsure where he was even heading, when all he wanted to do was run, run as far away from this as he could, but there was no running in him. Looking back to where the 7.32 to London Euston stood, or what was left of it, he could see the carriage he had only seconds earlier left was now a tangled mess, chairs, pieces of debris, and people littered the platform. Glass, bits of plastic, cable, clothing, metal, fragments of seats, and again lots of bits of people, yes that was people that were scattered all around.

He didn't know how badly hurt he was, at such a time as this would anyone recognise pain or be able to acknowledge the injuries, would they feel anything at all with adrenalin pumping through them at 300 mph, for he didn't feel anything tangible, except for scared, very bloody scared.

A paramedic ran past, then others, Police, Firemen and Rail staff, he could only presume he must have been comparatively OK, as they didn't cast him a second glance, but then again they hadn't stopped or even given a second look to the poor soul in what was once a yellow dress with her guts spewing out, so that was no gauge.

He again thought he should go to her, but why, she was dead, even in his current state he could see that?

He tripped on someone as he tottered around heading nowhere in particular, he looked down to see a blood soaked leg, a high healed shoe still attached to the foot, yet the rest of the body it belonged to was nowhere to be seen, the limb a frayed mess where it would have attached to the hip, the hip that was who knows where. And then he stopped dead in his tracks, just staring horrified at the mangled severed arm, a *Waitrose* 'Bag for Life' still being held in the disenfranchised hand.

Blood was everywhere, gore was everywhere, death was everywhere. It was as if someone had thrown buckets of offal all over the floor, then shrouded the entire scene in clouds of dust and smoke.

What the hell was happening?

Actually he pretty much knew what was happening, but why?

Arhh!

The pain had arrived, making itself all too recognisable after its delay in appearing, he felt a sharp stabbing sensation just above his left hip, looking down he could see the shard of glass, still with a *No Smoking* sticker attached, protruding from his side, blood flowing from the wound, flowing over the glass and trickling onto the floor, oh shit he hated blood, especially his own. He recalled hearing that if stabbed or impaled you shouldn't remove the thing inside you, leave it there to stop the blood, or was that if you get a nail in your tyre, he knew that was a fact, no he was sure it also applied to unwanted stuff stabbing into you.

Leave it there, wait until someone who knows what they're up to gets to you.

He kept walking, desperate to get away from the scene, tripping on unseen hazards as he went, not even looking down anymore, just wanting to ignore what it may be he was walking through, sure that the unseen obstacles were no longer living or breathing.

The screams, moans, and cries for help were all around now, a cacophony of pain and terror, slowly passing parts of metal and cloth rammed into the gaps on a bench he realised it was what was left of a pushchair, a pushchair

THE SHATTERED EAGLE

for God's sake, was there some poor little kid scattered around the platform as well as the disintegrated buggy?

His head was swimming, less and less able to focus on the events around him, how he wished he could be some kind of hero assisting others, the others that looked so much worse than him, the girl in the yellow dress, but now he could only think of himself, the blood on his hands from his head, the pain, and the glass, the glass sticking out of him, protruding ominously, it hurt like nothing he had ever experienced before. Please someone make it stop.

Police, Firemen and Paramedics were now all over the place, a Paramedic in green overalls and a white hard hat approached him, she placed her arm around his back.

"Are you OK love? Can you hear me?"

He could only point back to the girl in the yellow dress, and in a surprisingly polite tone requested.

"Please can you help her, I think she may be dead."

"No worries love, I'll get someone to help, but I want to see to you now, how are you? I'm Sarah, what's your name pet?"

"Gary," again the polite voice, the voice that most certainly didn't belong to him.

"Right Gary, you've been hurt, we need to get you to hospital, I want you to do exactly as I say Gary."

"But we need to help her, I wanted to help her, but..."

"Now Gary don't talk."

He could feel her, Sarah, supporting him, he wanted to talk, why couldn't he talk? He wanted her to make sure the girl in the yellow dress was dead, that there really was nothing to do for her, but he didn't feel in any position to argue, the thoughts were in his head but somehow the route from brain to mouth had been blocked. Sarah was waving a colleague over towards them, he was dragging a trolley, Gary thought of all the debris, human and non-human all over the platform and wondered how anything could possible wheel anywhere, he felt like he was swaying, moving from side to side, Sarah's grip tightened.

"Stay with me Gary, listen to me, I'm getting you something to lie down on, stay in there Gary."

The trolley was now beside him.

"Here I'm going to ease you over."

She edged him towards the trolley, he slid back, and was lying flat upon it, he opened his eyes, seeing Sarah talking to another paramedic.

"He's name's Gary, we don't know his surname yet, head injury by the look of it, nasty laceration to temple, bloody great lump of glass stuck in right side, appears lucid and coherent, but has lost blood."

A sudden rush of fresh air filled Gary's lungs as the other paramedic put a mask over his mouth, he appeared to be breathing OK, he felt so giddy though, he wanted to be sick. Sarah was now looking down at him.

"Right Gary my love, my mate here is going to take you to hospital, stay awake, and don't worry, I'm off to tend to that girl, so don't fret about her, just keep concentrating on yourself."

As he was being wheeled away he looked over and saw Sarah kneeling beside the girl in the yellow dress, although almost immediately she was back on her feet, she took her helmet off, ran her sleeve across her face, then put the helmet back on before moving to someone else.

His head was swirling, he was spinning, like he was on the tea-cups at some low rent theme park, he wanted to get off, let me off!

Right Gary me love, my mate here is going to take you to hospital, stay awake…

But he was falling, falling down a black pit, down, down, down…

-FOUR-
It's Definitely A Bomb, A Big One.

The dozens of electrical shops, chained restaurants, and themed pubs all too slowly passed by the dark blue *BMW*'s windows as it snaked between the stationary traffic down Tottenham Court Road, the blue lights flashing through the distinctive front grill and its ear splitting siren wailing to alert the other vehicles which were powerless to make way.

"For Fuck's sake, get out of the way you gormless prick! Get past him Felix, go through, go through!"

DCI Adrian 'Frankie' Howard was in the front passenger seat, directing DS Felix Fernando through the traffic, as he got ever nearer to self-exploding with uncontrolled rage. They could see the column of smoke emanating from Euston, thick billowing smoke, Frankie needed to be there, he couldn't be stuck in some never ending traffic jam, this was the real McCoy, what the ATU was about, and being gridlocked just wasn't an option. In the back of the car Detective Constables Sylvia Hardacre and Pete Daggett were strapping on protective vests, the sound of Velcro

THE SHATTERED EAGLE

vainly attempting to drown out Frankie's increasingly obscene ranting and raving.

"Move you daft bitch, move, for God's sake! Hardacre if that stupid cow doesn't pull over shoot her! I mean it, draw your weapon and blow her empty fucking head to bits! At last, yes and to you too love! Come on Felix, come on, it'd be quicker to get out and take the tube, honestly mate, make them have it, get past them."

As they went nowhere Frankie leaned across, he knew much to Felix's annoyance, and pressed the horn on the steering wheel repeatedly.

"Get out of the way!"

A path seemed to open up in front of them, although it was tight, painfully so, he could see the lights of several Ambulances ahead suddenly begin to move forward.

"Go Felix, Go! Follow them, don't give anyone a chance to box us in again, quick move it!"

"No Guv, it's too bloody narrow!" the driver argued, but he was wasting his breath.

"Bollocks is it, you'd get a bus through there, a big wide one at that, now just go!"

Felix accelerated ahead. The screeching of metal on metal left them in no doubt they may have got a bus through there, but not a six month old *BMW 5 Series*. The wing mirrors both tore off, one of which broke the side window with a loud crack right by Frankie's ever reddening face.

"Bollocks! Just keep driving Felix, maybe they didn't notice."

"There, keep going!" Frankie directed as Felix continued to drive through the snarled up morning traffic, the gap now big enough to pass through without damaging any more cars. The phone on Frankie's vest suddenly illuminated.

"Howard...Yes, yes... Casualties? Right, who we got on the ground? ... I'd say no more than a few minutes now, there's a channel opened in the road, hopefully we can go all the way without any delay, providing Felix doesn't wreak anymore mayhem and destruction that is. See you there."

Hanging up Frankie turned to address the other three officers in the car, "It's definitely a bomb, a big one. We got a high rate of casualties, they say it's chaos down there. This is big, bloody nasty. Felix, once we get near, park anywhere we can, I can't be sitting in this all day, whilst that's going on in front of us."

Approaching the junction with the Euston Road the traffic again ground to a halt, the line of Ambulances apparently now parking up wherever they could, Frankie was already opening his door shouting at Felix, "Over there, over there! Put it up on the pavement, we'll walk the rest!"

"But Frankie..." Felix tried to protest.

"No bloody 'But Frankies' just throw it up on the path will you, Jesus Christ Felix, just do it."

"As you say Guv," Felix pulled the car over directly outside of a *Starbucks*, the pavement was lined with onlookers, who shuffled along as the car inched into them,

THE SHATTERED EAGLE

Felix tooting his horn, in case the wailing siren wasn't enough warning that they were likely to get run over if they didn't shift.

"Move out the way you fucking retards," Frankie shouted, although the retards outside would have been oblivious to his insults due to the afore mentioned siren and tooting. One of the staff from the coffee shop came running out to remonstrate as they had almost blocked his doorway completely, but Frankie was having none of it.

"Police! So fuck off back inside your shop Espresso Boy and next year you be sure to pay your taxes!"

The whole road was now shrouded in a thick black cloud, as they ran towards the devastated railway station, the road outside was a mass of Fire Engines, Ambulances and Police Vehicles. Frankie's chest was heaving, partly from the sprint from the junction where they had abandoned their car, and partly from inhaling all the smoke that was laying so heavy in the air. As they ducked under the taped cordon that had been set up around the area they moved towards the doors to the terminus. It was a surreally horrendous sight, smoke and dust was still wafting around the concourse, which was doubling as a mobile field hospital. The smell of burning filled Frankie's nostrils, and the noise was truly disturbing, initially he could only stop and stare, turning to the other three who were all apparently rendered as immobile as their boss.

The view before them was one straight from some horror film, all around were injured people, the limbless, the bloodied, the dazed and the grazed.

"Oh Fuck-ing hell." Frankie mumbled to himself, this was after all Euston station, not Central Gaza.

As he brushed through the ticket barriers on Platform Eleven, the true horror of what had happened made itself all too evident.

As head of the ATU he had witnessed some terrible things in his life, dealt with stuff no one outside of those 'in the know' had even heard about. But this was another level. He looked out at the platform littered with so much human tragedy. Hundreds of horrific little dramas, personal tragedies played out in front of his eyes.

Firemen were cutting their way into carriages, paramedics were all over the place, and Police seemed to moving without any idea or guidance. But then what guidance was there to give, this wasn't a crime scene, it was a bloody battlefield.

To his right Frankie could see the sparks and smoke as Firemen cut through a tangled mass of metal where an arm protruded, it was miraculously still moving, how on earth could that be? A paramedic was crouched beside where they toiled holding the hand, mouthing words that the person connected to the arm had no chance of hearing. A group of Cub Scouts were being led single file by a Police Woman past the cutting of steel, none looked hurt, he guessed they had come from the other end of the train, but the terror and fear on their little faces was all too apparent.

THE SHATTERED EAGLE

Moving along he saw a man totally covered in dust, all grey bar the blood streaming from him, moaning and groaning, being tended to on the floor, tears leaving two clear trails through the otherwise totally grey face. And then he saw the girl in what was once a yellow dress, the paramedic who was tending to her apparently giving up, standing and wiping her tortured face with her sleeve, he moved to one side as they wheeled a bloke, covered in blood, a shard of glass protruding from his side across the platform.

This was just total madness.

-FIVE-
Bad News, Sore Eyes, And Pizza In Little Wayford.

Tears were streaming down Oli Allen's cheeks, he was near blinded, what kind of vindictive vegetable was this, he thought, as he stepped back from the plastic chopping board whilst wiping his eyes with the tea towel, desperate to escape the amino acid sulfoxides which were causing such an extreme chemical reaction. Unfortunately within the pokey kitchen he was working in there was little room for escape, in fact there was little room for anything once inside the tiny flat they were now renting in the equally small Northamptonshire village of Little Wayford. He was cooking the evening meal, well evening meal may have been a slight exaggeration, as was cooking, he was in fact adding extra cheese, onions and a few chopped chillies, to an *Iceland Four Cheese Pizza* before bunging it in the oven, but for Oli this was major haute cuisine.

Cooking - along with tidying, using a washing machine, making the bed, and leaving the toilet seat down - was a whole new experience for the twenty five year old Oliver Allen who had up until then resided in the protected sanctuary offered by his parents. He and Kate had moved there together once he had started the job at HMP Forest Green, the nearby prison about two miles down the road, and despite a couple of run-ins with the rejected Darius, who hadn't taken Kate's departure too well, the move had gone pretty much trouble free.

Whilst Oli was wiping manically at his weeping eyes, Kate was in the living room watching the News. She'd not been back from work very long, where she was employed as an administrative assistant at a local builders merchants - or general skivvy as she described it - a job she had managed to find almost instantly once joining Oli in the 'sticks'. But she reckoned it was a million times more rewarding than *Poundslasher*, where they had both previously worked in Enfield, and although hardly affording them the champagne lifestyle it paid moderately better as well.

"Hey Oli, quick come see this, it's bloody awful", she called to the kitchen.

Oli shuffled in, his eyes puffy and pink, although Kate didn't notice, as she focussed on the images on the TV screen before her.

"What is it?" he asked.

"Look, there's been a bomb in London, it was a train at Euston, they reckon over a dozen people killed, Jesus, we were there just last week, that could have been us. Oh my God look at it."

Oli watched the screen, the devastation and destruction being beamed out from the scene, he squeezed in next to Kate on the dark blue sofa that had only been delivered the previous day, and had looked so much bigger in the *Argos* catalogue when they had ordered it. The report went on to explain Police believed it was a terrorist attack, as footage showed Ambulances from earlier that morning queuing around Euston Square, and images of the walking wounded patched together with bandages and draped in blankets, blood showing through the makeshift dressings, victims shocked and battered, tottering around, being led to help.

Of course it was awful, but then Oli thought how shit happens all the time, yes this was particularly bad, but you have to distance yourself from the stuff like this don't you, otherwise you'd be worrying yourself sick about anything and everything, and that wasn't good for anybody. But unfortunately he knew Kate didn't have such a pragmatic view of world affairs, and glancing over he could see the concern on her face.

The report cut to views of the mangled and twisted wreckage of what was once a line of train carriages. The reporter saying '*authorities could not rule out al-Qaeda involvement, although it was of course too early to speculate on such matters, the attack does share similar hallmarks to that of the Madrid bombing in 2004*', before cutting to library footage of the carnage following that atrocity. Then once more back to Euston where the obligatory reporter stood outside the station, getting in the way, whilst regurgitating quotes from the Prime Minister and Queen, who were naturally devastated, shocked and sickened by the events.

"Wow that looks bad, poor bastards, the train must have been packed at that time of day," he said.

"Yeah," Kate replied, "What sort of animals do that?"

"I don't know, the world's a fucked up place. Still, not much we can do about it is there, I'll put that Pizza on, fancy a glass of wine or something, there's a bottle in fridge?"

"Oh go on then twat face, you've twisted my arm, I think it'd be rude not to."

With that Oli reached for the remote and switched to 'The Big Bang Theory', there's only so much carnage someone can watch in an evening, he didn't want to send Kate into a state of total depression, plus the weekend started here, he was off, they needed cheering up, not putting into a night of irreversible doom and gloom.

The weekends had become precious, since he worked every other one, and when they were both off he thought it was important to do something together, he remembered how Kate always used to moan about Darius just sitting on his arse all day, never wanting to go out or do anything other than watch TV, and Oli was all for learning from other peoples mistakes. They had taken to exploring the area, it was the total opposite to London, especially this time of year, and he had amazed himself with how he had adapted to rural life, previously walking was only something he did if he had missed the last bus after the pubs had turned out, only a few months back the thought of him and Kate enjoying a long leisurely stroll through some woods, or by the river would have been preposterous, not least as the thought of doing anything with Kate would have been. Yet here they were living together, and actually getting along nicely thank you very much.

He returned to the kitchen, he was hungry he needed to get that pizza sorted, why hadn't he just thrown it into the cooker as it was, saved himself a whole world of pain.

A couple of minutes later he was wailing, "Argh, argh, bollocks, shit, bollocks!"

Kate jumped up from the settee, and took the couple of paces required to come rushing into the kitchen, concern etched all over her face.

"What's wrong?" she asked, clearly expecting to see at least a severed finger based upon his pained reaction.

"Argh, I've put chilli in my eye, help me, quick wash it out!"

It stung like mad, he was sure his already red and irritated eyeball was melting, being eroded away by the toxic oils from the chilli seeds.

"You're such a twat Oli Allen, here, let me look."

She burst out laughing as she looked at his eye.

"It's not funny!" he protested, his left eyelid battling to stay open, as it desperately tried to expel what had attacked the eye beneath it.

THE SHATTERED EAGLE

"Yes it is dick face, just rinse it out and stop making such a fuss, ya big girl, honestly mate how on earth did you cope before I came along?"

"No really Kate, I think I'm blinded, you don't even care, help me will you, it stings!"

"Aw, look at my big rufty-tufty Prison Officer, ya big soft git, just rinse it out, and don't touch your cock whatever you do!"

"Why the hell would I touch my cock?"

"Because you're a wanker!" she replied, now laughing out loud at his plight.

Through his moderately good eye he could see her looking at him, that warm and loving smile on her face. "Look hold still you wuss, let Nurse Katie have a look will ya', you're acting like a big baby!"

As she tilted his head back by the sink, liquid spilling onto his tee-shirt as she poured the lukewarm water into his eye, he knew even more than ever that he loved Kate Wallander.

-SIX-
All He Wanted Were Some Of His Maltesers

He so wanted to be putting on the brave face, play the wounded soldier, but truth was he still hurt, in fact he wasn't going to even pretend to be in the slightest bit heroic here, he was in agony. Gary Westlake wanted the morphine, he wanted the brown little pills that gave him nice dreams, and he wanted the biggest concern in his life to revert back to being how he was going to get through a working day without actually doing any work.

As the blue nylon band tightened around as bicep he grimaced, whilst Harriett, the rotund nurse whose uniform was far too small for her, once again took his blood pressure, nodding sagely, but saying nothing as she jotted down the numbers on his medical chart, before returning it upon its clipboard to the end of his bed. He was lying in Bed Six, Ward Seven, of St Matthew's Royal Medical College. It had been four days since the 'Euston Bombing', and he had finally had the last of the multitude of glass shards removed from his lacerated and mangled hip. He had also found out where the blood from his head

THE SHATTERED EAGLE

had been coming from, fifteen stitches worth of cut on his now bandaged brow, and after watching the non-stop news bulletins he knew it was received as a result of a bomb exploding on the train he had only seconds earlier stepped off of.

Glancing around he could see the other five beds where victims from the blast were now situated. The man he knew only as Ted was over in Bed One, directly opposite him, a surprisingly still cheery middle aged man, his face peppered with shrapnel scars, Gary had overheard them telling him the previous day that he would be permanently blind in his left eye, which due to the fact that it was no longer there came as no small surprise to Ted.

Next to Ted was Mags in Bed Two, Mags who now had no need to ever go shopping for tights or stockings again, and certainly would never need to visit *Clarke's* shoe shop for the rest of her days.

Gary had no idea who was in Bed Three, as the curtains were always drawn, the only sign that someone was actually in there being the almost endless stream of nurses responding to his or her 'bell' every five minutes.

Bed Five to Gary's left was currently empty and neatly made by the nurses, Axel the teenage Jamaican occupant was in the operating theatre where they were digging around and stitching no doubt in the hope that they could restore something resembling a symmetrical face, something the bomb had robbed the kid of so cruelly.

In Bed Four resided Eddie, Gary looked across at him, sitting up upon the pillows Harriet had five minutes earlier plumped up for him, a vacant look dominating his craggy face, seemingly oblivious to everything around him, he must have been all of ninety years old. Gary had no idea what injuries poor old Eddie had sustained, but was pretty sure he would never leave that place breathing, in all the time he had been in there he had not had a single visitor, nor spoken a solitary word to any of them, just lying there laboriously breathing with *that* look on his face. He wasn't sure if Eddie had even been injured at all, maybe he was just travelling, or sleeping rough on the platform, but was in too bad a shape to be left anywhere else other than a hospital bed when the paramedics found him.

Through the news reports and newspapers he had discovered over the past couple of days that the Fat Accountant on the train was actually Simon Fisher, a structural engineer from Bletchley, unfortunately 'was' being the apt description for poor old Simon, although Gary had never rated his chances much, seeing as one of his abiding images of the carnage was the severed arm still clutching the rather inappropriately named 'Bag for Life', it shocked him no end to think that he was one of the last souls to see Simon breathing air, and he felt a pang of regret for developing such a low opinion of him.

He also now knew that Gill Montague was not in fact a Camden Council Diversity Manager, but a mother of a one year old daughter, called Kayla, she was from Milton Keynes and was on her way to London for a shopping trip, but alas Gill, like Simon and 16 other people just doing what they did every day, was blown to bits for no reason that made any sense what so ever.

He had watched the TV footage almost endlessly, unable to draw away from its spell, transfixed by some hypnotic hold on him. He felt so much guilt, not just for being alive, but that he was still focussing upon himself so much, not his good fortune that he was still there, but the wretched luck that he was on that doomed train in the first place. Was it selfish to have such thoughts? Should he feel more emotion towards the dead and maimed, and not just his own situation?

Stop it! It wasn't being selfish, he once more told himself, more pity for the now departed Simon and Gill, wouldn't bring them back, miraculously breathe life back into their mangled corpses, no they were his emotions, and his to fixate on what he pleased, and at that moment in time fixating on his misfortune was what he wanted to do.

And yet he knew he was kidding himself, because it wasn't just himself he was considering, he wished it was, but an even more vivid image kept surfacing, monopolising his mind, no matter how much he wanted to push it back, back into the compartment in his brain where it could be looked away and long forgotten. The look in her eye, almost pleading if not for help then relief, the intestines spewing forth like a long string of human sausages, the yellow dress, that damn yellow dress, haunting every dream and blighting his mind's eye in waking hours, he should have been helping her, even if it was just to put her out of her misery.

Then that other image surfaced, no longer guilt but anger, because once more he pictured the boy scurrying off without his bag, the naïve well intentioned call to him, the kid who had earlier had his sympathy, his concern, the kid who he was going tell the Police about in fifteen minutes, providing they bother to turn up this time, the kid who he was sure was to blame for everything!

Why haven't the Police been to see him yet?

Lying in his sterile prison, Gary sighed, he was tethered to his bed by saline ropes dripping into that little green tap thing they insisted on sticking into the back of his hand, causing severe disruption to his scratching routine, which as a side effect of the morphine was now worse than even he could have imagined.

His head was full of half prepared sentences as he contemplated what he wanted to say to the Police when they deemed him important enough to actually turn up, where the hell were they?

Then he heard those familiar tones coming down the corridor.

"No Josh, wait for heaven's sake, they're not for you, they're for Dad, no you can't open them now, I'm sure he'll let you have some, just be patient."

And through the door onto the ward they burst, Fran, Josh and Amy, he felt his face illuminate, a sense of reality returning to this messed up scenario he shouldn't be in, some semblance of normality entering the insanely unreal nightmare. Josh and Amy ran forward slamming a large

THE SHATTERED EAGLE

box of *Maltesers* into his lap, whilst both exploding forth with unintelligible chat he could have no chance of keeping up with, whilst Fran came over and planted a large kiss on his lips.

"How are you today Gaz? You do look so much better, you looked bloody terrible yesterday, didn't want to say anything though as I thought you looked miserable enough as it was," she laughed.

It was so good to see Fran and the kids, but it only made him think how desperate he was to leave this place and get home.

"They finally got all that stuff out of you then, is it sore love?"

"Oh it kills, just kills, I think I'm going to end up a smack head by the end of the week, I'm becoming a morphine fiend, but got to admit I love the stuff. Haven't had any for an hour or so though, I wanted to keep my head clear for you and when the Police come."

As he spoke Amy was beside him holding out a folded piece of paper, "It's for you Dad, I made it myself, can we have one of your sweets please."

"Sure pet, help yourself, but make sure you save some for me and Mum, don't be a greedy guts darling."

He leant over giving her a big kiss, and 'fist bumping' Josh, who had informed him that at 12 he was too old for kisses, then looked at the paper Amy had presented him with, it was a picture of him in his hospital bed, holding a bunch of grapes, well Fran told him it was a bunch of grapes, if grapes were pink, and he was sure it was him, even though in the picture he was either extremely tanned or of Afro/Caribbean persuasion, and why his arm was in a sling he didn't know, although to Amy's credit she had got the bandage on his head right.

"It's lovely darling," he said, meaning lovely in the way that all kids drawings are 'lovely darling', just like school plays are 'fantastic' and any story they write 'really good', although when it came to Amy's attempts at violin, 'perhaps you should stick to recorder, you're really good at that' was as good as he could muster at the time.

Whilst Josh and Amy munched as they raced their way towards the bottom of the box of sweets, which Gary really had been hoping to save until later as he had no sweet stuff left in his little hidey-hole cupboard, Fran told him about what she had heard they had missed at Sheila and Clive's social gathering.

He watched her rapt, this was just what he needed, her face was so alive and eager to tell him the story, he knew she'd burst if she didn't get it out immediately.

"Well Gaz, Debbie says it was the best yet, you know how Clive and Fiona's Paul don't get along, well they ended up in a Golf tournament on the *Nintendo wii*, Deb's says it was the funniest thing she's ever seen, they wouldn't let anyone else play, and as they got more and more pissed, they got increasingly competitive. Sheila told Clive to get off and let someone else have a go, and he told her to shut up, and that after ten years he couldn't listen to another one of her boring and whiney moans, she ran upstairs in floods of tears. At this point Paul, who Deb's reckons had necked the best part of a bottle of Scotch, told Clive exactly what he thought of him, called him a pompous, arrogant…"

She drew closer to him before whispering the "he called him the C-Word," and then returned to her normal tone.

"...and then offered him outside to settle it! Well she says they both bowled outside, pissed as farts shouting abuse at each other, and as Clive raised his fists and danced around like a cross between Mohammed Ali and a dressage horse, a suitcase hit him square on the head. Sheila had thrown it out the window with all his suits and stuff, just as he was stumbling below. Debs reckons it was bloody hilarious. Had to call an Ambulance, even as they shut the doors before driving off she could hear Sheila crying inside screaming how sorry she was!"

Gary winced as he laughed at the thought of middle-class mayhem in rural bliss, of Clive being flattened by a suitcase, it would have almost been worth not being blown up for.

"Oh Fran please don't make me laugh it makes me hurt like hell" he pleaded. But his beloved was a great believer in laughter being the best therapy, which it most certainly wasn't at this particular moment. Still it took his mind off the carnage and his self-imposed mental dilemma of whether he was feeling enough sympathy for others, which is just what he needed at that time.

"So what happened, how is poor old Clive?" he asked, although he was secretly hoping it was nothing minor, although couldn't say it in front of the kids.

"Oh he's fine, a small cut, luckily she didn't put too much in the case before hoofing it onto his head, I think it was one of her dramatic gestures, rather than a real attempt to evict poor old Clive, I reckon they're OK, Debs hasn't heard from them since, and Fiona and Paul are persona non-grata, but you know what they're like, they'll get over it."

"What about you love? How you holding up? It can't be too easy at home at the moment."

"Oh we're coping, these two…" Fran nodded towards Josh and Amy who were sitting at the end of the bed ensuring he would be chocolate-free that night, "…have been really good, local celebs at school, what with their Dad being blown up and all, plus your Mum's moving in to help out for a while, so…"

"Whoa! Stop, stop, you're kidding aren't you! Tell me you're kidding Fran!"

"Oh shut up, you know you love her really, and someone's going to have to bed bath you when you get home tomorrow, it'll be like when you were a baby again, you know how much she loves the photos of you being bathed, although I'll have to warn her your little winky has grown over them 46 years, though let's be honest Gazmo, not by much!"

Fran clearly thought that was hilarious, although Gary knew she would suffer as much as he would if his Mum came to stay, but apparently Fran was willing to take that hit, it appeared the ultimate in schadenfreude. Even though he had been impaled with glass within an inch of his life and probably experienced the nadir in his existence, she was actually delighting in the suffering that only his mother could inflict upon them. The thought of Mum nursing him through this filled him with dread, he loved her dearly, genuinely did, but why not just rub salt and vinegar into the weeping wounds whilst you're at it.

"When's she coming love?"

"Oh Gary, she's made me promise to call her the moment we know when you'll be discharged."

She couldn't hold back her laughter whilst saying that, wow he had married a sadistic cow!

"She doesn't want her boy to have to endure a moment without her," she was still laughing, lots. "Here Josh give your Dad a choccy, I think he needs something to put a smile back on his face."

As Gary laughed he heard a cough to his right, "Excuse us interrupting Mr Westlake, I'm DC Jay DeHavalland, and this is DC Peter Daggett, we've come to talk to you about Friday, are you able to spare us a few minutes?"

Gary turned to face the Policewoman who had spoken, he guessed she was in her twenties, her long blond hair was tied back in a pony-tail, she was wearing jeans and a fitted lilac shirt, she didn't look much like a Police Officer, more a primary school teacher. But when she ask for a few minutes it was clearly not a question, and he presumed translated to 'Please Mrs Westlake disappear and take your kids with you', a point that wasn't wasted on Fran as she gathered the children.

"I'll give you all space to talk, come on kids, we'll go and watch some TV in the day room."

Once they had gone the young Policewoman took out a small notepad, hardly even making eye contact with him.

"Is it OK to call you Gary, Mr Westlake?"

"Yes, please do, no worries."

"Right Gary I want to go through the journey with you from the moment you got on the train until the time you were taken to hospital, I appreciate you probably feel there's nothing new to tell us, but there may be something that can help us, so…"

Gary could barely hold it in, 'nothing new to tell us', he had plenty to bloody tell them!

"Look, for over a day I've been trying to get someone to talk to me, I do have something I want to say, I did see something, and I'm pretty sure it's something relevant. I think I saw the boy who planted the bomb!"

Both Officers were initially silent. DC Daggett, who it had to be said did look very much like a Police Officer in his crumbled suit and cheap tie, had gone from intently watching Eddie in Bed Four, probably wondering if he was alive or not, to staring at Gary instead, but with a look that was either disbelief or disdain.

"You saw the bomber!" he proclaimed. "You think you saw the bomber and didn't tell anyone!"

"Of course I told someone, I've been asking to speak to you since I came around, I've had nurses call for me, I've seen coppers walking past who have just shrugged me off telling me I'll be interviewed in good time, and to get

THE SHATTERED EAGLE

some rest, you may not have noticed but I'm doped up to eyeballs having been in surgery, I'm not exactly in a position to pop along to my local Police Station and give a statement. Thankfully you're here now, so please stop judging me and listen!"

All that good natured warmness and humour, and of course the dread of his Mum's visit Gary had been enjoying with Fran just a few seconds earlier had evaporated into the ether, how dare they judge him like that, did they really think seeing the kid who may be responsible for this shit storm is something he wanted to keep to himself, the cross he wanted to bear alone, No! He wanted to off load this as quickly as possible.

"OK, Gary, we're listening now," Jay said, drawing closer as she took her pen from her pocket. "Please tell us in your own time what you want to us know."

Where should he begin, getting on the train? Seeing him cramped between the late Gill and Simon? Calling after him? He'd had it all planned in his head, his grand statement, but instead decided to go for the abridged highlights, the sheer pertinent facts.

"I saw a boy sitting with a holdall on the train, once we got to Euston he rushed past me without it, I called after him then the bomb went off."

Hmm, he thought, perhaps that was a little too abridged, as both Officers initially sat there in silence.

"I'm pretty sure he made it away." Gary added, just to break the silence.

"You say you saw him, would recognise him?" Jay asked.

"Yes."

Daggett turned to Jay, "I'll phone Howard."

"I think you best," she replied.

Daggett scurried off, no longer disinterested, whist Jay now looked lost, her calm enthusiasm replaced with the weight of suddenly being out of her depth, confronted with the prospect of having a real witness to an all too real atrocity.

"Pete's just calling someone who's going to want to talk to you Gary, I'll wait here but I'll let you tell Detective Chief Inspector Howard, he's the one we report to, about all of this when he gets here."

At last he had got their attention, he could pass on the flame of knowledge, the black kid could fill someone else's mind day and night, not just his.

Jay smiled at him weakly, devoid of her pre-prepared questions she was unsure apparently what to say, an awkward silence had developed, but Gary was happy to let it exist, at least until her boss arrived.

Fifteen minutes had passed, Jay was still sitting on the chair, pretending to write something in her pocket book, every now and then flashing Gary a reassuring smile, probably just her way of coping with the silence which followed once she realised Gary actually may have been able to help, he could suddenly hear more voices in the corridor outside, an unrecognisable conversation as at least half a dozen pairs of boots clip-clopped at pace in their direction, the static squall of Police radios could be heard as well, Jay got to her feet and moved towards the doorway just behind her, Gary guessed her boss had finally arrived.

Only one of the unseen visitors came in, he was tall about 6'2" wearing a Fred Perry polo shirt, dark blue trousers, and a pair of well-worn but highly polished brown brogues, he looked about 40 years old, although it was hard to tell, he had one of those faces which were difficult to age.

"DCI Howard," he introduced himself as he walked towards his new star witness holding out a hand, which Gary shook.

Pulling up one of the plastic chairs he drew in close to Gary, before reaching out and helping himself to a couple of Gary's chocolates, "Hey DeHavalland, get these curtains closed, then sort me out a coffee, white, one sugar, and get Mr Westlake a drink, you are allowed a brew aren't you, not nil by mouth or anything like that?"

Gary nodded back, as Jay hovered around them drawing the curtains, as he answered, "The same please".

"So Mr Westlake, my colleagues tell me you may have seen something at Euston which is going to fill me with excitement. Now I'm not easily aroused when it comes to crimes, but I'm getting a little twitch on this one, so correct me if I'm wrong, but you saw someone leave a bag on the train?"

"I thought he'd just forgot it," Gary answered. "I'd been standing right near him the whole journey, I tried to call out to him but…" he trailed off like he couldn't finish the sentence, couldn't utter the words 'it blew up', why not he was able to tell the other two just a little while earlier, but Howard must have picked this up, taking on the conversation.

"Tell me about the journey, anything you noticed, anything you think was unusual, or indeed anything that was usual, this is your story, start where you got on the train."

Gary thought hard, to ensure it was actually the beginning, he wasn't missing something prior to the station.

"Well I got on at Leighton, the train was rammed with people, I just found a space where I could, as usual there was nowhere to sit down, all the seats were full. I remember standing at the side of the seats where he was sitting and thinking how cramped he looked."

"Good, tell me about him. You know, his age, height, ethnicity, what he was wearing, in your own time. But first build a picture in your mind, imagine he's sitting there, take a second to get that image, shut your eyes if it helps, really focus on that boy."

Gary closed his eyes, picturing him, squeezed in his seat between the faux accountant and non-existent council worker from Camden, those two people who would later be literally blown to bits. For a brief moment his picture was shattered as he heard the curtain open and Howard saying, "Wait a moment," to who he presumed was the Policewoman with his cuppa. He once more pictured the scene, the train speeding along, the smooth motion of the tracks, that boy sitting there, then he saw the guts spilling through the summer dress, limbs and bits of flesh everywhere, he winced, probably visibly as he heard Howard say, "It's OK Gary in your own time, keep focusing."

He was back in the carriage, before all hell broke loose, back to three commuters stuffed onto that seat which in reality could only ever seat two people comfortably.

He began again, talking quietly, his eyes still shut, his mind still focused on that train, "He's there in the seat when I got on, I'm sure he was. He was about 18 to 20 years old, black, thin, I reckon he would have been about 5'6", he wasn't tall. He was wearing jeans, a blue tee-shirt, it had writing on it, but I can't remember what it said, and a baseball cap, it was red, it had a logo I didn't recognise, I think it was a lion's head, or the silhouette of one, to be honest I wasn't really paying much attention to what he was wearing. He had a bag, a black holdall stuffed under his seat, or at least I presume it was his, I noticed it because I was wondering what he did, what he was doing on the train, it sounds silly, as there was no reason to wonder this, I just people watch I suppose."

He took a deep breath, to refocus, reboot the scene in his mind's eye.

"I didn't notice what he had on his feet, I must have seen as I saw the bag behind them, but I can't remember."

"Was there anything unusual about his appearance Gary, any scars, tattoos, birthmarks, anything that set him apart?" Howard asked, in almost a whisper, as if not to disrupt Gary's near hypnotic state.

"Not really. Wait yes, there were scars on his forehead." The image flashed into his mind, how had he not remembered them? "Three lines a couple of inches long, I think, I only saw them briefly when he took his baseball cap off, but yeah, he definitely had three scars."

"How did he seem on the journey Gary?"

"Normal. He looked uncomfortable, but he didn't show it, he didn't appear agitated, certainly not nervous."

"Was he alone?"

"I think so, there was no one else with him as far as I could see, he certainly never spoke a word to anyone else."

"Please, tell me about when you arrived at Euston."

"I recall going past the '1 Mile' sign, and making my way towards the doors, I wanted to get away quickly, I looked around and saw him stand up, it was only as he rushed past me as we left the train that I noticed he didn't have the bag with him, it was then I called out to him."

"Then what."

"Then it happened."

Gary was crying, he was initially unaware he was even doing it, concentrating so much on the pictures in his mind, but now he was actually physically sobbing, he could feel tears in his eyes as he was talking , but had no way of fighting it, he had to let it out.

THE SHATTERED EAGLE

"You're alright Gary, I'll get that drink, I'll be right back."

Sobbing into the bed sheet pulled to his face he wanted to control it, but he couldn't, it was like a pressure valve that has been blown out by an impossible to contain build-up of emotion. He just sobbed and sobbed.

Howard whispered to Jay, obviously he thought out of earshot, "Keep an eye on Weeping Beauty, I'll be right back."

Almost immediately Howard returned but it was not with a much needed beverage, but armed Police, three of them, all wearing flak jackets, and carrying what Gary presumed were some kind of machine gun. He suddenly felt embarrassed at his emotional outpouring, especially as he was now being referred to as Weeping Beauty behind his back, although that embarrassment was soon replaced by anger. He watched on in a kind of horror as two of the armed Police took up position at the foot of his bed, whilst the third positioned himself by Eddie's resting place, the old man oblivious to all the drama, still just staring at the ceiling, as the armed copper surveyed the room, his weapon arcing around with him as he turned.

Howard brushed past the new Kevlar clad bedstead, "Gary, we're going to move you to a private room for the time being, I've lots more to ask, and I'm going to want to go through some pictures with you, maybe some video footage, but I'd like to get some privacy before we start. OK?"

He felt almost dazed, had he taken too many of the brown pills without realising? Half hour ago he had been joking with Fran, now there were armed Police everywhere, for heaven's sake, was this real?

There was no time to wonder though, nurses were now scurrying around, the brakes were off his bed and he was being wheeled out, as they went the Police with guns were stepping backwards, their weapons slowly moving from side to side, he noticed Ted and Mags watching jaws dropped open, as he was wheeled out the ward, the third Policeman by Eddie retreated backwards following the procession. As he was wheeled past the nurses' station, he noticed more uniformed Police at either end of the corridor and others blocking entrances to the adjoining wards. Howard was talking to another man who was wearing baggy cargo shorts and a Hawaiian shirt, clashing with the tight flak jacket over his torso.

"Arrange the transport ASAP, I want the street cleared ready."

"Look Frankie, are you sure it's necessary? This isn't overkill is it?"

"He saw him Felix, I'm sure he saw him, I think he can actually I.D. him, I'm not leaving him here!"

Where were they taking him?

Where was he going?

He suddenly felt very scared, 'I'm not leaving him here' but this was a hospital, He was not going home until at least tomorrow, and then when he did leave he actually wanted to go *home*, this was all too fast.

THE SHATTERED EAGLE

"Gary, Gary!" It was Fran she was trying to push past a Policeman in the corridor, but there was no way he was letting her past. Gary saw him holding her back, then a female Officer joined him as they ushered her back away from his sight.

A wave of panic hit him hard, shit this isn't right, this isn't right at all.

"Fran!"

Sitting up he swung his legs around on the moving bed, he could feel the tube tugging on his hand, he pulled it out, blood spurted high all over his chest, as he attempted to jump free of the bed, he hit the floor with a bump, and scrambled to his feet, his armed escort swinging around, pointing their guns in his direction. Howard shouting, "For fuck's sake stop him!"

"Gary!"

He could hear Fran calling and shouting, but could no longer see her in the corridor, pushing forward he only took one step before he was flattened to the floor.

"Easy with him, be careful!" It was Howard speaking again, "Get him back on the bed, for crissake, what is this, the Keystone fucking Cops?"

Gary could feel himself being lifted, the fight already knocked out of him, he looked down at his hip, where there was now a big fresh patch of blood, as he was placed back onto the bed, he felt helpless, even to help the woman and children he loved more than anything in the world, totally helpless, no not helpless, useless. He lay on the bed being wheeled to heaven only knew where, he could no longer hear Fran, where was he going?

Howard spoke to him, "For fucks sake Gary, what was that about, you'll do yourself an injury, you're my star witness, I need you in top shape, not some wrecked heap on the floor. I'll have your family brought straight over, really there's no need to worry, we're going somewhere safe."

-SEVEN-
Welcome To Safehaven, It's A Lovely Day Outside.

Gary found himself waking in what appeared to be another hospital room, he guessed he must have been given something to get him off to sleep, as he couldn't recall much at all after he had leapt out of his bed like some demented Lazarus. But this time his was the only bed in the room, but he was not alone, Jay the Policewoman from St Matthew's was sitting by the door, in what appeared to be her off-duty clothes, well he assumed they were as he had not come across a Police Force yet who issue their staff baggy shorts and a Led Zeppelin tee-shirt. His head ached as he recalled the events before he went to sleep.

"Where's Fran, the kids, where's my family?" he asked groggily as he tried to sit up, but a thick nylon belted strap across his chest prevented him moving any more than a couple of millimetres.

"What's happening, why am I tied to this bloody bed, where's my family!"

He could feel his heart racing, beating against the thick nylon strap, what was the idea? He had done nothing wrong except be in the wrong place and get himself hurt, yet he was the one tied to the bed!

Jay walked over, smiling, but hardly convincingly, "Please Gary, remain calm, your family are here, I'll get Mr Howard, he's been…"

"Sod Howard, let me go, I'm out of here, I'm out of here do you hear me!"

They couldn't do this to him, he was strapped down like some psycho killer, it was tight, and it was uncomfortable, they couldn't treat him like this.

He saw her scurry to the door, calling out, "Guv, he's awake."

She returned, but before he could say anything Howard breezed in.

"Right Mr Westlake, I'm not going to…"

Gary tried to interrupt, tell him what was what, but Howard clearly wasn't someone who can be interrupted, not easily anyway.

"Shut up and listen Mr Weslake, I'm sorry about what happened earlier, but you have no idea, no idea what so ever of what we're dealing with here. Now I can pussy about all day being polite and civil, bowing to you, apologizing, hoping you don't report me to the Police Complaints Commission, or run crying to your MP, but that's not going to catch the person that put you and dozens of others in hospital, as well as killing eighteen law abiding, taxpaying citizens. I thought you were in danger.

THE SHATTERED EAGLE

Do you know what, I still do. As far as we know you are the only person, living and breathing at least, who saw the person that planted that bomb. Now I can bend you over, spread your cheeks and kiss your hairy arse all day, or I can find that boy you told me about. Now what do you want me to do?"

Gary again tried to speak, but before he'd even as much as opened his mouth, Howard was off again.

"Oh I'm sorry, I gave the impression you had a choice, actually that wasn't an open question, I was being, what's the word now, rhetorical, that's it, fucking rhetorical. I do that a lot, it annoys some people, but I think you'll be OK with me, considering I may have saved your life by pulling you out of St Matthew's when I did, are you OK with me Mr Westlake?"

Wow what an arsehole, Gary thought, who the hell does he think he's talking to?

"Is that a rhetorical question?" Gary answered.

Howard was silent for a second, then smiled and winked, "Good answer. I like that, good one, 'is that a rhetorical question', an attempt at humour, well done. Right before we do anything else let's get you unstrapped, something to eat and drink, and let you talk with your lovely family."

Howard moved over to the bed and began to unbuckle the strap, before pausing, "You're not going to put one on me are you Gary? Because I'm not undoing this strap to see you break my nose, and to be honest I will hit back, I'm very old testament in that respect."

How to answer that one, Gary thought, he had spoken to him like a piece of shit, had him strapped to a bed, and he had no idea where he was. He ached like mad, and felt crap. But then again was that one of his rhetorical questions, as he continued un-strapping him, obviously confident he would not be 'putting one on him'.

"I'm going to get a laptop, I've got some stuff I want you to look at, I'll be back in fifteen minutes, if you need anything ask Jay, she'll be outside your room. I'll get her to get your family too, they've been waiting for you to wake up. There you go you're free again."

And with that Howard was gone.

A wide line of sweat remained where the thick strap had been holding him pinned to the bed, the hospital gown he was still clothed in stuck to his skin, how long had he been there?

Within a few seconds Fran came in, running over and hugging her un-trussed husband tightly, making him wince, as he realised that his wounds must have been re-stitched after opening up earlier.

"Oh Gary, I was so worried, I had no idea where they were taking you, you're OK aren't you?"

"I'll be fine love, where are the kids? And where exactly are we?"

"It's like a hotel," Fran answered, "I've no idea where, the kids are in our room watching TV, I wanted to make sure you were OK before I brought them down, they said we'd be safe here, but I'm scared Gaz, I don't think they're telling us anything close to the whole story. That whole thing at the hospital, that was unreal. They took my phone you know, I've no way of letting anyone know we're here, they said we mustn't communicate with anyone, for our own safety."

Gary pondered, it was all too much, this sort of stuff didn't happen to the likes of them, they were just normal people, this wasn't the Westlake Story, 'Episode Three, Blown up and stuck in a secret hospital'.

"It's all messed up Fran, I don't know what the hell's happening, argh my head aches. Howard said he's coming back soon with a computer, he wants me to go through images, see if they can identify that kid I saw, I'm going to try and pin him down, get some answers, but to be honest Fran the bloke's a total arsehole."

Jay came back into the room with some toast and a cup of coffee for them both.

"There you go Gary, drink this, is there anything else I can get either of you?"

"No we're fine thanks," Fran answered, "If we can just have a little bit of time to chat, that'd be great."

"Sure," Jay gave her another one of her smiles as she exited, "Just shout if you need anything, I'll be just outside."

"So what is this place Fran, it looks like a hospital?" Gary asked while looking around his surroundings.

"Only this room, like I said the rest of what I've seen is more like a hotel, just we seem to be the only people here, well apart from Police and staff that is. I've asked loads where we are, but all I get is that we're safe."

"Hmmm, safe."

He didn't feel safe, didn't feel safe in the slightest bit, although at least they were all together now. He thought of their families out there worrying, turning up at the hospital with grapes and magazines to find just an empty bed, with Ted or Mags recounting what had occurred, what were they telling them? What elaborate story could possibly placate his mother when she found him missing? And what about Fran? He knew her well enough to tell that this was her brave face, she was no doubt feeling as scared as he was only with the added burden of not just being strong for him, but for Josh and Amy as well.

He needed to know what was going on, he felt himself becoming more agitated, uptight, yes he needed to know what was going on, he wanted to know straight away!

"I need to speak to Howard love, this isn't right," he could feel the itch coursing through his body, anxiety filling his mind. "I'm sorry Fran, can you get Howard now, I need to sort this out."

He didn't want to push Fran away, he needed her, but he could feel himself losing control, his composure vanishing as itchy stressed up hell wreaking havoc. Was this a panic attack? He could feel his breathing speeding up, heart racing, he needed to speak to Howard now, right away!

He could hear Fran talking outside the door, presumably to Jay, she was raising her voice becoming more animated, "Just get him now will you, get him please."

She came back into the room, her face unable to mask her concern for her husband.

THE SHATTERED EAGLE

"It's OK love, Jay's getting him, are you alright darling? Look Gaz, take slow breaths, you need to stay calm. When he does come I'm stopping too, I want to hear what he's got to say, I'm sorry but this affects us too, if he's going to give you answers I want to hear them."

But Gary wasn't arguing with her, in fact he was glad of her support, he felt a mess, he thought he should be the strong one here, but Fran was taking control. And he was glad she was.

"Right folks, DC DeHavalland tells me you want to talk to me, have some questions that can't wait," Howard had burst into the room again. "Go on then, fire away, I'm all ears."

Gary went to talk, but Fran beat him to it.

"We want to know where we are, we want to know why we're here, why we can't go back home, I want to know who's been told what, and…"

"Whoa, whoa, whoa." Howard interrupted.

"One at a time Fran, one at a time, give me a chance."

He walked over to the window, and pulled open the curtains, sunlight flooded into the room.

"Welcome to Safehaven, it's a lovely day outside. I will now try and answer any questions I can, you should know though that I won't be able answer all of them, and Fran you need to accept that."

Fran walked over to the window and looked out.

"It's just fields. Trees and fields."

Gary slid his legs around and hobbled over to join her, dragging a drip and monitor across the floor as he went, he ached like mad, and felt weak, but he needed to move his legs. She had described it perfectly, well almost, she had omitted to mention the 15 foot high razor wire topped fence about half a mile out, but there wasn't another building in sight bar what appeared to be a guard house in front of two large metal gates. Other than that they were literally in the middle of nowhere.

Fran again asked, "Where are we?"

"Like I said," Howard answered, "Safehaven, beyond that I can't tell you anymore, we need to protect you, but also once this is all sorted we need to protect anyone else who may need to come here. Only a couple of people know exactly where we are, DeHavalland out there doesn't, she really hasn't got a clue, and not just because she's a bit thick either. The guys on that gate don't, the lovely ladies who cook your dinner and clean up don't. They're bought here and stay here for two weeks, they live here like you, and when they go home they're none the wiser where they've been working.

"You'll have to realise that like them you are not one of the people that need to know, and before you ask me again, don't bother, because believe it or not I don't know either, and if I don't need to know I'm sure as bloody certain you don't. Right question one dealt with. Please don't ask that one again."

THE SHATTERED EAGLE

Gary nodded but was sure he was lying, both Howard and DeHavalland had to know where they were, of course they did.

"Next," he continued, "why are you here? You're here because - oh for God's sake sit back on that bed will you, you'll do yourself an injury - you're here because Gary witnessed the UK's worst fucking terrorist attack since 7/7, excuse my language Fran, not just witnessed the attack but I think you also got a damn good look at the perpetrator. This is great for me, really good, and in a short while I hope to find out just how good, but believe me Fran until the bomber is arrested, tried and locked up for a very long time, that is very bad for your husband. Yes Gary I am concerned for you, because you have no inkling of just how much some people are going to not want you to be able to stand up in court and point your finger at our man. No idea at all, otherwise you, or your lovely wife here, wouldn't be asking such a stupid question as why you are here."

"Right", he walked over to the end of the bed and glanced at Gary's medical notes, reading as he went on, "That's, where, and why taken care of, I know there are other questions you want to ask, but I want someone else to answer those. You're here under the Anti-Terrorism Witness Protection Programme. One of my colleagues will come and see you at some point during today and explain exactly what that means to you two and young Josh and Amy. I don't honestly know exactly how this works, my main priority is catching the one that did this, but this will be your home for some time, so please, get used to it. I'm not going to say any more, as I'll probably tell you the totally wrong information anyway. Now I'm off again, I'll be back in a short while with that laptop, and me and you Gary are going to look at some pictures, OK?"

Before they could answer Howard had left the room.

Gary was open mouthed, as Fran turned to him, "Oh shit, we're going to be here for ages aren't we. Please tell me he won't be here too!"

"Right Gary, I've got some video footage I want you to look at. It's from the platform at Euston." It had only been five minutes before Howard had returned, he pulled a chair up alongside Gary's bed, and plonked his laptop down on the table that slid over in front of him. Gary watched as he fiddled with some wires as he set it up, he could see he was trying to force the adaptor into the wrong hole, but said nothing.

"You'll have to excuse me, these things do my head in, everyone else seems to have no problems with this bloody machine, but I guess I'm one of those technophobes."

Finally he managed to get plugged in, and he pushed a button which filled the screen with a frozen black and white image.

"We'll take it from here," he was pointing at the screen, the picture began to play, a train is pulling up onto the platform. "Just watch it through once, take a good look then we'll go back and play it again."

THE SHATTERED EAGLE

Gary saw the train slowly coming into shot, he presumed it was his, the one he travelled in on that morning. The train drew to a halt, there was no sound, it all looked so eerie as Gary anticipated what was about to happen. The doors slid open and people streamed off, there was a slight stop motion feel to it, a little bit jerky, yet still a continuous film, he could see the first people running towards the barriers, moments later there's the lad who he was blaming for this nightmare, then he saw himself, it was from a distance but he could see his arm stretched out towards the bag-less murderer, then, well then he saw himself flying through the air. Also dozens of other people blown here, there and everywhere, he saw all what he didn't see on the day, he could see what was happening to everyone else. Howard pressed a button and froze the screen.

"Are you alright Gary? I appreciate this can't be easy."

He felt sick, shell shocked, he noticed his hands shaking, he'd seen all the aftermath on the TV, sketches and graphics of what had happened that day at Euston, but that two minute clip, devoid of sound or colour, was the first time he had seen the explosion as it happened.

"I think so, it's so bloody weird seeing it like that," he answered taking a large swig of water, to compose himself. "Yeah I'll be OK."

"Are you sure you're OK to continue? I can come back?"

"No, I'd like to go on."

And he actually did, he wanted to pass this on now, let him know who he saw, let him take the responsibility.

Leaning over the bed Howard pressed one of the keys on the keyboard and the footage returned to the beginning.

"Right Gary, I want you to talk me through it, take your time, I can slow it down or freeze it at any time. We can zoom in and out. You can watch it as many times as it takes. First I want you to tell me what you're doing as the film plays, OK."

Gary nodded.

"Right in your own time."

He again started the footage, Gary could see the train approaching.

"I'm in the carriage, as the train's coming in, making my way towards the doors probably at this point. It's quite packed in there, but I want to get off quickly as I'm going to walk from the station."

He saw the train slowing to a halt.

"I think it's around this point, as I get near the doors, I see him standing up, the boy who had the holdall, I don't take much notice really, it's just I remember how cramped he was. The doors open and I move out, as I go he pushes past me, he's moving quickly. It's then I notice he hasn't got his bag."

He could see his arm point in his direction on the monochrome screen.

"I call after him, and then…"

His voice trailed off as he stared at the screen. He had picked himself out, saw himself blown across the platform again, the bright flash from the carriage he had just come from and plumes of smoke blowing across the station like a tidal wave of dust. Then he disappeared from view.

"I'm going to zoom into the doors now Gary, I want you to take a good look, I want you to be sure that the kid who pushes past you, the kid you pointed out, is the one in the seat, the one with the bag. OK, hopefully I can do this anyway."

He again pressed a button, the train is approaching once more, as it stops Howard tapped several times on the keys and the image draws in, it's surprisingly clear. Gary could see the doors open, people come off, he saw himself shuffling through, then the would-be bomber pushing past him. Howard froze the frame. Gary could see the face clearly, the clarity was really impressive, no indication in it of what he was about to unleash, the baseball cap, the tee-shirt, it's him, no doubt, that's the person who was wedged between Gill Montague and Simon Fisher.

"That's him," is all he said.

"No doubt, no question?" Howard asked.

"No question."

"Right thanks Gary, Thanks a lot."

-EIGHT-
A Face A Name, A Genuine Suspect.

"Right people listen up"

The chattering continued.

"QUIET!"

DCI Adrian 'Frankie' Howard, stood in front of the huge array of whiteboards covered in photographs with masses of captions scrawled in differing colours, they were in a large well lit room within ATU headquarters, or the 'Red House', as it was commonly known. Tucked behind Charring Cross railway terminal, the building was once a typical London Victorian Police Station, constructed from red brick and large white stones around its windows and doors, but the traditional exterior was in stark contrast to the modern interior which housed the latest in hi-tech equipment, although as a nod to its history the antique blue lamp was still positioned over the entrance, as it had been since 1863.

About twenty jabbering Police Officers fell silent, as Frankie held his hands up. He looked out at his audience, and nodded.

THE SHATTERED EAGLE

"That's better. We've got a new face folks."

He waved a large A3 laminated photograph, in a dramatic flourish through the air, before holding it in front of him with his left hand.

"We've spoken to one of the survivors at St. Matthew's who is sure he saw this character on the train, and is equally sure he saw him making away from the scene. We now believe his name is Alaine DuPont."

Frankie gave the room a few seconds to digest the fact that from having nothing, they now had a face, a name, a genuine suspect. He stuck the photograph on the Whiteboard, and wrote with a green dry wipe pen 'Alaine DuPont - BOMBER?' above it before continuing.

"Here's what we know after a bloody long night's work. DuPont is a French National, he's wanted in France for the rape and murder of his then legal guardian. We don't know too much about this at the moment but we have got a French Officer flying over as we speak, so hopefully we can put some more meat on the bones of that. Now like I say, we've spoken to our witness at St Matthew's, who we now have tucked away somewhere safe, who gave us a damn good description of DuPont, we've checked CCTV and he confirmed it again. This kid is 18 years old, of Somali origin, as I said earlier the French want him already for a killing. That's how we identified him, we ran his face through the system and a red light flashed somewhere at Interpol HQ.

"Our witness on the Euston train recalls that, who we believe to be our boy, left a bag under a seat, he's in no doubt about that, even remembers calling to him to let him know. DuPont's now our top priority, we need to put everything into finding him, I want to know where he got on the train, where he's been, where he went to in London afterwards. I need all this. We now have a name, we have a bomber, who as far as I know is still breathing, we have a living perpetrator, and I want him, we're on Day Five, we now get busy."

Frankie walked back to his office, yeah that should do it, that should light some fires under arses. Sitting in his leather office chair he put his feet up on his desk and leant back, stretching his arms out as he let out a long yawn. He was tired, his eyes had that horrible gritty feel to them, and he was beginning to zone in and out as people talked to him, and a lot of people were talking to him since the Euston thing. He hadn't slept more than a dozen hours since the bomb, and it was definitely catching up, all that driving back and forwards to 'Safehaven' wasn't helping much either, but he knew it would be a few more hours until he would seeing his bed, the pieces were coming together, now wasn't the time for any of them to be closing their eyes.

-NINE-
A Very Peculiar Incident In Boots.

It had been a busy morning in the shop, it always was on Mondays, for some reason everyone in North London over the age of 65 seemed to materialise in one big scrum, desperately seeking flu-remedies, haemorrhoid creams or *Deep Heat*, following what had clearly been some uncomfortable weekends. Marianne Goodhall was working on the over the counter medicines section in *Boots* the chemist, and had been in the centre of the melee for elderly pain relief.

Urgh Jeez, she thought, she was so hungry and really looking forward to lunch, the diet had been going well, but it always left her drained in the mornings, perhaps something a bit more nutritional than a cup of coffee would have been a good idea for breakfast, but sod it, she had to shift those allusive last few pounds, the quick route was definitely the best route in this situation. The rush appeared to be subsiding a bit, at last giving her a chance to tell Julie about her weekend and the new club she had gone to, that had just opened off the Holloway Road.

"It was a really good night out Jules, although the drinks were extortionate! But we'd managed to smuggle a bottle of Vodka in, Mand' had it in her knickers, and you know, if anyone can stash a bottle where no one can find it, it's Mandy." Marianne laughed at this out loud, guffawing like a braying donkey, before continuing, "So all we had to buy all night were the mixers to go into it. The music was banging, really good, you must come next week, you'll love it."

Whilst she was talking she couldn't help but be distracted as she noted the young lad milling around in front of the counter, listening in to their personal conversation, not looking at anything other than them. Nosey bleeder, for a brief moment she looked him in the eye, he was just looking straight back at her, she had to avert her gaze, he was creeping her out, she thought he looked a bit weird, he clearly wasn't actually looking to buy anything, was just there, kind of staring at them.

"Can I help you?" Marianne asked, which really translated to 'if you're not buying, piss off, can't you see we're talking'.

But the lad said nothing, just continuing to look at them in that creepy way. Then without any prior indication he walked behind the counter.

"Excuse me you can't come around here," Julie explained to him, but he said nothing just walked up to Marianne, staring at her face. This is too bloody weird, she thought, stepping back and raising her hands before her, gesturing for him to back off.

THE SHATTERED EAGLE

"You must go back, staff only behind here, do you understand?" she said, her voice now raised, what the hell was he playing at?

Still he said nothing, but to Marianne's horror reached up and cupped one her breasts, just putting his hand upon it, not groping or squeezing, just literally cupping it. She instantly screamed, and pushed him away, continuing to scream as he just stood there, looking at her. The dirty bastard, the dirty horrible bastard.

Julie pushed him back from behind the counter as two of the male shop staff rushed over after hearing the commotion.

Marianne could only stand and stare open mouthed as Julie explained to her colleagues what had happened, it was all too mad, like some messed up dream.

"He just attacked Mari', he just groped her!" Julie was shouting to them. "Call the Police, filthy bastard, dirty little pervert!"

She could now feel Julie's arm around her shoulder, leading her away from where Tom and Jamie were holding her attacker, trying to console her, whilst still shouting insults at the pervert.

"You're alright Mari', the Police are coming to take him, the boys have got him, filthy little nonce, sick bastard, you're alright love."

Yet the attacker offered no resistance as he was bundled off to the manager's office to await the Police, just staring blankly back at Marianne, saying nothing, offering no explanation, no apology, no reason why he had just grabbed her like that, just staring at her, his head turning to look back as he was forced away. That stare, the long lingering stare that would give her so many bad dreams over the coming weeks.

But why had he done it?

-TEN-
Bonjour to The Men From France.

Frankie was again holding court in front of his team of Officers.

"OK folks, here we go, update time. The forensic guys have given us a quick idea of what they've got. The bomb would appear to be Semtex based, and they're sure it was in the carriage where DuPont was. It was probably detonated remotely, although they're still looking into it. It's unlikely our boy had any intentions of going up with the device, which is a bit unusual, as these things normally entail a bit of martyrdom, there's no shortage of volunteers, and it all adds to the effect, good for the cause. As for the bomber himself here's what we know. He got on at Milton Keynes, CCTV has confirmed this, he walked into the station before that, but we still don't know where from, Thames Valley are trawling through all their footage from the area to see if we can get a route. We know he had the bag with him when he went into the station, no sign of any other associates, just him from what we could see. He paid cash, no trail that way, he's pretty much under the radar.

"So, that's where we are then, if we're honest we haven't got a lot, but enough to get busy I'd say. We don't know why he planted the bomb, who was working with him, or where he went to immediately afterwards. We have absolutely no idea where our boy is now. We do know for certain he got on the train at Milton Keynes, has he gone home, back to MK? Hopefully TVP will come up with something, otherwise that's about it. I've got Hercule Poirot outside so…"

Howard looked up and saw Felix Fernando with his hand up.

"Yes Fernando?"

"Sorry Guv, but doesn't Hercule Poirot come from Belgium, not France?"

"Same difference, now stop being a smartarse and listen. So hopefully he will be able to enlighten us. I'm not sure if he speaks English, and as not all of us, well actually none of us, speak French, we've got an interpreter. We'll do questions and whatever after, OK?"

Frankie came back a few minutes later with two people following him.

"OK folks, let's have a bit of quiet! Can I introduce Captain Jean-Paul Matrice and his interpreter Carol Benning. I've asked him to brief us on what they've got on Alaine DuPont."

As Frankie talked Carol translated for the French Police Officer. Frankie observed his Gallic counterpart listening intently, he presumed Matrice was in his early forties, neatly trimmed hair, greying at the temples, he had either just returned from his holidays or resided in the south of the country, as he had a healthy tan, which he was sure women would describe as highlighting his good looks.

"Now as I said earlier," Frankie said, whilst actually thinking why he was scrutinising another male of the species and coming to the conclusion that he was handsome, "we'll hold the questions until the end, let our guest speak first, he has come a long way so listen carefully to what he says as I believe the Met are picking up at least some of his expenses for this trip, so without, as they say, any further ado I hand you to Captain Matrice."

"Merci Monsieur Howard, Bonjour mon amis…" the Frenchman said, his arms gesturing as he spoke, compensating for the language barrier.

Carol took up the translation, although even Frankie had got the gist of the opening part of what Matrice had just said.

"Thank you Mr Howard, hello my friends. Do excuse me not talking to you directly, I am most keen to ensure that we all understand what I am saying as well as possible. As way of an introduction I should explain that I am working on a murder investigation into a crime that occurred close to two years ago. Our only suspect was Alaine DuPont. He is wanted for the rape and murder of his guardian, Anna DuPont, at their home in Brittany. This was a horrendous crime, which shocked the most hardened of us. He disappeared completely afterwards, and until the unfortunate bomb on that train, we have had no genuine leads as to where he went. The events leading up to the crime are, how shall we say, complex, and really I should start at the beginning."

Matrice was drinking a glass of water whilst Carol caught up.

"DuPont, this was not his original name I must add, was a Somali child soldier, he was recruited when very young, we believe his parents may have been killed in the civil war, but we have no way of truly verifying this. At some point he broke away with several others and got involved in kidnapping tourists in Kenya, and selling them on to the gangsters back in Somalia who would ransom them back to their families, companies or governments. The Kenyan Police got wise to one of his raids, and he and his gang were caught up in a fire fight. Thankfully their target was freed with only minor injuries, but DuPont was taken into to custody by the Kenyans, and the trial was arranged.

Now at some point between his arrest and his trial a deal was done by *Compassion San Frontieres*, a French charity which happened to be run by Anna, and the local Kenyan authorities for young DuPont to be flown to France and live with Anna.

"The DuPonts were people with a great deal of influence back in Paris, particularly Anna's husband, Henri, who still works for the Government and is a man of much power. Clearly though three years of enjoying a privileged life with his new family did little to pass on the love and compassion his guardians were investing. After Alaine returned home from school for the summer, he raped

THE SHATTERED EAGLE

Madam DuPont in her own home, before brutally murdering her."

Whilst Carol was relaying his words Matrice was sticking photos to a large white board. There was a school photo of Alaine, a picture of Anna smiling in a rose garden. A shot of the house they resided in. Then crime scene photos, around half a dozen, showing the late Anna, no more than a bloody mutilated corpse, taken from various angles.

"As you can see," Matrice once more continued, talking through Carol. "This was a frenzied attack, our psychologists feel it was born through hate rather than being totally sexually motivated, although of course in any rape there is going to be some element of sexual gratification. As a child soldier in Somalia at that time he would have witnessed rape used as a punishment, a weapon of war. We believe this was aimed at Henri DuPont as much as his poor unfortunate wife."

Matrice took another drink, Frankie noted at that moment a sadness in his eyes that had previously been absent, no doubt born from still having the animal who had inflicted those horrific wounds they were now seeing running free, free to commit an even more horrendous act upon others.

"After the attack Alaine vanished, just disappeared. There were huge resources invested in his hunt, but nothing. It was always believed he made his way to North Africa, probably via Algeria or Tunisia, but that is just a theory, as I said he was never found. We are as keen as you are to see this man caught, and to answer for his crimes. Now I will hopefully answer any questions you may have. Thank you."

Frankie again addressed the room, "Thank you, Monsieur Matrice. I think we'll take a ten minute break before we bombard our guest with all our queries, we can have a drink, take a look at the board there, and we'll start again at quarter past."

Frankie took Matrice to his office, "Café?" he asked, utilising one of the few French words he was confident he knew the meaning of.

"Non merci, je souffre d'une indigestion, c'est que j'ai trop de caféine." Matrice answered.

Frankie was suddenly left feeling stranded, Carol was still outside, and apart from 'café', 'merci' and 'bonjour' he knew no French what so ever, why did he have to show off.

"Look Jean Paul, I'm shit at French, sorry, not very good at speaking the lingo, I should say. Just how much English do you speak?"

Matrice smiled and shrugged, "Mr Howard, I am fluent in three languages, German, Arabic, and English, please feel free to leave your phrase book in your pocket, I'm very happy to converse in English thank you."

"Then why the hell have I just spent £110 an hour on a bloody interpreter?"

"Because Mr Howard, you didn't ask. Presumption is the mother of confusion my friend!"

Frankie shook his head, in disbelief, was this bloke taking the piss, if so he quite liked him.

"Over three hundred quid she cost us in all, and you speak fluent English?"

"Why of course, you are after all part of Europe are you not?" Matrice answered.

"For the time being Captain Matrice, for the time being. Anyway, what are your plans, how long are you staying?"

"Personally I would hope to stay until you have apprehended Alaine DuPont, there are many questions that do need answering, and there is much I may be able to contribute to your investigation, but that is dependent upon the patience of my department."

"Where are you staying?" Frankie asked.

"I will find a nice hotel, the Department, and of course your Police force, have been most generous with the expenses for this visit. In fact are you free this evening? Perhaps we could have something to eat and discuss matters relating to DuPont, call it France's treat, you can choose the Restaurant, I hear English cuisine has developed considerably over recent years, I am very keen to test this out, I'm sure it can only have improved since my last visit."

"Jean Paul, you know what, that sounds like a very good idea, thank you very much, I think I know just the place, give me half an hour, we'll address the troops again, then we'll make a move."

***

As they walked out of the Police Station Jean-Paul Matrice followed Frankie, the English Policeman appeared keen to introduce him to the restaurant they were heading to, walking brusquely ahead, and that in itself wasn't a bad thing, he was hungry, and the meal he had been presented with on the short flight over was far from sufficient.

"Do we need a Taxi?" he asked, as he drew level with Frankie, adjusting his stride to match the taller man's pace.

"No Jean-Paul, we can walk it's not far, I think you'll like it, it's very traditional, very English."

Unfortunately *The Moon Under Water*, with its '£6.99 Burger and a Pint' wasn't what Jean-Paul had in mind with his quest for Great British Cuisine, in fact not what he was thinking of at all! Although the Department's financial office back in France would probably have been relieved at Frankie's idea of fine dining.

He should have got the idea when he asked for the wine list and was told by Frankie, who would clearly never make a fine sommelier, "*Echo Falls*, White, Red or Pink, makes no odds, they're all in the offer."

Jean-Paul felt horrified when he saw the menu, it had pictures of the food! He was 44, not four! He had said to Frankie money was no object, choose anywhere he wished, and he had brought him to place where he was offered 'pink' wine as it was part some Ten Euro deal where it was accompanied by a burger!

The English, he thought, they really have no idea when it comes to cuisine, a country obsessed with watching TV programmes about food, celebrity chefs, food

THE SHATTERED EAGLE

competitions, cooking quizzes, yet all it equated to was hundreds of hours sitting in front of a television, rather than extra time spent in a kitchen. It was like food was some kind of spectator sport here, people watching the rich and famous on TV dine on excellent meals, whilst they stared munching on potato chips and sugary snacks. He knew every house in this so called green and pleasant land had a TV, yet how many had dining tables?

"Frankie, are there no other wines? This is not a restaurant, this is a bar with a microwave. The food it is warmed not cooked, please let us go somewhere else, tonight I pay, we enjoy true cuisine, and fine wines, but not here I fear."

"Jean-Paul," his host replied, "this is a *JD Weatherspoon*, it probably has the best range of beers within a three mile radius, stouts, ales, and yes piss poor lagers for you my continental friend, tonight I'm giving you a little taste of England, fill your boots on burger, it's purely to line your stomach anyway, for tonight the boulevards and cafes are far away, tonight we drink copious amounts of beer, yes beer, we talk, we drink and we get very pissed!" Frankie stood up and moved towards the bar, "My rules, my round!"

As Frankie returned with two pints of lager, Jean-Paul knew that a night out with his English counterpart may not have been such a good idea, his vision of chateaubriand and a nice glass of burgundy, shattered, replaced by reconstituted meat and cheap lager.

"Bottoms up!" Frankie pronounced as he quaffed the best part of half a pint with one swallow.

Oh my God! Jean-Paul thought, we are about to become lager louts, still when in Rome... He drank a large swig of beer, tonight he would just go along with it, but then what choice did he have, he was sitting within what appeared to be a reproduction library, the wall to his left was lined with old leather-spined books, which he guessed no one ever read, he was going eat crap, and the wine was apparently sold solely on the basis of its colour, ha the things we do for a little Entente Cordial.

"So Jean-Paul, tell me about Alaine DuPont, what else do we need to know?" Frankie asked having wiped the froth from his lager from his lips.

"He is one bad person, I genuinely think he is evil. Monsieur and Madam DuPont took him in, cared for him, sent him to one of the finest schools in France, and in return? In return he brutally rapes the poor woman, mutilating her destroyed body, even post-mortem he defiled her. It is my biggest regret Frankie, the thing that haunts me still, not catching this monster. He was just a boy, but never have I witnessed such cruelty. And now, now he has killed eighteen more people, eighteen innocent people, just going to work, just travelling to your capital for a day out, just going about their lives. Perhaps we missed something, allowed him to slip away, didn't do something properly, in which case are we culpable?"

Jean-Paul could see Frankie's face it had changed, he looked genuinely moved by what he had just told him, then without warning he moved to his feet, "Ah, fuck it Jean-Paul, I was just shitting with you bringing you here, let's call it revenge over that translator, come on, let's go and get some food. Mind you that purse of yours better have some money in it!"

Jean-Paul was puzzled, but was glad to leave his gassy beer on the table and escape before something known as a 'Gourmet Burger' arrived, even in the picture on the menu it failed to impress.

A warm and bustling West End inched by as they both sat in the back of the cab on the way to what Frankie promised was the best Oyster Bar in London, it was hot in the taxi, even with all the windows open, the streets offering little in the way of cooling air, just noise and pollution as they discussed DuPont.

"Was there any indication this kid would turn into some suicide bomber, who didn't even have the decency to suicide?" Frankie asked Jean-Paul.

"No, nothing, we looked at his history in Somalia. When he was young he was fighting against the Islamists, although it wasn't his fight, he was, err how you say, press ganged into it. The first chance he got he left the militias and chased dollars kidnapping wealthy tourists over the border in Kenya. There was no record of any political or religious activity once under the care of the DuPonts either. Why he would plant a bomb is a total mystery to me. Although we must remember for the past two years we have no idea where he has been. If he went to North Africa as we suspect, then he may have come under the umbrella of al-Qaeda, that may be a logical explanation, but still a guess. Is there anything you know of him Frankie?"

"Fuck all. Sorry, nothing much at all. We didn't even know who he was until yesterday. Thankfully our witness identified him on the video and Interpol confirmed the name, and the next thing you're here. We know where he got on the train, but where he was before that, where he is now, is all one big mystery. We don't even know what he is known as, as I'd stake my mortgage it sure as hell isn't Alaine DuPont. For all we know he could be back in Africa, having a night out at the al-Qaeda Summer fucking Disco."

"I hope you don't mind me saying, but Frankie you do swear a lot my friend, some people may be offended by this, do you not agree?"

"Are you offended Jean-Paul?"

"No, well not much anyway, but some people may be."

Frankie shrugged his shoulders, "Well fuck 'em then, they're not here are they! Any way we're here now, I hope you like oysters, otherwise you're going to be pretty hungry."

Frankie presumed that Jean-Paul had been hungry. Very hungry, judging by the rate he had slurped oysters, frequently requesting more bread be brought to their table, whilst drinking £140 bottles of Champagne like it was the gaseous lager left on the tables at the earlier pub. He observed his new Gallic friend, who it had to be said was a very smart dresser indeed, his suit must have cost a month's salary alone. His tie was now loosened, his top button undone, he was leaning over the table pointing a finger at Frankie, slurring his words as he spoke.

"You, you are a fucking bad man Frankie, fucking bad. Look at me, one night with you and I say fucking lots of times. You are a bad fucking influence on people. You take me to that shit pub to eat your shit burgers and drink your shit beers. Then, then you fucker, you bring me here, and get me intoxicated, turn me into one of your lager louts, or am I a Champagne lout, ha ha."

He laughed at his own joke, a lot.

"Champagne lout, we French do things in style, errr sorry fucking style!"

Frankie laughed, the guy was class, pissed on bubbly, that's what you call sophisticated.

"Look JP, I'm going to call you JP from now on my continental cousin, two first names, two of them, that's just plain greedy, isn't one enough. Anyway did you book that hotel? Where are you staying?"

Jean-Paul slurred back, "JP is fine by me. Hotel? Hotel? I 'ave no fucking idea, tonight I sleep under the stars, I watch the sky, piss in your River Thames. Tonight London is mine!"

"No tonight you sleep at my place."

-ELEVEN-
The Morning After The Night Before.

Eurgh, what the hell is that, he thought as the alarm beeped in his ear. His head felt like shit, the alarm resonating like a horrible migraine in his wrecked and dishevelled brain. "Oh Jesus fucking Christ," Frankie muttered to himself, "I didn't feel that pissed last night."

He got out of bed and wandered naked out of his bedroom into the now brightly lit living room, scratching his crotch as he made his way to the bathroom.

"Good morning Frankie."

Oh shit! He'd forgotten all about Jean-Paul Matrice lodging on his settee for the night. He was sitting on the sofa, no sign of its dual use as a bed remaining, sipping from a glass of orange juice. He looked immaculate, even though Frankie knew he had had no opportunity to change. He scurried to the bedroom, and threw on a pair of boxers and tee-shirt, before returning to where Jean-Paul was watching him with such obvious wry amusement.

THE SHATTERED EAGLE

"For fuck's sake JP you could have warned me, I forgot you were even here. How the hell do you have the cheek to look so bright and fucking cheery anyway?"

Frankie was pulling his lower eyelids down and examining his bright pink eyes in the mirror over the fire place, whilst then looking at his lodger who, as he had correctly said, was all bright and cheery looking like he had taken twelve hours sleep instead of the four at maximum he knew they had both had.

"It's down to water Frankie, when out at night if drinking, every other glass must be water, stay hydrated my friend, stay healthy."

"Whatever, seems a waste of drinking time to me."

He walked to the kitchen a pulled a bottle of milk from the fridge, after a cursory sniff, he drank straight from it.

"We're off to Milton Keynes this morning, where DuPont got on the train, have a look at some CCTV footage, see if we can trace where he had been before he got on. Fancy a ride, you're more than welcome?"

"Why thank you, but unfortunately I need to return home for a day or so, it's related to another case I'm working on. But I will be very interested to catch up in a couple of days. Thank you for welcoming me into your home by the way, it was very kind. I am most grateful."

"No worries, thanks for the dinner yesterday, it was different, I've never got ratted on Champagne before, and the way my head feels I doubt whether I'll ever do it again."

Jean-Paul laughed, "Remember the water next time, it does help, honest."

"Yeah right."

Jean-Paul got up and walked over to Frankie, he shook his hand firmly, "I really did enjoy last night, I will see you when I return, although should anything of significance occur please call me on this number."

He handed him a business card.

"I will see myself out. Thank you again for your hospitality."

As he walked to the Red House he stopped off at a Newsagent for some much needed mints, his mouth tasted like a combination of fish and horse manure, he really could have done with a few more hours in bed, he had hoped that the walk would clear his head, bring him back to life, but it clearly hadn't.

Entering the open plan office where his squad were based he was really tempted to just walk straight back out again, head directly back to what was probably his still warm bed, but this wasn't the day for that, just as any of his other working days would never be.

"It's ten past nine," he informed the four other Officers who had managed to arrive on time forty minutes earlier. "No fucker talks to me until at least noon, unless I give my express permission. I know normally I'm a miserable old bastard, but today I'm off the scale. And before you say a word Fernando that especially applies to you and your awful fucking shirt! No one should have more than one of those things in the bottom of their wardrobe, yet you have one for every day of the week. Go and change it, you're one of my team, not the gay branch of Hawaii Five-O!"

"But Guv that's a bit homophobic, surely I have the right..."

"You have the right to remain silent until I advise you otherwise, I thought we'd already established that fact, which part of that didn't any of you understand eh? Now Daggett, put the kettle on, I'm bloody hanging here."

"Tough night Frankie?" Sylvia Hardacre asked with a smile that indicated she knew exactly how tough the previous night must have been. "Did you and Hercule hit the beers?"

"Oh if only, if only. Still enough of my hectic social life, I'm drinking my coffee, then it's Hi-Ho, Hi-Ho off to Milton Keynes we go. Pete, you can drive, I'm not having Felix wrecking another one of our cars. They're expecting us about lunchtime."

DC Sylvia Hardacre was wedged in the back of the *BMW*, the one which they had drawn from the motor pool to temporarily replace the car Felix had scraped and dented as they responded to the bomb. Along with Pete Daggett, Felix Fernando, and Jay DeHavalland - who was now looking after their star witness in Safe Haven - she was the fifth member of Frankie's team, and had been on the unit longest. Although she never acknowledged the fact, and only Jay was her junior, she had become the unofficial mother figure, though she wasn't sure if that was due to the fact they all looked up to her, or just that she was often accused of moaning at them all the time, whichever, it was a role she secretly quite enjoyed, and if she was totally honest with herself wouldn't have really wanted any other way. What she would have changed though was a snoring Frankie resting his head on her shoulder as they motored up the M1 at 80 mph, especially as she could see a small trail of drool running from his mouth and down on to his chin. She pondered waking him, or at least wiping the spittle away, but thought better of it, in his mood it was probably best to let him just dribble down himself, unless of course it took a detour onto her shoulder, then her DCI would be springing back to life pretty rapidly.

In the front of the car Felix and Pete debated the pros and cons of relocating to Milton Keynes, Pete rather unbelievably stating he would rather live in Peckham than the poshest part of the so called 'New City', it was just another one of their debates in a very long line of conversations they indulged in that very rarely had any real point.

"It's a bloody dump I'm telling you, you wait until we get there, you'll agree with me then. Sure it looks nice and clean, the houses are all pretty, but there's more to life than that, I bleeding hate Peckham but it's better than that place. They've got concrete cows and shit, what's that about." Pete spouted.

"They've got concrete cow shit?" Sylvia piped up from the back.

"Of course they haven't you deaf tart, I said concrete cows-and-shit."

"Well what shit is concrete then?" Felix asked, now aware that Pete was getting agitated, and happy to pour petrol onto his emotional fire.

"There's no concrete shit! Listen won't you. It's a bloody shit hole, that's as in real shit. And they have concrete cows, that's cows made from concrete, right, now can we forget about concrete, let it go, OK? I don't care, I don't like the place that's all!"

"That's it! That's enough!" Frankie had stopped snoring, Sylvia felt the weight lift from her shoulder, "All I wanted was a little nap, wasn't asking a lot was it, just keep your fucking mouths shut for an hour, but oh no, let's wake Frankie up by talking as much bollocks as possible. Let's really piss him off. Now please shut up about any of that shit you were harping on about, because I have a headache, it's doing nothing to improve my mood, and I outrank all three of you. So once again shut up!"

"Err Guv," Sylvia said.

"What!" he barked back.

"I thought you should know, you're dribbling. That's all."

-TWELVE-
How Those Tea Stains Got On The Wall Of The Reception Office

"And who's next? Hello there, your name and number please?"

Oli Allen was stood behind the old plywood desk in the Reception of HMP Forest Green, the room had definitely seen better days, and as far as a welcome to any prison went, it was not good. The posters apparently stuck up at random heights and angles did little to disguise the peeling pale green paintwork, and the cobwebs and dust that coated the barred windows literally prevented the sun from shining through. Before him stood a skinny black lad, staring defiantly, the surly attitude impossible to ignore. The warrant on top of a pile of papers bound in buff coloured card folders identified him as Abu Hussein Warsabi, aged 18.

Oli tried again.

"Hello, Mr Warsabi is it?"

THE SHATTERED EAGLE

Calling the prisoners Mister was a new addition to Prison vocabulary, introduced as part of a 'decency agenda', where to Oli's knowledge the decency only flowed one way, but it was a rule he found it easy to adjust to, not being in the job long enough to know much different. Warsabi still made no sound, his lip curling slightly as he looked at the young man in his crisp white shirt and polite enthusiasm with total disdain.

"Mis-ter War-sa-bi do you speak Eng-lish?"

Warsabi just glared back.

At this point the middle-aged Prison Officer who had been observing with wry amusement to Oli's left stepped forward.

"Oi cocker, let's get this straight, drop the attitude, you're going to need us before we need you, that's the one bit of advice I give you free. If you don't understand English, this ain't going to matter, as you don't understand a word I say, if you do listen up, Mr Allen there is here to actually help you, he's being a lot more patient than I would, and he's going to sort out your meagre possessions and assorted items of junk. Ignoring him and giving him the evils will get you bugger all, talking to him and saying please and thank you when you deem appropriate will smooth the transition from having fuck all, to having your property in your cell, no end. Now like I said if you don't speak the Queen's English, no harm done, but if you do then I would recommend being nice to Mr Allen, comprendi?"

Jim Bolton, who was 59, had glasses that were so thick Oli was sure they could start a fire on a sunny day, and hated everyone and everything. He had a way with words, not necessarily a good way perhaps, but Oli liked working with him. He was a bitter, miserable, old bastard, who hardly had a good thing to say to anyone, but everyone knew where they stood, if the prisoner played the game Jim would do everything he could to sort things out for them to ensure they got the bare minimum of what they were entitled to, if they chose not take that path, then they got fuck all, and plenty of it. That was the Jim Bolton School of Jail Craft, and although Oli was sure such a manifesto wouldn't work for him, it appeared to suit Jim just fine.

Abu Warsabi clearly didn't share Oli's enthusiasm for Jim's approach though, he just turned his head and transferred his attention from Oli to Jim, the look on his face leaving both men behind the counter in no doubt that whether he spoke English or not, Warsabi was what Her Majesty's Prison Service unofficially classified as a piece of shit, and a dangerous one at that.

"Hmm Mr Bolton, let's presume he doesn't speak English shall we," Oli interjected. "What I'll do is speak slowly, shout a little, point a lot, and avoid phoning *Language Line*, as I have no idea how it works."

He then pointed at a half full polythene bag lying at the kid's feet.

"Up here please," pointing again at the bag and then to the desk top in front of him.

THE SHATTERED EAGLE

The kid kissed his teeth, which made Oli suspect that he was understanding every utterance he made, before lifting the bag off the floor, at no point taking his eyes off Jim, who had clearly made an impression.

"Right Mr Allen, I'm putting a brew on, even though strictly speaking that's your job, do you want one?"

"Sure, thanks, coffee, white, one sugar please mate."

At that point Jim shuffled off to the adjoining room, shaking his head as he went.

"Don't wait for me, get his kit sorted, I don't know if my sides can take much more of his good natured hilarity, what a happy chappy our Mr Warsabi is."

Oli broke the plastic seal on the bag whilst Warsabi continued to stare at Jim who could be seen through an open doorway, whistling away to himself, rather amusingly to Kylie's 'I should be so lucky' which was playing on the radio, as he boiled the kettle. Oli had learnt early in his career that *Radio Two* was always a staple of the Reception regime in a morning, Jim insisted on playing along with 'Pop Quiz', even though he was always dreadful at it, usually ending each round with 'Well how I was supposed to know that, I don't know, all that modern music is right shite.'

"Right let's fill your prop card in then Mr Warsabi." Oli took a pen from his shirt pocket and began to fill a blue card in.

"Let's see, not a lot here mate is there. tee-shirt, blue, baseball cap, red, trainers, Nike, Black, one pair."

Warsabi ignored him, still focusing on Jim, who was now pouring the water into two mugs, which may or may not have been washed beforehand.

"Hurry up Mr Allen," he called stirring their drinks, "Pop Quiz waits for no man."

Oli took a small beige envelope out of the bag and tore the top off, with Warsabi still not looking anywhere but at Jim, inside was a chunky looking ring, it looked like it was actually real gold, was quite weighty.

Suddenly without warning Warsabi vaulted over the counter, his feet slamming into Oli's chest, knocking the wind out of him as he toppled back, before haring through the open door. Oli spun around but was unable to grasp the young prisoner as he sailed by. He saw Warsabi slam into Jim, it was all like a blur, he had been that fast, punching his colleague in the mouth, knocking the dirty looking mug against the wall behind, showering coffee everywhere.

"You bastard!" Jim exclaimed as blood sprayed from his lip as he said it.

Oli darted forward, instinctively pressing the green button on the wall alerting all via the alarm system, before grasping Warsabi by his hair, pulling his head down as he did so. Whilst Kylie still regaled the nation with *Lucky, Lucky, Lucky*, Jim, grabbed one of the arms flailing around, Warsabi still trying to inflict more damage on anyone within reach. The old warder was swearing and cursing whilst spitting blood onto his assailant, ramming the skinny limb into an arm lock that surely would see it burst free from the shoulder at any moment. Almost immediately he heard the sound of clanging steel gates as more staff arrived.

He felt his shoulder being tugged as someone else took control of the still struggling Abu Warsabi's head, pushing his hands away, "C'mon Oli, get away, they've got him."

He wasn't sure who was even talking, it was all so mad, just seconds earlier it was all OK, and now this.

"Allen move away!" The voice was raised and he saw it was Jim, a couple of feet away gesturing for him to follow. "Come on, help me get cleaned up."

Oli finally moved from the melee, "Jesus Christ, he's lumped you one." Oi said, as they moved away from the scene.

Jim was still cursing and swearing under his breath, as he walked by the half empty bag sitting on the counter he grabbed hold of the open top and swung it against the wall, the sound of the stereo sat at the bottom smashing, leaving no doubt that Jim was not best pleased with Abu Hussein Warsabi, not pleased at all.

Oli took Jim to the staff toilet, the sound of struggling well audible from the adjacent room they had just left. Blood was now flowing from Jim's mouth and nose, leaving large red patches down the front of his shirt, it sickened Oli, seeing staff injured always did, yet he knew it was part of the job, that one day it would be him bleeding, him being led away to get stitched or bandaged, it was what happened, although it hadn't exactly featured in the recruitment brochure they had posted to him when he had first applied for the job.

"Little bastard, little fucking bastard!" Jim was repeatedly saying, as he ran the tap in the sink and splashed water over his face.

As Oli stood by his bloodied colleague he felt a mixture of sympathy, guilt and anger, as Jim continued his relentless tirade, he was amazed, but no means surprised, that there could be a whole sentence consisting of nothing but profanities, yet still making perfect sense.

"Little fucking, shit wipe, bastard, fuckedy, fuckwit, prick!"

"Stay here Jim, I'll get a nurse."

Oli left Jim in the toilet, to swear away his pain, and surveyed the scene in the Reception Office, a trail of blood led back to where Jim had been assaulted, there were about a dozen Prison Officers standing by watching as three colleagues grappled on the floor with a still struggling Warsabi, who was spitting and cursing as they attempted to apply their HM Prison Service approved locks upon him, Oli looked around and saw two female staff in the dark blue uniform worn by Healthcare staff.

"Hey Jill," he called to one of them. "Can you come and take a look at Jim, I think his lip's split."

The nurse scurried over, "Where is he, is he alright?"

"In the loo over there, he'll live, but I think he's copped a good one."

The nurse sympathetically tended to Jim, as she uttered one of the two lines that the Healthcare staff always

THE SHATTERED EAGLE

delivered when confronted with an ailment, "You'll need to get that looked at." Clearly 'take two Paracetamol and leave your window open' was not entirely apt in this case.

As he walked down the corridor away from the now screaming and wailing attacker, he reached down and patted his pocket gently and realised that he had put the chunky ring in there, almost as an instant reaction as Warsabi had vaulted the counter.

Well a gift's a gift, Little Abu clearly wasn't going to be signing for it, Jim hadn't seen it, and for some reason it didn't mention it anywhere on the form that came with the bag.

He thought back to the days at *Poundstretcher*, when he used to supplement his minimum wage with the odd pack of *Mach 3*s or *Duracell* batteries, a kind of unofficial bonus scheme which he had himself implemented to compensate for being treated crap and paid the wages of a teenager. It wasn't really stealing, more a just and fair redistribution of wealth, a victimless crime for the benefit of all.

Just like with this ring, it ain't going to hurt anyone, old habits really do die hard.

-THIRTEEN-
All He Wanted Was A Quick Getaway And A Table For Two At Carlo's

"Oh c'mon Sir, do I have to go on this one, he's the one that assaulted Jim in Reception. I can't stand the little prick, there's got to be someone else, plus I'm supposed to be out tonight."

"Officer Allen, you are supposedly a professional Prison Officer, act a little professional will you. Every one of them in here has a victim, every one of them has a story, but as well as a story young Mr Warsabi has a broken wrist, or at least Healthcare say he has, we - as in Her Majesty's Prison Service - need two staff to come to St Hugh's with me on this escort. I've six wings out on Association and 22 Officers sick or suspended, well that's 23 now Jim's off, so do me a favour, put your tie on, grab the bag of cuffs and paperwork from Security, and meet me and Sergio in five minutes.

THE SHATTERED EAGLE

"Oh and Mr Allen, just for arguing with wise old George, which let's face it son is an argument you're never going to win, you'll be cuffed to him."

Oli sighed, he'd have to phone Kate, let her know, he should have learnt by now it was no use arguing with Senior Officer George Morton, twenty three years in the job and a pip on his shoulder will win any argument against a POELT, or sprog as he was more commonly known. Oli didn't really mind this though, George was alright, it was almost a badge of honour that he was happy to stitch him up, at least it meant he trusted him enough to take him along, even if he was on his uppers when it came to staff.

But that would be scant consolation for Kate waiting for him at home, he only had an hour and half until knocking off, he hadn't been in the job long, but long enough to know that any trip to St Hugh's Hospital with a prisoner needing an x-ray and possible treatment was going to take considerably longer than ninety minutes.

She was taking him out for dinner at *Carlo's* tonight, he'd skipped food to go to the gym during his lunch break, and was starving, a fact demonstrated by a timely loud rumbling of his stomach. Clearly a very loud rumbling as George called after him.

"That reminds me, whilst you're down that way getting the escort bag, pick me up a *Mars* Bar and a bag of Salt and Vinegar from the machine, we could be out a while."

***

Once he had got the escort paperwork and cuffs Oli and two other Officers went to collect Warsabi from his cell, the image of the young prisoner vaulting over the desk and slamming into Jim still buzzing around his mind.

What a little bastard, Oli could think of a million things he'd rather be doing than being cuffed to him. No, George had stitched him up, but then again he worked in a service where being stitched up was practically in the job description, wages, pensions, work conditions, Prison Service employees were well and truly used to being stitched up.

Warsabi appeared to cower a little on his bed, at first flinching as the white shirts entered his cell, as if he was expecting to be beaten, which wasn't an unreasonable reaction, considering the three staff at his door had no love for him at all. But then he was just one of a numerous number of staff assaulters within those walls, being a Prison Officer was a hazardous job at the best of times, but still a job they needed to keep all the same.

"Alright then Warsabi."

The mister now evidently absent.

"We're taking you to hospital, follow me." Oli told him.

Oli could see the young prisoner's demeanour change, once he knew the three Officers meant him no harm, or at least would not have the option of it, Warsabi soon reverted to type, as he arrogantly slid off the bed and slipped a pair of training shoes on. Ignoring the three men at his door he brushed his teeth and urinated in his toilet, before pulling a tee-shirt over his head, before eventually following Oli out of the cell, without saying a word, just sneering as he swaggered along the immaculately polished landings. Oli suspected any attempt at conversation was futile, but went through his standard speech he delivered to any prisoner he was escorting out of the prison.

"You're going to be handcuffed to me on this escort, you do exactly as I tell you, you don't mess me around, you don't mess the other Officers around, and you certainly do not piss the hospital staff around. Any crap like that and I don't care how bad that wrist is, we're coming straight back, alright?"

Again Warsabi didn't answer, instead choosing to bring up the contents from his nose through his throat and spit it on the floor, before turning to Oli slowly nodding his head.

At this point Oli would quiet happily have ensured that the trip to St Hugh's wouldn't have been a wasted journey, that there were some tangible injuries to treat, but instead contented himself with the knowledge that he'd be writing Warsabi up for another 'nicking' when they eventually returned.

Once back in Reception Warsabi was taken into a room by Oli and Sergio Pozzo, who had joined the Prison Service the same time as Oli and trained with him, where their reluctant travel companion was 'full searched'. Oli's mind once more flashed back to what had happened in that building just a couple of hours earlier, the tea stains still on the wall, Jim's blood spraying out as he cussed and cursed, and the almost feral struggling of the now semi-naked lad before them. Oli was never one for violence, neither the giving or receiving of it, especially the receiving, but a part of him almost hoped Warsabi would act up, he could feel the adrenaline coursing through him. It wasn't a feeling he was comfortable with, but he was feeling it all the same.

By the time his cuffs were checked, ID confirmed, and *I*'s and *T*'s of the reams of paperwork well and truly dotted and crossed, the Minibus, that *Q Cars* had sent to take them to St Hugh's, was outside in the 'sterile area' waiting for them.

"OK people let's go." George proclaimed. "Keys to me please, and don't forget your radios."

George appeared impatient, and Oli could see that he wasn't the only one who would rather someone else was going on the escort instead of himself, but George was obviously more used to having his social life wrecked and no doubt was well aware of the futility in arguing in such cases. The grey haired Senior Officer slouched as he led them out of the Reception gates to the awaiting taxi, taking a cursory glance at his watch, before shaking his head.

"Hey up, Rab," George clearly knew the driver as he patted him on his shoulder as he clambered into his vehicle, "they still letting you keep your licence, I thought they'd have banned you years back, what's in the hip flask today? All their real drivers busy are they?"

Rab, initially said nothing, but gave George a knowing wink and smiled, before good naturedly mouthing silently "Senile twat," although intentionally not silent enough that George couldn't fully understand.

THE SHATTERED EAGLE

George and Rab were laughing and joking as they were waved through the tall prison gates, which were closing again even as they were pulling out. Oli was a little crushed in the back, sitting beside the glass window which only appeared to intensify the afternoon sun that was beating down, making it far too hot within the van they were travelling, although Rab was somehow managing to still be wearing fleece, and apparently saw no reason to be switching on the switch that would offer some much needed air conditioning. As Andy Williams was singing about 'Music to watch Girls By' on the radio, Oli's nose twitched, the heat was doing little to mask the BO emanating from Warsabi's arm pits, not helped by the fact that the tee-shirt he was wearing was hardly clean on, it was really rather nauseating, with no prospect of any escape from it, as Oli was now manacled to him.

Warsabi was sitting between him and Sergio, all three had their backs to the driver, occupying the seats facing the rear of the mini-bus, George sat opposite them facing the front, his leg curled up on the seat, his belly uncomfortably hanging over his belt, as he sat at an angle. the leg acting as a table, as he filled in more of the paperwork, taking a break from his conversation with the driver.

"Paperwork boys, the real cornerstone of penal rehabilitation, you can lose a prisoner without worry as long as the paperwork is correct." George said, as they strapped themselves into the back of the minibus. "Did you get my *Mars* Mr Allen?"

"It's in the escort bag Sir." Oli answered.

"Lovely," George opened the bag, "Only one, didn't you get yourself anything?"

"Only had enough cash for that," Oli informed his superior.

"So I've no bloody crisps then? That's great isn't it, you need to always bring enough money to work to cover emergencies son, never know what'll happen, you were hungry as well weren't you."

George tucked into his chocolate whilst Oli's stomach just gave another loud violent rumble, Sergio thought this was most amusing, whilst Warsabi ignored the three white shirted prison staff, and just stared down at his cuffed wrist resting between him and Oli.

Forest Green Prison was situated pretty much in the middle of nowhere, St Hugh's being about 15 miles away through country lanes and minor roads until you almost stumbled, without much warning at all, upon the Ring Road. As far as Oli was usually concerned an escort to the hospital was normally a good little detail, a chance to get some fresh air on the way there and back, and perhaps a nice little opportunity of some easy overtime if things went bad and it turned into a bed watch. But now all he wanted to do was get home.

He had been living in the flat in Little Wayford with Kate for a while now, and though they had their moments, things were going pretty well, tonight was their anniversary, in that it had been a year ago since they finally admitted their feelings to each other in the *Rose and Crown*, or more pertinently twelve months since they got incredibly drunk, lost all their usual inhibitions and basically ended up sharing Oli's bed at his parent's house.

Hence the trip to *Carlo's* in town. But that was spoilt now, Kate's best made plans laid to waste, due to some ungrateful fucktard breaking his hand punching poor old Jim's face, he'd have to phone her from the hospital, let her know he would be a bit late, though hopefully not too much, he could use the mobile in the escort bag once they were there.

Oli thought how different it all was out here, compared to London, and how glad he was things turned out as they did. Kate was now working at a local Builders Merchant, she had made friends easily, as she would being the nicest person he had ever met, and life was pretty good. The job at the prison wasn't all he had been promised, at least the pay wasn't, with him finding out the delay in employing him was due solely to the Home Office imposing a new pay structure on fresh staff, which saw his expected salary cut by close to eight grand, still it was a secure job, and infinitely preferable to *Poundslasher*, so he'd stick with it for now.

On the journey George regaled them with tales of the good old days, all of which despite only being in the job a short while both Oli and Sergio had heard numerous times before, and at least 75% of them Oli reckoned had to be pure flights of fantasy. No one could possibly have done all that and still be employed, no way. Still George recounted them all the same.

For the trip to St Hugh's he again told the one about the prisoner found dead in his cell during the night, after the Officer who was supposed to check him regularly had fallen asleep, and of how to hide the fact he had a stone cold corpse on his hands, the hapless guard had dragged him under the hotplate in the servery for 15 minutes to 'warm up' before returning him to his bed and raising the alarm. Unfortunately the main stumbling block in his plan for poor old Bill Whetherby was the fact that the now warm, but certainly not breathing, convict had the word 'BARTLETT – ENGLAND' branded into his backside. Oli had heard this one before of course, but still laughed in the right places, and abided by the obvious rule of not asking questions that would trip George up and expose his tale as total bollocks.

At least George had lifted the mood, and the officers joked and laughed as they made their way to the hospital, by now ignoring Warsabi, and confident that at least half of what was being said would be totally incomprehensible to him, if not all of it.

With about five miles still to go, they drove through a ford crossing the road, the water splash up the side of the mini-bus, Oli was always amazed that there was a river which actually crossed the road, and that somehow it was normal to just drive through it. What sort of half-baked yokel logic was that? When it rained heavily you had to

THE SHATTERED EAGLE

take a three mile detour to find a bridge, why not just build a bridge there? Still he liked the ford, as when you could traverse it, it was always fun to do so at forty miles an hour and watch the water plume over your car, like some ride at a Theme Park. The first time he had bought Kate out this way he had deliberately lowered the window on her side of the car, and as they went through she got soaked. Somehow it wasn't as funny in reality as it was in his head beforehand, and it was safe to say that it had led to one of their first 'moments', and certainly the first time he had ever heard Kate use the C Word in anger!

And once more Oli was thinking of Kate, he was pretty sure that this was it, this was love, actual real proper *love*, the real McCoy, but his romantic thoughts were interrupted as he heard a small 'crack', and something warm and wet hit the back of his head. At first he was slightly puzzled, but only for the briefest of moments as the taxi suddenly veered to one side and crashed down into a ditch at the side of the road.

Warsabi was now pressed right against him, tugging at the cuffs, as if they would just fall off, Oli was swinging his head from side to side, trying to take in exactly was happening, what the hell was going on, because this didn't make sense.

"Rab!" George shouted, as he tried to stand, still buckled into his seatbelt, but there was another 'crack'.

Oli could only watch, now frozen open-mouthed as George slumped to one side, still held up by the seat belt. A red hole the size of a one penny piece in his forehead began trickling blood, which snaked to one side of George's nose, down a cheek and onto his neck, until he slumped forward revealing a crater in the back of his head, and a mass of brain matter and thick blood splattered over the rear of the vehicle.

Oh shit!

Warsabi was now on his feet, snarling and yelping like a wild dog, Oli was pulling at the cuffs desperately trying to pull him back down, to get down low, out of harm's way, his mind should have been all over the place, but he was clicking into some kind automatic calm, reacting now with a clear head, the terror being overtaken by a more powerful response, one that would hopefully keep him alive.

"Sergio help me! Quick get him down!" he shouted.

Oli could feel the cuffs pulling into his hand, searing as the steel pulled into flesh and rubbed against his wrist bones, he was now as much a prisoner as Warsabi.

"Sergio!"

But the door on the side of the minibus was already thrown open and Sergio bolted free, Oli could make him out rushing through a hedge, tearing the prickly branches apart as he scrambled through on all fours, but saw no more of him as he resumed his battle to bring Warsabi down again. His prisoner was screaming in a wild high pitched voice.

"Non, non, non!"

He considered following Sergio, it made perfect sense, but that notion was short lived, he was cuffed to the screaming animal clambering over him and the pair had no chance of getting out together. Warsabi was still screaming and hollering, the panic was primal, Oli knew that this wasn't something the prisoner had planned, and this certainly wasn't something he wanted.

Grabbing hold of the kid's legs he wrestled him to the floor, ending up almost straddling him, his knee on his chest, among the chaos his free hand got caught in the chain dangling from a very dead George, the cuff key!

Oli pulled the chain quickly, it initially snagged before coming free of George's pocket, he fumbled, his hand eye co-ordination shot to pieces, as he eventually removed the small brass key from the clip at the end of the chain, before placing it in the side of his boot, Warsabi was still struggling and wailing, eyes bulging, as he spat and spluttered.

"Be quiet!" Oli hissed. "Be quiet for god's sake and stay still!"

Then Warsabi went silent, was frozen, stupefied to the spot, at first Oli thought his orders had miraculously worked, but then he saw that in the door way stood a figure all in black, a gun with a large silencer, something Oli only thought existed in films, pointing in their direction. He or she looked something akin to Darth Vadar, their face behind what appeared to be some form of gas mask.

"Out, get out!" the figure barked.

Warsabi appeared to be whimpering, cowering on the floor, Oli wanted to join him, cowering and whimpering seemed as good idea as anything he could think of, bar perhaps begging and pleading for his very life.

"OUT! Before I blow your fucking heads off!" the figure shouted.

Oli held his one free hand up in a gesture of co-operation. "Alright, alright, don't shoot!"

His tethered prisoner was now lying perfectly still, just the sound of his fractured breathing replacing his yelps and frantic screams. The black figure had been joined by another, dressed identically, who entered the minibus, pulling Warsabi by the back of the collar on his stinking tee-shirt and by his hair, Warsabi suddenly kicked and struggled, whilst the cuffs again dug into Oli's wrist, it was so painful, but somehow he knew that was the least of his worries, as he battled to shuffle along having no chance to do anything else but follow.

Once pulled out of the vehicle Warsabi futilely attempted to break free, yanking Oli's sore wrist with a harsh jolt, that saw the prisoner spring back as if he had an elastic arm, before being grabbed by a third figure in black who slammed a syringe into his neck, he immediately crumpled to the floor jerking and spasming, forcing Oli to drop to one knee, as the cuffs pulled him down.

"You," the figure who had just injected Warsabi shouted to Oli. "Where's the keys, where are the keys to the cuffs?"

Oli knew where they were, he knew exactly where they were, digging into his ankle in the leg of his boot, but he was damned if he was going to say that, in his mind the fact that he was still attached to his prisoner was all that was keeping him alive at this moment, just seeing the fate of George and presumably Rab told him that. He had to think quickly, his life was dependent upon what he said next, how much did they know of prison procedure, who were they?

"They're back at the prison, we weren't to unlock him until we got back, Governor's orders."

"C'mon, we need to move, to get out of here," the first gunman said, the one who had the silenced gun. "We'll have to bring him along too. We can lose him once we get back, there's no time to piss around, let's go!" the figure shouted to the other two, before drawing a radio to his mouth.

"Gold Eagle, are you receiving, over."

"I'm receiving, send over."

"Gold Eagle, be aware prize acquired, we do have extra item which we are bringing with us, I repeat prize acquired, and one extra item. Two other items destroyed, one item lost. Eagle One Out."

Oli closed his eyes, *we can lose him once we get back*, Kate's face came into his mind, she had no place there at that time, would he ever see it again, see her again?

Grabbing hold of Warsabi under his arms two of the men pulled him up and dragged him across the road to a waiting Dark Blue *Range Rover*.

"Why don't we just cut one of their hands off, we're taking the screw for no reason?" one of the other two said to the first figure, who appeared to be the leader.

Oli shuffled behind, unable to do anything else other than shit himself, almost literally, they wanted to cut his hand off! Jesus Christ, he was unwanted baggage they were taking to God knows where.

"Just do as I say, we'll get rid of him when we need to, but no one's cutting any hands off, get me?"

Both Oli and his now very much unwanted prisoner were bundled into the back seat, where they were joined by one of the three, with the other two climbing into the front, he went to look back at the crashed Taxi, but before he could a black hood was placed over his head, he felt a draw cord pull tight against his throat, he had tried to pull his head away, but had no chance, it was pitch black, he felt so helpless, so lost, what were they going to do with him?

A voice from the front commanded, "Keep still you fucker, and shut up, we aren't going to hurt you unless we have to. My erstwhile colleagues want to cut your hand off, but I think that is not necessary at this here juncture of time. But you need to be sure of one thing, we need him, that ugly yoot on your shiny charm bracelet, and believe me we are taking him, but we don't need you one bit. So if you want to stay breathing, you better not do anything to arouse my anger."

Oli remained silent, silence always seemed a good way not to arouse anyone's anger, especially someone with a gun. He did a quick appraisal of his situation, well as good as he could being totally blind, he was wedged between the car door and what appeared to be a very much unconscious Warsabi, he was sure with one of his captors the other side of the slumbering 'ugly yoot'. He had no intention of stopping them from taking his prisoner, no intention at all, all he was concerned about at that moment was when, or how, he was going to get free, everything else - and he felt no shame in admitting it to himself - was secondary, it was harsh but George, Rab, Sergio, Warsabi, all came behind him when it came to a right to exist.

The engine started and they were on their way, to where he did not know, what should he do? *Shut the fuck up*, as instructed seemed a damn fine idea, or should he plead for his freedom and life, he sure as hell wasn't going to try and do anything heroic, they could do what they want with Warsabi, he had no intention of getting in the way of their plans for him. He just wanted to get out of this, get back to Kate, Kate who was still blissfully unaware any of this shit was happening, who'll be wondering why he isn't home on time. Why didn't he tell them where the bloody keys were? But too late now, they weren't going to turn around, pat him on the head and say no hard feelings, were they. It was out of his control now, he'd just stay shut up and hope that he may get a chance to get away before they discovered his lies.

Ten minutes must have passed, they appeared to be on a better road now, not so bumpy, moving faster. The three captors at first went quiet, saying nothing, just leaving Oli with his hideous thoughts, and Warsabi to blissfully dream whatever he wished, but as they went on they began to talk in hushed tones. Oli couldn't hear everything, but he was getting the general gist…

"Why did we bring him along, we should have freed the boy back there, we don't need no screw, we should have cut his hand off."

"The whole things a fuck up."

"One more word, just one more fucking utterance questioning me, and I swear I'll shut you both up. Now enough!"

-FOURTEEN-
Contain - Plan - Act.

Detective Inspector Craig Lovan looked at his watch, it had taken about quarter of an hour from when this happened to the arrival of the first Police car, their witness, Sergio Pozzo, had alerted them from a nearby cottage, but too late for anyone to have any hope of stopping the escape. By now, another fifteen minutes on, there were eight squad cars and three Ambulances present, Paramedics were fussing about, but all too aware that they were unable to do anything for either of men who had been shot, who it appeared had both been killed instantly. The Prison Officer, Pozzo, was again back from where he had earlier made his quick flight, pretty much injury free bar a criss-cross of scratches over his forearms and face, and they were now aware that they were looking for another Prison Officer, Oliver Allen, and prisoner Abu Warsabi, as well as at least three heavily armed men.

Surveying the scene from about ten yards away from the taxi, Lovan shook his head, wondering what the hell he was supposed to do, he was in charge of this, at least until someone who had a real idea of what to do in this situation arrived from Northampton, and he really didn't want to be.

The drone from the rotors of the force's helicopter could be heard overhead, competing with the chatter of radios, as it scanned the area for any sign of their targets, yet Lovan knew that they were now searching in the wrong place, their prey were long gone. Gold Command had been opened at HQ and had begun to co-ordinate road blocks throughout the county, liaising with neighbouring constabularies and bringing in the specialist resources which one of the country's smallest forces most certainly lacked. He scanned around looking at what he had, the taxi wedged into a hedge at the side of the lane, containing now just four paramedics and two corpses, blood and gore splattered within, offering a bloody big clue as to what had occurred. Oh Jesus, this sort of thing shouldn't be happening here, not half a mile out of Upper Wending, he needed to focus, he was in command, Bronze at scene, others would be looking to him for guidance, he wondered how much of that feeling of being so far out of depth was showing on his face, the face that usually gave nothing away, was always calm and reasoned.

He scraped his shoe over the loose grit of the road, it was just a country lane for heaven's sake, people murdered among blackthorn hedges, dandelions and the silver birches that lined the route, just over the hedge half a dozen cows were chewing the cud oblivious to what he was seeing, this wasn't Inner-city London, Liverpool or Manchester, this was the middle of nowhere.

SOCO were setting up, climbing into their white paper suits, he knew it wouldn't be long before the media began to arrive, he had stationed officers five hundred yards in either direction to keep them away, but he knew that it wouldn't be long before the helicopter overhead was joined by others, their cameras zooming in to try and pick out the gory and salacious details.

Contain - Plan - Act.

The three word mantra for any crisis, yet Lovan knew that already nothing was contained, the perpetrators were long gone, up to thirty miles away in any direction, he had no viable plan on the ground, and what he had to act with was no match for what appeared to be a small heavily armed army.

Staring down at the buff envelope, ripped open in his hand, he saw the prison's 'Escape Pack', a single A4 sheet of paper, describing the prisoner, a photo, half a dozen or so words detailing his appearance, date of birth and offence. What did it mean? A teenage foreign national on remand for sexual assault.

It didn't make sense.

It didn't make sense at all. He had two corpses on his hands, and a shit load of trouble, he was clueless on this one, and had managed to do nothing to sort it out. Perhaps he was being harsh on himself, he had sealed off the immediate area, contacted the right people, taken the correct procedures, initiated the appropriate contingency plans, but ultimately he was glad the Commissioner or one of her Assistants would be running this one, this was no job for the head of Zone Four, he was more used to investigating travellers having it away with farmers tractors or builders plant, or raiding the odd cannabis farm, but never murders? Well they just didn't happen on his patch.

-FIFTEEN-
Oliver Allen And The Desperate Grope In The Dark For Freedom.

Oli reckoned that they must have been travelling for over half an hour, judging by the sounds outside and speed they were now going he guessed they were in a town or city.

His wrist was hurting, he wondered whether there was some kind of damage to his tendons or ligaments, if he could have seen it he imagined it would be all bruises and swollen, it felt so sore, and it was hot, although he was hot all over, especially his head, the hood was thick and restricted the flow of fresh air. But he had no desire to say anything, still all too aware that keeping quiet was a good thing to be doing.

The three men that had taken him had said very little, and Warsabi certainly wasn't contributing to any conversation, although he could hear the occasional grunt or snort, so he knew he was still alive, plus his warm sweaty body was pressed against his, which only heightened that uncomfortable feeling.

Oli then heard a radio crackle, "Eagle One, are you receiving over?"

"Gold Eagle send over."

He presumed the reply came from the passenger in the front, although he couldn't be sure, it was a deep voice, how Mr T would have sounded if he had come from Essex or the East End of London rather than Chicago, it was the same baritone growl that had belonged to the one giving the orders back at the lane where this whole nightmare had begun.

"Eagle One, we were wondering on ETA and updates over?"

"Gold Eagle, be aware we are approximately figures five zero minutes from location. I say again fifty minutes. Prize is asleep, but undamaged, extra item awake, no damage to any Eagles. We are currently in Double N Over."

"That's received. Gold Eagle out."

Oli had made his mind up, he couldn't see a thing, but he had to get out, he had less than an hour to act, they had said fifty minutes ETA, but now was the time to do something, he could tell the traffic was practically stationary. Warsabi was between him and his captor in the back, offering him some kind of cover, or at least he hoped he did.

Without any further consideration, no opportunity to talk himself out of it, he ran his free hand down to his boot, trying desperately to remain upright, show no sign of moving, and slid a finger into the side inching painfully slowly into his sock, he felt his finger tip touch the small ring on the key and he gingerly pulled it free.

His heart was pounding, he was amazed the three men in black couldn't actually hear it, it felt like it was banging against his ribs like a huge bass drum setting the pace on a Roman galleon.

Boom-Boom-Boom!

Stay calm Oli, stay calm, he told himself, this was so far away from normality, was he doing the right thing? He was no hero, although he never considered himself a coward either, but certainly never envisaged playing out some scene from the 'Bourne' films, if this went wrong he was dead, Dead! That was something he never foresaw, had even considered, at least not for another sixty years, yet no doubt neither had George nor Rab gone to work that morning wondering if it may be their last.

But he wasn't going to die, not if he could help it, he had the key, it was clenched in his fist, he drew the fist across his lap to where he was shackled to the prisoner, terrified he would expose his play, he had no idea what his captors could see, whether their eyes were trained on him amused by his naivety and stupidity, or were they blissfully unaware that Oli Allen was making his leap for freedom.

He considered trying to pull off the tightly fastened hood, but knew that would immediately alert them, there was nothing subtle in suddenly pulling the velvety sack free and shouting 'Tah-dah, Surprise', no he would have to work in darkness, blind, but without as much as a white stick or friendly Labrador to help him.

The key appeared ten times bigger than he knew it was as he fumbled gently, silently trying to place it into the keyhole attached to his cuff, which had become near microscopic in comparison. Gently and slowly he blindly stroked it over the surface, again and again failing to get it in, he was committed now, he had to keep trying, he had past the point where he had any other plan, this was his one chance of survival, and the alternative was just not an option, any Plan B's no doubt ending with him getting a bullet in his head. It wasn't until the fifth or sixth attempt that it appeared to catch, he wiggled and stroked it around the keyhole before it cleanly slid in.

He paused, taking a big breath of warm air.

This was it.

Slowly, oh so painfully slowly, he twisted the key... *Click*.

It was unlocked! But with that audible click, it had made a noise, oh Christ he had to act, and now!

"What's that..." a voice, he couldn't tell which one had spoken, but it was now or never.

He lunged for the door handle in his total darkness, the man in the back, or at least Oli presumed it was him, grabbed hold of newly free arm, he felt the grip tighten, painfully squeezing deep into his bicep, no he was getting away, fuck this!

Oli swung round breaking free again, his fingers desperately groping in the dark, looking for that door catch, his route out of there.

He found it, the door was open.

THE SHATTERED EAGLE

"For fuck's sake! Get him, grab him!" 'Mr T' was screaming.

He tumbled free of the vehicle, his feet catching grip on the tarmac, he tried to run, but just propelled himself downward even quicker, he could feel his elbow scraping on the warm tarmac, skin peeling, but that was nothing to worry about, he immediately got back to his feet, were they out after him?

He was totally blind, but all he knew was he had move, get away, he stumbled forward, then he heard a blast of a car horn, a screech of tyres right in front of him, all he could do was lunge forward, getting free was everything, his legs buckled in pain, then he felt a hard crash against the side of his head. He rolled over a hot metallic surface, which he knew was someone's bonnet.

Through the blackness he could hear the sound of car horns, more screeching tyres, screams, he was lying on the floor, he reached for the hood, but however it was fastened he could not locate any bow or knot, nothing he could easily release, he pulled at it, but it was too tight. He tried to scramble to his feet again, to get away, put some distance between him and the 'Eagles' but his leg just crumpled under him as he collapsed once more in pain.

"Hold still, don't move, we've called an Ambulance." It was a female voice, concerned, compassionate, not coming from behind a gasmask or through a radio.

Was he safe?

"Someone help me get this hood off!" she called.

Oli could feel fingers picking around his throat.

"Who is he?" someone else was asking.

"I don't know he ran out straight out in front of me, lucky I wasn't going fast, he came out of a blue four wheel drive I think."

"Is he a Policeman?" another unseen man asked.

Oli's eyes were suddenly filled with the bright evening sunlight, he squinted. A large group of people were gathered around, he scanned quickly, he had to be sure no figures in black were present. He'd done it, he had gotten away, or more accurately his captors had. His right leg hurt like mad, and he touched the side of his head, a bump big enough to lift a straw boater Tom and Jerry stylee had made itself known, like a large hard-boiled egg, but he was definitely alive!

He could hear the sound of sirens, yes he was safe.

Back at the scene of the murders of Robert McKinnen and Senior Prison Officer George Morton, DI Craig Lovan received the news that Oliver Allen had been recovered in Northampton, having escaped from a Dark Blue *Range Rover*, and that the *Range Rover* had sped off down the wrong direction of a one way street. Gold Command had taken immediate action and were placing road blocks all around the town, this may all have a happy ending after all Lovan thought.

THE SHATTERED EAGLE

-SIXTEEN-
The Whole Thing's Gone To Rat-Shit.

"Eagle One to Gold Eagle, urgent extraction required, I repeat Urgent extraction required. 52°14'10" North 0°53'37" West. Three Eagles, and Prize, additional item has gone. I repeat additional item now gone. We have run into problems, need alternative exit plan!"

"Eagle One, hold one minute, will arrange to meet your request, over."

The radio went silent.

Parked on the third floor of a multi-story car park, close to a theatre in the town centre, it was clear to Auguste Fredericks that this had been a fuck up, and one of the highest order. The three gunmen were now out of the *Range Rover*, bickering, blaming each other, but this wasn't doing any good, he needed them to get a grip.

But still Jake continued, "For Fucks sake Gus, we're like sitting ducks in this car park, if the Old Bill turn up now we're trapped, we should have done as I said, cut the wanker's hand off, simple, job done. But oh no, we had to bring him along, take him for a joy ride to God knows where."

"Stop bitching Jake, I'm in no mood for your goddamn bitching, trust me, do as I say and we'll be fine, this is still on track, we still have the prisoner and we still can, no will, get out of this, the mission is going to be a success, providing you do just as I say. Hell man we've been in worse shit storms than this, do you hear me, stop bitching!"

The three of them were hastily stripping off their military fatigues, they changed quickly into a variety of shorts and tee-shirts, whilst Warsabi still lay unconscious in the back. Sean collected the discarded black outfits together, placing them in a big bin bag before throwing it in the back of the vehicle and covering it with a blanket.

Jake, now dressed in cargo shorts, and pink polo shirt, sandals and dark aviator sunglasses, was pacing around agitated, he pulled a pistol from the boot of the car and pushed it into the back of his shorts. "This has turned to total rat shit, total fucking rat shit, we should have just cut his hand off, I told you so, bringing a passenger along was madness. They're not going to be happy with us at all."

"Will you just shut the fuck up Jake, do you hear me, shut that great gaping mouth of yours, because we need cool heads here, and no head can be cool with such a fucking great mouth generating so much friction!" Gus, or Eagle One as he was known on this mission, replied.

He had about enough of Jake and his moaning, after all they had been through together Jake should know by now what he was about, and he wasn't about being bad mouthed and questioned half way through an operation. That it was taking an 'unexpected turn' only meant they needed to do as he said even more. He had considered, although only briefly, just putting a bullet through Jake's permanently open mouth, shutting him up once and for all, but this wasn't the time. Sitting on the passenger seat, his legs dangling out of the door, the stocky, stout, bald headed black man slipped on the khaki shorts he was changing into, he was now dressed with bare feet, similar shorts to his two companions, and a *Pepsi-Cola* tee-shirt which hugged his not inconsiderable chest, looking more suited to a beach than a messed up military operation in a car park in Northampton Town Centre.

"Now you just listen to me," he continued, "they'll get us out, we just keep our heads, do you hear me, stop bad mouthing me, and stay cool. We need to get another vehicle as quickly as possible, you do that Sean." He gestured to the third 'Eagle'. "Have a scout around, something that's not going to stand out in a crowd, I'm not after some pimp-mobil or brand new *Bentley*, do you hear me, we just need something a little bit anonymous?"

Sean said nothing, but scurried off.

Staring at the sky, reflecting on just mad all this had been, Oli was being loaded into the back of Ambulance on a trolley, two armed Police Officers was accompanying him to the hospital, whilst grilling him with questions. A host of emotions filled his mind, relief, of course relief at being free, he had no doubt that his days would have been truly numbered once he reached where ever 'Gold Eagle' was, but also immense confusion and sickening sadness at the demise of George, the great crater where his thinning grey hair once covered the back of his cranium. The three gunmen. Getting knocked down. Poor old Rab who he had only met that day. Sergio doing a runner. His thoughts were being interrupted as the Policemen grilled him, every answer was relayed over the radio, no sooner was he answering questions than more were being fired at him at rapid pace, his leg was killing him, his head pounded, and he needed a crap.

"Eagle One from Gold Eagle. We have an extraction point, head to 52°23'152" North 0°93'35" West. I repeat 52°23'152" North 0°93'35" West. Rendezvous with our vehicle there. They will make themselves known to you. Out."

Gus retuned the radio to his pocket, they needed to move, he could hear all the sirens wailing three storeys below, the 'screw' would have briefed them, made them fully aware of what they were dealing with, they needed to be citizens, civilians, not some paramilitary Most Wanted just there to be picked up.

A rusting *VW Polo* pulled up in front of them, Sean behind the wheel looking all pleased with himself, oh Jesus, Gus thought, that boy never fails to disappoint.

Bundling Warsabi into the rear foot well, they clambered in behind him, Jake sitting in the back with his legs spread wide in an attempt to hide the human bundle unceremoniously wedged on the floor.

"Is this the best you could find," Jake was complaining, his knees drawn up high by his chin. "Five grand's worth of hi-tech electronic key and you return with a shit heap like this, I give in."

"Hey, it doesn't stand out does it? Job done!"

"No not job fucking done, I'm getting cramp already, you bloody retarded mong, it ain't hard is it."

Gus turned to Jake, his voice quiet, but he wanted to leave him in no doubt that it really was time for him to be quiet. "One more word Jake, just one more word. It stops now. Are we clear?"

Jake said nothing, which in itself was a result.

They came out the car park into heavy traffic, the sound of sirens were all around.

"How far we got to go?" Gus asked Sean.

"About two miles, the extraction point is the football ground."

"Right," Gus stated, "No arguing here, do you hear me, no fucking arguing, I want no disagreement, no questions, you and Jake walk there, they're looking for three of us, plus him in the back, let's not hand them all of us in a car together, that would be total insanity, I'll drive, if I'm not there in 30 minutes get out any way you can, we'll meet back at the unit."

"Whoa, hold on," Jake cried, "why are we doing the walking and you're driving?"

"Because I've got no freaking shoes, and I sure as hell ain't going to fit in either of your little white boy Jesus boots am I! You both got weapons? Keep them well tucked away, this ain't the OK-fucking-coral. Don't do anything to give yourselves away whatever you do, now go!"

Jake went to speak, but was cut short by Gus, "Go! Don't you dare argue with me anymore."

As Sean and Jake disappeared from view heading out of the town centre towards the football stadium, Gus immediately turned into a side street, found a space and parked up. He looked back at the unconscious figure in the rear foot well.

"Those my little zonked out brother are two dumbass white boys, real fucking dumbass. Mind you, you're not the brightest bulb in the box are you?"

He again lifted the radio to his mouth, "Eagle One to Gold Eagle, be advised you have new extraction co-ordinates, I say again revised extraction point."

Back at the multi-story car park behind the *Derngate Theatre* a Dark Blue *Range Rover* exploded into a ball of flame. Thankfully no one was in the immediate area, as the intense fire popped windows and melted metal, the flames affecting both cars next to it as the searing heat destroyed glass, steel and evidence. Car alarms wailed and a fire alarm emitted three sharp beeps every five seconds, to warn would be motorists, and to ensure that the already alerted authorities arrived in swift time.

Gus smiled as he saw Police vehicles rushing by the end of the road, he saw two Ambulances zoom by heading towards where he had detonated the explosives in the back of the car, yeah that would keep them occupied for a little while.

Ten minutes later he could see another Ambulance at the bottom of the side street he was parked up, but instead of heading past the end of the road it turned into it and slowed down, sirens now silent and blue lights no longer flashing, there were two flashes of its headlights, which Gus returned.

"Eagle One, to Gold Eagle, much gratitude to you, extraction team on scene, I'll see you shortly, thanks my friend. Over."

-SEVENTEEN-
Not Such A Fruitless Day At Milton Keynes After All.

"What a complete waste of time, over six hours spent pissing around in that shit hole, see I'll give you that one Pete, I agree with you on that, to find out sweet Fanny Adam. Come on, put your foot down, don't make me swap you with Felix, I want to get back tonight."

It was coming up for seven o'clock, a fruitless afternoon trawling through CCTV and interviewing *Network Rail* staff at Central Milton Keynes Station had done little to improve Frankie's mood, in fact it had worsened it considerably. The other three remained quiet, Sylvia Hardacre, like Pete and Felix knew it was always wise to do so when Frankie was in one of his foul moods, sometimes he could be a right mardy grouch, she thought, and the rest of time he could be considerably worse.

"Are we going straight back Guv', or do you want to stop for some grub?" Pete asked.

THE SHATTERED EAGLE

"What do you think, do I look like I'm hungry or pissed off?"

"We'll go straight back then."

Sylvia smiled, yeah good call Pete, although she could have done with something to eat herself, they'd been flitting around the 'New City' all afternoon, checking the footage from not just the rail station, but also with the local council and police, and yet no one had as much as even offered them a cup of tea. She'd not even noticed how hungry she was until Pete had mentioned food, now it was all she could think of, perhaps when they got back she'd pick up a take-away or something.

The phone rang in the car, it was linked to Bluetooth, so they all could hear it as Pete answered.

"Hello, Daggett."

"Hello Pete," the voice on the other said. "Is Mr Howard available?"

Frankie spoke, "Yes Carla, what can I do for you this fine and lovely evening?"

Sylvia rolled her eyes, Frankie could be in one of his real ball busting, cock shrinking moods, but one word from Carla and he would go all sweetness and roses, he was so blatant.

"Well Sir, we've just had something come through. An eighteen year old male of Somali origin has just been sprung from a Prison escort. We've seen his picture from the prison. It's not definite Guv', but bloody hell, he don't half look like Alaine DuPont."

"Where did this happen?"

"He was on his way to a hospital from Forest Green Prison, they were ambushed, and he was taken by three armed men. They also took a Prison Officer who managed to escape in Northampton."

"When did this happen Carla?"

"About half an hour ago. There was all sorts of madness in the town centre, they also blew a car up in a car park."

"We're heading that way, Carla, find me someone to liaise with in Northampton, and keep us updated."

Sylvia knew what was coming next, and it certainly wasn't involving any take-aways.

"Pete," Frankie said, although it was clear that there really wasn't any need to, "come off at the next junction, and guess where we're going."

Pete switched on the sirens on the unmarked *BMW*, and accelerated to 120mph, Sylvia knew he liked all the high speed stuff, Felix, who had done the special course and had the frequently waved certificate to prove it, usually was behind the wheel for the 'Starsky and Hutch' routine, but that evening it was Pete's turn, and he was making the most of it. Reaching into his shirt pocket he pulled out a pair of mirrored aviator sunglasses.

Felix looked across, and shook his head, "And that's why I normally drive. What a wanker!"

They arrived at the scene of Warsabi's abduction in less than 30 minutes, it would have been sooner had it not been for the disagreement as to whether to go to the Town Centre or the country lane where the initial murders and

THE SHATTERED EAGLE

escape occurred. When they arrived Sylvia could see that the lane had been closed off and around half a dozen Officers in white paper suits were kneeling on the floor marking spots of significance and bagging the evidence relating to it, yellow numbered cubes dotted around to indicate where they had taken the items from.

She followed Frankie as he showed his badge to a uniformed Constable whilst ducking under the tape cordoning off the scene.

"Where's Lovan?" he barked, before following the direction of the Officer's outstretched arm towards a man in his late thirties, dressed in a short sleeved open necked shirt, who was stood by a *LDV* Police van briefing the staff beside it.

Sylvia scurried to keep up with her boss as he approached, clearly in a hurry.

"Inspector Lovan?" he asked the stressed looking DI, a little bit too rudely, Sylvia thought, as he interrupted the briefing.

Lovan ignored him, and carried on talking to the officers gathered by the van.

"DI Lovan?" Frankie again asked.

Lovan looked irritated at the interruption, barking back at Frankie, "Yes, can you wait a moment, you can see I'm talking."

Sylvia winced, the DI appeared to be stressed enough, without having to contend with what she suspected was now coming his way.

"No I can't!" Frankie fired back, in front of all assembled. "So please stop the talking and come over here, because as far as I can see none of these people need to speak to you as urgently as I do, and I am certainly not going to wait around any longer than I need to."

Lovan scowled, "Just who the hell do you think you are talking to? I have no idea what so ever who you are, but you are on my crime scene, a double murder investigation, and until told otherwise I'm in charge here, so with all due respect…"

"Don't you 'all due respect' me Inspector, don't even begin to go down that road."

Frankie held out his Warrant Card. "DCI Adrian Howard, Anti-Terrorism Unit. Now I'm not going to piss arse around here in the middle of Sleepy Hollow arguing points of order with you. Let's take it as read that I outrank you, my department is more high profile, and my agenda more important. Those are facts. Now I need to see a mug shot of that prisoner who escaped, I need to see it now. I need to see it because there's a good chance that he may be linked to the investigation relating to the slaughter of eighteen people. So please oblige my simple and humble request and show me that Escape Pack immediately."

Without a further word Lovan stormed off.

"Wow! That was a bit harsh Guv," Sylvia said as she watched him march away, "Poor bloke looks like he's got enough on his plate without you pissing him off. I've got to say as a motivational speech that was pretty poor stuff."

"Oh I'm sorry if you think I've hurt his feelings, we'll pick him up some flowers on the way home shall we?"

"Christ you can be a sarcastic miserable bastard when you want, and that Sir is without any due respect what so ever!"

She wondered how he ever got promoted to such a level in this day and age of so called political correctness and university educated senior officers. Sure she loved working with him, but he was like some prehistoric relic of policing from a bygone age, then again he cared, both for his people and for the job, plus her vocabulary had been broadened considerably, even if it was solely by profanities and expletives. He was alright was Frankie, although the way he spoke to that DI was just plain embarrassing, he really needed an 'off' switch sometimes, if for no other reason than to save himself.

A couple of minutes later a uniformed Police Officer came over to Frankie handing him an A4 piece of paper. The picture was indeed a remarkable likeness to DuPont.

ESCAPE PACK
HMP Forest Green

Name: Abu Warsabi'
Number: A5568GT
Age: 18 years of age
Height: 5' 7"
Weight: 9st 3lb

Place of Birth: Somalia
Build: Slim
Distinguishing Features/Marks: 3 Scars to Forehead.

"It's him!" Frankie exclaimed, "It's fucking him! Felix, call up the office, get some more bodies up here quick. Hardacre, go get me that DI you were so fond of, I need to speak to him straight away, schmooze him if necessary, as a very last resort apologise for me, but only if you have to. Pete, take those ridiculous glasses off, Felix is right you look like a wanker. It's him, we need to get busy on this."

THE SHATTERED EAGLE

-EIGHTEEN-
Own Goal At Sixfields.

They arrived at the *Sixfields Stadium* in good time, despite the mayhem of the previous hour or so, once they had got out of the town centre they had only encountered one disinterested Policeman, who happily pointed them towards where they wanted to go when asked for directions, whilst continuing his scan for would be paramilitary prison breakers, none too concerned about the two tanned guys in shorts looking for the football ground.

What an idiot.

Jake was concerned, there had been no contact with Gus, nor Gold Eagle, and it was eerily quiet as they wandered into the car park which separated the small stadium from the surrounding horseshoe shaped hill, topped with a host of cafes bars, and discount retail outlets. The day time traffic now gone, with the evening trade for the bars yet to arrive.

"What we looking for?" Sean asked.

"Not sure, Gus should be here soon, providing he hasn't fucked that up too, he's got the only radio. How much do you know about these guys Sean? Can we trust them?" Jake replied, because he sure as hell didn't know those paying them that well, and he had learnt from past experiences that trust was a virtue that could only be earned over time, especially in the game they were now in. He was in no mood for pissing around, he wanted away, he was still irritated and annoyed over what happened with the Prison Officer, they should have left him with the other two they had taken out, there was no reason to have dragged him along, now they were in the shit, especially as they were still only a couple of miles from where it had all gone tits up.

"I don't know, I know Gus," Sean said, "and he says they're alright, and I know they've got money, and plenty of it, I just want to cash in and be done now, this ain't what I do, this is wrong in so many ways. We don't kill innocents."

Really, *We don't kill innocents*, don't we? Jake thought, two tours of Afghanistan, doing what all three of them had to do, and Sean comes out with a phrase like that.

"No time to get a conscience now," he said, pulling his gun from the waistband of his shorts, then immediately putting it back, "too late for that, we'll soon be done, just deliver the kid to them, then California here I come. Don't dwell on a thing Sean, or you'll never get a good night's sleep for the rest of your life. It's business, just another deal."

Sean smiled, as if Jake's words had make everything in the world right again. "Hey Jake, I'll tell you another thing, if Gus don't roll up soon I'm going to that pub up there, and getting pissed."

THE SHATTERED EAGLE

"If Gus don't roll up soon, we're going to need a drink because we'll be fucked." Jake scoffed.

Jake was getting skittish, although he didn't want to let Sean see just how concerned he was, they were sitting by the entrance to the Car Park, throwing stones to see who could get nearest to the kerb the other side, but Gus should have been there by now. This wasn't good, they didn't need 'extracting', not now, they could just ditch the shooters and go home, they had no extra baggage, didn't have what was now no doubt Britain's Most Wanted in a car, they were invisible.

But it wasn't right, something stank, and he knew it. Gus going it alone, making them walk, sure it made sense, but where was he?

Where was Auguste Fredericks?

The two sat in silence, Jake's mind now full of scenarios, what if he had been caught? How long before the Police were coming for them?

Finally Sean spoke, "Jake, I'm not liking this, we need to move. If the law have got them, they're going to come looking for us, and we're sitting here waiting for it."

Jake became animated, "I fucking know that, don't you think I'm thinking the same, don't take me for an idiot Sean. Either Gus has been nicked, which I very much doubt, he's too shrewd for that, or, or he's done us a good one, left us here high and dry."

He felt mean sounding off like that at Sean, he was a good friend, and they had been through a lot together, all three of them had, and in reality he knew that they both owed Gus their lives, their old Sergeant twice going back into the *Mastiff* and pulling them out whilst the Taliban took pot-shots at them.

"Sorry mate," he said to Sean, his voice displaying an almost apologetic tone, "Too tense, come on let's ship out, get some space between us, he better pray he's been nicked, because I'm cutting his big black bollocks off and feeding them to him raw if he's done us over, I swear it, I'll kill him."

"Come on Jake, don't talk like that, Gus wouldn't do that, you know that, you know what we've been through together, he just wouldn't."

"Oh yeah? No Gus I can understand, but where's the bloody extraction. There's no helicopter, no fast car, no motorbikes, not even a fucking tandem, it's not right Sean."

They had been through much together, Sergeant Auguste Fredericks had earned his Military Cross after saving the lives of Privates Sean Cavanagh and Jake Murray, after their *Mastiff* Personnel Carrier was blown from the road by an IED as it returned to Camp Bastion, Helmand Province, on the 7th March 2010. His citation read that he had twice returned, under heavy Taliban fire, to retrieve two injured and immobilised colleagues, from their wrecked vehicle and placed them in the safety of the following *Mastiff*, as a result of his actions no British lives were lost on the mission.

THE SHATTERED EAGLE

During this heroic act of bravery Sergeant Fredericks sustained a gunshot wound to his left leg, yet still continued with his rescue. There was no doubt that had he not taken this action both his colleagues would have perished, and rather than returned home to be met by loving families at Heathrow would have been driven through Wooten Bassett at 5mph whilst mourners tossed roses and tributes in their direction.

It was such a debt that led to both Sean and Jake agreeing to leave the Regiment and join Gus in his new Private Security venture, *Blackwatch*.

Playing bodyguard to Arab Royalty and Russian Oligarchs had proved most lucrative, especially as most of the time it involved no more than waiting around casinos, the finest restaurants, or lavish hotels. Gus was well connected, he clearly knew people in high places, as the work seemed to come in almost immediately.

But the nice evenings out to Park Lane, Chelsea and Mayfair suddenly halted, Gus said he had subbed them out, taken on new contractors to look after the rich and dishonest clientele, and that *Blackwatch* itself would be attending to the interests of a single paymaster. It all became very hush-hush, secret squirrel stuff, with Gus referring to their new employers as no more than the 'Connection'.

A factory unit was rented outside of a rural village in Surrey, and a makeshift barracks, for just three, installed within it. Military equipment was procured, hi-tech electronics installed, a small well stocked armoury, incorporated into a concealed room. The three did no more work, Gus declaring they were on standby, that when needed the 'Connection' would be in touch. Fractures appeared between the group, it was as if the two of them weren't trustworthy, they were preparing for a mini-war, and apart from Gus, didn't even know who they were fighting for.

Then after seven weeks of kicking their heels, a call came, 'Gold Eagle' had activated the mission, it was time to earn that money.

And now Jake and Sean were walking away from the rendezvous point, no Gus, no extraction, no plan other than to put as much mileage as possible between them and what was now a murder scene a couple of miles away.

"What do you reckon Jake, take another motor, bus, or find the train station?"

"Let's find a bus, how many wanted men travel public transport, come on, let's go home."

-NINETEEN-
Going Home In An Ambulance.

Unwrapping a large cigar, Gus examined it closely as he rotated it in his hands, sitting in the back of the Ambulance as it sped down the M1, blue lights flashing, its oblivious patient lying on the bed in the back. Even he didn't imagine things would pan out this way, everything working out so damn well. Not only was he sending his hapless ex-partners off to oblivion, but getting clean away like that was a thing of beauty. Those guys who were paying the bills knew how to do things in style, he seriously doubted that had it been the entire resources of the British Armed Forces at his beck and call they could have pulled off a sweet extraction like that, just out of nowhere, in such a short timescale.

He lit the cigar and breathed the smoke in, awarding himself a moment of pure indulgence, before blowing it out in a long and continuous motion onto the unconscious form lying beside him.

"Well my little Somali jail bird, I have no idea why they want you, or what the hell they want you for, but you have just earned me a pretty sweet little one and half million, I should be kissing your little skinny black arse in recognition of services to my bank account."

He laughed to himself, before coughing, having not completely cleared his mouth of the cigar smoke.

"Yeah mother fucker, one and a half goddamn million, someone must really love you, or you must have sorely pissed someone off, either way they are going to be mighty pleased to see your sorry face again."

Sitting back in the seat adjacent to the bed, he swung both his feet up on the rubber mattress, wiggling his toes as he drifted back to the endless days during that last horrific six month tour. Out on patrol every single day, not knowing whether he would return with his legs still attached to his body or not. He remembered that young kid from Cardiff, no more than eighteen, literally blown in two as he walked through what they thought was a deserted compound, routine stuff, a supposed bolt hole to get their feet up and have a drink in comparative safety. How they were pinned down for over three hours, two more of the patrol dying at the hands of an unseen sniper, the fucked up rescue which saw the helicopter brought down and exploding into flames. The whole patrol looking to him for the non-existent way out, young teenage kids, and men with ten years in, all terrified and at the mercy of the Taliban. They were all expecting Gus to get them out safely, when he himself only wanted to dig himself a great deep foxhole and hide.

Day in day out that shit happened, for thirty two grand a year, every single day of those six months. And here he was in the back of an Ambulance looking at earning what it would have been impossible to earn in the army. They were paying him 45 years money for one operation. 45 years!

That was why it was easy to have no conscience on this one, that's why he could put bullets in innocent heads, kill people who had done him no harm, if this was what you had to do to earn that sort of money, then so be it. He had to admit though that he was almost glad the Prison Officer got away, one less civilian to terminate, no harm done. In fact it all worked out for the better, he was never happy with the part of the plan where they were to separate, it just didn't ring true in his mind.

From the darkened window he saw the sign for the exit to Hemel Hempstead, and the Ambulance turning into the slip road as they pulled off the motorway, the siren went silent, they continued for about half a mile before reaching a roundabout, where they turned off down a country lane.

Gus was anxious, it was prime time for double crosses, for back stabbing and Machiavellian treachery, the irony of which wouldn't have been wasted at all, had he found himself on the receiving end.

He had no idea who was in the front, or even how many of them there may be, he did know they were good at what they did, but certainly that didn't make them trustworthy, on the contrary it made them dangerous, very fucking dangerous.

As they drew to a halt, he pulled the pistol out, and tucked it beside his leg furthest from the door, he wanted it in easy reach. He could hear the handle being pulled, then the door swung open, two men filled the exit, both looked like they were forces, or had been, they were dressed as Paramedics in Green overalls but they were soldiers for sure, neither appeared armed though.

"OK," one of them said to Gus, "this is where we go our separate ways, all your fees and expenses have been paid into the specified destination, and our employers thank you for all you've done. There is a car over there, the driver will take you where you wish. Oh and please don't forget your weapon by your left leg, but I assure you that it is no longer needed, they are honourable men."

Gus nodded back, his eyes never leaving the two forms as they moved from the open door, he still felt uneasy, just one bullet from either of the two phoney Paramedics would save someone a bloody great heap of money, and end *Blackwatch Enterprises* there and then. But he had no choice, he shuffled out of the back of the Ambulance and picked his way across the gritty road, like a lizard on hot sand, still regretting not bringing any shoes to change into, and got into the back of the waiting silver *Audi*.

Before he was even in the car the Ambulance was driving off.

"Where to Sir?" the driver enquired.

"Do you know Leatherhead?" Gus answered.

The driver nodded.

"Then I'll show you where when we get there."

THE SHATTERED EAGLE

The driver said no more and pulled away. Gus had one last job to do that day, just to ensure that a couple of loose ends were well and truly tied up.

-TWENTY-
A New Arrival Comes To Safehaven

It was hard to see much from the window, it was starting to get dark outside, the lights in the gatehouse were glowing, a dull amber shade, but beyond that there was very little to break the oncoming gloom. Gary could see the road that led past the gates slowly disappearing into the evening, he had no idea where it led to, just as he had no notion of where he actually was. A dog was furiously barking somewhere out there, but not a lot else, they appeared to literally be in the middle of nowhere.

Fran had left to get the kids off to sleep back in their room, no doubt struggling, she said that their whole routine had gone to pot since the bomb, and that they had slept very little, just couldn't settle. But then Josh and Amy weren't the only ones struggling to settle, he knew he should be resting, it was what he was told every day, but he needed to walk around a bit, stretch his legs, he couldn't just lay there, thinking, remembering, reliving it all again and again, he needed distraction. Staring through the unrelenting darkness beyond the fence he could just make out three sets of headlamps in the distance, approaching down the fast fading road, he watched them fixated by their glow as if they had some magical hold over him, as they got nearer he could see that two pairs belonged to Police Cars, which were sandwiching an Ambulance, they appeared to be moving at a fast pace, although no blue lights were on.

As they approached he could see the metal gates opening, automatically, and the vehicles gliding into his world, the gates immediately closing behind. As if synchronised to the metal gates his door opened exactly as the vehicles drove through, a nurse entering the room.

"Hello Gary", although she pronounced his name 'Gurry', "I am sorry to disturb you, I have very good news, we moving you to a normal room, you be with your wife, the doctor says you are well enough to move now, I get bags together, and I get a wheelchair, I will not be a minute."

He didn't want to question her, there was nothing more he wanted than to be with Fran, Josh and Amy, but what happened to 'You need to rest Gary', 'Please get back in bed Mr Westlake', 'Gary you really mustn't walk around', and the host of other well-meaning orders he seemed to be issued at five minute intervals?

But he wasn't arguing, he had missed sharing a bed with Fran, although if he was honest there was some merit to single sleeping arrangements, after over twenty years of marriage the ratio of blissful post-coital sleep filled nights, to being woken by graceless snoring and subconscious farting, had shifted quite disturbingly.

With remarkable swiftness the nurse, Polina, who Gary was sure was Polish, but with a credible grasp of English, returned with a wheelchair, and ushered him into it.

"OK then Gary, let us go to room."

As he was wheeled along a narrow carpeted corridor, he got his first real chance to look around beyond the room he had been 'imprisoned' within, Fran was right, this place did resemble a hotel, a nice one at that. There were prints on the walls, rural scenes, landscapes, and coastal views, and the navy blue carpet appeared new, the walls were papered in a pale gold print, large flowers embossed upon it, it looked expensive. They came to an elevator, and Polina pressed the 'up' button, seconds later there was a ding, the sound of Adele, wafting out as the doors slid open. He looked at the illuminated panel, 3-2-1-G, she pressed 3 and the doors closed and they rose up to the strains of 'Chasing Pavements'.

"I guess this sudden move out of there is more to do with that Ambulance arriving, than my miraculous speedy recovery?" he asked Polina.

"I'm sorry Gary I cannot answer such things, but you are getting a lot better," she replied. "Plus if you need anything there is bell in your room, we can come and help you whenever you like, the rooms they are very nice here, I am sure you will like it."

Hmm he was not so sure he would like it. What about work, he hadn't really considered it, not until now he was

THE SHATTERED EAGLE

deemed 'fit' again. Then there was Fran's job, the kids, how long would they be there, they were due back at school in early September?

'Ding' the doors slid open again, the corridor seemed very similar to the one two floors below, in fact he wondered whether the elevator had just remained still, it was pretty much identical, the same paper, the prints on the walls appeared to be same, spaced in the same order, with the same idyllic vistas, and the same carpet beneath him. Polina wheeled him out of elevator and about half way down the familiar corridor until they stopped outside a room, 307.

"Here we are Gary," Polina tapped gently on the door, a moment later Fran opened it.

"Sur-prise, sur-prise! Heeerrre's Gary!" he said, although hardly with the conviction of Jack Nicholson, but then Jack wasn't recovering from surgery.

"Blimey that was quick, Jay has just phoned and said you were on your way. Amy, Josh, come quickly look who's here!"

The kids came running, both crashing into the wheelchair as they threw their arms around their much missed father.

"Be careful kiddies," Fran told them, although it appeared to be falling on deaf ears. "Dad's still our little wounded soldier, you must be careful with him."

"Dad, Dad," they were both shouting at once.

"It's a hotel!"

"We've got Sky!"

"There's a swimming pool!"

"Wow, a swimming pool, have you been yet?" Gary asked.

"No, but we've seen it, it looks great Dad, can we go tomorrow, please, please, please!"

"We'll see, I'm hurt remember, don't know if I'm up to swimming myself, maybe I can just watch."

Fran wheeled him into their room, as Polina said her goodbyes and scurried off, Gary presumed to meet whoever the new arrival was.

The room was far bigger than he imagined it would be, in fact it was a suite of rooms. He was in an extremely spacious living area, and could see leading off of it there were three bedrooms and what he guessed was a bathroom.

"Well this is bigger than I was expecting, it actually looks pretty plush," he climbed out of the wheelchair and hobbled over to the window, it was now really dark outside, there was no moon to offer illumination, and with the lights on inside there was nothing that could be seen outside at all other than his own reflection, and that didn't look particularly good.

He guessed they were the opposite side of the building to where his hospital-like room was, as there was no road or gatehouse to see, and certainly no Ambulance.

"Someone else has just arrived," he told Fran. "I think that's why they've kicked me out of the other room, I saw an Ambulance and a couple of Police cars pulling up."

THE SHATTERED EAGLE

"I know," Fran replied, "Jay pretty much said as much, although you know what they're like she hasn't exactly told us a lot."

"Hey Dad, Dad…" Josh was tugging at his sleeve. "Dad, we can have food whenever we like! We just have to phone, do you want some chips, you can have chips, and puddings, it's all free too!"

"Wow that sounds great Josh, I'm not hungry now though. I'll tell you what we'll do, you and Amy go back to bed and get some sleep, and in the morning we'll go exploring, what do you say, is that a plan or is that a plan? We can stuff chips once we've had a good lookey around."

"Oh do we have to go to bed?" they both whined in perfect unison.

"Yes, me and Dad need to talk about things," Fran told them as she ushered them off. "And if you're going exploring you need to have lots of energy!"

After much tucking in, re-tucking in, hugs, and further tucking in, Josh and Amy finally settled down for the night.

"Cor my side's aching like billyo, I think I've been on my feet a bit too long." Gary was holding his side, where the glass punctured his flesh to such spectacular effect.

"Oh surprise-surprise Mr Genius, what did you really expect, Oh no you're Gary Westlake, you can't rest up when told to! But of course you can when the garden needs doing, rooms need painting or the toilet seat replacing, but not when you're told to by the doctor can you? I bet you haven't taken all the pills you should either, crikey Gary don't turn me into a nag!"

"Too late for that darling, see like I've told you hundreds of times already, you're becoming my Mum!"

"Shut ya' face you fat tosser! Now get sat down, I'll sort us something to drink."

He flopped into one of two brown soft leather sofas, Fran offered him a drink, but he was on too many pills to quaff alcohol, so she just sorted him a *Diet Coke*, apparently the fridge was stocked with all sorts of stuff, fizzy pop, fruit juices, spirits, wines, beers, it was all in there.

She poured herself a large glass of white wine, and settled down beside him.

"How are you love?" he asked, as he placed his arm around her as she snuggled against his chest, she felt so good, she fitted in there just right, he could smell the wine on her breath, but it wasn't unpleasant, blending nicely with the slightly floral fragrance of her hair, it was the first time in days he had felt comfortable, not so much physically - as he still hurt like mad - but mentally, at ease, or as close to at ease as was possible in this mess.

"All kidding apart. I'm not sure Gaz, this is all so surreal. I've no idea where we are, we can't phone anyone other than the people in here. Mum and Dad don't have a clue we're here, my work, your work, friends, family, no one. They'll be worried sick. You know your Mum, she'll be climbing the walls. I tried to walk outside earlier, they wouldn't let me, wouldn't even let me outside for heaven's

THE SHATTERED EAGLE

sake, we're like prisoners in here. I'm so glad you're now with us, at least we're together. I think back to yesterday at the hospital, those Policemen with guns, you trying to get to me, it's a bloody nightmare."

"I know love, I know, I'll try and find out more, but they seem to only tell us as little as they need to, I suppose we're safe here though, and the kids as well, that's got to be the main thing. Once they find this boy I saw I guess we can return to normal, or at least I hope so, because I know one thing for certain, we can't live like this forever."

-TWENTYONE-
A Family Reunion.

They drove onto the small airfield just North of Watford, it was dark, but the *Embraer Phenom 100* was clearly visible waiting on the tarmac.

The Ambulance drove across the shortly cut grass until it was alongside the small jet. The steps were down already and Henri DuPont, dressed in a dark suit with an open necked black shirt, walked down to greet his estranged adopted son. He moved to the back of the vehicle, where the two green suited 'Paramedics' opened the door. Looking inside at Abu Warsabi, or Alaine as he was known to him, he gave a cursory nod to the men either side of him. Alaine was now awake, strapped to the trolley, struggling, his mouth gagged.

"Hello my son," he said in French, "I'm sure you are just thrilled to see me again. It's been a long time Alaine, a very long time, yet I hear you've been up to so much of late. Let me assure you we will catch up on that soon, I think though you would have disappointed poor Anna so much if she knew what you have been up to. But then you never cared much for my wife did you? In a moment you will be moved onto that plane, and we will fly home, but first I have one question. Where is my ring?"

Alaine continued to wriggle and struggle, desperate to get away, but knowing that there was no escape.

Henri entered the Ambulance, he pulled the black tape from Alaine's mouth, skin remained on the adhesive side, like someone had kissed a tissue, Alaine winced, his mouth bleeding where chunks of his lips had been torn away, but said nothing, as he had said pretty much nothing to Henri from the moment he had entered his house five years previously.

"Where is my ring, Alaine? Where is it?" Henri whispered in his ear.

Again silence.

He raised his tone slightly, just enough for Alaine to hear above the whine of the two jet engines which had just fired up yards away. "You can hear me, I know you can hear me. You will tell me, you will tell me personally, because I will be the one asking you this question again and again. I will get great satisfaction from getting the answer. This Alaine is personal, this is something we've both been waiting for, for very different reasons. And believe me when you've told me where the ring is, you will tell me what happened at that school you went to. And then me and you will be done."

Henri stood up and stepped back out onto the tarmac, he nodded once more to the two men outside, one of them administered another injection into Alaine's neck, who immediately stopped his struggling and went limp.

"Put him on the plane," Henri ordered, as he climbed back up the steps.

About five minutes passed, the volume of the engines increased considerably, the plane began to slowly taxi into position before suddenly accelerating and taking to the air.

Inside Henri lifted open the laptop on a small table in front of him. He pressed some keys and the screen was filled with the image of him and Anna on their wedding day. She was beautiful, so radiant, so very happy. The ivory silk dress accentuating her wonderful figure, her lovely hair framing the face so full of joy, she was just the image of perfection. He was there in his uniform, the proudest man in the world, nothing could have made him any happier than he was that day. He remembered watching her coming down the church aisle, walking through flowers that lined her path, the sun bursting through the large doorway behind her, tears were rolling down his face as he stared at the screen.

His Anna, his lovely Anna.

-TWENTYTWO-
Back At Blackwatch HQ

Jake felt exhausted, he just wanted the day over with, a quick shower and then to bed, everything else could wait until the morning, or more precisely later that morning. They were just outside of the factory unit which doubled as *Blackwatch* HQ, it was three o'clock AM, and he had a lot of stuff running through his mind, the most important of which was where the fuck was Gus?

It had been a long journey back, the buses in the evenings were hardly regular, and they ended up having to go miles out of their way, a lack of money meant they were unable to get a cab, and Sean ended up stealing a car, which in turn broke down just outside of Leatherhead, leaving them no alternative other than walking the last six miles in the moonless pitch black through country lanes and overgrown footpaths.

Neither of them were in the best of moods, nor were they dressed anything like appropriately, shorts, tee-shirts, and sandals weren't the ideal choice of clothing for a cross country trek the wrong side of midnight. Both were cold, hungry, and scratched to bits by brambles, whilst Jake had trod in some rather offensive dog shit, which had also managed to coat the toes on one foot, before he had realised what it was.

Yeah, he thought, that about topped the day off nicely.

Cussing and cursing he unlocked the steel door at the side of the unit, and walked in, Sean following, wisely saying nothing, as Jake was not in a conversational sort of mood. Oh Jeezus, he thought, as once inside the stench from his soiled sandal became evident, he really needed that shower. Fumbling in the dark he pulled down the large lever adjacent to the doorway, but instead of the place illuminating welcomingly, nothing happened.

Pulling out the gun which was tucked in the back of his waistband, he held his hand up to Sean, something was very wrong, two tours in Helmand had gifted him a sixth sense for danger, though not for dog shit, and alarm bells were ringing loud and clear in his head.

Backing out of the doorway he hissed back to Sean, "Something's up, it's not right, Gus not turning up, no extraction, and now the power's out here."

"What shall we do?"

"What do mean, what shall we do, we can't do shit right now, but I'm not happy stopping here, let's get some clothes, cash, and a bit of grub, and get out, we can take the van round the back, and head somewhere we can lay low, at least until we find out what happened with Gus, but stopping here ain't happening."

Sean drew his gun and they entered the building, Jake thought back to Afghanistan, moving through the villages, not knowing who was in a doorway, who was watching from one of the low roofs or windows, he never liked that, and he definitely didn't like this. Slowly and deliberately they moved towards the offices, which doubled as their living quarters, their eyes struggling to adapt to the total lack of light within the building.

They inched forward.

"Shit!" Jake exclaimed, his bare shin had scraped against the sharp edge of what he now knew was a small stack of pallets. He could feel the splinters digging in, a small line of blood flowing to his stinking foot, he couldn't see jack shit.

"You alright?" he heard Sean whispering.

"No I'm fucking not!" Jake hissed back, what a stupid bloody question that was.

Jake continued to make his way across the unit, step by step, Sean following, their guns scanning around, yet they were unable to see anything. Fanning his free hand in front of him he groped in the black thin air for dangers, or the wall he knew was approaching, the wall that contained the glass doorway to their living area and store, where he knew there were warm clothes, food, drink, and most importantly at this time, at least three 'Dragon Lights' just one of which would illuminate the entire unit.

The hairs on the back of his neck were on end, his bare arms speckled with goose bumps, adrenalin was now kicking in, yeah every part of him knew this was wrong, why were they doing it, he suddenly asked himself, yet onwards he went.

At last he felt the flat cold surface of the painted breeze-block wall, "Nearly there," he whispered to Sean.

Shuffling sideways he kicked an unseen bottle across the floor, he thought he was going to shit himself, but all that training had kicked in, his mind disseminating what it was given to process and evaluating the threat it had been presented with. He heard a scampering, probably a rat that was spooked, and continued feeling and groping in search of the door way. This was ridiculous, his shin was stinging, he smelt of shit, and he couldn't see a fucking thing. Where was Gus?

Or more importantly at that moment where were the bloody electrics in this place?

What was wrong with this picture?

At last his hand found the frame, the door was already open, he slid in, as he did so, he felt the taught pull of the wire against his ankle.

The phrase 'What was that?' would probably have been his last thoughts, Afghanistan had made him wise to booby traps, he should have been more aware.

But unfortunately time deprived him of the luxury of last thoughts.

Over thirty thousand tiny ball bearings shot out in all directions travelling at hundreds of miles an hour. Neither of them had a chance, confronted with the steel wind that came their way, Jake's face was stripped from his skull as he instinctively ducked, turning much of his head into a fine mist of flesh, sinew and bone spraying across the

THE SHATTERED EAGLE

darkness, Sean being further away from the point of release found his body peppered with the steel balls, the equivalent to being shot by over a dozen shotguns at close range.

Jake was dead instantly, having one's brain disintegrated has a habit of doing that, poor old Sean took several minutes to perish, his eyes turned to mush, face peppered, body ripped to bits, but his internal organs intact, he had to wait to lose enough blood to enable his euphoric release from unimaginable pain and suffering. As he passed into blissful ignorance he was aware of the flames crackling, wood spitting and hissing, he couldn't see it of course, his eyes pulverised, but the sound was unmistakeable, the whole building was on fire.

Blackwatch had lost two thirds of its ownership, all fees were now payable solely to Auguste Fredericks.

-TWENTYTHREE-
Another New Arrival Comes To Safehaven

Oli was shattered, both physically and emotionally, his leg felt like it had been hit with a sledge hammer, and his head ached like mad. He kept reaching up to touch the bump, it wasn't getting any smaller.

His mind replayed the images of the day before over and over, from kissing Kate good bye and dashing out of the flat with nothing more than a dry variety box of *Coco-Pops*, which he dipped into as he drove in, to Jim getting assaulted, and then where it all went into the nightmarish, unreal, murderous trip to a hospital. George - again and again he visualised the gaping hole in the back of his head, the glistening brain matter, or what hadn't been blasted over the back of the taxi, revealed where the bullet had smashed the back of his cranium out. Dead. George was dead, Warsabi shrieking and screaming, struggling for his wretched life, looking down at his wrist Oli could see the thick purple welts where the cuffs had twisted into his flesh as he struggled to stay in control. Then there were the three guys who took him, why?

THE SHATTERED EAGLE

Where was Warsabi now?

Where, more importantly, was he now?

He remembered in the Ambulance he had asked one of the Policemen escorting him about Kate, told him how she was supposed to meet him at *Carlos*, about how he was worried about her. The Policeman said he would sort all that, and made a couple of calls to someone to arrange for her to be transported to wherever they were heading, where was she?

Having looked around as he was wheeled off the Ambulance just hours earlier, he knew he wasn't at a hospital that was for sure, unless it was one of those fancy *BUPA* ones, but the place looked more like a big country home, the sort of mansion that would host one of those Murder Mystery Weekends or a high class Swingers Orgy, how very appropriate he'd seen enough murder and felt well and truly fucked.

He recalled how he was wheeled up a makeshift ramp which had been placed over the stone steps leading up to the entrance, a pair of lions standing guard either side of the doorway. When they had entered the lobby, he had looked around, it was all quite modern compared to the grand stone facades outside, a glass wall one side appeared to have an indoor swimming pool behind it, whilst the other side housed what looked like a row of offices, it was well lit and spacious, but once more he pondered if it wasn't a hospital, then where the hell was he?

***

He was now lying in bed, within what he was told was the Medical Centre, which appeared no more than a large bedroom which was painted white and occasionally went 'Beep'. A man, who Oli presumed was a doctor, shined a bright light into both his eyes, felt around his battered leg, and then confirmed that he had no major injuries, before scurrying out, leaving Oli to lay on top of the sheets and blanket, still in his uniform. A nurse had flitted in and out, but had said very little to him other than inform him she was just taking his blood pressure and checking his temperature, one of the Policemen who had escorted him there had popped into the room, but only stopped for a couple of minutes, apparently just staring at him, saying nothing at all when Oli had tried to strike up some conversation.

But none of them had answered the question he asked each of them, where was he?

There was a knock on the door and a tall man entered, he was wearing a smart blue suit, and a polo shirt, and smiled as he came in, he was followed by a dishevelled looking character, in jeans and a Hawaiian shirt, probably in his late thirties or early forties.

"Hello Mr Allen, DCI Adrian Howard, although my friends call me Frankie, and DS Felix Fernando, do you mind if I call you Oli?"

"No worries, sit down if you like." Oli nodded towards a pair of chairs, though he had to wince as even that small motion felt like his brain was being hit by a huge wrecking ball.

THE SHATTERED EAGLE

"Do excuse us calling so early, but we've some very important questions to ask you, we'll try not to keep you too long, I appreciate you must be very tired, youi've been through a lot."

"You're not far wrong there, didn't sleep at all, it was all running through my mind." Oli yawned as he answered, not to make any point, but because he was plain shagged.

"That's good for us then Oli, nice and fresh in the mind, eh," the one called Felix said. "Obviously, we're here to talk about yesterday, you had some ordeal there mate, couldn't have been easy, I'm not surprised you had trouble sleeping, anyone would."

Frankie again took over, "Yes, you're one lucky young man, kidnapped, run over, and you walk away with only scrapes and bruises, a very lucky young man, wouldn't you agree Sergeant Fernando?"

"Yes Guv, very lucky."

"I don't feel that lucky." Oli answered.

"Well that's open to interpretation isn't it?" Frankie said, "I'd say the two people who were killed were unlucky, wouldn't you? I'd say being shot in the head is pretty unlucky. Very unlucky compared to not being shot in the head, having the key to the handcuffs, and rolling out of a slow moving vehicle in Northampton Town Centre, and sustaining just a couple of bumps and bruises. Now some would say that was pretty lucky."

Frankie was up pacing around the room as he spoke, Oli was startled, the bloke's whole demeanour had changed, he was no longer reassuring, kind, tactful, no longer any of those at all.

"Hey Felix, who would you say was the luckiest person in that Taxi?" Frankie said nodding towards Oli, as if a clue was needed.

"I'd say Mr Allen Guv."

"So would I Felix." He then turned to Oli, "You see my problem is I'm from the Anti-Terrorism Unit, I don't think I included that in our introduction did I, I've got someone who I believe to be the Euston bomber, being sprung from a bloody Taxi in the middle of nowhere. I've got dead bodies, I've seen them, very dead I'd say. I've got big bad men with guns, and I've got you. Now what I'm asking myself, and what any five year old retard with half a brain would ask themselves, is how those big bad men knew Abu Warsabi would be going to hospital in a taxi, at that exact time?

"They may also ask why you are sitting up in that bed and not in a morgue at this very moment. Why you were able to walk out of that *Range Rover*, just walk out like it's the number twenty two bus or something. This doesn't add up for me Oli, this all appears a bit wrong. What do you think Felix?"

"Very Wrong Guv'. Very wrong indeed."

"No!" Oli shouted back. "Are you mad, are you both out of your minds?"

He was shell shocked, there was no indication this was coming, that this was even being imagined by anyone, how could anyone even suppose for one second he would be capable of having anything to do with any of this?

Frankie was raising his voice, moving closer to Oli, leaning over him in his bed, his face just a couple of inches from Oli's, "Then tell me what happened, what really happened, because at this very moment you young man are all I have. Now I don't know whether you're my suspect, a fucking good witness or both, but believe me you've got a long day ahead, because you're going to talk to me until I know either way."

Frankie stood up and took a couple paces back, before taking a buff coloured card folder which Felix had handed him, he took a set of photographs from it, and held them out in front of Oli, "Look at them, is that him?"

Oli picked the small stack up, there were five photos, they were black and white, but that was Warsabi, he was sure of that. They showed him getting off a train, he recognised the hat and clothes from the property, and there in the fourth picture on his third finger right hand, the ring. Oh shit the ring! It was still in his pocket, he felt his heart beating faster, he still had that bloody ring on him!

"That's him, that's definitely Warsabi," he told the man standing over him, although as he was speaking he was thinking not of the Somali kid, but the item he had in effect stolen from him. "They're the clothes he came in with, I'm sure of that. Look I had nothing to do with…"

"Yeah, yeah, not now. Tell me about when he came in, when you first met him." Frankie said, taking the photos back from Oli and pushing them back in the folder.

"He came from court. I think he was remanded, had a real bad attitude. I wasn't sure if he could speak English, he just ignored us, kissing his…"

"Us?" Frankie interrupted, "Who's us?"

"Me and Jim Bolton, another Officer, we were working reception that morning."

"Please go on," Felix said, a lot calmer and friendlier than Frankie could muster.

"Well like I was saying, he had a really shitty attitude, kissing his teeth and staring, you know giving us the eyeball. I tried to speak to him, but it was a waste of time, he was having of none of it. I was sorting his property out, going through what he had and recording it."

Oli thought for a brief moment, should he mention the ring? Of course not, he still needed a job, he would completely leave it out of his account, not even allude to it, it wasn't on the prop card, so nothing could tie him to it, he just needed to make sure it wasn't on him, wouldn't trip him up.

"Look can we stop for a moment, can I have a drink, it's been hours since I've had a drink, I feel a little faint."

Frankie looked a bit put out, but didn't argue, it was after all a reasonable request, "OK, we'll get someone to get you one. Tea or coffee?"

"Either, I really don't mind, as long as it's white and got a sugar."

Going to the doorway Frankie called out, "DeHavalland, DeHavalland!"

THE SHATTERED EAGLE

Felix was looking at his boss, Oli took the opportunity whilst their backs were turned, hurriedly taking the ring from his pocket and sliding it under his pillow.

"Yeah Jay, can you get me get me two teas and a coffee, all with sugar, and some biscuits, quick as you can please."

He returned and drew a chair next to Oli, a bit too close Oli thought, it made him feel a little awkward, closed in, but then that was probably how this man wanted him to feel.

"Right, where were we, you went through his things, that's it, anything out of the ordinary? Anything to set him apart?"

"No, nothing at all really, just clothes and a stereo, I think, I never got to finish sorting it all."

"And where would they all go, you say it's the same gear as in the photos, we really need to get that." Felix asked.

"They'll be stored in reception, every prisoner has a prop box, it'll be there I guess."

"You say you never finished sorting it?" Felix asked.

"No, he jumped over the desk and attacked Jim, had to be restrained."

"And?" Felix was looking at him, like he was expecting him to say so much more.

"And what? I was with Jim after that, that was me done with him."

"Well Oli it obviously wasn't you done with him was it?" Frankie was again on his feet. "I'd say far from done wouldn't you? So go on what happened next, how come you were done with him one moment, and then you're going on the Magical Sodding Mystery Tour, with no John, Paul or Ringo, but a very fucking dead George. Go on please tell us, because this is what I really don't understand, this is the bit that's putting a great big illuminated sign with 'suspect' written in neon above your head. No please tell me."

"I don't understand?"

"You don't understand?" Frankie laughed, but it wasn't a friendly laugh, there was no humour in it. "Let me help you, why were you, you in particular, in that taxi? Why are you still here? Why are you breathing, when if I was one of those bastards with guns, who have already killed two people, I'd have made pretty damn sure that you wouldn't be talking to me in a secure safe house, do you understand now?"

Oli understood fully what he was alluding rather blatantly to, but this man was so wrong. He felt his anger welling inside, his mind flashed with images of George, Rab, men in black, guns, chaos, his fear, his very real fear that he was going to die, and this bastard was somehow saying he was in on it, was somehow to blame!

He couldn't listen to him anymore, there was no calm left in him, he exploded, "Because I got away! I'm not going to feel guilty that I'm alive, fuck you, I'm not! Yes I'm lucky to be alive, but George is dead, the cabbies dead, do you honestly think that's anything to do with me, anything at all. Are you mad, or just stupid? You don't know me, you don't know me at all. What do you take me for? Now, I do want to help you, I really do, but get off my back, I'm the victim here, get it, I've done nothing wrong, treat me right, you don't treat me like this!"

Oli was irate, there was no need for this. He was also scared, he knew he needed shot of that ring, it was the only thing he had done wrong, the only untruth, yet if discovered would make him a liar, illuminate Howard's sign to dazzling proportions.

"Look," Oli continued. "I went on that escort because George told me to, I begged not to go, I was supposed to meet Kate later, she's my girlfriend, we were supposed to be going out, I couldn't afford to be pissing around at St Hugh's. I didn't want anything to do with it, I've no time for the prisoner after what he did to Jim Bolton, I told George that, but they were strapped for staff."

Felix was watching Oli intently, running his fingers through his mop like hair before asking, "How soon before you left on the escort did you know they were going out?"

"Only about quarter of hour, I just had time to fetch the escort bag and pick Warsabi up from his cell, it was all rushed, I didn't even know he was injured, honestly I had no idea."

"So tell me about the journey, start from the prison," Felix said.

"Well he was searched, and cuffed, then loaded on the taxi. It was pretty much standard stuff, same as usual, although not friendly Warsabi was quiet, didn't give us any trouble to speak of. Me and Sergio, Sergio Pozzo, were sat with the con facing George. We took the usual route, through the lanes, it was just normal I guess. Well it was until we crashed."

"Go on."

"I heard a noise, I think Rab, the driver, had been shot, something hit my neck, it was warm and wet, we then came off the road. It was madness, George was trying to get to his feet, but then he was shot."

"Could you see anyone outside at this point?" Frankie was again asking the questions.

"No, no one, but then I wasn't looking, I was fighting with Warsabi by then, he was going mad, I really reckon he had no idea he was going to be taken, he was frantic. Well by now Sergio had done a runner, across the field I think, I don't know if he got away, I guess he did, as they said something later about it on a radio. But it was manic, really manic. Anyway I'm fighting to get Warsabi to stay down, then there's someone at the side door, with a gun. From there we're taken to the *Range Rover*, well I am, Warsabi's drugged or something, they put a needle in his neck and he was sparko."

"Why do you think they didn't do that to you?"

"I've no idea."

"So why did they take you?"

"I think because I was cuffed to him, well I'm pretty sure that's why they did it, they didn't have the key to the cuffs."

"No you did."

"Yeah."

THE SHATTERED EAGLE

Frankie looked confused, "That's not right is it though, you wouldn't be cuffed and have the keys to them surely, even in the Police, and we're famed for our natural stupidity, that wouldn't happen?"

"No George did, on his chain, I took them while I was struggling with Warsabi, hid them in my boot, they asked me for them, but I knew once free of Warsabi I wasn't needed, I saw what happened to George, what they did, so I said they were back at the prison."

"They believed that?" Felix asked with feigned incredulity.

"I don't know, you'll need to ask them."

"Then what?"

"Then they put a hood on my head."

Frankie was again asking the questions, it was like a tag team Oli thought, only instead of good cop, bad cop, they were both bad, only Frankie was really bad! "You must have seen them before that, seen something about them?"

"They had like gasmasks on, they were wearing army stuff, all black gear."

"So tell me about the journey, how you got from there to laying in a road in Northampton?"

"They talked at one point about cutting my hand off, and they argued a bit about it, there were radio calls, they were 'Eagle One' and they were talking to 'Gold Eagle'. Warsabi was out of it, I really can't say much. When the traffic slowed down I could hear we were in a town or something so I fished the key out of my boot, un-cuffed myself, and got out."

"And they just let you go?" Again Felix and his exaggerated doubtful tone.

"They tried to stop me, grabbed me, but I was out. Look I can't tell you what they did, I couldn't see anything, I got out, that's it!"

"Quite the James Bond aren't you Oli," Frankie's sarcasm was unmistakable.

Oli knew they didn't believe him, in fact after hearing himself telling the story like that he doubted whether he would have believed it, the whole story sounded ludicrous.

But it was the truth.

"Right," Howard said, "Let's hear it all again from the beginning please."

For another hour Oli went over it all, and with each telling Frankie appeared to be just as cynical and Felix just as sceptical, and both just as sarcastic, it was clear they didn't think much of Oli, or his story. Finally around lunchtime they left.

Thank God! They had made feel like he was the criminal, yet he knew he had done nothing wrong, why would they possibly think that his story was anything other than the truth, because that is what it was, the truth, well 99% of it. It was that other 1% he needed to put right, looking around the room he saw the black *Adidas* holdall in the corner by a soft chair. Sliding out of the bed he hobbled over to it, lifting it on to the chair. It contained a towel and some underwear, as well as a few toiletries, he had to do something, and this was as good a plan as he had at that moment. He placed the ring deep into the bottom of the bag, under what was a stiff card like base, he looked at the end of the bag, a small card showed through a plastic window, 'GARY WESTLAKE'.

As Frankie and Felix entered the lift, the DCI asked, "Well Felix what do you think?"

"It's all a bit far too fortunate, there's a lot of luck, and he's hiding something, I could tell that, but he may be telling the truth."

"Yeah, it'd be a lot simpler if he wasn't, I reckon he'd crack pretty easily, but you may be right."

As they exited the lift Howard's phone rang.

-TWENTYFOUR-
Sergio Pozzo Goes To Pack His Bag.

Craig Lovan splashed the ice cold water over his face, looking at himself in the reflection of the mirror in the Gents, he was about done in, but knew that he wouldn't be getting any sleep for hours yet. He needed to find some toothpaste and a brush, his mouth tasted crap, and he could feel that furry coating over his teeth, it had been a long night. He had spent much of it in the company of Sergio Pozzo at Northampton Police Station, they'd gone over it all again and again How Pozzo had struggled to assist George Morton until it was clear he was dead, how he had tried to help Oliver Allen, but realising that the gunmen were almost upon them, he had made a break for it, to attempt to get help as quickly as possible to raise the alarm, and most relevantly how he was lucky to be alive.

Lovan was sure that anything Sergio Pozzo had to tell them was by now well and truly told, what he wasn't sure of though was whether Sergio was a national hero or merely a snivelling coward, there was something not all there about the story, something incomplete. He had reluctantly liaised, as instructed to, with DCI Howard of the Anti-Terrorism Unit, who he had taken an instant dislike to from the moment he had been so bloody rude in the lane the evening before, the man was pig-ignorant, rude to the extreme, and incapable of finishing a sentence without peppering it with profanities and obscenities, a typical Met Senior Ranking Policeman, full of bravado and crap, nothing to convey but his own egotistical importance. But Howard outranked him, and that still meant something to Lovan, so if the man said he was sending a car to take Pozzo to somewhere safe then he could have him, besides he needed to go with them, he wanted to speak to Allen, no needed to, but had received nothing but excuses and obstructions as the ATU fobbed him off.

But why should he be worrying? It was certain that Howard would be taking the case, he was adamant it was linked to terrorist activities, and seeing the state of his two murder victims, he wasn't doubting it, although pretty sophisticated terrorists they must have been.

Pozzo was once more sitting in the interview room, it was well into the morning, the sun was shining outside, illuminating the previously dingy room with its bright rays. Lovan entered, he would just let him know where he was going, then it was just a case of waiting for the car to arrive.

"Right Mr Pozzo, my colleague I was talking about earlier is keen to speak with you, he's sending someone to pick you up, I believe due to the nature of the case they may be taking you somewhere safe for a couple of days, I'll accompany you, but that's about us done with any questions we may have had, although I'm sure Detective Chief Inspector Howard will want to go over what we've already talked about."

"Why?" Pozzo asked. "I've told you everything I know, I need to get home."

"I appreciate that Sir, but he wants to ask you questions personally, and although I can't go into it in too much depth, there may be security issues, you were there, after all this was no ordinary crime."

"I can do without this. Look I need to get some stuff from home before I go anywhere, I'm in my uniform still for heaven's sake, this is crazy. I don't live far, I've done nothing wrong, at least let me sort out some gear, you know clothes to change into."

Lovan wasn't particularly bothered, he could see where the lad was coming from, he needed some clean clothes himself, and the car wasn't due for an hour, it would be good just to get him out of his way for a while, Pozzo had something about him, a self-assured cockiness that just grated a little bit.

"I can arrange a lift back home for you, get what you need, but you need to be quick. Then we can come back here and wait for their car, how does that sound?"

"Shit, whatever. I just need a change of clothes and a shower."

Yep, he did have an attitude on him, Lovan considered how he was putting himself out, he was stretched for staff,

THE SHATTERED EAGLE

he was having to free up a car to act as a taxi as it was, a thank you wouldn't have gone a miss.

PCs Holdsworth and Crossly waited in the yard in their patrol car, they really didn't need to be acting as some glorified private chauffeurs, there was plenty to do as it was. Sergio Pozzo was led out by Inspector Lovan, and got in the back of the car.

He was living about half way between Northampton and the prison, in a village called Hubble, it only took about twenty minutes to get there, the journey time helped no end by Crossly putting on the blue lights to speed things up a bit.

As they pulled up outside his house, Holdsworth looked at his watch, as Sergio told him, "I won't be a minute, just get some clothes, toiletries and stuff."

"Yeah keep it quick mate, the Inspector needs you back as quickly as possible." he replied.

The two Police Officers watched from the patrol car as Sergio entered the house and they saw the curtains draw inside.

"This is a bloody joke," Holdsworth complained. "We're supposed to be on a break and we're running around the countryside to pick someone's clothes up."

"Yeah, yeah, yeah," Crossly answered. "A Policeman's lot is not a happy one, happy one."

"What?"

"Gilbert and Sullivan my son, you really should…"

But before he could finish his sentence a motor bike accelerated from the side of the house, passing them, its engine roaring as its fleeing rider increased in speed.

"Shit!" Crossly exclaimed.

He immediately threw the car into a three point turn, and switched his sirens on, as he pulled away in the direction of the bike, which was now out of sight. As the car turned out of the cul-de-sac into the other residential road they came to the junction, "Left or Right?" Crossly asked, "Quick left or right?"

"It's 50/50 mate, makes no odds either way he's gone. Go left, I'll call it in."

"Sierra Oscar to Control, be aware, errr, be aware there's a very fast motorbike heading we don't where from the village of Hubble. No index number, although it's light green we think, and that's about it. Over."

"Sierra Oscar, please repeat your last transmission, over."

"Control please disregard last transmission, will contact Inspector Lovan by land line. Out."

It was a call Lovan really didn't want to make, how was he going to explain giving Sergio Pozzo a lift to a high performance motor cycle, thus enabling him to make his exit instead of being handed over to the secure custody of the Anti-Terrorism Unit?

How indeed.

"Good morning I need I speak to DCI Howard urgently."

-TWENTYFIVE-
Tell Me About Sergio Pozzo.

Frankie placed his mobile phone back in his pocket, not saying a word he turned around in the lobby, by-passed the lifts and sprang up the stairs back to Level One. Polina was walking down the carpeted corridor with a large jug of water as he swiftly walked towards her, Felix Fernando following getting the general drift that his boss wasn't happy at all.

"Good morning Mr Howard, how are you this morning?"

"Pissed off," he replied, he marched on pushing the door to the medical room wide open, barging in to see Oliver Allen just nodding off.

"Oi, sleeping beauty, wake up, the ugly sister's here and he ain't pleased!"

Oli grunted opening just one of his eyes, oh no, he thought, not him again, "What do you want I thought we were done?"

"Tell me about Sergio Pozzo."

"What?"

Oli was so tired, he felt shattered, he needed the sleep, not another large dose of DCI Howard in his face.

"Pozzo, tell me about him, tell me everything, start where you like, end with him pissing off out of the taxi. But make sure you don't miss a thing out. Come on, come on, I'm on the fucking meter here, talk!" Frankie ordered.

"I, errr, I trained with Sergio, he joined the Prison Service at the same time as I did. He was born in Italy but said he lived in Brentford since he was a kid, before moving out to Forest Green. He's OK. A good lad, well he was until he left me and did a runner, but then I'd probably have done the same in his shoes."

"Is he married? Girlfriend? Boyfriend?"

"No, he's single, likes to put it about a bit, but no one serious I know of."

"How did you get on? Was he a mate, a good friend?"

"A mate I guess," Oli wasn't sure what was going on here, Frankie was firing questions one after another, hardly taking time to either digest the answers he was being given or even breathe.

"Mate? What does that mean?"

"Well, we went out a bit whilst training at Newbold, but I don't see much of him out of work now, I've sort of settled down, and he does his own thing. But we had a laugh at work, yeah, normally he's alright."

"What about money, does he gamble, do you know of any debt?"

"What's this about, why you asking about Sergio?"

"I'm asking the questions, you're answering them, carry on, money, debt, gambling, we're on a roll here, don't spoil it." Frankie was rotating his hand as he spoke, Oli could see he was keen for him to carry on, although he had no idea why Sergio was all of a sudden so important.

"No, not that I know of, but I doubt he'd tell me anyway, we weren't that close, we just got on, that was it really."

"Yesterday, anything strange about him? Did he say, act, or do anything out of the ordinary?"

"No, nothing."

"OK, I haven't got time to piss around, here's the million dollar question, do you think he was capable of being involved in what went down yesterday?"

"Jeez, what's with you, not ten minutes ago you were accusing me, now it's Sergio, what is it you're on?"

"On? What am I on? I'm on a quest for the bloody prisoner you un-cuffed yesterday Mr Allen, the same oxygen thief who killed eighteen people the other day. I'm sorry if I hurt your sensitive sensibilities with my frank and brutal questioning technique, but fuck it, grow a pair and play along with me will ya. Now, was he capable, in your opinion, of being involved in what happened yesterday? Because someone was. Someone in that prison you work in told someone else Warsabi was going out, and I may not be Sherlock Holmes but I think it's fucking elementary my dear Watson that, with George losing the best part of the contents of his skull, it was either you or Sergio Pozzo, and as much as it grieves me that at some point I'm going to have to apologise to you for getting it wrong about you, I'm now leaning towards your mate. Your mate who pissed off a few minutes ago 100 miles an hour on a motorbike, rather than come here with us. So what do you reckon?"

"I honestly don't know, I really don't, I don't know much about him other than work. Don't get me wrong I'd love to blame him, just to hear you say sorry to me, but I'm afraid I can't."

"Fair enough, that leaves me pretty much none the wiser, but thanks for your time, oh and by the way, I'm having your girlfriend brought here she's on her way, should be here within the hour."

"Kate's coming here!"

"I fucking hope so, otherwise I've got some explaining to do to someone being driven down the M1 as we speak. Have a nice day Mr Allen."

With that Frankie left the room in pretty much the same style he entered.

-TWENTYSIX-
At Home With Jim Bolton.

Sitting in his armchair Jim Bolton pulled the top from another can of *Stella*, letting out a long and continuous belch, which ended with him wincing as a little bit of vomit diluted by the last gulp of gaseous lager briefly came back up into his mouth. He was flicking through the channels in search of something to act as a diversion to the realisation that his life was turning out exactly as he was expecting it to, which was not a good thing as his expectations were depressingly low.

It wasn't that he enjoyed work particularly, but the prospect of retirement was not something he was relishing, and being on the sick, only meant he got more time to spend at home.

Swigging from the can, he stared trancelike at the TV before him, his other hand subconsciously dipping into a giant bag of Beef and Onion crisps. On the screen an almost naked out of work lap dancer gyrated her scrawny arse, Jim reached into his pyjamas and fondled his penis, although more out of habit than any quest for sexual self-gratification, inadvertently rubbing crisp crumbs and beefy onion flavour into it whilst doing so.

Another night in the company of *Babe Station*, another night hating himself whilst getting pissed.

This had been his routine pretty much since Ella left him, and why not, who else was there to worry about but himself, why should he care if no one else did. Beer and soft porn, what more did he require at home in an evening, he didn't need anything else. Ella had become nothing but a moaning old harpy anyway, even if she had been still willing, which she certainly hadn't been for at least the last ten years of their time together, he wouldn't have wanted to have shared a bed with her, couldn't stand her, miserable old cow, well rid of that whinging bag of shite. All he had, and wanted, now was his beer, TV and that job.

Hah! The job, the stinking rotten job, what had become of that? You couldn't even trust your colleagues anymore. They'd drop you in it sooner than look at you, university educated Governors, snotty nosed young Officers, and soft as shite do-gooders. The cons had it all, did as they pleased, they'd give staff a good kicking, and they would give them *Playstations* in return, *Playstations* for God's sake.

He drained his beer, and instantly pulled open another, the empty can just thrown through the air towards a pile of tins, pizza boxes and old newspapers in the corner of the room. Looking around he could only feel sadness, well that and a large dollop of self-sympathy, the dust covered photos of his three children he never saw anymore and pictures of him in Ulster with mates from his days in the army. Look at me, he thought, so young, so happy, whatever became of that boy? And then his wedding photo, all those years ago. Oh Ella, why did you go? But then he knew all too well the answer to that one.

On the TV two girls, well they would have been girls thirty odd years back, fondled each other's breasts, whilst both licking their lips, and making gestures with their hands imitating a phone, the script at the bottom of the screen indicated Jim could talk to them for just £1.50 per minute, he was low but not that bloody low. He flicked the TV over to another channel, a dismembered corpse lay on a metal table as some beautiful American TV Cop sliced the chest open to a Who soundtrack, well that pretty much got rid of his lazy lob on.

He settled back, took a long swig from his can, and removing his glasses, lightly closed his eyes, he thought of Ella, before it all went wrong, before he became this. Then with his thoughts of what was, and what could never be again, he slowly fell asleep in his armchair.

Who the hell could that be, it's nearly midnight?
Bang, bang, bang!
Again another knock, hard and in quick repetitions, was it the Police again? He'd already told them everything he knew, which was pretty much nothing. He had bugger all to do with that little bastard, other than get smacked in the

face by him. He got up, brushing the crumbs from his chest, and shouted "Alright, alright, I'm coming!"

Bang, bang, bang!

"Who is it?" he shouted as he hobbled to the door, still half asleep.

No answer, just another loud round of banging.

"Who's there? Who are you?"

That was it, he'd not get off again now, he could feel the acid reflux in his chest, what sort of person calls at this time of night?

"Who's there?" he again called, not even attempting to disguise the irritation in his voice, but as a way of an answer there was a sudden thud, someone had bashed his front door with something heavy, he saw it vibrating from the shock, what the hell was happening? He stood back, as an instant reaction, then another thud, wood splintering and splitting as the door burst open.

Jim turned and rushed towards his kitchen, but whoever it was pulled him down to the floor, their arm tightly wrapped his neck as they went down with all their weight, he had no chance of staying on his feet.

He lashed out with his fists, he didn't know what this was about, but it sure as hell wasn't good. Despite nearing retirement he could still handle himself, but this bastard was strong, and had put him down on the ground with ease. He could feel something damp smothering his face, his assailant was rubbing some kind of chemical over his mouth and nose, it burnt and stung, causing him to cough and wheeze. He felt the grip around his neck loosen and he stumbled forwards, he was blind, couldn't see a thing without his glasses at the best of times, but now his eyes were streaming, he was totally disorientated. On all fours, a long line of snot flowing from his nostrils to the grubby patterned carpet Jim crawled pointlessly, now just wanting to get away from this nightmare that had kicked his door down.

For a brief moment he was unsure where this intruder was, had he gone? Then he found out exactly where he was, a hard kick to his ribs, he heard the crack, the actual sound of bone cracking, and felt the searing pain of having at least one rib broken. Collapsing flat to the floor another kick followed, already winded and breathless he fought to fill his lungs, to get air, but he was helpless, all he could do was lay there, waiting for the next blow.

"Hello Jim. I believe you may have something that belongs to me, or at least you better hope you do."

A figure stood over him, Jim couldn't see who his attacker was, his eyes still full of the involuntary tears.

"Don't try and talk yet my friend," the deep voice commanded, "I want to be able to hear your answers good and clear, I need to have no doubt about what you tell me, no doubt at all."

Between coughs, wheezes and splutters Jim whispered in broken tones, "Who are you?"

"That Jim, that Jim is a good question, probably the first question I would ask, even if I was told not to talk. I am a bad mother fucker Jim. Seriously if I were you I'd be wetting my pretty patterned boxer shorts at this point. I really would. Let me introduce myself, my name is Auguste, Auguste Fredericks, and someone is paying me a shitload of money to come and be relentlessly bad to you, so bad that you will tell me anything."

At this point the man, Fredericks, walked into Jim's kitchen and returned with a pine chair, which he placed beside the still incapacitated snotty mess on the floor.

"I gotta say Jim, I like what you've done with this place, all this filth and rubbish everywhere, makes it very homely, very lived in, it's definitely you, it suits you." Jim heard a booming laugh, although he could find nothing amusing in any of this, nothing at all.

Through a blurry glaze Jim saw Frederick's get up from the chair and walk around, he picked up the photo of him in Ulster, with his comrades, stood by an old *Land Rover*, a prized memento from better days, the best of days.

"An old soldier, eh, I was in the army you know, just a couple of years back, doing my bit for Queen and Country out in Afghanistan. It was hard. You served in Ireland eh? It's a dirty business fighting people who don't wear uniforms ain't it? I got used for all sorts of bad shit. Once you start punching the truth out of someone it all gets blurred Jim, so blurred. You don't notice whether they're the Taliban or some kid with a few goats, al-Qaeda or someone's Grandmother, all you see is the quest for the truth. That's what I'm looking for here, the truth. I'm sorry but I don't see an old soldier laying where you are, an old brother-in-arms, I should I know, but sorry Jim I see someone who needs to tell me something, and you know what, you will, you'll be glad you did."

Jim had recovered a bit, the breathing once more returning to something akin to normality, but his ribs were searing with pain, he shuffled and dragged himself across the floor and leant against the wall by the kitchen door, this Fredericks character apparently happy to let him do so. He could now make him out, a well-built man, black, shaven headed, he was once again sitting in a chair.

"What do you want? Why are you here?" Jim croaked, surprised that his voice was so weak, barely above a whisper.

"Those Jim are the right questions to ask in these circumstances, good open questions, I can answer without any misunderstanding. After all we need to have no ambiguity here, do we?

"Right, what do I want? I'll answer that one easily, I want the ring you stole from Abu Warsabi the other day. I want it now. That is what I want, do you understand, well do you?"

Jim looked confused, or was it still pained.

"I don't have a bloody clue what you're on about, now get out of my house!"

Fredericks sprang to his feet and threw the wooden chair at him, he tried to move, but had no chance of avoiding it, one of the legs caught him above his left eye, opening up a cut, which began to bleed instantly.

"No, no, no, wrong answer! Where's the ring?"

His tone had changed, although not shouting he left Jim in no doubt he was angry. But Jim didn't have a clue what he was on about, he needed to get away, as he attempted to stand Fredericks sprang forward punching him hard in the solar plexus, leaving him winded and crumpled on the floor again.

Fredericks stood back a moment, just looking, watching him, apparently calming down again.

"Look we seem to have met an impasse, here's what is going to happen. I will, have no doubt about this, keep asking, you will eventually answer, and answer truthfully. Then I will leave. Now where's the ring?"

Jim looked up, he could feel the blood now streaming down his face from the cut, he coughed, and spat to one side, "I don't..."

Whack, Fredericks punched him across his cheek, hard, his head reeled to one side with the force, Jim barely had the strength to it draw it back up again, his head just lolling to one side.

"Wrong answer, don't give me fucking I don'ts, I don't isn't the right response to my question. Now let me help you here, only you and Allen were dealing with Warsabi when he arrived at your prison, I know Warsabi hasn't got the ring, I can be sure of that, I know it was bagged at court, so where the hell is it?"

"I... don't... know, I really... don't..."

Smack, a punch square onto Jim's nose, his ears were ringing, instantly he could taste the blood, he had no idea what this lunatic wanted, he knew of no ring, he couldn't

THE SHATTERED EAGLE

even tell him that at this point as his mouth was incapable of speech. *Bang*, another blow to his face, and again, and again, this maniac was pummelling him, he had nothing in response. He couldn't fight back, he had no strength, his head just swung with the blows, couldn't even plead for him to stop, then he drifted out of the room, as if floating away, he could see Ella, as she was the day they got married, as she was forever captured in the photo just feet away. The pain was subsiding, as he called to her, Ella, oh Ella…

August Fredericks stood back his fists covered in blood, splashes and spots covered his face, it took him back to that day in the small village in Helmand, when he was first utilised in interrogations, when he had beaten the location of a massive IED out of a Taliban fighter, saved lives, prevented loss of comrades, it was a totally justifiable action. But then this was justifiable too, enough Dollars paid into a Dutch bank account could justify anything.

He looked down at Jim Bolton crumpled and bloodied on the floor, whimpering as he stood over him again.

"Right, that's it Jim, do you have the ring?"

Jim just stared blankly ahead, seemingly now oblivious to what he was saying.

"Thanks." Gus whispered.

He now knew he wasn't lying, because he was good at his job, not just the violence, but perception for the truth, there was little point in inflicting anymore pain on this old soldier, no need to pluck out eyes or break fingers, it was just unfortunate that he had talked to Jim Bolton before Oliver Allen, if it had been the other way around then Jim wouldn't be lying there covered in blood.

He looked down as the poor pathetic man curled into a ball, whimpering the words, "Ella, oh Ella."

The single bullet fired through his temple from a silenced pistol killed him instantly.

Auguste Fredericks walked out of the house, once back in his car he removed the latex gloves, and shoe covers, and pondered what a waste of time that was, it had caused him no joy, no pleasure. He wished he had thought it through beforehand, he should have worn a mask, perhaps it would have meant he wouldn't have had to kill the old soldier. He had had Oli Allen, and let him get away, with that damn ring, or at least the knowledge of where it was.

Now he'd have to find him again.

-TWENTYSEVEN-
Why Would Alaine DuPont Get Himself Arrested?

Back in London Frankie gathered his team again, the 'Prison Break', although now allowing them the luxury of at least knowing that their suspect was alive, had created far more questions than revealing answers.

The meeting was combined with a literal bun-fest, as it was Sylvia's birthday, and due to an ATU tradition which it appeared only she adhered to, she had brought a couple of boxes of cream cakes into work with her. This was only fair though as she normally lived by the Hardacre rule that any food in any fridge or lunchbox was ripe for taxing, and that she was entitled to help herself to as much as she liked.

"As mysteries go, this is a good one for you." Frankie opened proceedings, a small dollop of sugary cream and jam nestling on the corner of his mouth. "Why would Alaine DuPont, who for the benefit of simplicity and lack of confusion shall now be referred to as Abu Warsabi, blow up a train full of people one day, and within the same week, get himself arrested?"

Frankie walked to the large white board and scrawled *ABU WARSABI* above where the name *Alaine DuPont* was already written.

"It doesn't make sense to me, not at all. If I had just killed that many people I sure as hell wouldn't be groping the tits of some girl I've never met before in *Boots* the Chemist. No I'd be hiding away somewhere pretty damn secluded, keeping my head well below any minor sexual assault parapet. So why did he do it?"

"He wanted to get nicked." Daggett said, shrugging his shoulders as he said it. "There is no other reason, he didn't run, try to get away, did it in broad daylight. For some reason Guv' our boy had given himself up."

"Then why not just hand himself in to us, let's face it I'd have snapped his bloody hand off if he had come bowling in here shouting 'I Surrender, I Surrender'. But he didn't do that did he?"

"Just an idea Guv'," Felix said, "but he probably thought he'd not be connected with the bombing, where better to hide when Police are looking all over the country for you than in a Prison? Hardly do door to door enquiries around B Wing do we. Quite a good idea really. But why then escape?"

"He didn't escape, he was taken," Frankie answered.

"Same thing isn't it?" Sylvia said.

"Only if he wants taking. But Allen, the Prison Officer, told me it was like he was terrified, genuinely scared shitless. Why someone would take him I don't know, but I do know that our boy is still out there, and I want him!"

"Well I wanted that éclair Guv, you knew that, my birthday, my choice!" Sylvia said, rather spoiling the emphasis of Frankie's last line.

"Tough luck, although I do have a present for you, let's call it a day out, a little birthday treat shall we say."

-TWENTYEIGHT-
My Money's Saying It Wasn't The Cat That Did It!

Pete Daggett and Sylvia Hardacre were once again motoring up the M1. Driving under what was another clear blue sky, Sylvia was pondering the number thirty nine, it wasn't a high number was it? People lived to their nineties nowadays, loads reach a hundred, thirty nine - that's not old, she didn't feel particularly old. Glancing down at her legs hanging out of the cargo shorts she was wearing, she did a quick appraisal, they were definitely the legs of a young person, still firm, no varicose veins, slender around the ankle, and her stomach hadn't given in either, that little roll over her waistband was just due to how she was sitting. Yeah thirty nine is just a number, and low one at that.

Then her mind flitted to what she was doing on her birthday, not now, but when she got home. There would be no surprise parties or romantic meals out later that evening, Graham had made it clear he was going to the football, and although it saddened her to think it, she was pleased, because if there was one thing that did actually make her feel old it was her husband.

She glanced over at Daggett, he had those stupid aviator sunglasses on, she wondered why he didn't go the whole hog and buy himself a crimplene suit and grow a moustache.

"This seems like a complete waste of time to me the local boys have already spoken to him yesterday, he had nothing to tell them, when will Frankie learn to trust people, accept that others can do Police work as well as we can? This really isn't my idea of spending my thirty ninth year on this earth," she said to Daggett, who only appeared to be half listening as he fiddled with the radio, trying to get something else to tune into.

"Bloody local yokel news," he moaned, "who cares how much dog shit is in Luton Town Centre, it's another shit hole. I'd rather…"

"Yes," Sylvia finished. "You'd rather stay in Peckham, I know, I know. You say it wherever we go, instead tell me why we're going to Northampton again?"

"I don't know, he wants us to sniff around the Town Centre as well as talk to this Bolton fella, see if there's anyone that witnessed the Prison Officer getting away. You know what he's like, he'd do it all himself if he could, if not it'll have to be one of us, he's always been like it, you should know that, you've been on the Unit longer than I have."

"It just seems like a waste of time that's all."

"No some old biddy talking about dog shit in Luton is a waste of time, this Sylv' is what pays our bills."

They arrived at Jim Bolton's house at about 11.30, the street was quiet, it looked quite a nice area, although Sylvia thought that number seven, Jim's house, could have done with a lick of paint, all the window frames were peeling and what was once a white wooden door was a dirty grey where it had weathered over the years. They parked up by the rusting front gate and walked up the path through the over grown garden, it clearly hadn't seen a lawn mower all summer, just a mass of weeds and tall grass.

"Oh balls" Daggett exclaimed, "I've left my folder in the motor." Sylvia smiled as he turned and went back to the car for his precious bloody leather folder, which he always insisted on taking when interviewing people, he said it made him look more professional, all official and organised.

Sylvia tapped on the door, which pushed open slightly, a warm waft of stale air hitting her in the face as she peered in.

"Hello Mr Bolton, hello?" she called.

There was no reply, she called again, "Hello, anyone home?"

She presumed there would be someone there, it was a reasonable enough area, but hardly the sort of place you would go out leaving your door unlocked. She heard a scratching, and looking down she saw a cat clawing at the carpet by her feet, it sidled up to her, rubbing around her ankles, meowing.

"Hello Darling, what's your name then, oh you are pretty aren't you." Sylvia said reaching down and stroking it, she liked cats, always had, but unfortunately Graham was allergic to them, or at least claimed he was, so she couldn't keep one at home. But as she lifted her hand she noticed the sticky blood on her palm, then the splintered wood and bent screws around where the lock sat.

Oh bloody hell!

Daggett was still leaning into the car, no doubt sorting out his professional looking folder. "Pete!" she called over showing him her hand.

"What's that?" he yelled back, squinting his eyes unable to see what she was showing him.

"It's trouble!"

They both cautiously walked in.

The house smelt of a combination of cat's piss, onions and Chinese food, it was a disgusting pit, Sylvia had always said you could judge a person's cleanliness by the state of their light switches, in this case no one in their right mind would have even dreamed of touching them without the aid of *Marigold* Gloves and barrier cream, dirt was everywhere, Sylvia saw the Cat litter tray in the hall, ironically it looked probably the cleanest thing in the house.

"Hello, Mr Bolton!" she called out again, but still no answer.

COLIN PAYNE

***

It was Pete Daggett who found Jim Bolton lying on the floor in his dingy living room. The blood that had emanated from the hole in his temple and his smashed nose was smeared across his face where the cat had brushed against him, vainly looking to get fed.

Sylvia could only watch as Daggett knelt beside the still body, his index and forefingers pressed against where Jim's jugular should have been pulsating. Inevitably she knew that her colleague was touching nothing but an extremely unpleasant cold clamminess, it was clear that the man before them was well and truly dead.

As he got up Daggett nodded to Sylvia, "Call it in Sylv', I need to wash my hands," before walking to the kitchen, and rinsing them off just above the huge pile of food encrusted crockery and pans that filled the sink.

Sylvia looked at Jim Bolton, crouching down just inches from where he lay, it was clear he had been horribly battered, his face a swollen mess of bruises, cuts and abrasions, the blood creating a dried mask that offered so many clues as to how he died, but none as to why.

Daggett walked back in, his fingers still dripping water, "Well this adds another piece to the puzzle. What do you think?"

Sylvia stood up, surveying what they had before them, "I don't know what to think, but I know one thing for sure, my money's saying it wasn't the cat that did it."

-TWENTYNINE-
The Safehaven Residents Association Inaugural Meeting.

"Oh Fran, did you really have to?"

"Come on Gary stop being so unsociable, it'll be fun, she seems nice, she was at the pool yesterday, we got chatting. I mean it's not like there is anything else to do is there? Hardly having to shuffle around the social calendar to make some space are we. We've got a fridge full of booze, people will cook the food for us, Josh and Amy can amuse themselves in their rooms, it'll be good to have adult company. If it goes on too late, do your usual, you've got the perfect excuse now, just say your wounds hurt or something. Besides I've already invited them."

"But I can't even drink."

"You never drink anyway. Come on it'll be good, it'll be a proper Saturday night, snap out of it!"

"But…"

"No buts Gary, if you make it past midnight there's a chance that the High Class Hooker may come tapping on your door tonight, whilst I'm not there. Now you don't want to miss her do you?"

Ah bollocks, Gary was caught off guard, Fran was playing the role-playing card and the High Class Hooker always equalled some imaginative dressing up, was he really that easily swayed?

Hell yeah!

"Of course," Fran continued, "She'll only come tapping if you give little Gary a thorough scrub, she's high class after all."

Oh Fran, how to spoil it, he thought, but then again High Class blooming Hooker, that's normally the stuff of Birthdays or special nights away, let's not over react here.

"OK Fran, if you should see her wandering the lobby let her know Big Gary and Little Gary both agree to her demands."

"Oh Westlake, you're so bloody predictable."

Gary watched her, those little wrinkles at the corner of her eyes and her near perfect teeth revealed as she laughed that infectious laugh, he really didn't fancy company, but then even in normal circumstances if given the choice he would prefer to spend an evening with just her. Did that make him anti-social, or just still in love with this wonderful woman?

But tonight they were to be hosts, although in truth it was already a done deal an hour earlier when Fran had invited Kate and her mysterious boyfriend for dinner. Well he wasn't really mysterious, it was just neither of them had seen him since his arrival two nights previously.

THE SHATTERED EAGLE

***

At that same time a dozen or so yards down the corridor a similar conversation was taking place.

"But why?" Oli whinged. "X-Factor's on the telly, and there's that latest Bond film after on *Sky*. I'm injured Kate, I should be resting, I need to recuperate, recharge the batteries."

"Injured, you daft sod, you've a bruised leg and a tiny bump on your thick head, you didn't even need to spend the night you did in that bloody medical room. Oli you really are a soft shite, are you sure you escaped from that motor, and they didn't just throw you out because they were sick of your whining and moaning, because I would have."

"It's not funny, you know what happened, you know about the others."

Kate Wallander suddenly felt very guilty, looking at the wounded look on his face, she was such a silly cow making a joke about it, she knew he hadn't slept more than a couple of hours since it happened, haunted by what he had seen, two men murdered in front of him. What he had witnessed was horrendous, as well as the anxiety of being where they were now, because he was in so much danger, she hadn't allowed for that, what was she thinking saying yes to Fran when she invited them around for dinner. Oli wasn't up to it. Sure he acted like his old self, but she knew he wasn't right, that the demons from just two days earlier had far from vanished, instead tormenting him at every opportunity, and there she was making light of it.

Stupid, stupid cow!

"I'm sorry, I wasn't thinking. Don't worry about tonight, I'll let them know we can't come, I'll make it another time, are you alright Oli?"

"Ah it's just me being moody, forget it, I'll be OK. Of course we can still go, they better have drink though, I'm not leaving our fridge to go to some Quakers slide show, they do have booze don't they?"

"I'll tell you what, we'll take some with us, there, see I've got an answer for everything."

Gary had to admit Fran had been right, as he lay in bed thinking back over the past few hours, he was glad he had gone along with it. Oli had been a good laugh, and Kate was just lovely. They were a great couple, they reminded him of how he and Fran were when they first met. All that possibility in front of them, the chance to live life how they pleased. Though he couldn't remember being quite as immature at that age, not as much as Oli was, or perhaps it was just times changing, it was as if nothing was off the menu of conversation.

He wished he could have drank something, as the night had worn on he had felt on a different plane to the other three, who were semi-pissed and giggling, as their two guests regaled them with tales of how they first got together, a drunken night of lost underwear and inevitable infidelity.

THE SHATTERED EAGLE

Fran in turn retold the much worn story of how they both worked for *BT*, the months of flirting and yearning leading to another tale of drunkenness, in that following a bosses retirement party they had got their mountain bikes and rode down the canal tow path, venturing on a cross country pub crawl, ending with an explosion of pent up emotions, and a life of being together.

Oli had told them all about prisons, it seemed like a different world he was describing, but a fascinating one, he could tell a good tale, and the time seemed to fly by. Somehow Gary's stories of recovering corrupted data from ruined hard drives didn't quite have the same intrigue and fascination.

They had ended the night playing board games, Gary pondered how neither he nor Fran were intellectual giants, but they were positively geniuses next to the young couple that had been competing against, although their young naivety was extremely endearing. After all how could you fail to like people who thought the Crown jewels, were safely stored in the Blackpool Tower, the famous mythical creature from Scotland was the Skegness Monster, or that Jackie Collins wrote 'Great Expectations'. He was hoping that alcohol had a played a big part in some of the answers, but rather feared it hadn't.

He closed his eyes, his side was still aching, but nowhere near as bad as it had been, he thought of what special thing he could arrange for Fran once free of Safehaven, money was so tight though, but then it always was. He didn't even know what was happening with his job, he was told not to worry about it, that the 'Powers That Be' would deal with that, but he was still in crippling debt, even with his wages being taken care of. Although being at Safehaven was saving him some money, all the food paid for, no petrol, dinner money, bills. Ha, there was a bright side to being blown up after all.

He could hear the shower running in the bathroom, thank God she was still there, the constant in his life, the rock his world was built on.

As he turned in the bed he heard a knock on the door, damn, Fran was in the shower, he'd have to get it. Gingerly swinging his legs around he slid out of bed, throwing a robe on, tying the towelling belt as he walked to the door. He opened it to find Fran standing in the corridor, certainly not in the shower, a long coat on, her stocking clad calves and high heels hanging from the bottom.

"Hello, Mr Westlake is it?" she purred.

"Err yes, can I help you?"

"I do hope so, I'm told you require my services."

She let the coat open and then drop to the floor, right there in the corridor. She was totally naked except for her stockings.

"I do hope Sir is going to be happy with my services. I can assure you I am very, very good."

-THIRTY-
Mouse Trap, Operation, Monopoly and Trivial Pursuits.

Over the next few days the two cast away couples got to spend more time together. Both Josh and Amy loved Kate, and she in turn enjoyed spending time with them especially in the pool, teaching Amy how to swim properly on her back, and participating in swimming under water competitions with Josh.

She was a natural with children, and Fran had told her on more than one occasion when it was all done she ought to look at working with young people, whilst making sure she never hinted at actually teaching, as she didn't want to be unrealistic.

They had learnt how to break the increasingly long days down, how to pass the time without going mad. Jay DeHavalland, who was a God send, had arranged for video games to be brought in for the two young Westlakes, but even for them there was a limit to how much time could be spent on them. They were now allowed to walk around the grounds, although not beyond the fence, and Fran had taken to helping the gardener, Sidney, maintain the flower beds, the kids at first helping as well, but then rather predictably preferring to go swimming after just an hour or so.

The evenings developed into sitting outside until dark, bringing the contents of the fridges down with them. They had claimed a pergola with grape vines growing around it as their own, naming it the 'Pub', then becoming more imaginative and giving it the moniker of 'Howard's End', in honour of their great protector.

The kitchen staff had got used to their new habits, and now served the evening meals al-fresco. Gary had stopped taking the medication, partly to enable him to drink again, and partly due to the fact that he was healing nicely, although still suffering at nights, the anxiety ruling what should have been his sleeping hours when other distractions were absent. The itch was still very much part of his life.

The Westlakes continued to marvel at just how bad Oli and Kate were at board games, and even though Jay had bought them a whole heap of the things, ranging from *Monopoly* to *Operation*, the unfortunate young couple couldn't win any. Fran had told Gary they needed to give them at least one game, let them win without their knowing they were going easy on them, just to throw them a bone, but he couldn't do it, what was the point of playing to lose. They had even played *Mouse Trap* one evening, a

THE SHATTERED EAGLE

game devoid of any skill or prior knowledge, just twist the bloody handle when the time came, but even that failed to give them their allusive victory, with Amy beating Oli into second place. Kate nearly broke her duck taking on the kids at *Snakes and Ladders*, until robbed at the end by a particularly cruel snake, taking her from 97 back to 22 to ensure their heroic losing streak remained intact.

Occasionally Jay would join them for the evening, stopping over in one of the rooms, after all there were plenty spare, they were the only residents there. She had a lot in common with Kate, and had become good friends, being of a similar age, but she appeared to get on without any problems with all of them. She would often go swimming before the evening meal, and both Fran and Kate would join her to swim lengths without the need to entertain children.

It had been nearly a week since they had last seen DCI Howard, which was no bad thing. Jay had assured them that he was actually alright, and was really a good bloke, but Oli in particular remembered how he had accused him of all sorts of stuff, taking no time to consider his feelings or how upset he was, just steamrollering over him.

They had learned through Jay that the investigations into both the bombing and what happened on the way to the hospital were still moving at a good speed, which didn't actually tell them a lot. What was a good speed when it came to finding murderers, and getting the six of them back to their real homes?

They had been allowed to contact loved ones and families, who it transpired were partially aware of what the score was, although it had been pointed out to them that the phone could only be used at appointed times, and all calls would be monitored. Life was certainly getting easier, but it still wasn't good.

But Safehaven was becoming home.

-THIRTYONE-
Here's To You Mrs Green, Jesus Loves You More Than You Will Know.

Sergio Pozzo cupped his hands around the blue glowing screen, checking the cash point to make sure it was really still there, a big broad smile dominating his face as the machine confirmed there was £492,873 in the brand new bank account under the name of Sergio Pragua. He was staying at *Lilliput,* a B&B in Bournemouth, spending his days lounging on the beach, the evenings partying like a madman. He knew he should be keeping a low profile, avoiding attention, but damn, it was hard having half a million paid into your account. He still didn't have his plan fully sorted, so he would just enjoy life until it was finalised in his head, it was down to a three way choice between Spain, Italy or Australia.

He ran the options through his mind once more, as he took the £300 from the machine, Spain would definitely be easier to do, they would probably be looking for him in Italy, obviously due to his family connections, and he was going nowhere through an airport, not with his passport and let's face it Australia was hardly easily accessible from the back of a forty foot trailer. No Spain was definitely the best choice, although when was now the question. But for the moment he had something else to sort out, he was sure she was up for it, he hadn't read the signs wrong, it was more than just flirting…

Lying upon his bed watching TV, pondering when best to make the move, Sergio felt the surge of electric excitement when heard the tap at the door. Oh yes, he thought, that's for me. He definitely hadn't read it wrong, and wrapping the bright red satin robe around his otherwise naked body he opened his bedroom door, allowing Lillian, the B&B owner's wife to enter his room. She was dressed in a white cotton blouse, knee length skirt, which was just a tad too tight, and what he hoped were black stockings – he had no time for tights, with her feet within a pair of highly polished black high heels.

"Hello Sergio, I got your text. Oh you are a naughty boy aren't you, using such shocking words when addressing a lady, you do realise I'm a married woman?"

"I do apologise Mrs Green, my mistake, I hope I haven't offended you."

"Oh no, not in the slightest, I'm very broad minded."

She slowly closed the door as she walked into the room, walking over to Sergio and brushing herself against him,

THE SHATTERED EAGLE

for a woman nearing fifty he had to say she still had a nice body. This was number seven about to be crossed off the wish list.

She reached down and rubbed her finger tips over his groin, gently, teasingly, Sergio let out a little groan, she felt his erection and her fingers followed its satin clad outline.

"Oh Sergio, you like that don't you!" she gave a little giggle.

"Hell yeah," he answered.

"Mmm, it feels good."

Turning her back to him she lifted her skirt, revealing her bare buttocks. "Oh dear, Lilli seems to have forgotten her panties, aren't I a silly girl. I hope you don't mind."

He didn't mind, he didn't mind at all! "Well, you are a bad girl, but what kind of bad girl needs panties anyway?"

"Quite right Sergio, let's find out shall we."

He was no longer able to play along with her flirtatious game, he clumsily began to fumble around with the buttons of her blouse, undressing her with an over eagerness, that slightly disappointed her.

"Oh Sergio, slow down, take it easy, Lilli's got all afternoon."

But it didn't matter to Sergio, yes that's Number Seven! Shag the room service in a hotel, well it was close enough, even though she hadn't brought his breakfast up. In fact that was Number Four as well, he wasn't sure if she was a mother, but well, what the heck, she'd count as his MILF.

COLIN PAYNE

***

The wish list, ten challenges he had set himself to help make his time in Bournemouth a bit more enjoyable, add an element of competition and fun. Lillian, through her energetic actions had just joined Gayle and Chelsea (Number Three) the unusually generous twins from Tuesday night, and Phoebe (Number Nine) the receptacle for his Champagne slurping the night before that, as ticks on a scrappy piece of paper, well a man has to keep himself occupied doesn't he.

Lillian had actually been very nimble, quite athletic even, she seemed to live up to and even surpass his older woman expectations, he considered her as a cross between Jane MacDonald from 'Loose Women' and Sybil Fawlty, although the Sybil bit was purely down to her occupation, rather than any physical attributes.

As he lay next to her, trying desperately to avoid the now cold wet patch they had created on the off white bedding, he planned the rest of his day in his head. He would go shopping later, get some decent clothes, then in the evening out to somewhere a bit nice, fill his wallet with some more cash and have a bloody good night out.

But first he needed to shift Lillian, come on woman, he thought, when are you going to go?

She was still lying beside him, naked on top of the bed, stroking her nails gently over his chest, somehow Number Seven didn't seem such a good idea now, he had got quite

THE SHATTERED EAGLE

settled at *Lilliput*, now he'd have to find somewhere else to stay, it would be just awkward otherwise, he couldn't have her tapping at his door every time her weedy looking husband had to go to *Costco*. This was a one off thing, no seconds, no extras, no repeat performances.

No he'd have to do a flit in the morning, leave the money in an envelope on the side. Jesus, she's still stroking away, it's getting really irritating now, please for God's sake Lillian when are you going to go!

He turned to her, he had to say something he wanted her gone, nonchalantly announcing, "I've really got to make a move soon, sorry."

"Oh Sergio, my little Italian Stallion," she said in a really irritating affected voice, which he guessed was supposed to arouse him, well actually it had forty five minutes earlier, but somehow now only made him want to tell her to shut the hell up. "Do you have to, Lilli would like some more, he isn't due back for at least another two hours. We could stay in bed. Hmm have a little more naughty fun, what do you say, would you a little more naughty fun?"

She was circling her finger nails around his chest hair.

Sergio noticed her nicotine stained front teeth, and her overpowering bad breath, things he had strangely been oblivious to whilst she was mercilessly humping his brains out.

"No Lilli, I'm sorry I really must go, it's been good though."

"Oh do you really, really have to go, I'm feeling so horny, so very horny."

She took his hand and placed it between her legs, "Feel for yourself Sergio, I'm so very horny, so wet. Go on Sergio, feel my naughty little pussy."

Sergio wasn't sure just how much she was horny or how much of it was his own seminal fluid, either way he had no desire to venture back into her 'naughty little pussy', no desire at all.

"Sorry, but…"

"Oh please," she purred in a disturbingly nauseating manner.

"I'm sorry Lilli, I really…"

"Oh come on Sergio," she reached down as she spoke and cradled his testicles in her hands, giving them a firm squeeze, "Please for Lilli."

As she cupped his balls she leant over and put her tongue in his ear. Sergio thought he was going to throw up, he reeled away. Suddenly she sat up. The whinny naughty girl voice now abandoned.

"Oh screw you then, you little wanker!"

She climbed off the bed stomping around as she started to put her clothes back on, clearly none too pleased with her little Italian Stallion.

"It's your loss kid, and you better be sure to keep you're bloody Itie mouth shut, you greasy little prick!"

Wow! Whatever happened to the Mrs Robinson act?

"And make sure you're gone by tomorrow you ungrateful little twat."

With that she was out of there, slamming his door behind her, buttoning the last of her blouse buttons as she went.

THE SHATTERED EAGLE

***

He was quite relieved at his unceremonious eviction from *Lilliputt*, he never particularly wanted to stay there anyway even though he was settled. It was his idea of keeping a low profile, it was a bit of a shit hole after all, he could now move to a proper hotel, perhaps keep Lillian as just a Number Four, and hunt down a genuine Number Seven.

Now the raging woman spurned had departed he decided not to wait until the morning, he packed his bags there and then, and headed off. He left the money at the small reception which doubled as a bar, making sure that other people were about before saying goodbye to Lillian, and thanking her for the excellent service, he couldn't resist the wink as he said it, seeing as Lillian was unable to express her feelings in return.

He hailed a taxi, his motorbike ditched miles away, and told the driver to take him to the *Marriott*, which turned out to be a good choice. He got himself a sea view room, on the top floor of the large Victorian palatial hotel. As he stood at the window looking out over the calm sea, there was a knock at the door.

"Room Service."

-THIRTYTWO-
Was This Really Howard?

After not seeing them for over a week Frankie walked up to Gary and Oli who were sitting in 'Howard's End' reading newspapers whilst drinking coffee. He had a broad smile on his face, and rubbed his hands together as he spoke.

"Good morning Gentlemen, and how are we today?"

"Hello Mr Howard, I'm fine thanks" Gary replied, still wary of him, still not happy to demonstrate any warmth or put on any display of apparent forgiveness.

"Me too, but what have I done now?" Oli looked concerned, Gary knew that his new friend had an even lower opinion of the Chief Inspector than he did.

"You Oliver my friend have done bugger all, well nothing wrong anyway. You really need to let our little misunderstanding go you know, ask Gary, he's of the age now, all that pent up tension, it will only lead to grey hair, ulcers, and a premature colonoscopy, you must learn to release."

THE SHATTERED EAGLE

Gary said nothing, he was well aware of what pent up tension would cause, and was in no mood for joking about it, another night fighting the nightmares, then that damn itch, had left him tired, very tired.

"No I'm just here to update you on the investigations, and also while I'm here I have a little suggestion. Firstly the bombing, we're now 100% sure that thanks to you Gary we know that Abu Warsabi is our bomber. Unfortunately we still haven't got him, nor what I think is more important, those who conspired with him, and until we do I'd feel happier if you and your family stayed here. The other investigation is being headed up in Northampton by an Inspector Lovan, I know you've met him Oli, we're working closely with them as we know that this is the key to finding Warsabi. Whoever killed poor George and Rab also has him, or at least can lead us to him. And as I said to Gary, the same applies to you Oli, until we have them I'd be a lot happier to keep you here at Safehaven. Sorry folks but that is where we are."

Frankie sat down at the table with his two star witnesses', taking the last three biscuits from the plate in the middle, he popped one whole into his mouth. He called out towards the girl who was working in the kitchen.

"Can I have a coffee please!" Before addressing Gary and Oli again, "These biccies are nice aren't they, I'll tell you what, the food isn't bad at all is it?"

"Yeah it's alright," Gary answered, "Although I'd still rather be at home."

"Of course you would Gary, who wouldn't, but better here at the moment, it's safe. Anyway, about my idea, how to cheer you up a bit. I've had DeHavalland on the phone, she's very caring is our Jay, she reckons things can get a bit boring here, a bit monotonous. How about we get out of here tomorrow for a few hours, do something different, break the old routine. I've a rest day, and even God needed one of them, fancy it?"

"What like a day out?" Gary asked.

"Yeah, why not," Frankie answered. "You've been here without as much as a glimpse of the outside world, it'll do us all good. We'll have to be back before midnight, don't want to turn into some pumpkin or anything like that, the ladies can do something with the kids, DeHavalland can go with them, I'll come with you two. What do you reckon?"

"Where are we going to go then?" Oli enquired, clearly more than a little excited at the prospect of day away from Safehaven.

"I don't know, obviously somewhere no one's going to know you, we have to be realistic here, you're not hiding away from the world for nothing. We can't have Gary suddenly roll up at Leighton Buzzard, where ever that is, where everyone knows him, with the local in-breds carrying him on their shoulders whilst chanting his name celebrating the return of their local hero. Nor you Oli, walking into your pub of choice like some episode of 'Cheers', every one standing up and raising their glasses in the air whilst shouting 'Oli!' With the local dope dealers

THE SHATTERED EAGLE

celebrating seeing the sudden economic downturn in business ending after one heavy night. That my friends is not keeping a low profile. No we've got to go somewhere a bit off the beaten path. Think on it."

Both Gary and Oli looked at each other just a little perplexed, was this really DCI Howard in front of them? Days Out? Actual pleasantness? They both knew they had to act a bit quickly, before he reverted back to his old miserable self, no time to think about it, get something arranged.

As if synched they both said together, "Fishing!" "Watch a Match!"

"Oh No! I hate bloody fishing, and despise football. You're just saying it to punish me aren't you. Let it go boys, I've apologised to both of you already, I thought we were mates now. I know, do either of you play golf?"

They both looked at him silently.

"Good there you go, golf it is, it'll be educational."

"What happened to think on it?" Gary not unreasonably asked.

"Sorry lads, you couldn't agree, so I took the executive decision. I'll sort you out some clubs, we can grab a bite then a pint afterwards, it'll be fun. I think you'll benefit from the fresh air as well. You both look a bit pasty. Besides I've already booked the course, it's miles from anywhere, but I can sort someone to drive, so we can let our hair down. I'll pick you both up at 10 O'clock tomorrow."

With that Frankie got up from the table and was gone.

-THIRTYTHREE-
This Is Not An Acceptable Situation At All.

In the large well lit room, with its panoramic views over almost all of the Parisian city centre, four men were gathered around a highly polished boardroom table, sitting upon Mahogany high backed chairs padded with dark blue leather. Two sides of the room consisted entirely of glass, constituting the corner of the top floor of the large office block, whilst on the other walls were framed photographs of what appeared to be Special Forces personnel in desert locations, portraits of historic French Soldiers, and a large Napoleonic map of the world, detailing the French Empire of the time. Without exception they were dressed in business attire, and by the door leading into the room stood two guards, also in dark suits. The eldest of the four dismissed the guards with a cursory wave of his hand before speaking.

"Gentlemen as you are all aware events in England have not gone as we would have ideally wished. After two years

THE SHATTERED EAGLE

of evading us, our young fugitive was repatriated as planned, although he did not have what we required of him. He was though, Henri informs me, most helpful in pointing us into a direction where it could be located. Since then there have been further developments, which I feel it would be appropriate for Henri to elaborate upon. Please Henri continue."

Henri DuPont cleared his throat before speaking.

"Thank You Claude. It would appear that the ring was taken from the boy, who now calls himself Abu Warsabi by one of the guards at the prison. It may even be correct to say it was stolen by him. Unfortunately for us this individual was also present at the scene when our people took Warsabi. Through a combination of events that still puzzle me our people allowed him to escape. The guard in question has been placed in protective custody. We do not know if he has it with him, and if not where it may be. This is not an insurmountable problem Gentlemen, and I am confident that this whole situation can be resolved to an acceptable conclusion. I am working on it as we speak, and expect good news very soon."

One of the others present gave a derisory snort.

"Henri, you talk of what is acceptable. This is not an acceptable situation at all. You know how we all mourned for your dear wife, and the circumstances leading up to all of this have been truly tragic, but you were careless. I know it was agreed to take precautions, yes we all agreed that was only right, but to allow this to happen has been madness, utter lunacy. I'm sorry to be so harsh, but Henri you now need to get a grip on this, bring it all to a resolution in as timely a fashion as possible. We have much to lose, not just personally. We have supplied you with the funds to make it happen, yet we watch on as you report this comedy of errors, this incompetency. I do very much fear you are not in control, and that is not an option we can tolerate."

Henri showed no sign of emotion, no response to the attack that had just rained down upon him.

"As I said Gentlemen I will recover it. I can ascertain where this individual is being held, he is accessible to me, very easily accessible. I admit to being a little offended at being doubted by you Michel, so readily, so easily, are we not about more than just apportioning blame and pointing fingers when things are bad? Have I not always served not just the Republic, but our fraternity, so loyally, and if I may say so, effectively?"

Michel again spoke. "Effectively? Is that what we call losing something that could see us all go to Prison for life? Is that effective? Henri, you appear to be minimising what has happened, we've lived with this for two years, we've been patient, but now it needs sorting, rectifying, and that is for you to do. If you are not, and no offence is meant here, capable, then please say so, I would gladly proceed with this if you cannot."

Henri's composure was clearly being tested by Michel, as Henri considered this was all motivated by their ever clashing personality's as much as actual failings on his part. Michel and Henri had never really gotten along,

THE SHATTERED EAGLE

Henri considering himself the loyal soldier, servant of the Republic, whilst he thought of Michel as no more than a Politician, a soldier by title only. In Michel's case Henri thought the ring they all normally wore with so much pride was not earned by personal merit, but by ruthless decisions being made without the burden of empathy or conscience. Whereas Michel had given orders that many would have found indefensible, it had been down to Henri to actually get dirty carrying them out.

"Yes," he now angrily responded. "I appreciate what those two years have meant to us all, none more so than to myself. I have invested much in tracking him down, travelling the world in search of him, and believe me the fact we now have him has done nothing but illuminate my life with joy. But the ring, my ring, is my priority, it is mine to recover, and I certainly do not need your assistance, but thank you for your offer. Already plans are in place to recover it. No one knows of its greater importance other than us. I have never tried to keep that from you have I? Please just be patient."

Claude the most senior of the four again spoke.

"Henri, please do not think anyone is doubting you, we all know how important this is, but not just to you, but all of us, let's be clear on this. Plus the ramifications of you being unsuccessful in this will be long and far reaching. So you must understand Michel's anxieties over this matter. But I do think it right that we allow you to continue overseeing this to its conclusion. With the sacrifice you bear, we do owe you that much."

-THIRTYFOUR-
Très Très Merde Au Golf

Gary was waiting in the lobby of Safehaven, he was actually quite looking forward to their day out, for the first time since the Euston bomb he was going to escape for a few hours, get out of there for just a day, but that would do him at this juncture, it would be sufficient to keep him going. Jay had already left with Fran, Kate and the two children, they were off to an unspecified town for a bit of shopping, then the cinema and a Chinese meal to finish off their day.

It amused him no end that they still hadn't been told where they were, that phrases like 'Unspecified Town' were still being bandied around, yet the moment they came to the first road junction all would be revealed, why hadn't they just told them when they first arrived where exactly they were, it would have improved his trust of them no end.

Frankie had of course got his way, as it was inevitable he would, even though Oli had never played golf at all, and Gary had only ever been on a course half a dozen times in his whole life, all of which had ended humiliatingly bad, their host for the day was never going to back down.

Ping.

Gary turned from where he was sitting on the small sofa, to face the lift doors as they opened, seeing Oli come out, grinning as he waved a across the lobby. Oh you are shitting me, he thought, though the words escaped his lips as an unintelligible whisper, the young Prison Officer was dressed a pair of running shorts - which appeared too small for him, a faded tee-shirt and a battered pair of training shoes.

"You're joking aren't you?" Gary said to him as Oli walked over and sat down on one of the arm chairs next to him. "Tell me you're joking, please!"

"What?" Oli answered.

"That get up, you can't play golf in that! It's all dress up in the right gear mate. Have you never seen golf played at all?"

"Yeah of course. But it's only a friendly, no one will care."

"Of course they will! Howard's taking us to some swanky Golf Club, you're supposed to be a member and all that crap, they're not going to let you in the bar dressed like Linford Christie, these people are hard-core snobs. They take it really serious mate, honestly you won't be allowed on the course, you'll have retired Majors and blue rinsed Headmistresses blowing their fuses. Look at me."

Gary stood up revealing a neatly pressed pair of light brown trousers and a black cotton Pringle shirt, "You have to make a bit of an effort, do you really think I'd go out like this normally?"

"Bugger it Gary, I'll be OK, if they don't like it stuff 'em. To be honest mate I'm really not too worried what they think. Anyway heads up, here comes Sherlock Holmes."

Gary followed Oli's gaze, he could see through the window it was slightly overcast out, it made a nice change, as the mini-heat wave was getting a bit draining. Frankie was outside walking towards the entrance, before bounding up the stone steps. He was dressed in beige golfing trousers and tartan jumper, like an elongated Ronnie Corbett, though certainly not running shorts and a tramps vest. He was with someone else, it was someone Gary hadn't met before.

"Do you know the other fella?" he asked Oli.

"No he doesn't look like anyone who's been here before."

Frankie came through the front doors, a broad smile on his face.

"Good morning, Good morning," he breezed in, in remarkably good spirits for a confirmed miserable bastard of the highest order. "All fit and keen I hope, let me introduce JP, Jean Paul Matrice, he's over from France investigating Warsabi with us, I hope you don't mind, he came back over yesterday and is at a loose end today, so I invited him along. He tells me he has never played seriously, so hopefully we can win a few drinks off him, though I should say he's not been that honest with me in the past, so don't take that as fact."

JP shook hands with Oli and Gary.

"I hope you don't mind me joining you, I apologise in advance for the poor standard of my golf, but I'm told the food at this Golf Club is very good, so a little humiliation on the course in exchange for a good meal seems like a fair deal to me."

"Hey Oli," Frankie barked with a look of judgemental distain on his face. "Are you really wearing those shorts to a Golf Course?"

"Why what's wrong with them?" Oli replied.

"You're joking aren't you, tell me you are. Hey Gary this boy is joking isn't he, he is having a laugh?"

Gary shrugged his shoulders in mock ignorance.

Frankie continued, his critical gaze giving way to apparent amusement. "They're more like hot pants! We're playing the sport of gentlemen, not hide the sausage at a Barry Manilow concert! You need to dress the part, this is a decent club I'm taking you to, it's not the Crazy Golf Shack at *Butlin's*. Quick go and change, something that at least covers your hairy scrotum and arse cheeks, because there's no way I'm driving you there like that, why not just put a leather harness and gimp mask on, just in case anyone's in doubt!"

"We should have gone fishing, a carp ain't worried what I'm wearing!" Oli answered, with a mock sulk on his face.

"Just get fucking changed will you!"

About five minutes later Oli came bouncing down the stairs in brown chinos and a Ben Sherman polo. Frankie cast an eye over him, the trousers were rolled up so they were above his ankles, revealing he had no socks under a tatty pair of espadrilles.

"Oh for Heaven's sake," he muttered with exasperation, "JP do you still have that bottomless credit card from your over generous department?"

"Of course Frankie, you don't think I'd travel without it do you?"

"Good, when we get there will you kit out numb nuts here from the club shop, there's no way I'm playing golf with Andrew shit-for-brains Ridgley!"

"Who's that?" Oli asked.

"Never mind, let's get out of here."

Once through the gates it took just three minutes for Gary and Oli to establish that were staying at an old RAF station just outside of a village called Great Barham, Frankie told them it was in Buckinghamshire, quite near High Wycombe, and that it was originally owned by a Lord Meltham, who sold it to the Ministry Of Defence during the Second World War.

It had been affiliated to Bletchley Park, and was utilised for code breaking. Apparently the Police had been using it since 1972, and among the previous residents had been IRA Super Grasses, Russian Double Agents, and more recently people foolish enough to cross the London based Tri-ads or Albanian Mafia. They were being driven by someone they had never seen before, but presumably he was one of Frankie's men. After about twenty minutes they arrived at the *Cedar Hills Golf Club.*

"I've arranged for three sets of clubs for you guys, we'll pick them up, and sort Andrew Ridgely out some clobber, Jesus Oli I can't believe you really were going to go out in public in those shorts, let alone imagine for one single second it would be with me."

"Look Mr Howard, I'm willing to let you dress me up like Alan Titchmarsh, but who the hell is this Andrew what's-his-name?"

"Two things Oli, one please call me Frankie, now I'm 100% sure you're OK I'll allow you that, and two you know who George Michael is don't you? You know how he wanks people off in park toilets."

Oli nodded, Gary was cringing at the thought of what was to follow.

"Well that was probably Andrew Ridgley's job before George became famous!"

Gary laughed, although JP and Oli both looked totally bemused. It was strange thinking they were out with Howard, or Frankie as they were apparently now allowed to call him. The bloke had been a total cock to them since they met him, and suddenly here he was, demonstrating a new side, now he deemed them OK everything else was to be forgotten, he trusted them so they could be matey. What if they didn't want that?

But Gary knew that didn't matter, what they may want was of secondary importance, because it had become clear that at Safehaven it was Frankie's way or no way.

Frankie grabbed his bag of clubs from the car boot. "Come on Oli, let's go shopping, JP, bring that card."

The other three laughed and joked as Oli was handed some of the most extreme golfing clothing imaginable, although in the end he was dressed in plain dark blue trousers, a plain white polo, and, although he never admitted it to Frankie, a *Lyle and Scott* pale yellow lamb's wool jumper which he later confessed to Gary that he really actually liked. They collected their clubs and headed out to the course.

By the third hole it was clear that the golf aspect of their trip was going to be a disaster. Oli was truly atrocious, but Gary realised still infinitely better than he was, the supposedly more experienced player. He had endured a nightmare, he had barely hit any ball straight, more than seven yards, or putted anything more than 6 inches from the hole. Balls were going in all directions, the rough claiming more than any holes were. He tried to blame it on his bad hip, but he knew that had nothing to do with it, he was just plain appalling at golf. JP, although putting on a better show of enjoying himself than his two hopeless companions, was also what the French would describe as 'très très merde au golf'. By the seventh hole Oli had already secretly cheated at least three times, and that was just what Gary had silently witnessed, and Gary himself

THE SHATTERED EAGLE

had taken ten shots more than what a reasonable golfer was expected to use on the whole eighteen holes.

Frankie unfortunately could play, and could play well. Of course it wasn't in his nature to ease up, to make his fellow players feel better, which only heightened Oli and Gary's desire to call it a day after the ninth, which they had voiced at every hole since the fourth.

Frankie of course wanted to continue, so according to the golden rules of democracy it was down to JP to decide. Good natured, accommodating tactful JP.

"It's up to you," Frankie said to the Frenchman, "we go on like men, show our grit, look adversity in the face and play on. Or wimp out only half way through, like those two little girlies. What do you say JP, Man or Mouse?"

"Oh Frankie, what can I say, as much as I have enjoyed this humiliating lesson in your sport of gentlemen, let's go and eat, drink and vow never to play this awful game ever again!"

Gary and Oli fist bumped each other, then JP, laughing, cheering and making squeaking noises. Frankie mumbled something about France, a lack of gratitude and the war, which appeared to be only half in jest, whilst the other three guffawed at his expense.

An hour and half earlier than Frankie had planned they made their way to the club house, Gary felt knackered, thankful the other two had backed up his suggestion to call it day on the course, because there was no way he could have played another nine holes.

Once in the 'Cedar Lounge' they ordered the first round.

"Four lagers please." Frankie called to the smartly dressed steward. "Yes JP, that's lager, no bloody champagne today my friend."

The four of them sat round a table, Gary thought how good it was to be out, as horrendous as his skills with irons and woods may have been, he had to admit it had been fun. The drinks arrived and were duly despatched in double quick time, as Frankie called for the same again.

"So gentlemen." JP said after sipping the glass of water he insisted on having between pints. "Frankie tells me this is the first time you have been away from that place since you both arrived. It must be good to see, how you say, a change of scenery. He has told me all about what you have been through, you Gary, that awful bomb, that must have been pure hell, was it not?"

"You could say that JP, in fact pure hell is an understatement." Gary answered, there was something about JP which he found extremely likeable, there was a twinkle in his eye, which hinted at good natured mischievousness, like he knew exactly how to handle Frankie, without Frankie even knowing, but also he was sincere, his concern appeared genuine when talking of what Gary had been through.

"I can but imagine, you found yourself in a situation no man should." JP continued, "The world can be a cruel place, what you saw, what you smelt, what you heard, it cannot be unseen, unsmelt, unheard, the wounds from such a thing last longer than we imagine."

THE SHATTERED EAGLE

JP paused a moment, taking another sip from his glass of water before turning to Oli, "And you Oliver, you also have experienced horrors no one should ever witness, seeing your colleague and the driver killed, taken away as you were, cuffed to DuPont, I'm sorry I should say Warsabi, that is truly awful, just awful."

Oli nodded, before taking a big swig of beer.

"Yeah, but on the bright side I got a new set of clothes out of it, cheers!"

He laughed and held his glass aloft, the other three followed suit.

Three pints later, dinner had turned from a table for four in the posh looking restaurant next door, into steak sandwiches where they were sitting. The conversation had shifted to families, with JP questioning all on their marital status whilst chewing on what was a good half a pound of meat stuffed into two thick slices of bread.

"I've been married for over twenty years now," Gary started, slightly slurring his words as he spoke. "Two kids, Josh and Amy, and still madly in love with Fran, my very, very, lovely wife, I really love that woman! When this is all over I'm going to treat her to something special, well I would if I had more than two pennies to rub together, but I'll sort something out, she deserves it."

"That's lovely Gary, it's a rare thing to maintain the love after many years, you truly are a lucky man indeed." JP told him.

"Luckier than me mate!" Frankie said, putting his sandwich back on his plate. "Two wives, two children, two divorces. Fuck 'em."

He picked the sandwich back up and tore a chunk off with his teeth, before continuing to talk whilst chewing vigorously. "Fuck 'em both, took me to the cleaners the pair of them, in fact I think Lyn, my second wife, who left me, then became a Vicar, learnt everything about having me over from Amanda, my first, who pissed off and took up with some big hairy arsed lesbian who should have had bigger bollocks than the four of us put together. The two boys are grown up now, one at University and one works at *Waitrose*, see them about half a dozen times a year, usually when they need money. Yeah you are a lucky man Gary."

The four fell silent, wow, way to lift the mood Frankie, Gary thought.

After a short awkward moment, JP asked Oli, "And you Oli, is there a lady in your life?"

"Sure is, her name's Kate, we used to work together, she moved out to the country with me when I started at the prison. We're not married or anything, but yeah, I think she's the one, she's a good girl is Kate. But what about you JP, who's waiting patiently back home for you mate?"

Jean Paul, looked down at his glass, Gary could see the happy smile disintegrating as that twinkle in his eye extinguished.

THE SHATTERED EAGLE

"Alas I am a widower, my wife died a few years back. We had no children, although we always planned to, but an awful disease took her from me."

He was silent for a moment, staring into his glass of lager, no doubt reflecting on his loss, Gary looked to Oli, then Frankie, but no one spoke, leaving JP to think of his now gone wife.

"But now I am married to my job." JP smiled, shrugging his shoulders, "It will never leave me, become a Priest, nor run away with another woman with giant testicles. That gentlemen is true love."

He raised his glass, "To our current, past and future women, oh, and to my job!"

The four all raised their glasses again.

"Cheers!"

Gary felt considerably worse for wear, they had gone onto shorts, he was never a big drinker at the best of times, but now he felt decidedly queasy.

Oli had tried to introduce them all to Jager-Bombs, but a decidedly sniffy Bar Steward had suggested if they required such a beverage then perhaps they would be more suited to drinking elsewhere, which in truth they were in no fit state to do, well Gary wasn't any way. It felt like he was now spectating, although still there in the mix, his mind was watching from somewhere else, offering him a slightly skewed version of reality.

"And tell me gents, what do you do to make life special?" JP enquired.

They looked at him blankly, well Oli and Frankie did, Gary wasn't sure what he was looking like anymore, he wondered just how obvious it was that he was now out it.

"I for instance," JP continued, "collect antiques, it is a pastime I find most rewarding. As Frankie will testify Police work does not come without its stresses and traumas, and I find searching out curios from Brocants and Markets a most relaxing pursuit. Now you Gary, what do you like to do?"

Gary was struggling to function properly at this stage, his head was swimming and he wanted to throw up, but he didn't want to kill the day for everyone else, so he played along.

"I enjoy going to the football mate. I also like doing stuff with the family, you know things and stuff, and things like that." The part of the brain affecting his vocabulary had clearly been attacked by too much beer. "Oh, and I'm writing a book, but don't tell anyone, it's not very good."

"Oh really?" JP seemed enthused by Gary's drunken confession of a literary bent.

"What's it about?"

"I don't know yet I'm only on page 15."

Gary then emitted a prolonged belch.

"And you Frankie, do you have any, what you call, hobbies?"

"This is between us four right?" Frankie looked around the table for confirmation that whatever was revealed was for their ears only. Gary wondered what it was going to be. Cross Dressing? Stamp Collecting? Bee Keeping?

THE SHATTERED EAGLE

"I go dancing."

Oli who had just taken large swig of beer, blew it back into his glass. "You what Frankie. Dancing! What like Strictly or something?"

"No you little prick, not like Strictly! Northern Soul, real dancing, always have, since I was a kid. I used to go to all-nighters, and go all around the country, still go when I can, it's keeping the flame alive, can't beat it."

Gary visualized Frankie gyrating and throwing himself around some sweaty dance floor, a dopey smile spreading across his face.

"Fair play to you Frankie, no really, sounds good." Oli offered, although even in his current inebriated condition Gary could see he was taking the piss.

"And another thing." Frankie was now on a roll. "I've got two scooters, one *Lambretta* and one *Vespa*, proper genuine models, rebuilt them myself, see you never knew that about me did you?"

They had to admit they didn't, it was hard to picture Frankie speeding down to Brighton or wherever on his scooter, he was hardly Phil Daniels in 'Quadrophenia'.

"And what of you Oli?" JP asked.

Oli appeared to think for a minute. "I've taken to exploring the countryside, lots of walks around where we live, well normally live. But really as hobbies go I'm doing it now, you can't beat a good night out with your mates can you?" He paused for a moment, then winked, "Even if one of them is the Dancing Queen!"

***

As they drove back to Safehaven Gary pondered how Frankie had, since they had met, got so much wrong and yet got that day so very right. It had been just what he and Oli had needed, well maybe not every part, they had to stop three times so far in order for him to jettison the evening's food and ale, but for what he needed at that time it had been better than any pill or medicine, and he had known a few in his time. His whole opinion of Frankie had altered, the bloke had been funny and really entertaining, a right good laugh, and Oli had got a new set of clothes out of it, even if he would only ever wear the jumper again.

-THIRTYFIVE-
The Black Rhino Versus The Middlesex Under 18 Champion

His room was unbelievable, the view on a good clear day stunning, Sergio was definitely enjoying his new surroundings at the *Marriott*. Lying back on his bed, his hands behind his head, he congratulated himself on how things had turned out very nicely indeed, he had achieved a new Number Seven on his wish list, Emma, a local girl just about his own age, and although it was strictly against the rules - as she kept telling him - she was happy to spend her nights in his bed. In fact he had abandoned the rest of the list completely. What's happening to me, he thought, he was really struck with her, and he had even felt a pang of guilt and shame, almost a totally new sensation for him, over how he had behaved prior to coming across her. What he wasn't feeling any guilt about though was what had happened on the way to that hospital, he knew he should, should be enduring sleepless nights and all manner of problems, but somehow he was coping very well with it, hmm life's strange, but sometimes very good indeed.

Unfortunately for Sergio he was blissfully unaware of a clean-up operation that was now taking place. The nice kind people who had paid him half a million pounds, were now panicking, as they hadn't actually got what they wanted.

Five storeys below whilst Sergio had moved from his bed and was now looking out of his window, totally naked, safe in the knowledge that no one could see him, Auguste Fredericks was enquiring in the Lobby whether his dear friend Sergio Pragua was staying at the hotel, as he was very keen to surprise him. A £20 note handed over the counter confirmed he was, and was in room 503 if 'Sir wished to call up'.

Sergio had the *i-Pod* he had brought the previous day on full blast as he danced around his room, stark bollock naked bar the strap around his bicep, cradling the MP3 player, and a pair of head phones running to his ears. Hopefully Emma would be calling up at some point if she got a chance, they could have a quick kiss and a cuddle and work out what to do over the weekend, it would be nice to enjoy a bit of time together away from the hotel that bound them. He paused his thoughts for a moment, a kiss and a cuddle and planning ahead, these were not the actions of Sergio Pozzo, well they never used to be.

THE SHATTERED EAGLE

***

Auguste Fredericks banged on the door.

No answer.

Inside Sergio obliviously bopped around his room.

Gus banged again, still no answer.

Patience wasn't Gus's strongest attribute, never had been, so he then kicked the door open, he sure as hell wasn't going to piss around out there all day.

Sergio saw him smash through, like an angry black rhino, charging towards him, there was a knife in his hand, who the hell was this?

Instincts kicked in, instincts honed from hours spent in gyms and dojos, this man meant him harm, and by the look of it serious harm. It wasn't Lillian's husband, was it some other boyfriend, husband, father or older brother, there were enough reasons for aggrieved menfolk to be coming after him, but there certainly hadn't been any warning. He immediately bounced on his toes, as Gus came into range he swung around kicking him in the head, sending his attacker reeling backwards, Sergio instantly taking up the ready stance again. Years of kick-boxing, becoming Middlesex Under-18 Champion, was now being put to good effect.

The attacker got up, shaking his head, clearly surprised, he obviously wasn't expecting that, he again charged forward swinging with the knife, arcing it towards Sergio, who bounced back momentarily, as the blade swung within millimetres of his chest, before once more springing forward, punching Gus hard around the head, as he moved back through the force, Sergio gave another kick, this time with the heel of his foot, blooding Gus's nose in the process.

Sergio, knew he had to get away, he could knock this big lump around all day, but he had no guarantee that the bloke only had a knife, and he had no intention waiting to find out if he was going to pull a gun on him. This wasn't some hard done by loved one from one his romantic conquests, this was *him*!

Why was he here? Who had sent him? They had paid him the money, and he had stuck to his side of the bargain, why do this now?

He continued forward and ran into the corridor, naked, he hadn't even pulled the headphones out, Girls Aloud still singing their Greatest Hits directly into his ears. He ran for the stairwell, he heard a shot and wood splintered around him, shit, just as he thought, no looking back, just keep running, he swung around the corner and leaped down the stairs, taking three steps at a time, desperate to get away.

He now knew for certain who his attacker was, and he sure as hell wasn't going to hang around to engage in conversation, the last time he saw him he had just murdered two of the people he had been travelling with. Again a shot, plaster turning to dust on the wall just beyond his head, he kept running, running for his very life.

THE SHATTERED EAGLE

He reached the third floor, he was getting away, his pursuer was at least a floor above him now, he couldn't let up, now on the second floor, run Sergio, run!

He continued to leap the steps three at a time, he stubbed his toe landing, initially stumbling, almost tumbling down the rest of that flight, but it didn't slow him down even though judging by the excruciating pain it was broken, but adrenalin is wonderful thing to be full of in such a scenario, he was only concerned with his exit.

He ran through the doors at the bottom of the stairwell, straight into the large spacious hotel lobby, crowded with people, clearing aside for him as he bolted, they were staring, pointing, some of them laughing, it was a naked man running through Bournemouth's most expensive hotel after all! But he wasn't about to stand around and apologise for his outlandish appearance, offer a plausible explanation for having his cock out in such a public fashion, he just had to get away.

He was outside, clear of the hotel, the pavements were crowded, he just dodged through people, families, holiday makers, a group of young girls photographed him using mobile phones, before he had even left their sight he would no doubt be being 'liked' on *Facebook*, or 'trending' on *Twitter*.

He didn't know if the man who was so keen to kill him was still chasing or not, he just kept running. He was all too aware of the state of undress he was in, what was he going to do once he was clear? Bournemouth was hardly full of washing lines full of clothes he could pluck from them. All he could do was keep running, where to he didn't know, then as he sprinted past the end of a side street, he ran straight into the bonnet of a Police Car.

THE SHATTERED EAGLE

-THIRTYSIX-
I'll Talk To Start With, You Better Be Ready To Help Him Stop Crying!

"What happened to his clothes?"

Sylvia had a puzzled look on her face as she asked the Custody Sergeant the question that had been on her mind since she had first seen Sergio Pozzo being led through the holding area wearing a paper suit. "Were they taken as evidence?"

The Sergeant laughed.

"If only love! They picked him up totally naked, wearing nothing but an *i-Pod* and a smile, sprinting down the Sea Front like Leaping Lenny. We presumed he was just pissed, on a stag do or something, we get a lot of that, but he was begging for us contact Northants, saying he was involved in all sorts, and wanted to give himself up. Our CID have been there, to the *Marriott*, they are treating it as a crime scene, there's a couple of bullet holes, they've already spoken to him, but we are going to need him back at some point. But he's all yours for now."

"Well thanks, we'll be sure to look after him," she said as she guided the terrified looking young man into the back seat of the silver *Ford Mondeo* they were transporting him back to London in. Frankie had been most eager for them to pick him up soon as possible sending her and Felix down there within minutes of getting the call from DI Lovan from Northampton. She had hoped it would perhaps turn into some sort of over-nighter in a good hotel, a nice dinner out, full English in the morning, then pick Pozzo up and get him to Frankie before his first cup of coffee, especially as it was gone seven before they had even left, but alas Frankie was having none of that, he wanted him back ASAP, didn't care how long it took, he'd stay up for this one.

It took the best part of two hours for them to get back to the Red House, but in that time Sergio hadn't stopped talking, barely pausing to take a much needed breath, despite being told repeatedly to save it for the formal interviews. He was clearly terrified, and by the sound of it with good reason, after hearing what he had said Sylvia had her doubts about moving him in the unmarked car, the man that had come after him was still out there after all, but Frankie lectured her on the fact that both her Felix carried firearms for a good reason, and he 'didn't need to be calling SCO-bloody-19 whenever I need something doing'.

Once in London Sergio was initially placed in a holding cell, where he was given a drink and some sandwiches, it

THE SHATTERED EAGLE

was coming up for midnight, and Sylvia suddenly realised just how peckish she was.

But Frankie was already chasing her, apparently showing no concern for his DC's energy levels, so on leaving their suspect she went straight to Interview Room 2, or at least after a very short detour to the vending machine, where she picked up a couple of bags of crisps and a *Twix*.

"He's going to talk like a good 'un Guv," she told Frankie whilst tipping her head back and pouring the last of the crumbs from her first packet of Smoky Bacon into her mouth, before continuing whilst chompsing on her crisps, "Honestly he wouldn't shut up all the way back. He's their boy on the inside of the jail, that's for certain."

Frankie, gave a gentle nod, "Oh yes! Come on Hardacre let's get him in, give him no time to have second thoughts, I'll talk to start with, you better be ready to help him stop crying."

Sergio walked into the interview room escorted by Sylvia, Frankie was already sitting down.

"Sit down over there." Frankie said to him, looking up as Sergio entered the room nodding towards the solitary chair on the other side of the table, bolted to the floor.

"I'm DCI Howard, you've met DC Hardacre. Let's start with recent events first shall we, why the hell were you running naked down Bournemouth Seafront? Call me a traditionalist, old fashioned, but that's not right is it Sergio?"

"I was escaping from someone, someone who was trying to kill me."

"You're good at that aren't you Sergio, bloody good. Escaping that's your forte isn't it son, your very special skill in life, escaping from Taxis whilst everyone else is being murdered, escaping on motorbikes instead of coming to see me, escaping in Bournemouth giving loving old ladies heart attacks and strokes - no pun intended, because believe it or not I am not in a very jokey mood. Look Sergio, I may as well be honest I've never met you before today, but already you're on my Top Five list of little wankers who I really don't like. In fact you're Number One at this very moment, quite an achievement as there are some people who I fucking detest who now find themselves below you on my afore mention list."

Sylvia pushed back into her chair, this bloke was practically signing the confession in the car on the way there, he didn't need Frankie's Top Five speech, although she never tired of hearing it in interview rooms, sometimes she wished Frankie would just stay quiet and let her do the questioning, as in this case it would have been so much easier.

Sergio looked stunned, "Are you even listening, I said someone was trying to kill me. I don't care if you like me or not to be honest, in fact I'm quite glad you don't. But you really should listen to me, because I've nothing to lose, and am happy to help you, but that is likely to change if you intend to continue talking to me like that."

THE SHATTERED EAGLE

"What is it you want to tell us Sergio?" Sylvia cut in, keen for Frankie not to antagonise Sergio anymore.

"The business with Warsabi, I want to tell you everything, well everything I know. The man that tried to kill me, he was one of them there, he was the leader."

"Go on," Sylvia offered, her voice calm, friendly, "start at the beginning, tell us how you got involved?"

"I was at work, it was coming up for lunch time, we had fed the wing when I got a phone call in the Office, everyone else had headed off for lunch and I was the Patrol Officer working on my own. I didn't know who it was, they just called themselves a friend. They came straight to the point offered me quarter of a million, just to get something from Reception for them. That was it."

"What did you say?"

"I thought it was a wind up, said no of course, you know, laughed it off, asked who it really was. He then began to trot out details of how he knew where my family lived, even said the actual address over the phone, where my niece went to school, stuff like that. Told me how he didn't mind making me rich for this one little thing, but that I would do what they asked anyway, and he wouldn't take no for an answer. I wasn't sure what to do, how to play it, I mean, it's not the sort of stuff that happens every day. I still said no, but then he became really threatening, said what would happen to people, including me, and all I had to do was lift one thing from Reception. Just one thing and he'd pay me a fortune."

"So you got it for him?"

"No, it wasn't there, and there was no record of it."

"What was it?"

"A ring, but it wasn't on the prop card, or in his stuff, there was no sign of it."

"Then what?"

"Then he called back about ten minutes later, said that something had been put on the Prison Incident Reporting System, stating that Warsabi may have a broken wrist. He said that I was to make sure I was on any escort that may go out, and that I should contact them as soon as I got word about any developments. He said the reward was doubled if I did as they said, half a million. He gave me a number to phone him back on."

"And you did?" Sylvia said, trying hard to mask her contempt for the man before them. "Why?"

"Because the number was my landline! They knew where my parents lived, where my niece went to school, and had the front to phone me from my own house. I was scared."

Frankie couldn't help himself, he had to chime in, he couldn't stay quiet, "And they were paying you half a million quid, that must have sealed the deal eh Sergio, eased the anxieties a bit?"

"It helped," admitted Sergio.

"Go on," Sylvia said.

"Well then it happened, George asked me to stay on and go out on an escort. I didn't even need to do anything to make it happen, they were that desperate for staff. I knew straight away who it was for. I phoned my home number, a different voice answered, but I told them where we were going, and what time we were leaving. They told me once they stopped the taxi, to run for it, get clear, like I had gotten away. They then said the money would be paid into an account, the details of which would be texted to me."

"And you trusted them, believed they would actually do it?" Sylvia scoffed, amazed at Sergio's gullibility.

"They did do it though, they paid the money in, and sent me a debit card under a false name. I was as surprised as you are to be honest. I was just glad to still be breathing. That was the last I heard of them. I saw him, the black guy, at the scene, I was hiding just the other side of the hedge, in fact I saw all three of them, they were wearing masks and stuff but once they were in their car they took them off. I didn't get that good a look, but the guy with the knife in my room was definitely him."

"So you were happy for them to kill your buddies, murder two people as long as you got half a million, you're a bit of a cold one eh Sergio. I wouldn't want you as my best man at my wedding, probably shag my missus, eat the cake and steal all the presents!" Frankie said, whilst sipping from a mug of coffee.

"No! They had said no one would get hurt, they said they were going to use some form of incapacitant. I had no idea they would actually kill anyone."

Frankie again chimed in, sarcastically, "Oh that's alright then. DC Hardacre please release Mr Pozzo and apologise for any inconvenience we may have caused him, he's clearly one of the good guys. Or then again, let's continue. Names?"

"I don't know, honest, I only spoke to them on the phone, and even then only for a few minutes."

"What did they look like? Start with the one who attacked you in your room?"

"He was about 5' 8", a bit hench, you know well built. He was black, no hair on his head, but he did have a beard. I suppose he was in his mid-thirties, but I can't be sure, he was scary, you know what I mean, looked proper mean. He came at me with a knife."

"So," Sylvia asked, "how did you escape? I mean this guy clearly meant business, my guess was that he wasn't coming to pay you a bonus for a good job well done."

"I fought him off, I used to kick box, so I was able to get out. Shame I didn't have any trousers on at the time, but I wasn't exactly in a position to say, hold on can I get dressed first, really was I?"

"No, I guess note," Sylvia replied before taking a bite from her Twix, "I guess you weren't."

THE SHATTERED EAGLE

-THIRTYSEVEN-
Your Mum's Got Fat Pants.

Oli and Kate were returning from one of their evenings at 'Howard's End', it had been a good night, the kitchen had made up a large vat of chilli and tacos, which although messy had created a great base for a night on the drink. Once the kids had been packed off to bed, they had indulged in a rather vigorous evening of cocktails, which had then been narrowed down to a session on Margaritas, they had gone down easily, a bit too easily, as they had left Gary suffering with raging heartburn, seeing him and Fran have to make an early exit to pour *Gaviscon* down his neck, a by-product, Fran had informed their younger friends, of being an old miserable git who eats too much.

"See Kate, we can beat them at something. What's four games of *Pictionary* compared to having your arse whipped at Margarita downing!" Oli gloated.

Kate was in the bathroom, cleaning her teeth, calling back through foamy saliva, "It wasn't a competition Oli, sometimes you're such a competitive little bell-end, but yeah, we whooped them didn't we!"

Coming out in a pair of tartan flannelette pyjamas she slumped into the settee next to Oli.

"Put some music on will you babe, something a bit quiet," she asked as she lay there cuddled up to a pillow. Oli put a CD, a compilation of acoustic cover versions, into the machine, before re-joining Kate on the sofa, she had claimed a bit more of it whilst he was up.

"Move over fat pants," he asked.

"Piss off, who are you calling fat pants, you big knob head? Your mum's got fat pants!"

Oh dear, she had launched into the inevitable game of matriarchal insult tennis.

15-Love. To Wallander.

"Oh yeah very mature," Oli laughed, "you really want to go down this road do you?"

Kate shrugged, "Well she has got very big pants Oli, gotta call it as I see it haven't I."

"Yeah. Well they're your mum's hand me downs, you know, where she's grown out of them, because her huge arse is so big."

15-All

"Well your mum don't need them anyway, she's always being given a really good seeing to by your dad, and your Uncle Eric, he's having a good old dabble on Mummy too, I bet they're at it now. Picture it Oli, in your imagination, go on Uncle Eric make her have it!"

Oh good one 30-15 to Wallander.

THE SHATTERED EAGLE

"Yeah, well the only reason your Mum's so fat is every time she gets shagged by Fat Barry he gives her a slice of cake, oh and the 50p she charges of course!"

30-30. Ms Wallander to serve.

"Uncle Eric and your Dad are double teaming your Mum as we talk!"

"Yeah, yeah…" For a brief moment Oli appeared to be lost for words, before turning to Kate with a doe-eyed face she didn't know whether to slap or laugh at, at least until he spoke. "Marry me Kate. I mean it marry me. I love you so much, always have, you mean the world to me, please be my wife."

"Oli, what are you saying? Are you serious?"

"I've never been more serious, nearly two weeks ago I almost got killed, I don't want to waste my life doing things I don't want to do, compromising, achieving second best. You're the best thing that's ever happened to me. I mean it Kate, this is me being dead serious, will you marry me?"

"Yes. Of course I will, of course I bloody will!"

Game set and match to Allen.

-THIRTYEIGHT-
Jay DeHavalland And Kate Wallender Leave Safehaven To Get A Cup Of Coffee.

"What! You're joking!" Jay DeHavalland screeched as Kate told her the news as they prepared to dive into the pool.

"No, last night, he actually proposed, got down on one knee and everything." Kate replied, a huge smile dominating her face.

Jay took several paces back from the edge, now focussed on Kate's news, rather than swimming fifty lengths of the small pool.

"You said yes didn't you? Of course you did, otherwise you wouldn't be so excited. Oh Kate I'm so pleased for you." Jay threw her arms around her, "Come on let's get dressed, never mind the swim, I want to take you out, just us this time, we can grab a coffee and a cake, look around some shops, maybe look at some rings!"

THE SHATTERED EAGLE

"But Oli's..." Kate began.

"But Oli's asleep, will be for hours, come on, I'll check with Howard but I'm sure he'll be OK with it." Jay was pulling her by her hand, not taking no for an answer.

She was right, Kate thought, it would be good to get out again, and she really liked the young Detective Constable, although Fran was lovely, Jay was more her own age, they had so much more in common. And Jay was spot on about one thing, Oli would be dead to the world for hours yet.

"Oh go on then."

Jay loosened her grip on Kate's hand, "And you may as well be honest, you didn't fancy this swim any more than I did, did you." She laughed out loud, "I knew it! Just how much did you put back last night?"

"Oh one or two," Kate said, whilst hurriedly rushing back to her room. "I'll let Oli know where we're going."

"No," Jay said, "Let him sleep, you've got your whole life to wake him up now, let him have one last lay in."

"Alright I won't be a minute."

"I'll meet you out the front, I'll just give Howard a bell and get my clothes back on."

The engine was already running in Jay's car as Kate bounded down the steps, she had one of those 'new' *Mini's*, bright red, with a soft top which was down. Kate could see her new friend still looked excited, a big broad toothy grin on her face as she turned to her, "Wow, I can't believe he asked you last night. Did you know he was going to?"

Kate shook her head, "Nope, one minute he's insulting my mother, the next he went all loved up and soppy. It was lovely really."

"I bet!"

As Jay drove through the automatic gates she gunned the accelerator, the car instantly responding. Kate could feel the wind blowing her hair all over the place, but it felt good, exhilarating, she was so happy, so incredibly happy.

She thought back to the previous night, that dopey git actually asking her to marry him, and once more reflected on the surreal life they were both living, was it only a year or so back they were working at *Poundslasher*, selling bad imitations of famous brands to the great British poor in return for a zero hours contract and minimum wage. The thought of her being with Oli back then was ridiculous, he was such a knob, and she was stuck with Darius, yet was it really that ridiculous. It was only with hindsight that they both realised just how much each of them was keeping to themselves, how they both had secretly fallen for the other, yet bound by the constrictions of social mores, modern etiquette and not wanting to look totally stupid, had kept their opinions and feelings to themselves. Fortunately alcohol had no respect for such inhibitions, and so it was they were brought together that rather special night in the *Rose and Crown*.

"Hey Dolly Daydream, wake up!" Jay was again laughing, "Look at you, oblivious to everything other than Oli."

THE SHATTERED EAGLE

Kate smiled, as she was doing a lot this morning. "Sorry miles away."

"I know. I said is it OK if we just stop off somewhere, I need to pick something up, it's a bit of a trek, but we've got all day. In fact it'll be nice to a have a good drive."

"Sure, no worries, like you say, Oli won't come to life for hours, what else have I got on."

"Oh thanks Kate, I've got something I've really got to do."

-THIRTYNINE-
It's Simple X+Y=Z.

Sometimes a man has to do work he wouldn't normally enjoy doing, dirty his hands in affairs he shouldn't be touching, make concessions due to necessity and need. For Auguste Fredericks this was certainly one of those occasions.

Gus wasn't a particularly squeamish person, his moral compass was hardly focussed pointing North 100% of the time, but he did have his own guidelines, standards he tried to adhere to. Sure he had, in the course of his duties and certainly not for pleasure, inflicted some pain compliance on the female of the species. It came with the territory, he didn't enjoy it, in fact he enjoyed little in the way of the work he was now finding himself doing, but then again in these economically troubled times one sometimes has to be prepared to branch out, embrace the idea of travelling down alternative avenues, seeking out fresh opportunities.

Kate Wallander was a prime example of such diversification in his career path.

Unfortunately for Kate, less than eight hours after probably the happiest moment of her life, she was now one

THE SHATTERED EAGLE

of just two people residing at Fredericks Towers, the name Gus had given to his new company premises, if only in his own mind, even though it was severely lacking in any form of tower, and was actually a rather shabby looking small industrial unit, a poor replacement for the one razed to the ground in Surrey.

The other resident of course being Gus, after all it would be a poor party without a host.

Kate was tied to a swivel chair, her feet bound together and hands behind the back of the seat all tethered with cable ties, she couldn't see the purple welts on her wrists due to the black velvet hood over her head, although he was sure she could feel them. She had been there for well over a couple of hours, since Jay had brought her.

He was sitting on a similar chair about five feet in front of her, drinking a pint of milk straight out of a carton, watching his 'project', mulling over his dilemma.

"Well Kate, I guess it's time I gave you an explanation."

They were the first words he had spoken since he had brought her there, she had no doubt heard him moving around, she had begged him to speak, but he had responded with only silence. It was what he had been trained to do, part of the process, confuse, disorientate, soften them up ready for whatever you need them for.

"What's happening, please let me go, please don't hurt me, what's happening?" she whimpered in a pathetic tone.

He wheeled his chair forward, so he was just inches from her hooded face, he took another swig from his milk, then leant back in his chair, his head cocked to one side, studying the form in front of him.

"It's like this Kate, I have no issue with you, I really don't, in fact I'm sure if I got to know you I'd like you, I'm a sociable kind of guy. But, and this Kate is a very big but, your boyfriend, partner, cohabitating lover, let's call him what we will, has something I need. Now let me explain. Normally in these circumstances it's simple, painfully simple. Someone has something I want, be that information, or a possession, or whatever, it's all semantics, the equation is straight forward. $X+Y=Z$. This is all very educational Kate, stay with me.

"X in this equation is fear. Y pain. And Z, well good old Z is the resolution to the problem, it's all just mathematics really. Do you follow?"

Kate just sobbed, "Please, please don't hurt me, what do you want, why am I here?"

Gus ignored her pleading and questions, continuing with his little speech. He liked the little speeches, it made him feel like he was offering something special, something besides mere brute force and ignorance, a certain little bit of intellectual reasoning.

"But Kate, here things aren't so simple, there's plenty of X, I can hear that by your pleading and begging, the tears you weep and sobs you emit, believe me X isn't my problem in this case. Unfortunately I may soon be utilising Y, although I genuinely hope I will not need to, but our problem is I don't think you can supply me with old Mr Z. No Z, the solution to all our problems, can only be

THE SHATTERED EAGLE

supplied by your man, your Oliver. Now don't get me wrong, you are a good means to obtain Z, and I am sure I would have no problem getting Z. But no matter how much misery and genuine unpleasantness I bring your way, it isn't you who can give me what I want."

"W-w-hat do you want?" Kate enquired between tears.

"I want the ring Kate, I want the ring."

She was silent, as he expected her to be, she probably had no notion of what he was on about, her thieving boyfriend keeping her blissfully ignorant as to what he had done, what had landed her into this predicament she now found herself within.

"Now Kate, I don't want to keep you all tied up like this, blind and incapacitated, this is no way to treat anyone, especially someone who has basically done me no wrong, an innocent bystander so to speak. So here's what is going to happen. Now listen good Kate, stop sobbing and listen, are we clear, because if I think you're not listening to me I will leave you like this, do you understand?"

Kate sobbed back, "Yes."

"No, we're obviously not fucking clear are we Kate, you're still crying, stop the crying and listen."

It wasn't that hard to understand was it? He had been clear, Jesus sometimes people could be so relentlessly stupid, although Kate was now slowing down the pace of her breathing, the sobs being stifled back.

"That's better. Now Kate in a moment I'm going to take that hood off you, you can't live like that, you need to eat and drink, breathe air, see the light. But when I do take the hood off, you will see me. Now there is a problem with that, a fucking gigantic great problem with that, the issue being that if you see what I look like I will have to kill you."

Kate recoiled back, "Oh no, please don't!"

Gus had learnt the lesson from the incident with Jim Bolton, he was a bad arse, sure he was, but really he regretted killing poor old Jim, he only had to because the old veteran had seen his face, well that and the fact that he had introduced himself by name, hmm got a bit carried away with the speech on that one. He really didn't want that to happen, at least not needlessly, in this case.

"Shut the fuck up Kate, and listen! I do not want to hurt you, no that would not help anyone, unless I have to, but let's not dwell on that. Now Listen! When I take your hood off I will be wearing one of those ski masks. This is solely to prevent me from having to kill you, not because I'm in the IRA, a rapist, or I want to go skiing. So like I said, don't be alarmed."

He got up and slowly removed the hood from her head. Her eyes were red, bloodshot from her crying, and her hair matted across her face from the sweat generated from being enclosed within a black velvet hood. He could see the fear on her face, she would tell him anything he asked, she was ready, but had nothing to tell him, she was just leverage.

"Don't hurt me! Don't hurt me!" she pleaded.

"Kate, Kate, don't you listen to a word I say. Jeez. Now in a minute I'm going to untie your feet and hands, now

THE SHATTERED EAGLE

don't run or do anything stupid. Chances are your legs have gone to sleep and you'll just collapse in a heap anyway, but even if you can run the doors are locked, you can't get out."

Kate looked around, avoiding the gaze of the monster in the black ski mask, standing just inches from her.

What did he want from her? What was the deal with the ring, Oli had only proposed earlier that morning, yes it was still the same bloody morning, he hadn't even got her a ring. What was this about, it didn't make any sense.

She could see she was in what appeared to be an empty store cupboard, there was a bed made up one side of the room, it looked new with equally fresh bedding on it, there was uncovered bulb hanging from some flex on the ceiling, and a TV in one corner. There was a small table with some folded clothes and underwear on top, and in the another corner a bucket. It was like a prison cell, or what she imagined a prison cell would look like.

Why had Jay done this to her, why had she brought her here? Who was this man? What did he want, and what was he planning to do with her? Oh God, was he some kind of rapist, a sex-beast or something, she began to cry again, then she remembered his words, not just the warning about tears, but his explanation for why she was here. Oli had something, something this man wanted.

"Why am I here, what do you want from me, please let me go," she said, desperate not to cry.

"Right Kate I'm going to tell you some of the story, not all of it, because hell I don't know all of it, I don't need or want to know all of it, but let me cut your hands free first, they're looking uncomfortable."

The man before her took a long pair of scissors, she recoiled back, but he grabbed her hands from behind the chair, firmly, saying nothing as way of reassurance, just cutting the tie that bound her hands so uncomfortably. As he did so she could feel his breath on her neck, her skin crawled, goose-bumps popping up all the way down her back. She felt the blood rush back in past where she had been so tightly tethered, and as she drew her hands around she could clearly see the dividing line between purple hands and white wrists.

He then stood back. "I'm going to cut your feet free now, but remember what I said, stay sitting."

Kate nodded, as the man dropped to one knee, cutting the ties around her ankles. They hurt, they really did hurt, worse than her wrists, and her feet had gone numb, he was right she wouldn't have got far if she had tried to run.

He stood back a bit, she was still scared, no terrified would have been a better description.

"All this shit, all this unnecessary inconvenience is down to Mister Oliver Allen taking something that in all reality did not belong to him Kate. Wasn't his to take. Now the Police have put our little thief where they thought he would be safe, where you both would be safe, but the person paying my wages is some powerful mother fucker, who it would appear has friends in all sorts of places.

THE SHATTERED EAGLE

Thus, unfortunately for you and your thieving boyfriend, that means that the place you thought you were safe in wasn't very fucking safe at all. Now obviously time is of the essence, meaning it's very valuable to me, I'm going to talk to your Oliver and let him know just how important time is to you and him, and how even more important that ring is to me. Are we clear so far Kate?"

Kate nodded.

"I'm sorry Kate, are we clear, because at this point we should be crystal fucking clear. I do require a verbal response in this situation. Now are we clear?"

"Yes," Kate answered still almost inaudibly.

"That's good Kate, that's very good. Now I'm going to leave you with your thoughts for a few minutes, to ponder the situation so to speak."

He reached into a rucksack by his feet and took out a couple of packs of sandwiches, some crisps, and three bottles of water, and placed them on the table besides the clothes folded neatly.

"In the meantime have something to eat, I hope you're not a vegetarian, otherwise you are going to be one hungry lady."

She saw him leave the room, her eyes not leaving him, making sure he was really gone, as he went she could hear the sound of bolts sliding shut. What the hell was happening to her?

She was emotionally drained, the only feeling being one of empty sickness, dread leaving her devoid of any positive emotions at all. What had Oli done so bad to bring this upon her? This man, the man with the mask, he wasn't anything to do with the Police, that was blatantly clear, then why had Jay delivered her into his clutches?

What was this ring he was so bothered about? What was he planning to do to her, do with her, what sort of harm was someone so clearly bad capable of?

She gingerly walked to the bed, lay down and buried her head in the pillow. It smelt new, but not in a good way, there was that plastic aroma that came with cheap fabrics, almost chemically, it wasn't pleasant, but then neither was anything about this situation. Everything had come tumbling down around her. The new life in the country, her relationship with Oli, the dreams and aspirations of someone who just months earlier had felt trapped within *Poundslasher*, it had all turned to mud, she was there at the mercy of some of some lunatic, and she had no control over anything.

THE SHATTERED EAGLE

-FORTY-
That Was The Sound Of Non-Compliance.

Stretching his arms out wide, Oli began his 'getting up' routine, the yawning stretch being followed by a good old scratch before shuffling off to the bathroom to wake himself up under a moderately warm shower.

That had been a good night, although his pounding head was telling him that perhaps they should have called it a day an hour or so earlier, but he was now engaged! Going to actually get married. Of course he had thought about proposing many times before, including those long lingering daydreams whilst working at *Poundslasher*, staring like some love sick puppy towards the then oblivious object of his romantic imaginings, but it had ended up kind of just slipping out. Up until the minute the words left his lips and he fell to one knee he didn't plan on actually expressing it, making that giant leap into romantic bliss and a lifetime of commitment. Yet he had no regrets, none at all, just relief that Kate had actually said yes.

He opened the small frosted window, and looking out could see a combine harvester in the distance, a long plume of dust trailing behind it as it hoovered up the wheat, or whatever the hell that yellow stuff was. In an adjoining field a couple of horses galloped around, no doubt spooked by the huge monster causing such devastation just a couple of dozen yards away. It was all idyllic, and yet with all that space, just the other side of the high chain link fence, he was stuck within these four walls, as nice as they may be, still a prisoner. He thought about laying out in the gardens, catching some rays, perhaps reading one of the dozens of books Jay had brought for them. Oh Jeez he must be bored, reading a book, what was happening to him.

"Kate, Kate!" he called out, perhaps she fancied an afternoon of sunbathing too, although like him she was hardly the world's greatest reader, as far as he knew the last book she had read was some 'Tracy Beaker' story in her early teens.

No answer.

Bloody hell is there ever a time that girl isn't in that swimming pool, she'll wrinkle away to nothing if she isn't careful, there's only so long people can spend in chlorine water before they begin to mutate into some aquatic creature. Switching on the shower he grabbed his razor and a small cup, which he half filled with water.

Looking from the bathroom to the living area he saw the clock on the DVD machine, 12:33. Twelve Thirty Three! Why hadn't she woke him? She didn't normally let him sleep in past eleven.

Stepping into the shower he let out a small whoop as the colder than expected water vigorously expelled any last

THE SHATTERED EAGLE

traces of sleep he still had, realising that Kate must have used it earlier that morning, he hastily fumbled to adjust the dial, the powerful jets instantly warming to a more appropriate temperature. Safehaven didn't have much going for it, but this was a damn good shower, at home if someone in the flat below flushed their toilet or did the washing up he'd either get blasted with ice cold water or scalded, depending on the mood of the antiquated plumbing system, but here you could luxuriate in the firm jets as long as he liked, with no fear what so ever of an aggressive swing in temperature.

Once he prised himself out of the shower he ran the razor over his face, it was funny but since coming here he had developed a regime, he guessed it was just to pass the time, fill the long repetitive hours, but he now shaved daily. Pondering his genius money making plan he smiled to himself, seven blades!

It was inevitable anyway, the razor manufacturers always got all orgasmic every couple of years as they invented the new razor, identical to the old one but for an extra blade and an even slimier strip running along the top, by-pass the six blade revolution and go straight to the ultimate seven-blader, change shaving forever!

He wandered out of the bathroom wet and naked, a towel over his shoulder and walked to the fridge, pulling out a yogurt, stripping the top off and drinking straight from the carton, when all your food is free why bother scraping around the bottom of plastic pots with spoons, it only creates washing up after all. He drained what of the thick liquid was going to flow easily into his tipped back face and tossed the carton into the bin. Wrapping the towel around his waist he laid upon one of the leather settees, flicking the TV on with the remote control.

Ah daytime TV, auctions, house buying and in one case a combination of the two, what sort of diet of entertainment is that to feed the great unemployed of Britain. Oli watched as a middle class woman in her fifties told how she planned to sell her Grandfather's Great War medals so she could use the money towards buying some new conservatory furniture. Why did he watch this shite, it only made him angry, for pities sake, where's her morals? Of course Gloria Hunniford was most impressed with this plan, as was some twat in a tweed jacket and ludicrous yellow waistcoat, oh they should fetch well into three figures. Three figures, it's your Grandfather's war medals you heartless cow! Oh why did he let things like this wind him up, why was he even watching this crap?

He flicked through the channels for something more engrossing, but it was clearly going to be in vain, as he always ended up watching this repetitive toss.

So there he lay, watching television, whilst pondering why he was still lying there watching television, but this was different, this was Oliver Allen, fiancée to Kate Wallander lying down doing absolutely nothing, and that appeared to make the whole world a better place.

It was then he heard a faint ringing, like a mobile phone.
What was that?

THE SHATTERED EAGLE

***

It was the golden rule of Safehaven, no mobiles, laptops, no internet, no nothing that connected you to the outside world. Yet there it was ringing. He stood up, the towel falling to the floor, he left it there, if you can't walk around naked here, alone, where can you walk around naked.

The ringing appeared to be coming from his bedroom. He moved over to a chest of drawers, he was curious, what could it be? Opening the second drawer down the ringing became louder, he could see it glowing, shining through from under a pair of Kate's knickers.

He picked the mobile up, it was an old one, still had a keypad, he answered, cautiously, where had a mobile come from? "Hello?"

"Oliver Allen?" the voice on the other end replied.

"Errr yeah."

"Good. Listen Oliver Allen. I have Kate, you now need to listen very carefully…"

"Whoa, whoa, what did you say? You've got Kate?"

Was this some sort of wind up, but then who was there to wind him up?

"What part of listen carefully do you not understand, now be quiet, listen, and you take in every single syllable I say."

"But…"

"No fucking buts Oliver, no ifs, buts or fucking maybes, I said you listen, you better damn listen."

"OK, OK!"

"Good, hopefully we can now establish a meaningful dialogue, productively come to a resolution of what is a big problem for you Oliver, and an even bigger one for Kate, sitting here next to me.

"It's the ring, I want that ring. Don't bullshit me you don't know what I'm on about here, don't insult me with some arse wipe attempt at ignorance, because your lady here is in what I would describe as a pretty vulnerable situation, which will only be worsened considerably by anything I deem to be non-compliance on your part. Now Oliver I will ask a simple question. Have you got the ring?"

"Look, I don't know..."

"Arghhhhh!"

Oli heard a scream down the phone, it was female, it was Kate!

"Did I say answer me with a 'Look', you dumb prick, did I? That, that was the sound of non-compliance."

Oli could hear Kate whimpering in the background, horror had filled his every thought, that was Kate! This man had Kate. Oh God.

"That was the sound of Kate being punched in the face by yours truly, by someone who quite frankly doesn't give a shit what happens to your girlfriend, as long as he gets what he wants. Now what I want is that ring. Oliver, my dear Oliver, the next words you utter better be honest insightful words, they better be the fucking truth, so God help me if I hear anything other than the truth Kate here is not going to be happy, not happy at all. So you listen you little prick, you listen good. Do you have the ring?"

Oli was sitting on the floor, leaning against his bed, his guts were clenched up, he wanted to vomit, he wanted to scream, that was Kate he heard, that was her. How the hell did this arsehole know about the ring?

How was he getting out this?

Only one way.

"Yes. I have the ring. Please let me speak to Kate, let me…"

"That's a good answer Oliver, very good. Now I need to know we are talking about the same item here, because my guess is that someone in your situation is hardly likely to say 'No, I don't have it'. So please describe it to me."

Oli scrunched his eyes shut tight, pictured the object that was now causing him so much pain, he hadn't exactly scrutinised what he had in effect stolen from Abu Warsabi, he had only briefly looked at it, but it was distinctive.

"It's gold, thick, there's the French flag with an eagle on it."

Oli could barely talk, it was like his world had collapsed. But then he didn't actually have it, this ring. Gary had it, unknowingly, but he had it all the same. But he couldn't say that, not to this man, this man that had already hurt Kate, this man that could do anything he liked to her on a whim.

"Oliver I do believe you are telling me the truth, that my boy is very good news for you. This is a champagne occasion, a light a big bad fat cigar moment, because it means you have just saved Kate from a shit load of trouble my friend."

Oli heard him then talk to Kate.

"See it's all good Kate, dear little Oliver hasn't let you down, sure he shouldn't have stolen the God damn thing in the first place, but this has all the hallmarks of a happy ending."

He then continued to talk to Oli.

"I was just informing Kate here of the good news, she doesn't look as happy as I thought she would, unless those are tears of joy, you know what, I think she may be blaming you for her current predicament, that's a shame. She should focus on the bright side, accentuate the positives, but I suppose a smack in the face does that to people, loved ones keeping secrets does too. You really should be more honest with her Oliver. When this whole sorry mess is resolved you should have a good long chat, talk about honesty in a relationship."

Again Oli heard him talk to Kate.

"It's important isn't it Kate, honesty, trust, being straight with each other."

"I think she's agreeing with me Oliver, it's hard to tell, she seems so upset with you, I think this one may take more than a bunch of flowers from *Texaco* and some £3.99 bottle of wine, this is a biggie! So here's what will happen. You will not say a thing about this to anyone. I will repeat this just to make sure there is no confusion, you will not say a fucking thing about this to anyone. Now repeat that,

THE SHATTERED EAGLE

and say nothing else, to me Oliver to ensure we have a full understanding here."

"I will not say a thing to anyone." Oli answered his head bowed staring at the carpeted floor, the dejection and hopelessness evident in his broken voice.

"Good! See already we have an understanding, because I will hear if you tell any of those Policemen about this, I will hear, be sure of that, and if I do hear that you have spoken to anyone about this I will kill Kate. I will first inflict unimaginable pain on her, this is biblical shit Oliver, and then I will kill her. You need to understand that, this is the rule all our dealings will be built upon. There is no half ground here, talking to the Police ends things for Kate. I will still get the ring, but you will not get your girlfriend back. But that isn't how this is going to go down is it? That isn't a scenario any of us envisage. What will happen is you will leave the ring where you found this phone, it will be there by six o'clock tonight. At that time you will go swimming, far away from your little love nest. If anyone asks where Kate is you say she is asleep, she doesn't feel well, she's in bed. To keep things nice and simple that's it, there are no further instructions. Kate will then return to you by nine o'clock, and our business together is done. Clear?"

"How do I know you'll return Kate, please don't hurt her, but how can I trust you?"

"Oh you can't Oliver. This is what's called a leap of faith. But believe me if that ring isn't there at six o'clock this evening you can trust me on one thing. You won't have to worry about explaining a God damn thing to Kate. You can be sure of that!"

With that the phone went dead.

THE SHATTERED EAGLE

-FORTYONE-
Oli Hiding Under A Bed Where He Really Shouldn't Have Been.

"Shit, shit, shit!"

Oli was crouched on the floor, naked, his head buried in his hands, eyes scrunched shut.

What to do, what to do?

Think Allen, think!

Don't say anything to the Police. That was clear, but how could he be sure he was going to get her back, back safely, that was all he was concerned about, preserving that job at the prison was no longer his priority, he would have no qualms at all about fessing up to being a petty thief, it was the right thing to do surely?

But he couldn't take the chance, honesty was not an option he had the luxury of considering at this point in time. He had to get the ring back. He didn't even know if it was still in Gary's bag, what if he had found it already, was keeping it for himself, like some real life Gollum coveting his 'precious'. He only had a few hours, a few hours to leave it in the drawer, he thought of Kate, being hit or whatever, on the other end of a phone line, he had no idea where. He had to keep her safe, but he had no control, no power, no input into her destiny at all other than some 'leap of faith'.

What to do, what to do?

First he had to get some clothes on, he sprang to his feet, he only had a few hours, and sitting curled up feeling sorry for himself wasn't going to solve anything.

He pulled a tee-shirt on over his head, and put on a pair of football shorts. He needed to find that holdall of Gary's, preferably without him knowing, no definitely without him knowing, Gary was a bit of an old woman there's no way he could know about any of this he would definitely go to Frankie. Oli paced the room, think, think, you need to get the bag, chances are it's in Gary's room, the room where Gary is also likely to be, and his wife and kids. Think, you need that bag, no you need the ring, there's no choice.

Oli knocked on the door of room 307, there was no reply, he knocked again a little louder, and again no one answered. Were they still in bed, no it was gone midday. He reached for the door knob, and gently twisted it, as he suspected it was unlocked, why lock your room here, where you were allowed nothing of value, phones, laptops and any decent electrical kit was prohibited, what was to steal, and who was there to steal it?

This may transpire to be easier than he thought, just go in, find the bag, and get out. He entered the room, cat

THE SHATTERED EAGLE

burglary wasn't his speciality, he was scared shitless. He looked around, as usual when he went into the Westlake rooms he felt a sense of unfairness, why was their accommodation so much better than his?

But what did that matter, why was he even letting that enter his mind?

He scanned the living area, his eyes checking for any trace of that now priceless *Adidas* bag, there was no holdall there, he moved towards the bedrooms, Gary and Fran's room first, it was so bloody tidy, walking in he again looked around the floor, no bag, he opened the wardrobe door, Gary's clothes one side, all neatly pressed and Fran's the other, actually set out in a colour coded order like a cotton rainbow, creams through to blacks.

Wow! These people were tidy. Shoes neatly paired up at the bottom, jumpers and sweatshirts perfectly folded on the top shelf, but no holdall. Then he heard it, the door opening.

Damn!

He darted for the bedroom door, closing it silently before anyone could see it had been opened.

Shit!

He heard them entering the suite, muffled laughing, Amy boasting, "Yeah, well I swam ten lengths, when we go back to school I'm joining the swimming club, aren't I Mum."

"Yes darling," he heard Fran answer. "But you can keep practicing here, get really good and fast, that'll take your friends by surprise. Right, what are we going to have for lunch, and before you answer it's not going to be chips again, there's no point swimming everyday if we all come out of here looking like big fat chippy chips is there!"

Oli was pushed flat against the wall in the bedroom, he barely dare breathe, his heart pounding, what the hell was he thinking, what was he doing here, in someone's bedroom, like some out of control pervert. He sidled over to the immaculately made double-bed, this was something out a nightmarish 'Carry On' film, lowering himself to the floor like a caterpillar he inched under where Gary and Fran slept at night.

"If we all get changed, I'll phone for lunch, but no chips! I'll get us some sandwiches, alright?"

He could still hear Fran arranging the family's meal, he hadn't eaten since the previous night, and was now all too aware of just how hungry he was, yet it was far from his biggest concern just now.

"But Mum can't we…"

"No Josh, you can't have chips, there I'm psychic now, you don't even need to speak. Let's get changed, and Amy I'll brush your hair when you're dressed."

Oli heard the bedroom door open and close, and looked out from beneath his hiding place. He could see Fran's feet from under the bottom of the valance, a white towelling robe fell to the floor, followed by her stepping out of a black swimming costume.

Oh no, please no!

This was wrong, so bloody wrong, in so many ways. He heard Fran humming a tune and the mattress push down as

THE SHATTERED EAGLE

she sat on the side of the bed, he could still see her feet, just inches away from his face.

"Amy! Have you seen my hairbrush?" Fran was calling out to her daughter in the next room.

"No, it was in your room, when I last saw it."

"OK love." Fran called back, then under her breath he heard her mutter, "You didn't even look."

He saw the feet moving again and the mattress return to its previous height.

Fran was talking to herself.

"Where is the bloody thing?"

He could hear her checking around the room, the feet moving from one point to another, and as his head twisted to follow her movements he noticed silhouetted between him and the three inch gap where the valance allowed him sight, a hairbrush about five inches under the bed.

Then Fran's feet were running along the underside of the bed, her toes blindly searching for the elusive brush, he recoiled away from them, silently shifting out of reach, he could see the bloody hairbrush, at the foot of the bed, it would be just out of reach, he gently pushed it with his foot nearer the edge, as he could see Fran's foot searching around working towards it. He was lying rigid, hardly allowing the air to enter and exit his lungs at all for fear of giving himself away and starting a sequence of events that was never going to be sufficiently explained away.

At last Fran's feet found the brush, thank God! Her toes curled around the plastic bristles as she pulled it free from under the bed. Oli inched further towards the middle as again the mattress lowered. He heard the TV coming to life, it was a music channel, Fran was singing along, very out of tune, presumably as she brushed her hair, her feet no longer visible. As he turned his face away his cheek brushed against something, cold and rubbery. Bugger me Fran, if you had to smuggle something in with your personal possessions, it takes a certain degree of balls to make that one thing a bright blue *Rampant Rabbit*!

Oli thought how at some point in his life he may find that really funny, but this wasn't that time, it made him feel even dirtier, even more like some voyeuristic sexual deviant. That was Fran above him singing along to 'I'm sexy and I know It', unaware that for all innocent reasons he was violating her privacy, intruding and crossing all boundaries.

The main door opened again.

"Fran!"

It was Gary.

"I'm in here love," she replied.

Oli saw the Robe elevating from the floor, then Fran's feet reappearing, as the bedroom door again opened and closed.

"Why hello Mr Westlake, I've been expecting you."

He saw the robe fall to the floor. Oh no, oh no, please in the name of God no!

"Mmm, Mrs Westlake, so you have, and what do you expect me to do?"

THE SHATTERED EAGLE

Oh shit, Gary was speaking in the world's most unconvincing Sean Connery accent, surely not, please don't let this happen!

"Well Mr Westlake."

Oh bollocks Fran was now speaking like some pantomime villain, but also not a very good one.

"I expect you to scratch my back, then order the kids some food, you pervy old bastard!"

"Damn, you're such a tease."

Oli then saw it hit the floor, the bag, the *Adidas* holdall, it was there!

But then the bed sunk another level, oh no, he's on it too, he heard them laughing, Fran giggling. For crissake Gary, just scratch her back and piss off and get the food!

As if his wishes were granted Fran cut Gary off in his prime.

"That's it Gazmo, off you go, I need to dry my hair, I'll be out in a bit, go order us some food, and don't let them soft talk you into anything with bloody chips, and that goes for you too fat boy!"

"But Mrs West…"

"Never mind that, you can interrogate me all you like later, we need to get on, now get that food ordered."

As Gary left Oli heard the hairdryer go on.

Phew!

Within five minutes he saw Fran's feet slip into a pair of fluffy slippers and leave the bedroom, and thankfully the door shutting behind her. That had to be the longest twenty minutes of his life, he imagined he would be stuck there all day whilst Gary returned for an afternoon of spy based copulation.

He needed to get what he came for and get out, and quick, the sooner the ring was in that drawer the sooner Kate would be coming home, and that was all he wanted.

Peering out as he drew level with the valance he made sure it really was clear, but the room was thankfully empty, Oli slid out from under the bed, and grabbed the holdall, hurriedly unzipping it. Please God let it be there, please, he thought, as he peered in to see Gary's sweaty gym kit. He reached inside and ran his finger along the thin card base, groping along the edges, there it was, pulling it free he hastily inspected it before placing it on his middle finger. He returned the bag back to where Gary had left it, and walked to the window only to see what he knew he would, a straight drop three floors down, I don't think so, he thought, no way was he getting out that way.

He had no choice but to crawl back under the bed, he would just have to wait.

Two hours he had to wait, two long hours, praying Fran wouldn't come back in, two hours worrying himself sick over what would happen to Kate, two hours busting for a piss.

Then he heard them leaving, the Westlake clan off for one of their walks, even though they weren't allowed much further than the lawns in front of the house, the same

THE SHATTERED EAGLE

lawns he and Kate should have been lying upon sunning themselves, they went every day, just walking around.

He wondered what they found so fascinating, they must know every blade of grass, every petal on every flower by now, but to Fran and Gary it was an essential part of the day.

He gave it a couple of minutes, before he crawled out from under the bed, then through the window saw the Westlakes outside, thank God, he watched the kids run ahead, whilst Gary and Fran strolled behind hand in hand. He wondered if he and Kate would still be walking hand in hand in twenty years' time, for a brief moment he wondered whether he and Kate would ever be walking anywhere together again.

Like he had done so many times over the past couple of hours his mind went to a very dark place, he shuddered, what was she doing now? What was happening to her? He remembered the mocking voice on the phone, her captor, saying how unhappy she was with him, how he was to blame.

He was.

He knew that, but he had no way of knowing this would all pan out this way. He moved out of the bedroom, through the living area and after gently opening the door sneaked into the corridor, silently closing it behind him.

He breathed a long sigh, he had done it, he could now leave it where instructed, there was nothing more he could do but wait, wait and hope. Suddenly he felt a hand gripping his arm, the grip was hard, forcefully hard the strong fingers digging into his bicep, the surprise causing him to jump near out of skin.

"You, you're coming with me!" Frankie, maintained his hold on his upper arm. "This way, let's go."

"But, but…"

"Come on Oli, do me a favour, just shut up until we're away from here."

He dragged him along like some naughty schoolboy being taken to the Headmaster's Office until they reached the end of the corridor, Frankie opened what appeared to be a cupboard door, still holding him tightly, but Oli saw that it was in fact a darkened office, with the bank of TV screens lining one of the walls offering the only illumination.

As they got inside Frankie pushed him towards one of two office chairs.

"Right Casa-fucking-nova, sit down!" he pulled up the other chair. "We've got two female guests here and you're shagging both of them? Both of them! That's a 100% record! What's your deal Oli, are you Michael Douglas or something. Can't live without it, an addict for shagging or something is that it?"

"No!" Oli fired back. "It's not that at all, you are so far off!"

"Oh shit, I was hoping you'd say yes, because that was our best scenario, because now I'm going to have to ask why the hell you were breaking into someone else's sodding room, and then sneaking into their bedroom like some Peeping Tom, are you a Peeping Tom Oli? Is that

THE SHATTERED EAGLE

what we're talking about here, because I'm not that comfortable with that my friend, I'm not very fucking comfortable with that at all. That is not normal run of the mill behaviour for someone your age, and in a relationship, it's wrong, are you a wrong 'un? Well are you?"

"It's not like that. I didn't go into…"

"Look at the screens Oli! Look at the TVs, there's a camera in every bloody room, well except for the bedrooms and bathrooms, and that reminds me wear some clothes when you're parading about won't you, it's not nice for anyone that. Now please enlighten me why you were in the Westlakes bedroom this afternoon, because if you weren't shagging her, or cracking one out behind the curtain I'm curious as hell to establish what you were doing there!"

If you talk to anyone about this I will hear, and I will kill Kate! He had made it clear on the phone, but what to do now, if he couldn't tell Frankie the truth?

"OK, I was spying on Fran!" Oh shit did he really just say that! "I couldn't help it."

"Bollocks!" Howard replied. "You know that's bollocks, I know that's bollocks. I know that's bollocks, because in my line of work I get a feel for people. You know that's bollocks because you're lying through your crooked teeth. Your eyes are all over the place, your sweating the sweat of a liar, not a nonce, your leg's twitching like you're working a jackhammer with Parkinson's disease. Now you better start telling me the truth, which I guess is going to be something special if you'd rather make out you are some freaking pervert, because you're not leaving this office until I hear it."

Oli bowed his head, in a forlorn whisper he answered, "I can't."

"Oh Oli there's no such thing as can't, didn't your mother teach you anything? This is the land of Cans, of Wills not Won'ts, this is the Kingdom of Yes and definitely not No, now I'll ask again what the hell were you doing in the Westlakes bedroom, whilst poor old Fran was in there I might add?"

Oli felt like he was falling into a black pit, one lined with misery and despair. He began to sob, almost silently, sod it he couldn't keep this to himself anymore, he had no way of knowing whether Kate would even be freed if he did as he was told, what did he have to lose, well except for Kate that is. And forever?

"He'll kill her. He said he'd kill her if I tell you!" Oli blurted the words out, the words he knew he mustn't say, yet was so relieved to be able to speak out loud.

"What Gary? Gary will kill Fran?" Frankie's face was a picture of confusion.

"No, No! Someone has Kate, he phoned me."

"What!" Frankie stood up. "What do you mean someone's got Kate?"

"You're the one with the TVs, do you see her? Can you see her there?" Oli pointed at the screen that showed his living room, then tapped it, "Do you see Kate?"

Frankie picked up the phone.

THE SHATTERED EAGLE

"No!" Oli shouted. "Don't! Don't tell a soul, you can't, he said he'll know if I talk to anyone."

"Who, who said that?"

"The bastard on the phone, he hurt her," Oli shouted, then a lot quieter tone continued, "I heard it, he's got her."

"But that's not possible this place is safe, no one comes in, no one goes out, unless…"

"Go on, unless?"

"Unless they're Police." Frankie answered slowly, his voice trailing off as he spoke the words.

"Exactly, so now tell me how they got Kate out? Go on. That's why you can't tell anyone, so put the phone down please Frankie, I beg you."

"Shit. What do they want from you?"

"I don't know, I…"

"Come on Oli don't mug me off, they asked for something, or why else take her, now what did they ask for?"

Oli shrugged, his eyes now avoiding Frankie's gaze, the gaze that Oli knew was burning into him.

"Well go on," Frankie pushed.

"A ring." Oli mumbled, he knew now the truth was his only option. Frankie was the one person he thought he could trust, the one person who was so bloody obnoxious and brutally frank, that he had to be genuine, no one could be that convincing unless they were real.

"I took a ring, from Warsabi at the prison. Stole it whilst he was fighting with staff."

"Oh no, please, you're not telling me Warsabi has your girlfriend?" Frankie groaned, leaning back against a desk as he spoke, rubbing his face with both his hands.

"No it wasn't him, it was one of the blokes who sprang him, I recognised the voice."

"This isn't happening Oli my boy, this isn't bloody real. I'm in some far away parallel universe populated by stupid fuckwits who act like total retards. That can be the only feasible explanation for this shit you're telling me! In a minute Doctor-fucking-Who is going to land in his Tardis and bring me back to earth, far away from the planet Mong and its retarded king Oliver bloody Allen!"

Frankie paced around, he kicked his chair and it wheeled across the floor into a bank of electrical hardware, all the screens flickered off and on again. He was making no attempt to disguise his anger, his face had reddened, a vein on his temple almost visibly pulsating, "I don't believe you, well actually I do believe you, which is even more disturbing. One of the three fucking horsemen of the apocalypse phones you, and you don't think this something you ought to tell me? He tells you he's taken Kate, the woman you supposedly love, and it doesn't enter your tiny teeny shitty little mind to tell me that either? And I don't even want to know about a bloody ring you half inched!"

Oli sat there his head bowed.

"Go on," Frankie spoke up, calmer and softer, almost as if he cared, "Tell me Oli, tell me about it all."

THE SHATTERED EAGLE

"I got the call about eleven thirty, it was a mobile, in one of the drawers in the bedroom, when I answered he told me he wanted the ring, he said he had Kate, I heard him hit her, her crying. He kind of taunted me, but said I was to leave it there, in the drawer and make sure I was out of the room at six. He told me not to talk to anyone, he would hear if I did, and he would kill Kate."

Frankie sat down in the chair he had moments earlier kicked across the room. The aggression was now completely gone, he was concerned. "There's someone on the inside," he said to himself, almost as if Oli wouldn't hear. "One of us."

Tapping his fingers on the table, sucking on a biro, he turned to Oli, "Tell me about the ring?"

Oli looked up, ashen, the shame and guilt written across his face, "I was processing Warsabi the morning he escaped, going through his property, he didn't have much, I was opening an envelope with the ring in it, when he went for Jim, Jim Bolton, who I was working with."

Frankie pricked up, like Oli had plugged him into the mains, the mention of Jim shocking the caring concerned look from his face.

"Go on," he said.

"Well…"

"Go on Oli just say it."

"I put it in my pocket. Stole it."

"Jesus Oli, you never disappoint do you?"

Again Frankie was on his feet, still sucking on the biro, "Why the hell were you in the Westlakes bedroom? That's puzzling me. I'm sorry to jump ahead, but I really want to clear this one up before we go any further?"

"It was the ring, when I arrived I stashed it away in Gary's bag, he'd left it in the medical room. I needed to get it back, so I went to find it, they came back whilst I was looking. Look, I shouldn't have said anything, he said not to, he'll kill Kate."

"No, no, I wished you'd told me about this ring earlier, I really do. You should know, Jim Bolton's dead, he was murdered at his house, had seven shades of crap knocked out of him first, now I'm no fucking Einstein but I'm guessing this ring played a big part in Mr Bolton's demise. Where is it now?"

Oli held his hand up.

"Let me see." Frankie held his hand out.

Oli pulled it free of his finger and handed it over. Frankie walked over to another desk and switched a lamp on, "Hmm," Frankie held it close to the light, and spoke, again as if thinking aloud. "It's nice, in fact it's pretty impressive, but why would anyone kill for it?"

THE SHATTERED EAGLE

-FORTYTWO-
Oli Confides In Yogi-Bear And Mummy Smurf.

Oli left the small darkened room in a state of stupefied shock.

Jim was dead?

Killed, by the same people who took Warsabi and Kate. This was a nightmare that knew no limit, that never ceased to horrify and scare. He wandered down the corridor, tears moistening his bloodshot eyes, he was an emotional wreck. He stopped by a water cooler, and rested his back flat against the wall as he lowered himself down into a crouch, his arms tightly embracing his shins as he cried into his knees.

He heard the ping of the lift, and the sound of the doors sliding open, as the Westlakes emerged from inside, he looked up, his face red, and streaked with tears and snot, he felt so helpless, so lost.

Gary rushed over.

"Oli? Oli are you alright, what's up mate?"

Oli sobbed, "Please Gary just leave me alone."

But Gary continued, clearly concerned to see his new friend in such a state.

"Is there something me or Fran can do, what is it?"

Oli stared at Gary, looking at the genuine concern on his face, he was like a father figure, well maybe uncle, there wasn't much wrong with the Dad he already had. He was a friend, yes, even though they had only known each other such a short time, but he admired him, admired the relationship he had with Fran, the way he interacted with Amy and Josh, his always positive take on things.

He and Kate had spoken just the other day and decided that if Gary was to be a cartoon animal - it was a game they used to play at *Poundslasher* - he would probably be Yogi Bear, only even cuddlier, whilst Fran would probably be Mummy Smurf, the as yet un-invented matriarch of the little blue people, who would be, well she would be bloody lovely, that's what she would be.

Another wave of guilt surged over him, the thought of intruding in their bedroom, violating their trust. He needed to be honest with these people, they deserved it, he was also all too aware that if Safehaven was the most inappropriately titled place in the world, then Gary should know, it wouldn't be fair to not tell him.

"Sorry Gary, can we talk?"

Gary led him back into 307, his arm around his shoulder as they went, whilst Fran hurried the kids into their bedroom, to watch TV, as 'Mum and Dad need to speak to Oli.'

THE SHATTERED EAGLE

Over the next ten minutes Oli retold his story to them both, well almost all of it, he wisely omitted the part about not actually having the ring until he stole it back from Gary's bag, also leaving out hiding under Gary's bed whilst Fran stripped off, that would have been awkward, in fact that would have been a bloody great deal breaker for their embryonic friendship.

But he did tell of Kate's disappearance, the phone call, Frankie finding out. How he thought they weren't safe there, didn't know who they could trust, well apart from them of course, and he was pretty sure Frankie.

"I'm stopping with you Oli," Gary said, "at least until Kate's back. What's Frankie planning? What's he going to do?"

-FORTYTHREE-
Not a very Safehaven.

Frankie paced around the empty office, shit crap shit! It was one of his own behind it, one of his people who had handed over Kate to some deranged lunatic who was willing to kill her for a bloody ring.

He had rewound the CCTV over and over, Jay DeHavalland of all people, there she was leading Kate out to her red *Mini*, clear as bloody daylight. He had big plans for that girl, supposedly off for the day to visit her seriously ill mother.

Lying bitch!

She was a bent copper, the worst thing in the world, well the worst thing, apart from Paedo kiddy fiddlers, filthy rapists and murdering bastards. But still close all the same.

But was she working alone?

Whoever this kidnapper was, he had connections. Pozzo, Jay, who else was there lurking out there, taking a government wage whilst betraying colleagues and the very people they were paid to protect? These guys were like a small army, they seemed to know everything, could even waltz someone clean away from a place that was supposed to be so secure they called it Safehaven.

THE SHATTERED EAGLE

How did they know Oli was even there?

That was need to know stuff, of course he and DeHavalland knew, as did Pete, Sylvia and Felix, but someone else must have pointed them into Jay's direction, like they must have given them Sergio Pozzo, surely those two weren't already on the pay roll? What sort of money does it take to corrupt people within minutes of needing them, turning decent honest coppers into lying scum?

Who could he trust?

Oli had made it clear the person that had Kate had said he would know if he spoke to anyone, and kill her. How many others were in this deep pocket? He only had to alert the wrong person, and that was it.

What to do?

It was well gone four, they were coming for the ring at six. Presumably Jay would be returning from a miraculously cured Mrs DeHavalland Senior. He couldn't call it in, could he?

It was too risky.

Should he confront DeHavalland, pile so much pressure onto her she would have to tell him everything? But what if she didn't know everything, didn't know where Kate was, was just a mule, carrying the goods from A to B?

What if it wasn't even her collecting the ring? Should he leave the ring in the drawer, play along? But how could he follow it, tail DeHavalland wherever the treacherous bitch went, he couldn't even follow her out of the gate without it being impossible for her not to see him.

Damn it!

***

Forty five minutes later Jay DeHavalland returned to Safehaven. Frankie saw her car coming through the gate, and then at that moment he decided what he was going to do, how he was going to play it.

Walking to the lobby he sat down in one of sofas, watching the door, Jay was bent, it was just a mess, the whole thing now thrown up in the air.

Jay ambled through the entrance, she looked dejected, concerned, worried, like any daughter should with a seriously ill mother, but then her mother wasn't ill, it was all a lie.

"Ah Jay, how's your Mum?" he casually asked, rising to his feet and walking beside her.

"Not so good Guv," she replied. Oh she was good, that concerned look etched into her face, playing the worried daughter perfectly.

"I'm going to have to go back in a bit, they want me there, for the operation, it's pretty touch and go, I hope it's OK with you, but really I have no choice."

"No, no, of course it's OK, family must come first in my book, I just hope she's going to be alright, you must be worried sick."

"You've no idea Guv."

Oh he had an idea, he had a very big idea.

"Look Jay, I want to sort out some leave for you, give you a bit of space with your Mum, come to my office a minute, we'll go through what you need."

THE SHATTERED EAGLE

"I'm a bit pushed Guv, can we do it when I get back?"

Frankie's tone changed, his face no longer caring, no longer wearing a mask of kindness.

"Bullshit over DeHavalland, come with me!"

She turned to move away.

"Now!" he called to her.

He grabbed her wrist and ushered her through to one of the glass fronted offices in the lobby, she looked confused, puzzled by what was happening, he pulled a cord which closed the venetian blinds.

"Sit down."

Jay hesitated.

"I said sit down!" he snarled.

This time she perched on the edge of the seat, her hands clenched tight together in her lap.

Frankie wasted no time. "We can either dance around together for an hour, pissing about playing games, pretending we don't understand what we're both on about, or we can cut to the chase. Now I'm going to take that latter path, which by my reckoning means you better do so too. Now I don't want you to say a solitary word until I finish speaking, then when you do speak it better be worth hearing. Have no doubts your career is fucked DeHavalland, really fucked, what we're dealing with here is just how long you are going be locked away for, how many years of being finger fucked by some butch bitch with facial tattoos who hates coppers, but really despises bent coppers even more. Because that is your new career path darling. There is no negotiation. Now here comes the bit where you talk, and remember cut to the chase because I'm hanging you out no matter what, but this does definitely make a difference, OK. Now one simple question. Where's Kate?"

Jay was physically trembling, her eyes pink and swollen, full of saline tears, flowing silently down her cheeks.

"I don't know, honestly Guv, I don't know."

Frankie looked at her, his eyes looking through her, penetrating her very being. "Don't you ever refer to me as Guv again, ever! Now where is she?"

"I'm telling the truth I don't know."

Frankie picked up a hole punch from his desk and, without any warning or indication of what was to follow, threw it at Jay, it smashed into her upper body, she recoiled, then crumpled forward, her hand clutching her shoulder.

"You can't do that!" she hissed. "You've fucked it up Frankie you bullying bastard, fucked it up big time. Either arrest me, and make sure you get my lawyer, or let me go, either way nothing's going to happen until after six."

Frankie pulled his chair up close, her head was partly turned away, she was actively avoiding the gaze, the gaze that could whither stone if ever unleashed in its direction. He drew his face in near to hers, speaking directly into her ear. "That was a big mistake DeHavalland, that was probably the most stupid thing you have ever done, even more so than kidnapping my witness's girlfriend, that has just pissed me off, that has just shown me what a stupid bitch you really are. Now let's imagine you never said that

THE SHATTERED EAGLE

last sentence. Let's imagine we can turn back the clock two minutes, let's remember in this room there is no tape recorder, no video equipment, no little blonde secretary taking down notes, just you and me. Now I'll ask again, and you better give this some serious consideration, where is Kate? Where is she Jay?"

"I really don't know." Jay sobbed, "I don't."

"Then where are you to take the ring?"

"I can't say, I can't, he's got my Mum." Jay broke down in tears, she was sobbing uncontrollably, "He's got my Mum!"

Frankie stood back, looking down on the Detective, who until just an hour or so earlier he trusted as much as anyone he knew, her face in her hands, he gently shook his head.

"No he doesn't does he?" he said quietly and slowly. "He hasn't got Mummy at all. No more than she's seriously ill. I spoke to your dear old Mum not an hour ago, that's why I know she's not in hospital having a brain transplant, open heart surgery, or a redundant womb ripped out. That's how I already knew she wasn't wrapped in gaffer tape with a bloody claw hammer on the floor next to her. No she was watching 'Deal or No-fucking-Deal' whilst filling her fat face with *Chocolate HobNobs*, so either you start giving me the truth, or you are going down for the rest of your life, because if for any reason what so ever Kate Wallander doesn't come back tonight you're doing life, and I mean that!"

Jay stopped sobbing, she turned to face him and reluctantly spat out, "I'm to take it to a car park, at a Motorway Services. He will hand Kate back. I was to leave her at the next junction, give her a mobile, then I was gone."

"Gone?"

"Oh then I was gone so far away you would never find me."

"Where's the meet?"

"Oh come on. Give me something to bargain with Frankie. If this is so bloody off the radar, no rules, no regulations, the Frankie Howard School of Doing it Bad, then I want some of that leeway, I want some of your rule bending, because when they find out I've had them over I don't want to be in prison, just waiting to have my throat slashed by some dirty slag for two hundred quid. Do you hear me, they've already shown how far they reach, what they're capable of. Do you think I'm the only one they've paid off? They've got millions, and I mean millions, how do you think they found me in the first place?

"Your squad's rotten, bent, they're paying people from the top down, you stupid ignorant wanker, do you really think you can do anything to stop it? Think about it Frankie, who else is in their pocket, Sylvia? Pete? Felix? Think about it hard, they're untouchable. The only reason they've not paid you off is that you're so bloody stupid you'd probably declare it on a tax return.

"Now you've got less than an hour, you need what I know more than you need me in prison. Now I may make

THE SHATTERED EAGLE

you feel sick at this moment, absolutely revolt you, but you better realise you need me Frankie, so now you shut up and listen. I'll deliver the ring, what happens after that I don't give a damn. But if you want that girl back you better play along. You can follow me there, do what you like once it's done, but I'm going to be out and on my way. That's my deal to you. Now, as much as I think you are a truly unpleasant prick of a man, and I really do, I do think you are also a man of your word. Here's my deal, and you better listen to it. You swear that you'll let me walk. In return I'll take you to the drop, and once away safely I promise to tell you everything I know. But only once I'm away. I'll tell you it all, who else on the squad is bent, who isn't. Now you want that don't you? So swear it Frankie."

He was stunned. "Shit."

"Yes, shit. But one more thing, you better be sure you actually want to know everything, because once you do, you'll be as damned as I am."

-FORTYFOUR-
The Three Stooges Go To Newport Pagnall.

Auguste Fredericks watched as the rain streaked down the windscreen, forming rivulets as it neared the bottom of the glass, next to him sitting in the passenger seat was Kate Wallander, her hands again bound by cable ties, the bruise on her cheek swollen and raw, accentuated by her pale pallor. Gus stared straight ahead, silent, just watching the large drops of water converging as they raced to the bottom of the screen. He was reluctant to talk to her, all too aware that the last thing he needed was some form of relationship, an understanding, because he didn't need to understand how she was feeling, he was sure it was shit, but that wasn't his concern.

They were parked up at the edge of the large car park, just a few yards to one side the host of picnic benches, which were crammed with hungry families just a couple of hours earlier, but were now empty. An endless stream of traffic drove by, a relentless procession of diesel fumes and pollution, each one throwing up mist and spray, and slightly rocking the van as they went. Newport Pagnall,

THE SHATTERED EAGLE

one of the busiest Motorway Services in the country, it truly was an odd place for such a transaction, you couldn't have made it more public if it had been in the middle of Oxford Street, yet they were invisible, totally anonymous, no one noticing the kidnapper and his victim in one of the hundreds of vehicles parked up.

"You know, I ought to kill you now Kate, I really should." He couldn't keep his silence any longer, it had really annoyed him, gripped his shit, did Allen really think he wouldn't hear? "I know that boyfriend of yours has broken the terms of our agreement, a little bird has told me that much. There's a good chance when this goes down they're going to want to turn it into some sort of fucking circus, and you know I ain't no clown. I'm here for one thing only, and when I get it I'm off. They're not taking me for some fool, it ain't happening. No way."

She said nothing, just sat silently gazing into whatever was in front of her. She hadn't spoken a word since he had punched her whilst he was talking to her boyfriend on the phone, she hadn't pleaded, begged, or as much as whimpered after that, he had to admit he admired her for it, she had grown strong, defiant. He knew in reality he didn't plan to kill her, that would have served no purpose, although he liked the idea of hurting Oliver Allen, there was nothing to really gain by it, and every one of his actions had to have a reason.

His phone rang, he allowed it to ring five times before picking it up. "You got it?... Good... No there's been a change of plan... What do I mean? What I mean is there's been a fucking change of plan, rearrangements amendments, strategic alterations... No you listen. You see that bridge that goes over the road, you walk over it, come to the other side of the road, and walk straight out. I'll tell you what to do next. Now I'm watching, I'm watching very closely, make sure you're alone, I appreciate this has been a difficult situation, people may be with you, or listening in, so I'll say it clearly, so any eavesdroppers are sure on this, I only want a little ring, an inanimate object of very little worth, everybody else wants Kate here, they want her back safe and sound, now that sounds a fair swap to me, in fact they're getting a lot more than I do. Don't let anyone's quest for justice go clouding what is a very simple fact."

With that he hung up.

Frankie was sitting in the front of his car, six speeding lanes between them and Fredericks, saying nothing to Jay as she got out, slamming the door behind her, then running towards the bridge, he just watched her run, her head leaning forward into the pouring rain, not even looking back at them.

"He's a clever Fucker," he quietly said to his two companions who were sitting in the back.

"What does that mean, did you hear Kate? Did she say anything?" Oli desperately asked.

Frankie suspected he shouldn't have brought Oli along, in fact he knew he shouldn't have, it was obvious he'd react like this at every opportunity, he was too personally

THE SHATTERED EAGLE

linked, and how the hell Gary joined the party he still had no idea, yet that was who he was with.

Why did he agree to it? He had three perfectly good Officers, who had guns at that, kicking their heals back at the Red House, and he turns up to some messed up hostage exchange with nothing but the victim's boyfriend and some computer repair man. He needed his head examining.

"Of all the misguided fuck ups I've been involved in during twenty years on the force this has to probably be the biggest." He announced whilst banging his hands against the steering wheel of the car they were sheltering within, not answering Oli at all.

Gary spoke, before his friend had a chance, "Yeah, never mind that, you had no choice, but did you hear Kate?"

Frankie ignored the question again, as if only talking to himself. "Look at us, I'm with Laurel and fucking Hardy, or is it the Three Stooges, with me the biggest comedian of all. What a balls up, why didn't I see this coming, why?"

"What do you mean?" Gary asked, leaning forward between the two front seats.

"A bridge over the motorway, no way to follow without being seen, no way to pursue afterwards, he's on the wrong carriage way, of course he is, why the hell wouldn't he be. Bollocks, he's right, it is just a ring, and Kate's all that matters now, we were never going to nick him anyway. I knew we'd played this wrong!"

They had to go through with it, Frankie knew that, let Jay take the ring. He was right when he had said they couldn't do any harm just observing, being there to bring Kate home when it was all done, but now they were actually watching from the other side of the road, totally and utterly useless, it all seemed shit. Still, doing as the kidnapper said wasn't a bad thing for Kate was it? If there were no problems for the kidnapper surely he would be more likely to release her. Wouldn't he?

Yeah, in some dreamland, but Frankie had though played an altogether different hand, couldn't let Gary or Oli know, but really he had no choice.

He watched as Jay walked into the buildings, past the *Burger King* and *M&S*, on her way to hand over the ring, that blasted bloody ring, to hopefully set Kate free, return her to the stupid dick sitting in the back of his car.

Once she was out of sight he closed his eyes and sighed, the other two had immediately darted out of the car, over to the wooden fencing that separated the car park from the grass verge which led to the heaving M1. He slowly stepped out of the *BMW*, turning the collar on his Harrington Jacket up around his ears. Instantly he felt sodden, the greyness all around perfectly encapsulating his mood, as he strolled over to where the others stood. In his hand he had a set of binoculars which he drew up to his eyes, the relentless gloom becoming literally magnified through the lens. Past the clouds of water thrown up by the speeding motorway traffic he saw Jay emerge from the other side, breaking into a hurried jog, as she made her way to the grey van parked by the picnic area, her head still bowed to shield herself from the rain. The passenger door of the van opened and something was bundled out onto the tarmac.

Oh no, please no, he thought.

"Kate!" Oli screamed in vain, the cars, lorries and coaches drowning out his desperate call.

Immediately Jay got in and the van sped off on its unimpeded journey to the slip road.

"No, no, no," Frankie hissed under his breath, he couldn't see the bundle anymore, it was obliterated by the traffic re-joining the road onto the heaving motorway, God please let her be alright.

Oli and Gary ran for the foot bridge, Frankie just stayed there leaning against the fence watching the kidnappers disappearing down the road.

"Oh baby, you played that well, that was a thing of sheer fucking beauty," Fredericks boomed. "We had them over Jay-Jay, good and proper, are you sure it was just them."

Jay was laughing, "Of course, Howard is paranoid, doesn't trust anyone. I couldn't believe how stupid that arrogant prick was, he bought the lot, he really thought I'd fuck you over for…. Look out!"

A blue transit van over took them at speed and swerved in front of them, the back doors swinging open instantly. Another two unmarked cars, blue lights flashing, swung in beside and behind them.

"Armed Police, Armed Police! Do not move, put your hands on the dash board. Armed Police!"

At least a dozen Policemen surrounded the van, weapons pointing at the two people within. Gus knew not to react, these weren't Community Support Officers, or local plod on push bikes. He just slowly raised his hands.

"You fucking bitch, I'll kill you!"

"No, this wasn't me, I swear, this wasn't…"

But before Jay DeHavalland could finish explaining away her part in this betrayal the doors to the grey van were pulled open and both Gus and her hauled out and laid flat face down on the floor, into the puddles and oil soaked pools of the road. Cuffs were thrown on both of them as Police stood guard, their *Heckler and Kochs* pointing at the prone prisoners.

"Stay still, do not move!"

One of the Officers rubbed Gus down, he passed a pistol to another, who placed the *Beretta* into a clear evidence bag. Another colleague, in plain clothes, but for a protective vest and a Police baseball cap, was handed a wallet, he opened it and scanned the contents.

"Auguste Fredericks, I am arresting you for the murder of Robert McKinnen, George Morton and James Bolton. You do not have to say anything. But it may harm your defence if you fail to mention when questioned anything you later rely on in court."

Inspector Craig Lovan had never arrested anyone for murder before. It felt good, saying those words. His mind darted back to the corpses, first the two at the scene of the minibus from Forest Green, then being called to Jim

THE SHATTERED EAGLE

Bolton's house, the poor man tortured and beaten before being executed in cold blood, and this was the person responsible.

He then moved to the bedraggled, treacherous Policewoman lying face down in the filth and muck. "Jayne DeHavalland, I am arresting you for Kidnap, False Imprisonment and Improper Conduct in a Public Office. You do not have to say anything. But it may harm your defence if you fail to mention when questioned anything you later rely on in court."

Oli ran to where Kate was already being attended to by Paramedics, he fell to his knees beside her.

"I'm so sorry Kate, I'm really sorry, I had no idea, I can't say just how sorry I am."

The rain was soaking his tee-shirt and his hair was matted to his head, it was impossible to tell tears from the rain running across his cheeks.

Kate looked at him, he felt sick seeing her like this, her eyes appeared hollow, empty, she looked ten years older, her face was bruised, those eyes full of so much sorrow.

"This is down to you Oli, he was right, do you even care?"

The words had been delivered quietly, barely audibly, but he had heard them as if they were screamed in his face.

"Please Kate." But he knew no there were no excuses, this was all down to him, she could have been killed, for what, his light fingered greed and selfishness. He wanted to say so much more but instead just muttered, "But I love you."

"No Oli, leave me alone."

She was lifted into the Ambulance, he went to follow, stepping up, but was stopped by one of the Paramedics, as Kate declared, "No, I don't want you to come, I really don't. Please just leave me alone."

With that the door was slammed shut, and the Ambulance pulled off, the blue lights illuminating the grey gloom all around.

Oli turned to one of the Policemen standing by, "Where are they taking her?"

"Sorry Sir, I really can't say, but she'll be safe. I promise."

"But I'm her fiancée!"

"I know Sir, like I said, she'll be safe."

Gary stood by, he put his hand on Oli's shoulder, giving it a reassuring squeeze, "She'll come round mate, the main thing is she's alright."

Frankie walked over the bridge, and made his way through the now backed up traffic, towards Craig Lovan, his arm extended, "Thanks Craig, I can't thank you enough." He said, shaking the DI's hand firmly.

"No not at all, the pleasure was all mine."

"I've got a couple of things to sort out, I may be an hour or so, can you hold on talking to them until then?"

Lovan smiled, a big rain drop dripping from his nose as he nodded, "Don't worry, you won't miss a thing."

THE SHATTERED EAGLE

-FORTYFIVE-
We're Upping Sticks, Moving Out.

"Sylvia, listen carefully…," Frankie wasn't sure about everything, but he was sure that those remaining at Safehaven were at risk, and a serious one at that, he had to move them and it had to be done by someone he knew 100% was incorruptible. He'd like to have thought that all his team came under that umbrella, but the actions of Jay, and what she had said, had made him ask questions, which deep down he knew were just ridiculous. So he had phoned the one person who he was positive he could genuinely rely on, although he was still so angry with himself for doubting the others.

"Are there people around you that can hear?" he continued, standing to one side of the sodden picnic area, away from anyone else, his hair soaked flat to his head, and his jacket proving totally inadequate to the prevent his shirt from becoming waterlogged.

"No Guv' I'm at home, Graham's out, what is it?"

"I need you to pick up Fran Westlake and her two kids from Safehaven, it's urgent, we need to get them out. Phone me when you've got them."

But Guv…"

"We need to do this straight away, it's been compromised."

"Compromised? Are you OK Frankie?"

"Yeah I'm fine, but it's all got very messy, we've just nicked Jay, I can't talk now. Look Sylv' this may sound a stupid question, but I can trust you can't I?"

He heard Sylvia's voice take on an angry tone, "What do you mean can you trust me! Of course you bloody can. What's this about?"

"I'll fill you in later, but for the moment don't tell anyone where you are going, no one at all, not Felix, not Pete, nobody. Do you understand?"

"Not really, but I'll do it all the same."

Frankie walked back over the bridge with Gary and Oli.

"We're upping sticks, moving out, it's not safe back there," he said as they moved away from the scene of the dramatic events that occurred not half an hour earlier.

"Where to?" Gary asked.

"I haven't a clue, but I've arranged for Fran and your kids to be picked up."

"What about Kate?" a very wet Oli said, he wasn't even wearing a jacket, just a drenched tee-shirt, ironically emblazoned with a giant sun with a big smiley face and sunglasses, "I can't just leave her, I can't!"

"I'll sort something out with Kate." Frankie replied, although with not a little bit of irritation coming through.

THE SHATTERED EAGLE

He liked both of them, even Oli - and he was a knob, but they needed to let him think, get his head together.

What to do now? It was about to open up for him. He had Auguste Fredericks, his route to Warsabi, cuffed up in the back of a van on his way to a holding cell in Northampton. He also had Jay, although he'd be damned if he was letting her walk no matter what he had said, he'd find out who the wrong 'uns were, but she wasn't getting off, not after what she had done. Usually his word was everything to him, but she had crossed a line that meant he wouldn't lose any sleep what so ever about lying to her.

But Kate, what to do about her? There didn't appear to be any physical harm to the girl, but would he be able to get her to come back to Oli, he didn't really know her at all, but she had to be put somewhere safe. It would be so much easier if she was with the boy, as he was now struggling to find one safe house, let alone two.

Then there was his team, he trusted Sylvia he had worked with her for over ten years now, he had to trust her, he had put Fran and the two Westlake children into her care, but the others? Before this he would have put his very life in their hands, no doubt, but now? Stop it man, he told himself, you're over analysing everything, Jay was fucking with your head, of course Felix and Daggett are straight. But he had used Craig Lovan, not just because he was practically in place already, just a few miles down the road, but because he had more faith in the man he had only met for a few minutes than he did the team he had been working with for years.

What had the bitch done to him, he was so used to being in control, being the one in charge, pulling the strings, not dangling from them.

Where was safe for him to send Oli and the Westlakes? There were a couple of safe houses they used regularly, but if either Pete or Felix were bent then they were non-starts. His place, his home, was neither secure nor big enough.

He turned to Gary, who was still consoling Oli.

"Gary we need somewhere safe for the next few days, somewhere you, your family, Oli and eventually Kate can stop. Is there anywhere you can think of, anywhere at all?"

He phoned Sylvia back.

"Sylv', it's Frankie, when you pick them up I need you to take them to this address…"

THE SHATTERED EAGLE

-FORTYSIX-
Hello, Henderson Residence.

Clive Henderson was in his living room, smoking a large cigar, *Sky Sports* was showing the golf from Atlanta on his 62" 3D television. Of course the luxury of the cigar would mean a rushed ten minutes of frantic hiding the fact later, spraying *Febreze* around, burying the evidence at the bottom of a bin, cleaning his teeth and sucking a packet of mints, but a small price to pay for keeping Sheila oblivious to the fact that he actually had something he enjoyed in his life, something that was truly his alone.

The phone rang.

"Hello, Henderson Residence, Clive Speaking."

Jesus, Gary thought, it's like going back in time, what's wrong with just saying 'Yeah, who is it?'

"Hello Clive, Gary here."

"Gary! Thank heavens, we've been so worried about you both, where the Devil are you, how is Francess and the children, what on earth's going on?"

"Look Clive I can't talk too much now, I need a huge favour, and it's a big one."

"Of course, whatever, just say."

"We need somewhere to stay for a few days."

Gary heard fevered coughing, as Clive inhaled too deep on his cigar, then the line went quiet.

"Hello Clive?"

"Oh yes, sorry, errr, yes, that would be great. Yes why not? When are you coming?"

"We're on our way."

There was a pause, probably Clive realising what he had committed to, before he replied in what Gary perceived as being a curt manner, "Oh right."

Gary winced on the other end of the line, hesitation in his voice as he asked, "And Clive, will it be OK if a friend joins us, you have plenty of room haven't you?"

"Why not," the 'pleased to hear from you' voice had certainly disappeared somewhere between the words 'huge favour', and 'we're on our way'.

Clive and Sheila lived in one of the more expensive areas of Buckinghamshire a small village about three miles outside of Leighton Buzzard, Fran and Gary had nicknamed them Lord and Lady Mentmore, as they couldn't go more than 10 minutes when introduced to new people without mentioning that they lived there. In truth Sheila and Clive's was probably the last place Gary would have chosen to stay, no matter for how short a period of time, but when he was asked by Frankie it was all he could think of, the only place he could imagine no one would believe he was hiding away in, including gun toting

THE SHATTERED EAGLE

homicidal maniacs. It was miles from the nearest shop, the Post Office had long gone, and even the village pub had closed down, it was the ideal location to become invisible within.

Frankie had phoned Sylvia and directed her to take the Westlakes straight there when she picked them up, they would meet them at the Hendersons. He planned to drop Gary and Oli off, then head straight back to Northampton to meet up with Lovan. From the Motorway Services they were only about half an hour away from Clive's, but he was keen to get back, so he travelled with the blue lights on his unmarked *BMW*, hammering through the lanes once off the Motorway.

Sheila and Clive's house was a large converted estate workers home, overlooking a picturesque village green and the fields beyond, although there was no view to be seen by the time they arrived as it was dark and still raining, Gary knew that on a clear day you could literally see for miles. Clive greeted them at the door.

"Come in, come in, please get in the dry."

They walked in, and as they entered, Clive made a poor attempt at clearing his throat, whilst nodding at their feet.

"Oh of course." Gary said, as he slid his shoes off.

Oli did likewise, whilst Frankie simply said, "Right I'm out of here, you've got my number."

Without even saying a hello, goodbye or how do you do to Clive he was jogging back to his car and driving off.

"Well come in, come in, I'm Clive Henderson," he said to Oli whilst holding out his hand, Oli shook it, whilst introducing himself.

"Oli Allen, I'm a friend of Gary's."

"Great, any friend of Gary's and all that," he said, not exactly 100% sincere, but still welcoming enough. "Good to see you Gary, great, really great, I must say wasn't expecting you to call like that, where is the lovely Francess, and Josh and Amy?"

"They're following on Clive, should be a couple of hours or so, I'm sorry to be a nuisance, I'll explain all. Sheila not at home?"

"No not yet, she's at her *Zumba* class, please come through sit down."

Gary noticed a small scar on Clive's forehead, he guessed it was related to the suitcase incident Fran had told him about back in the hospital.

"So how are you and Sheila?" he asked their new host.

"Oh we're fine, just great," Clive kind of tailed off mid-sentence, Gary knew they were fine, but recognised Clive was probably exaggerating just a lot when he said great.

They went through to the living room, Oli was just following, he felt totally lost, he still wanted nothing else other than to go to Kate, beg her forgiveness, and bring her home, to their real home not this place.

It had to be noted that the Hendersons house was wonderfully decorated, the carpet was deep as un-mown grass, the walls covered in a paper which Gary reckoned cost more than his car was worth, and the TV was to die

THE SHATTERED EAGLE

for, even if it was unfortunately showing golf, but he knew that staying here would come at a cost, and that cost would soon be returning from her *Zumba* class.

"Sit down my friends, I'll get some drinks, scotch OK?" Clive offered, breaking Gary's train of thought.

"Yes fine by me, thanks." Gary said.

"And me too, thanks," Oli piped up.

Clive scurried off, they could hear him in the kitchen, as the front door opened, and a rather haughty voice declare, "My God Clive have you been smoking? It smells like some wretched Cuban bar, what have you been up to?"

"I'm in the kitchen darling", he called back, "We need to talk."

"Talk? Talk about what?"

They heard Clive walking out to the hallway and whispering in hushed tones just out of their view. Sheila didn't appear too overjoyed at the news that they were now staying, as they heard her raise her voice above the whispers she had initially been using. "What do you mean stay a few days? Well what did you say? And a friend? Oh really Clive!"

A couple of minutes later she breezed into her living room.

"Oh Gary darling, it's so good to see you!" she gushed as she leaned over and left a big lipstick print on his cheek.

"We've been so worried about you, it was like you just vanished from the planet. I must say we expected a phone call, but never mind here you are."

She turned to Oli, "And you must be Gary's friend, so nice to meet you."

A few minutes later Oli made his apologies and went to bed, it had been a terrible day, and all he wanted was some solitude, he knew he wouldn't sleep as his mind replayed over and over again the day from hell. He kept visualizing the look on Kate's face, totally rejecting his attempts at being with her, preferring to head who knew where, with total strangers. He was hollow, empty, he had no idea where he was now, but he did know he was sharing a room with china dolls and embroidered pictures of dogs adorning the walls.

Although 25 years old, he had managed to go those two and half decades without ever sampling the joys of whisky, and now his chest was burning. Why the hell would people drink that for pleasure? He wondered whether he would be able to get any sleep, between reliving the past few hours and internally combusting, he couldn't envisage sleep whisking him away from it all anytime soon.

Downstairs Gary wasn't doing too well either. The atmosphere was just that bit strained, laboured, the pauses in conversation that bit longer than they should have comfortably been, as the three of them struggled on without their common denominator.

Gary had only ever been in Sheila and Clive's company with Fran, and then it was always a case of surreptitiously

THE SHATTERED EAGLE

checking his watch at regular intervals to ascertain when that golden hour arrived when he could come out with the 'sorry we must be making a move, the baby sitter needs to be back by…' line, and thus make his escape.

He knew Fran was due any time now, the Detective, Sylvia, had been in touch to say they were nearly there, and he couldn't wait, he wanted them there with him, to know they were safe, Kate being taken had brought it home to him just how vulnerable, insecure and at threat his family really were, how through no fault of his own his world had fallen in. And yet when he did reclaim some of that world he chose Sheila and Clive's of all places!

He could see the furtive glances between Mr and Mrs Henderson, without words Sheila castigating her husband, he could imagine the later conversation, her ripping into poor old Clive, not phoning her, keeping her in the dark, but he also knew that she would have done the same, not for him, but for Fran.

The silence that had enveloped them was suddenly broken by a tap at the door, it was like Sheila was racing to get it, as keen as he was to see Fran again.

"Ah Francess! Lovely to see you, Josh! Amy! Come give Auntie Sheila a big kiss."

The remaining Westlakes entered the house, followed by Sylvia.

"Clive and I have been so worried, so terribly worried, Gary has kind of explained things, you poor, poor thing, it all sounds absolutely ghastly!"

Fran introduced Sheila to Sylvia, who received a none too complimentary glance over from their host, before she asked, "Sheila, if it's not asking too much can Sylvia stop the night, it's late and she has a long journey home?"

Gary could see the look on Sheila's face, it said all they needed to know, it was doubtful she actually wanted him stopping, let alone Oli, and now this Policewoman, dressed like some teenage boy in jeans, bomber jacket, and wet trainers, which she had yet to take off as well.

But of course Gary knew Sheila couldn't say that, not to her longest serving friend, and he had no doubt that she did consider Fran a genuine friend.

"Why of course, it's no problem at all, please feel free to leave your shoes there with the others my dear."

"Thank You Mrs Henderson, that's very kind," Sylvia answered.

"No problem, and please call me Sheila, and that's Clive," she gestured towards Clive who was hugging Fran. "My husband. Now can I get anyone a sherry?"

THE SHATTERED EAGLE

-FORTYSEVEN-
No Comment

Frankie had hardly had any sleep at all, he felt dead on his feet, after leaving Mentmore he had headed straight up to Northampton, where he liaised with Craig Lovan over the events of the day. He had stayed at the local *Holiday Inn*, but hadn't got to his bed until well into the early hours. He was keen to get stuck into their suspects, so next morning he made his way to Northampton Police station, too early to even avail himself of the formulaic breakfast that was included in the price of his room, but he could eat later, he wanted to hear what *she* had to say first.

Jay DeHavalland was sitting in the interview room, looking round at the ceiling, she knew someone would be watching from the small office the other side of a thick Perspex panel, which was mirrored the other side in the interview room. Of course knew she was being watched, she'd been the other side of such a panel on numerous occasions, normally with some terrified foreign national sweating it out just inches away, who chances was innocent of any wrong doing. But, as Howard had repeatedly told her in the past, counter terrorism involved percentages, you pull enough religious extremists in and sooner or later one will have something to tell you.

This though was different, she knew she was guilty of something, Howard knew she was guilty of something, how would he play it?

She understood there was no good cop bad cop routine with him, she'd watched, and yes admired, his interviewing techniques on numerous occasions. He worked on the law of attrition, wear the suspect down, intimidate, dominate, catch them out, confront the weak parts of any story until even the truth becomes a lie in their mouths. And here she was, she was sure he was the other side, watching her, waiting for her to be ready for him.

The door opened, he waltzed in, that smug 'I knew as much' look on his pock marked self-satisfied face. He was followed by the Policeman who had arrested her back at Newport Pagnall.

"Hello Miss DeHavalland I'm Detective Inspector Lovan, I'm leading the investigation into the murders of James Bolton, George Morton, and Robert McKinnen, and the Kidnapping of Kate Wallander. I believe you know Detective Chief Inspector Howard, he will be sitting in for the duration of this interview. Before we start can I get you a drink?"

Jay shook her head. "I want my solicitor." There was no way she was saying a word without a brief. Howard may not be talking, but he was the puppet master, he was pulling this clown's strings.

THE SHATTERED EAGLE

"OK," Lovan continued. "Let's go over what we've got. Yesterday morning you drove Ms Wallander from Safehaven to an as yet unknown location, where you left her with Auguste Fredericks. Am I right?"

"No comment."

She looked around the room, she knew what was happening, what was coming, she knew they wanted her to drop herself in it before her legal representative was there, give them a toe in, a good head start. Did they really think she was that stupid? It wasn't happening, even though she was damned already. She wanted that brief. She needed that brief because this was now her on her own. There was nothing she could say that could make her life any easier, any less threatened. If Gus even suspected she was talking she was done for, he'd pass it on, tell 'him', and as shitty as the next few years of her life were going to be, she would rather spend them breathing without the aid of a machine, with her face still intact.

"Why did you do it Jay? Why ruin your career and do that?" Lovan pressed on.

"I want a solicitor." No way was she going to say anything, Gus had made it clear, the rewards were massive, but the consequences of failure were even bigger. There was nowhere she would be safe if she implicated anyone, explained where the money was coming from. This was the deal she had made with the devil, the pact where she sold her soul for a massive great pile of cash.

"What was the motivation for a serving Police Officer to become involved in a kidnapping for God's sake?" Lovan continued.

"No comment."

This can go on all day, all night, all week, even when the solicitor arrives, this is what they would be getting, nothing.

"Why did you take Kate Wallander, Jay, Money?" Lovan persisted, his calm Scottish brogue was reassuring, inviting her to help herself, but then she looked over to Howard, she was keen not to make eye contact, be drawn by his withering gaze, but she had to see what he was doing. He was just sitting there, keeping quiet, obviously having briefed this other one, the questions no doubt his, just waiting for his moment.

"No comment."

Of course it was for money, it wasn't for the thrill of it! But that will never be admitted, because once that is admitted, then it leads on to other questions, and those questions will lead to trouble. Worse trouble than six years, serve three, kind of trouble. These were bad people.

"Come on Jay, give us something?" Lovan said, he was still polite, there was no aggression, no raised voices. She again looked at Howard sitting there, she could almost hear the grinding of his teeth, waiting for the explosion where he could no longer sit back and watch Lovan's softly-softly patient approach. She remembered the hole-punch flying into her shoulder, the purple-black bruise was there in case she forgot, if he had his way now her nose would be bleeding after smashing it into the desk, or some other unimaginative thuggery. Yet he was just watching, almost with no show of emotion.

"No comment."

Howard stood up, she flinched, just the slightest bit, but enough for him to notice, yet he appeared to ignore it. "I think that'll do for now Inspector Lovan, can we arrange for Miss DeHavalland to contact her solicitor?"

"No problem Sir, I'll sort out a phone call for her. We'll reconvene when her legal representative is present."

With that they both left the room.

Jay leant back in her chair, she would have almost welcomed Howard hitting her in the mouth, rather than that. That wasn't him, yet he only knew the one way, he couldn't play mind games, what was he up to?

Frankie entered the room next door again, he slumped in a chair.

"Well done Frankie, you were the model of restraint," Lovan said as he hung his jacket on a hook and sat beside his superior, both watching DeHavalland through the one way screen.

"Restraint! You have no idea Craig, no idea. That two bit crack whore is going to get it, I swear, next time it's my show, if I have to smash her lying face through this window I will, and I'll throw her fucking brief through after her! What did that achieve Craig, what? Please tell me, because I really want to know."

"It made her think. Look at her, her minds not thinking how much she hates you, how you've smashed her face in, how you've screamed at her until she burst into tears. She still would have lawyered up anyway, would have hit us with no comment after no comment, but now she's pondering her fate, seriously thinking. She's ours no matter what, she doesn't need to admit to what she's done, we know that. We need her to tell us why she did it, which I don't really care about to be honest. But once she has said why, then we've who. It's the who I want Frankie, the who, and we don't get that by shouting at her. That's why next time I'm still the one going in, and you Sir, and yes I'll say it with all due respect, will keep your mouth closed and kindly refrain from throwing anyone through my windows."

"Bollocks, let's go and talk to Fredericks, can I shout at him?"

"Feel free Frankie, he's your show."

THE SHATTERED EAGLE

-FORTYEIGHT-
The Irresistible Force Meets The Unmoveable Object.

They walked down a corridor to where Auguste Fredericks was sitting in Interview Room 5 within Northampton Police Station. Frankie entered the room, followed by Lovan who didn't say a word as he moved to sit down, shuffling papers on the desk. Frankie looked at Fredericks sitting before them, leaning back in his chair, feet on the desk, he was a big unit that was for sure, not tall, but wide.

Nothing was said for about thirty seconds, before Frankie finally broke the silence, "Sit on that chair properly please."

"Say what?" Gus answered back.

"I said sit on that fucking chair properly, you do speak English don't you Auguste? You're not a cretin are you? Some sort of dribbling idiot, is that it Auguste, is that your story, too stupid to understand?"

The broad ex-soldier laughed, still leaning back in his chair, "Oh very good Mr Howard, very good, a little bit of intimidation to start with, a little bit of big man talk, that's probably what I would have opened with, a bit clumsy though, you need to work on that a little bit. In fact if I was you I'd be kicking the mother fucker's chair from under him, you know, start some kind of instant understanding, leave the bitch in no doubt you're the man." Fredericks continued to laugh, "But you're not in this case. You're nothing, in this here relationship in fact, you're the one who should be scared."

"So," Frankie went on, "stupid it undoubtedly is then. That would account for a lot, a whole lot. That would explain why after killing three innocent people you go and take someone under my witness protection scheme, then lead us straight to you. That is the work of a truly stupid moron, wouldn't you agree big man?"

Gus just continued to rock on his chair, he smiled at Frankie, "This isn't how you talk to me, Mr Howard. This isn't how you are going conduct our business."

"Auguste you need to understand this is exactly how I will conduct my business, if I so choose to, because I am a Detective Chief Inspector, and you, you are a worthless piece of shit."

Suddenly Gus stopped rocking and leaned forward, bringing his face closer to Frankie's.

"You had better understand you jumped up lanky streak of piss, I'm going down for life, I fully appreciate and understand that clear fact, you've got me for three murders. Now in my position it doesn't make a whole lot

THE SHATTERED EAGLE

of difference if I reach across and snap your scrawny rotten neck, do you hear me you arrogant arsehole."

"Sit down Auguste, I said sit down!" Frankie's voice was raised, Lovan sat there still, watching intently.

Gus suddenly jumped to his feet, pointing down at Frankie, "You better listen to me you lump of fucking dog shit, you mother fucker, I can snuff out your worthless shit life like it's nothing. Do you understand! Do you!"

Lovan had got up and rushed to press the alarm on the wall, Frankie just sat there, he hadn't even flinched. Four Police Officers ran in, whilst Gus was still on his feet pointing at him.

"I'll fucking disembowel you and throw your entrails to your dog…"

The incoming Officers piled onto to Gus, he tried to brush them aside, but more arrived, even whilst he was struggling his tirade continued, "You think I'm stupid, you think I'm a moron…"

He was tossing the Policemen around the room as they attempted to restrain him. "I'll show you, I'll show you who's a… Arghhhh!"

Gus received a long burst of pepper spray, as his eyes began to burn and his nostrils fill with the incapacitating fumes, he toppled to the floor, unable to place his hands to his face as they were pulled behind his back, as once again he was lying face down with hand cuffs slapped on. He was coughing and spluttering, "You fuckers, I'm going to kill you all!"

Howard walked over to Gus, tears, drool and mucus flowing from his facial orifices, fighting for air, struggling to breathe.

"Why didn't you just sit properly you dumb fuck."

Frankie and Lovan left the interview room, leaving the uniformed Officers to tidy the mess, which to be fair was of Frankie's making.

As they walked down the corridor Lovan turned to Howard, "Well, I'd say that's 1-0 to me."

Frankie winked, "It's still early in the game my friend."

THE SHATTERED EAGLE

-FORTYNINE-
Grand Theft Auto

Oli and Gary were sitting in the Hendersons back Garden, drinking Orange Juice, neither though were particularly saying much, each lost in their own thoughts. Oli's mind was inevitably focused on his estranged fiancée.

Fran, Josh and Amy were cooking lunch inside, it was the afternoon after Kate had been taken, and a bigger contrast in the weather couldn't have been imaginable, the sun was beating down, and Gary had resorted to borrowing one of Clive's panama's, protecting his head from the UV rays in his host's absence. The fact that a man could in fact own more than one of these straw hats had at least caused Oli a moment's amusement, although it was short lived, he knew he had been like the proverbial bear with a sore head, but he saw no point in putting on a brave face. This had been the first opportunity he had got to speak to Gary properly, express how he was feeling to the only person he was able to at that time, although he had been putting it off, a couple of times moving to speak, before changing his mind at the last moment. He didn't want to come across all needy, but that was what he was, because he needed to offload. He leaned forward one more time, but before he could speak, Gary beat him to it.

"For God's sake Oli, just say it, spit it out man."

"What?" Oli replied.

"Whatever it is you've been wanting to talk about the last ten minutes."

Oli shrugged, "I need to find her, it's been over a day now, I've got to make it right mate, I can't just stand back and do nothing. It was only two days back she agreed to get married, now I haven't a clue where she is, and for all I know she's through with me."

"Well Oli, I'm sorry to be the one to tell you this, but we're stuck here, you know what Frankie said, we can't even go into town, we've got to stay hidden away, they're still out there."

"But they don't need me anymore, I've not got the ring, I'm no use to them."

"Oh come on," Oli could see the annoyance in Gary's face at the comment he had just made, "don't be so bloody naive, you know you witnessed that bloke Fredericks take Warsabi, he's up for murder, you're no way safe Oli, any more than I am."

"I'm sorry Gary I need to find her, I've got to."

"Look, talk to Frankie or Sylvia about it, they may be able to contact her for you, but until then you've got to get her out of your mind, she'll be safe wherever she is, you've got your whole lives to argue about it, she'll come around, after all like you said it was only a couple of days ago she was agreeing to marry you, God help her."

Oli fell quiet again, he was far from convinced, he stared into his drink, mesmerised by the cloudy fruit juice,

THE SHATTERED EAGLE

wondering what Kate was doing at that exact moment, how she was, how she was coping, how she felt about him.

He felt so guilty, so incredibly responsible, which once more he reminded himself he was, after all if he hadn't stolen that damn ring none of this would be happening to them, or would it? He was still a witness, but there would have been no need to have kidnapped Kate, involved her in this whole nightmare, and that was all he wanted at this moment, for her to be safe, although safe with him rather than wherever else she may be.

He got up and walked back into the house, ignoring Fran as he walked through the kitchen, not even acknowledging her cheery attempt to ascertain whether he wanted beans with his lunch or not.

He really didn't want to be there, they were Gary and Fran's friends, those people, not his. All he really wanted was to see to Kate, because that was all that mattered, everything else of secondary importance.

Walking into the hallway he stopped by the neat row of shoes, all banned from the house, and he slipped his trainers on, he'd go for a walk, get out of there, maybe it would clear his head, he couldn't play happy families with the Westlakes, he knew he would just be dragging them down too. As he looked up, after straightening the backs of his *Adidas Gazelles,* where he had squeezed into them without undoing the laces first, he saw bunches of keys hanging from hooks spaced along a wooden sausage dog. The *MG* logo was on a fob hanging on the middle hook.

Shit. What kind of person was he? But he couldn't just stay there could he? He had to do something, something to find Kate. Looking around first, he took the keys, hurriedly placing them in one of the pockets in his shorts, before calling out to Fran. "I'm just going to clear my head for a few minutes, back soon."

"OK Oli, remember I'm doing lunch, don't be too long darling."

But he was gone before she had finished speaking.

Whilst Fran cooked sausages, sizzling and spitting in the pan, and Gary listened to the radio in the Garden dressed like some character from 'A Passage to India', Oli opened the garage doors, checking himself for a moment, was this really what he wanted to do, was this really what he was, a dirty thief?

Of course not, but he had to do it, he had to find her. So taking the keys from his pocket he unlocked Clive's pride and joy, a racing green 1969 *MG Roadster* with a pale cream hard top roof. He hesitated, this was so ungrateful, Clive had, even if reluctantly, offered him a bed, safety, a place to stay, even some of his scotch, which he didn't particularly enjoy at all, and in return he was stealing his car.

But then again it was only borrowing, he'd return it before the rightful owner was even home from work, Clive would, hopefully at least, be none the wiser. Sure technically it was a crime, but a victimless one, and one only he, and hopefully Kate, would know of, it was like

THE SHATTERED EAGLE

that thing about a tree falling in a deserted forest and no one hearing it, well actually it wasn't but he'd cling on to any justification he could.

Turning the key in the ignition the recently rebuilt engine fired up, it sounded good, really loud within the low roofed garage it was parked within, and he pulled out, hastily shutting the wooden garage doors behind him, leaving the Westlakes blissfully unaware that he had committed Grand Theft Auto with their friends much loved and cherished classic car.

He had no idea where he was heading, nor indeed where he was, as he drove away from the house, only that he had more of a chance finding Kate away from that village, than he would moping around the place like a lost puppy.

As he headed for, well he wasn't quite sure where he was heading, he mulled over in his head how to find her. Was she still in a hospital or was she somewhere else?

He pressed his foot hard down on the accelerator, the windows were open with the wind blowing around the interior of the car, it felt good, like a freedom he had been missing ever since that day in the taxi. The warm air cooled as it rushed around him, for a brief moment he let it clear his head, blow away the anxieties and worries, he even managed a smile. Reaching over he put the car stereo on, it was one of Clive's CDs playing, The Beach Boys - Pet Sounds, not normally his cup of tea, but he turned it up loud anyway, singing along, wondering how it was he knew all the words, as Brian Wilson harmonised with him on 'Wouldn't it be Nice.' With his west coast soundtrack and weather to match he hammered through the country lanes, well he was only doing fifty but it appeared much faster on the bumpy road from such a low vantage point. Resting his elbow out of the window, the light flashed in bright blasts into his face as the little sports car sped along the tree lined roads, he pushed his foot even harder onto the accelerator, the engine responding with another blast of British automotive power. Looking at the speedo, he could see it was now showing just over sixty five miles per hour, it felt exhilarating, he could see why Clive loved the little car so much, it really was a joy to drive, then he noticed the petrol gauge.

Bollocks it was nearly empty.

He had no money.

Bollocks, bollocks, bollocks!

His mood had plummeted as fast as it had risen, what the hell did he think he was playing at? He was never going to find her anyway, what was his plan after all? To walk into all the local hospitals and ask them if they had Kate Wallander, pretty girl, about 5' 6", likely to have an armed guard at her door as she's under Police Protection. Oh really, you can't answer my question, why would that be?

As ideas went this wasn't his best, he slowed to a stop, parking just on a bend, and put his head in his hands, Allen you knob end, what are you playing at.

Once again stealing something that didn't belong to him, Stop Thief! "Oh God," he said to himself, "I'm a walking disaster, a fucking liability of the highest order."

THE SHATTERED EAGLE

Pulling the car around into a three point turn he knew it was time to go back, he should never have left, but it was all recoverable. He'd beg Gary and Fran, if they were aware he'd even taken the car, not to tell Clive what he had done, that was his worst case scenario, they may not have even been aware of his stupid joy ride.

He pushed the leather topped gear stick into reverse, yeah even the bloody gearstick was class, then heard the screeching tyres...

He could do nothing to get out of the way, he was right across the road, a Dark Blue *5 Series BMW* had swerved around the corner, he heard and felt the sickening metallic crunch simultaneously as it clipped the front bumper of Clive's pride and joy, tearing it clean off. Then the sound of brakes screeching, before he saw it plough into the verge, the front end disappearing into a bramble hedge. The driver got out, she looked furious.

"You bloody idiot!" she screamed at the *MG*. "Are you some kind of.... Allen? What the hell are you doing here?"

It was Sylvia Hardacre.

But Oli was looking beyond her, instead staring inside the beleaguered *BMW*, it was Kate!

As emotional reunions went it was slightly ruined by Oli almost killing her before they had a chance to even speak. He ran to the car, but was stopped by Sylvia, "Hold on, get this motor out of the road first, before you actually do kill someone, go on, get it moved quick!"

He pulled the only slightly battered *MG* away from the middle of the narrow carriageway, where it had been located on a sharp bend, which on reflection wasn't the best place for it. Sylvia pulled the dented, but still shining bumper from the hedge it had ended up in, and placed it on her back seat, before getting back behind the wheel of her car and reversing it from out of the thick foliage where it partly resided, to just in front of Oli's stolen classic, now a hundred yards or so down the road.

Sylvia stayed in the car as Kate got out and walked towards him, the Detective giving an exaggerated grimace, as it was clear this wasn't the stuff of orchestras and Happy-Ever-Afters, as Kate slowly moved towards him with her head bowed.

It was awkward, there were no hugs or kisses, just a strained conversation.

"I was on my way to look for you," Oli said to his none too happy fiancée.

"Well I guess you found me didn't you, well done." Her face was blank, he couldn't read it, the bruising was still there, but she appeared to have a bit more colour to her, she looked a lot better, but he couldn't tell if she was happier.

"Are we OK?" he sheepishly enquired.

"No Oli, we're far from OK, a bloody long way from it you stupid, stupid, twat, but I'm here aren't I, you're not getting out of buying me a ring that easily. I'm really pissed off with you, more than you can imagine, and you are going to find out just how pissed off, probably for the rest of your pathetic little worthless life, but I've got to ask, whose car is that?"

THE SHATTERED EAGLE

"That's Clive's, and he's going to be pissed as fuck, when he finds out I borrowed it!"

"Who's Clive?"

"He's Sheila's husband, but you'll meet them soon enough. Anyway I hope so, you are back aren't you?"

"I guess I am, where else am I to go, although you're going to wish I wasn't by the time I'm done. You can thank Sylvia for persuading me, I'd have happily let you stew for a few more days, although I was getting a bit bored and lonely, she said we aren't far from where we're staying, are you going to give me a lift in your new toy then?"

"Only if I can have a hug."

Kate looked him in the eye, "Twat-face."

"Shit for brains," Oli answered.

With that Kate smiled and gave Twat-face a hug, before saying, "Come on then take me home."

Oli drove back to Mentmore, he was pleased to see Kate, and despite all she had been through she appeared to be at least talking to him, which was far more than he was expecting. He looked at the bruising on her face, most notably her cheek, but could see that it was really nothing serious, although he then felt a surge of guilt, how could being punched whilst tied up by some psycho, who he had already seen kill two people, be anything but serious?

On the drive home he had explained how they were now residing at the Hendersons, friends of Gary and Fran's, which surprised Kate as she remembered Gary talking about these friends from hell one evening at 'Howard's

End', hearing the tales of long painful nights around their place and of the suitcase incident.

"What's he going to say when he finds out you've pranged his motor?" Kate asked him.

"Hmmm, he didn't even know I was borrowing it! Although before you tear into me, it was only to go hunting for you!"

-FIFTY-
What Clive Did Say When He Found Out Someone Had Pranged His Motor!

"You did what! In my car. Why the blazes were you even in the bloody *MG*? This is my home Gary, my garage, and my bloody car. Really I am so disappointed in you."

And that was the solution, Gary agreed to take the blame for the accident, it appeared better than letting Clive know that the young man who he didn't know from Adam, who was residing in his home only because he had stolen something that didn't belong to him, had now nicked his car too.

Gary wasn't particularly pleased with the plan, he suspected that neither Clive nor Sheila had any affection for him anyway, but it was the best that the combined IQs of Fran, Kate and him could come up with at such short notice. Oli was all insistent on telling the truth, keen to demonstrate to all a more responsible side, but it was a bit late for that, a good time to have done that would have been before taking the car in the first place.

"I can honestly say Gary," Clive was far from finished, "that this is one of the more foolish things you have done, it shows no respect. You know if you had wanted to drive Old Meg I would have gladly let you, but to just take her, really that is beyond the pale. If you hadn't crashed her, would you even have told me?"

Gary was now seriously regretting taking one for Oli, and the worst was still to come, he was looking like some pathetic school child being chastised by the teacher, he was trying not to look in Sheila's direction, but unfortunately he made eye contact. He momentarily closed his eyes and took a deep breath, drawing strength in preparation of the inevitable onslaught, now bring on the worst.

"I knew it when Francess married you, from the very minute she told me she was to be wed. I should have said something. You were always so irresponsible, look at you, having to come to us for a roof over your head, can't even look after your own family. Your money sense is appalling, you make no effort to improve your social standing," she turned to Fran, although not taking a breath, "Honestly Francess if I didn't love you and the children so much I'd have to ask you to make alternative arrangements."

Gary could see that Fran was now also seriously regretting the idea of Gary taking the blame, very

THE SHATTERED EAGLE

seriously, as no doubt did Kate and Oli who he knew were listening from the landing upstairs.

He could see that look in Fran's eye, he didn't see it often, but could tell she was about to fire back, but before she could Gary held his hand up to stop her, saying as he did so, "Look Clive, once again I just want to say how sorry I am, I only wanted to find a gift for you, for both of you, to let you know how grateful we all are for having us stay, especially now Kate's here as well. You really have been so kind to us. That's why I borrowed Old Meg, it was my only way into town, I really wanted to show how appreciative we are, but wanted to keep it a surprise. I am sorry, I genuinely am, the last thing I wanted to do was upset you both in this way. I feel so bad, absolutely terrible."

Fran stood by as Gary bowed his head, he wondered if the face he was pulling was one of a naughty repentant puppy, or just the village idiot. But apparently it had worked, he had just scored the goal of the season, he knew Fran was about to unleash verbal Armageddon on her long term friends, but instead he had - despite being almost destroyed by Sheila's evil tongue - magnificently pulled one out of the fire.

"Oh." Sheila replied, "that's really, errr, sweet."

"Humph, why didn't you just say so in the first place? I would gladly have lent you the car," was all Clive could manage, still not overjoyed at having his beloved Meg debumpered, but knowing he had to take the lead from Sheila.

"Sheila, Clive," It was Fran now speaking, "I know we've imposed on you, what with Oli and Kate, and the four of us, we really are grateful, but really I feel it may be fairer on you if we perhaps arranged to move somewhere else. I'm sure the Police can organise another safe house for us, I believe they have one on an estate in South London, I really don't want to outstay our welcome."

"No, no, no!" Sheila replied. "I won't hear of it, this whole matter is now closed, just a misunderstanding, it's only a lump of old rusty metal anyway, our friendship is nearly as old, and far more valuable to us, really Clive why were you making such a fuss?"

Clive said very little other than grunt, clearly the value of the two ladies friendship wasn't as valuable to him as it was her!

"And as for staying on some horrid estate in South London, really, do you honestly think we would stand by and let you do that. You do know what kind of people live in places like that?" Sheila's face was a picture of the ultimate in middle-class snobbery, Gary knew what kind of people lived in such places, but was sure that Sheila Henderson had no idea, other than many of them weren't white, rich, or likely to vote either Conservative or UKIP in the next general election.

"I'll tell you what," she continued. "Let's open a couple of nice bottles of wine, get your friends down from upstairs, and Clive can order us an Indian meal, they deliver out this far you know, one of the joys in living in Mentmore."

THE SHATTERED EAGLE

"That sounds lovely," Gary answered, although still wondering whether Fran's idea to move, even to some shitty council estate in South London, may not have been the best course of action after all.

-FIFTYONE-
Let's Not Spoil It By Insisting I Supersize The Meal.

Craig Lovan was curious as to why Frankie had left it over 24 hours before returning to talk to Fredericks, he thought the whole point of pissing him off so emphatically the previous day was to somehow put him off guard, make him susceptible to mistakes, stick him on his back foot, yet it now appeared it was purely and simply to solely piss him off after all. They both entered the interview room, Fredericks was now cuffed to the table, by a chain secured so it gave him just enough movement in his arms to bring his hand to his face for the purposes of drinking.

Lovan again sat down and remained silent, even when the first thing Frankie did was to go and un-cuff Fredericks, although the words, 'Why the hell did you do that?' were very hard to suppress! Fredericks remained in his chair though, saying nothing.

"Right Auguste, let's start afresh shall we. Just to reintroduce myself I'm DCI Howard, Anti-Terrorism Unit, and once again this is DI Lovan, of the Major Crimes Unit, Northamptonshire Police."

"Good day to you Mr Howard, may I introduce myself," Fredericks was smiling, in total contrast to his mood the previous day. "I am Auguste Fredericks, murderer, kidnapper, and one bad mother fucker. And I think the fresh start idea is a pretty good one. Yeah I like that, I think we may have had what I would describe as a chemical reaction yesterday Mr Howard."

Frankie smiled back, Lovan could see he was clearly happy to follow the path that had been set before him, let things remain all civil and polite. "Good. So let's begin. Where's Abu Warsabi? Where is he Auguste?"

"I have no idea what you're talking about, no idea?"

"Oh come on! Let's not start so negatively, I thought we were doing so well. Look, I know you were one of the armed men who took him, you've already admitted to the murders. The Prison Officer has confirmed it, you've quite a distinctive voice Auguste, not a man to blend into the crowd are you? So where did you take him?"

"The thing is Mr Howard, I'll admit to killing those guys, I even admit to taking the little Somali, but I am not saying where to. We need to get that clear, because you're going to waste a lot of breath chasing after that information, and believe me you are on one massive great fruitless quest with that one. The trail stops with me, I'm going down, I'll take the rap for it on my own, I accept that."

Frankie leant over the desk, not threatening nor intimidating, but to stress his next point.

"You were out there, in Afghanistan weren't you, fighting the Taliban, keeping us safe at home, protecting us from unseen horrors and fundamentalist suicide bombers. People don't do that for money do they Auguste, it's in you, you believe in what you do. Warsabi placed a fucking great bomb on a train, killed a load of people, that's not what you believe in is it? You've seen what bombs do to people haven't you, how they work, why did you free that kid? Who paid you to? How did you even know he was there?"

Fredericks laughed, a loud booming laugh, and shook his head. "Do you think I did what I did to help that little skinny mother fucker? Do you really think that? That I would actually kill two decent people, just to release some worthless terrorist piece of shit arsehole? You are so wrong.

"What were the other questions, oh yeah, who paid me? That is not of your concern, believe me, you are better not knowing that shit. How did I know Warsabi was in prison, was going on that ride in the taxi? That is why you don't want to know who I work for, because in this case ignorance really is some kind of fucking bliss. Because if you don't know who, and you certainly don't want to know why, then they will have no reason to harm you! I'm doing you a big favour, I'm protecting your arses by saying nothing. I don't want a solicitor, I don't want to argue guilt or responsibility, while you're at it I've another

THE SHATTERED EAGLE

two names of recently deceased persons to give you, call them ex-associates. I'm helping you here, giving you my balls stuck between two sesame seed buns, with a large dollop of fucking relish and a gherkin stuck in there, let's not spoil it by insisting I supersize the meal, be grateful for what you've got."

"We are Auguste we are, you say two other bodies?"

"Bodies, hmm, there ain't a lot of body left with them poor boys, but yeah, I'll give you them."

For over an hour and a half Gus talked, told them everything he had done, whilst continuing to refuse to implicate anyone else, even keeping Jay out of the picture. It was clear that he no longer had Warsabi, and even more clear that the ring was strictly off topic.

-FIFTYTWO-
The Man From The Bullingdon Club.

"She's got who in there? Sir David Pascall-Shaw. How the hell has she managed that? That parasite is the lackey for A-List kiddie fuckers and hook handed clerics avoiding being kicked out of the country, not a bent copper on under thirty grand a year. He certainly doesn't do Legal Aid. What's he doing here for crissake?"

Frankie was infuriated, DeHavalland had been hard enough to crack without her brief, now she was going to be sitting next to probably one of the country's top legal professionals, they had no chance of getting anything out of her.

"It'll be just the same as if she was with some student lawyer from the local Ambulance chasers," Lovan assured him. "We'll ask the same questions, and she'll no doubt give us nothing. Let's find out anyway."

They both walked in to the room.

"Good afternoon. My name is DI Craig Lovan, and this is DCI Adrian Howard. It's 14.25 on the 16th September. Also present are Jayne DeHavalland and her legal representative Sir David Pascall-Shaw. Right Miss DeHavalland…"

"If I can interject here?" Pascall-Shaw interrupted, leaning back slightly in his chair, looking over a pair of half-moon spectacles. "My client would like to make a full statement. I do have a written copy to present to yourselves, but I have also asked my client to read it out aloud, for the benefit of the recording. Once she has done this, under my instruction, she will make no further comments. Please Jayne continue."

Jay looked at her brief nervously, he nodded and she spoke hesitantly reading from the sheet of paper she was holding.

"I would like to voluntarily present this statement as my account of the events I am charged with. I do so with my own volition and present this as a truthful record." She hesitated whilst she took a sip of water, then continued, "Four days ago, on the 12th September I was approached by Mr Auguste Fredericks, who offered me a sum of money to take Miss Kate Wallander to a location where he was residing. I agreed to do this, the motivation of which was purely for financial gain. Mr Fredericks assured me no harm would come to anyone. He also required me to leave a mobile phone secreted in Miss Wallander's room. Later that day I was to collect an item from the same location and deliver it to Mr Fredericks. After carrying out the first part of this I was approached by Detective Chief Inspector Adrian Howard. Mr Howard confronted me about what I was doing, and I answered questions asked of me. Mr

Howard promised me immunity if I carried out the rest of the plan. At the time I expressed my concerns and reservations about this, and clearly stated I did not wish to continue with this criminal act, but he made it apparent that if I did as he instructed I would not face prosecution."

She looked up at Howard, who was impassive, bar an almost imperceptible twitch in his left eye, she continued reading. "At this stage I did not wish to continue in this venture, and was keen to report the matter to the correct authorities, but due to his assurance of immunity I continued with Mr Fredericks initial plan. I followed all Mr Howard's instructions and did nothing to alert Mr Fredericks of any Police involvement. That I now find myself charged with offences relating to this matter is of great distress to myself, as stated earlier I was informed by Mr Howard that this would not be the case. I know of no other persons involved in this crime other than Mr Fredericks, and would like to stress no other involvement other than that already described."

She put the paper down and lifted her head to face the two Policemen on the opposite side of the table.

Lovan spoke first, "Miss DeHavalland you say you were approached by Auguste Fredericks, can you tell me where this occurred please?"

"No Comment." Jay replied.

"OK, you spoke of a financial payment, how much would that have been?" Lovan's tone was calm, Frankie was watching, bursting to let her have it, the lying two faced bitch, it was as much as he could do to share the

THE SHATTERED EAGLE

same air as the conniving cow. But Lovan, just maintained the same level of calm serenity.

"No Comment."

"Where were you told to take Miss Wallander, once you took her from Safehaven?"

"No Comment"

"How aware were you that Mr Fredericks had been involved in at least three murders at that time?"

"No Comment."

"Excuse me Inspector," Pascall-Shaw butted in as Lovan prepared to ask his next question. "My client has made a statement and we have reiterated that she will not elaborate any further, as is her right. I appreciate you may require further information, but my client has been advised not to make any further comments at this point, and I can assure you she has taken that advice on board, so unless…"

Frankie couldn't listen anymore, the twitch had become unbearable, it was his psyche's way of telling him he had heard enough bullshit.

"For fucks sake you jumped up little turd. This woman next to you here kidnapped an innocent young lady and delivered her to a murdering psychopath. She needs to answer questions, telling us why, when and who, because that lunatic was also being paid by someone, and that someone is a very dangerous individual we need to find. Now I'm guessing this is going to get me a phone call from some other toffee nosed twat who also got buggered in the toilets of the Bullingdon Club, then so be it, because finding these people is key to two crucial investigations, which for the good of me, you, and a lot of decent people in this country is very important. She needs to speak, she needs to talk to us. Now I haven't promised her jack shit, and you know that, but if there's an ounce of common decency left in that lying bitch then now is the time to show it!"

Pascall-Shaw just smirked, leaning back in his chair as he played with his pen, clicking the button in and out on the top. He really was a smug arrogant prick. "Hmm Mr Howard, you can rest assured that you probably will be getting a phone call from someone at some point soon. But as far as my client is concerned I suggest we finish this interview now, and resume at some future point, perhaps when you remember that you are in fact a professional Police Officer, and as such I would expect you to behave like one next time, if indeed there is a next time. With that Gentlemen I thank you."

THE SHATTERED EAGLE

-FIFTYTHREE-
The Penny drops.

Sitting in the otherwise deserted offices of the ATU, within the Red House, Frankie stared at the white board. He had travelled back from Northampton a couple of hours earlier, but had too much on his mind to just go back to his flat and try and get some sleep, no matter how tired he was. It was coming up for midnight, but his head was whirring, it didn't square up at all, it was all too random. Why would someone horrifically rape and murder a woman out of sheer spite? The woman that had done him no wrong, the woman who had taken him in, in all probability saved his wretched life? Then just disappear off the face of the planet, only to return blowing up a train in a city he had never been to. This kid apparently wasn't a political or religious extremist, prior to the murder of Anna DuPont anyway. Then he goes and commits a minor sexual assault, which bore no resemblance to the attack on the French woman, and just waits there, waits to get nicked, the same kid who evaded capture for over two years whilst France's Most Wanted? Then a small army comes along, pays probably the best part of a million to previously honest people, corrupting them instantly, before getting hold of Warsabi. Wow, that's fucked up logic.

The lines on the whiteboard led from photo to photo, linking them, but for no apparent reason. This was a terrorist investigation, it should all be linked, cemented by ideologies, extremism, misdirected belief and faith, an invisible enemy, but one with reason, they *always* a reason.

There was no link to al-Qaeda, the Taliban, ISIS, Hamas, Palestine, Iran or any of the usual suspects. All that was constant here was a ring. Warsabi or DuPont, the bomber or the murdering rapist, had it. Fredericks wanted it. Oli had stolen it. Kate was kidnapped for it. Jim Bolton was murdered just because someone thought he may have it. The ring, that damned bloody ring.

He took a sip from his coffee, and pulled out the large pack of colour photographs, all depicting the ring from various angles. He took his reading glasses from his pocket and closely examined them, the eagle on a French flag inset into a thick gold band. Along the side in ornate lettering *Avec gratitude, qui ne peut jamais être évoqué*, which JP had informed him meant 'With gratitude, which can never be spoke of.' It was an impressive bit of jewellery, there was no doubting that, hardly subtle, but he was sure it was valuable. But not that bloody valuable, not worth killing for and paying millions to get hold of. It was now securely locked away in a safe, being held somewhere only he and Lovan knew of, but what was so damn special about it?

He had trawled the internet looking for something on it, countless searches revealing fruitless pages of images.

THE SHATTERED EAGLE

Experts on jewellery and French history had been enlisted to help, but had drawn a complete blank. He'd emailed pictures to JP, who had scoured around for answers, but he too came up with a big giant nothing, no one in France appeared to know anything about it either. He needed to know what the ring was, what it meant, because he was sure someone knew.

He stared at the whiteboard, the host of faces previously unrelated.

Warsabi, the boy that got away. Twice.

Where was he now?

What was he doing at this very moment?

Who was he with, are they the ones who gave him the bomb, the bomb that wiped out so many lives?

Fredericks a war hero, someone who risked his life to save others, even got a nice big shiny medal for his efforts, yet was now just a murderer, refusing to explain why he had changed from one to the other.

Why would someone who so nearly died in Afghanistan fighting against terrorists and extremists free Warsabi from Custody?

Anna DuPont, murdered by Warsabi, even whilst he was using her surname.

Why?

He remembered JP saying it may have been as much to spite her husband than for sexual gratification.

Where was the husband on the whiteboard?

What had he done to deserve finding his wife in such a horrific fashion?

He walked to one of the computer terminals, and opened up *Google*. HENRI DUPONT he typed in. A host of stories came up, relating to Anna's murder, pages of them, from the sombre reports on the day of the murder, to the grotesque, salacious and macabre retellings that came after, as the internet followed the trail of blood and gore.

There were plenty of pictures of Anna, but none featuring Henri.

He changed the search parameter to just images. There were Henri DuPonts, lots of them, but none appeared to be the one he was searching for. This man was supposedly in French Government, a man of power and influence, there had to be some images of him on the internet for God's sake!

He tried HENRY DUPONT, still no husband to the late Anna. Other variations of what was a name without too many ways of spelling it followed, but each time nothing. He was perplexed, he didn't like being perplexed. This man wasn't a ghost, he had existed, still existed, he had to be out there somewhere, so many pictures of his wife, but none him.

He typed in ANNA DUPONT, again under images, and once more hundreds of pictures appeared. He went through them, photos of her in Somalia, relating to her charity work, at various functions in long ball gowns, posing with three teenage African boys outside a centre in Paris. She was a beautiful woman, but one who clearly wasn't photographed with her husband. He went on, by page seven of the results other Anna DuPonts were appearing,

THE SHATTERED EAGLE

Facebook photos of a teenage girl from Lyon, and an old lady from Toulouse who was celebrating her one hundredth birthday, a driving instructor from Lille, and at least half a dozen others.

Frankie, made himself a coffee, wondering if he was over-tired, would be better leaving it to the morning when his head cleared, clear of some ghost that had no face?

It was gone half one in the morning, yet still he trawled on, there had to be a picture with Anna and Henri together. He came to one at the President's residence, a party outside, he again saw Anna, mixing with the great and good, no doubt to raise funds. He clicked on the image to make it bigger, a trip to the President's Garden Party, what sort of husband wouldn't go to that?

He zoomed in on the image, she appeared alone. Suddenly there was something in it he certainly wasn't expecting, Well bugger me he thought, there's JP in there, standing behind her, Captain Jean Paul Matrice as clear as day, wow the old dog, he certainly knew how to mix did JP, no doubt with the Department's credit card in his pocket at that. Look at him, Frankie smiled as he realised JP was actually talking to the President in the shot, Nicolas Sarkozy, the then President of France!

He smiled to himself, wondering if JP had got pissed on the president's champagne, sipping his glasses of water as he went. Who'd have thought it.

The clearly high-flying Frenchman was due over again in a couple of days, Frankie saved the image to *Paint*, and cropped the picture so just JP and the President were in it, he pressed the print button, he'd have some fun with this! He was looking forward to winding JP up a good one.

The image began to jerk out of the printer, his quest for the allusive Henri DuPont momentarily forgotten as he again smiled at seeing his new found friend mixing with one of the most powerful men in the world. Excellent it was a good copy, once printed he'd pin it up on the wall, see JP's face when he walked in. He took the picture, and went into his office, he pulled some notices off the blue felt notice board on his wall, and freed a drawing pin, piercing the top centre of the sheet, and placing it onto the board, he stood back laughing to himself, suddenly he went cold, very cold, goose bumps appeared on his arms.

"Oh shit. Oh fucking shit. No."

He looked at the picture.

He felt sick, actually physically sick, JP shaking hands with the President of France. The very hand he was using, on his finger. It was there, it was the ring.

THE SHATTERED EAGLE

-FIFTYFOUR-
The Eagle, The Eagle Is Moving!

Frankie walked into Lovan's office, "Get that ring Craig, I need to see that ring now?"

Lovan was sitting at his desk studying some papers, he looked up over the top of his glasses, "Why hello to you too Frankie, don't worry about phoning, letting me know you're here, or even knocking, just come right in. What the hell are you doing here so early anyway, I thought you went home last night?"

"Never mind that, look!"

He held out the sheet of paper he had printed out just seven hours earlier.

Lovan pushed his glasses further up his nose, and studied the picture.

"Hmm I see the President of France, and if I'm not mistaken that's your French friend from Brittany, Jean Paul. As impressed as I am that there is only one degree of separation between you and one of the most powerful men in Europe, I fail to see why you've travelled over 100 miles first thing in the morning to show me this, go on give me a clue, what am I missing here?"

"His hand Craig, look at his fingers!"

Lovan held the paper closer to his face, examining it to ensure there was no mistake, "Oh my God, it's the ring isn't it!"

"It must be. Why is Jean Paul Matrice in a picture with the President of France wearing that ring?" Frankie then held out a second picture, the original before he zoomed and cropped, with Anna DuPont in the foreground. "With Warsabi's first victim."

"We need to be asking him that I think." Lovan had pushed his chair back and was walking towards the office door, "Come on let's go and have another look at that ring."

They walked down a corridor, neither saying anything, then into a room full of filing cabinets, where in the corner stood a large old fashioned safe. Lovan took out a long brass key and unlocked it and pulled out a clear plastic evidence bag.

"Please shut the door Frankie," he requested before sitting at a leather topped desk. He switched on an angle poise lamp and placed the bag beneath it, looking at the contents within, through the clear plastic.

"For fucks sake give it here!" Frankie said as he pulled it from Lovan's hands. He tore at the top with his teeth and ripped the bag open, tipping the ring onto the dark green surface of the desk. He pulled a pair of latex gloves from his pocket and slid his hands into them.

"Right what have we got Craig?" he asked, but it was clear it was one of his rhetorical questions, so Lovan just

THE SHATTERED EAGLE

waited for him to continue. "It's obviously French, it's not that old by the look of it. There's the writing down the side, which we know translates to *With gratitude which can never be spoke of.* A gift then, given to someone, is it official, some kind of decoration, award, like some medal? I've asked around all over the place but no one knows of it. JP played ignorant, but then he crops up in a photo wearing the bloody thing! Is it the same one? Is this JP's ring we're holding? Oh Christ, is he really tied up in this?"

"Of course he is!" Lovan said, seemingly not wishing to say it too obviously.

Frankie winced, this was someone he had brought right into the investigation, been out drinking with, had opened the case up to.

"Sorry Frankie, but that's too big a coincidence, he's wearing the same ring on his hand for heaven's sake. You asked him to look into it, and he said he came up with nothing, yet look for yourself!"

"I know, I fucking know!" Frankie stood up and paced around the small room, he held the ring in his fingers, like the answers to all his questions were suddenly going to come tumbling out through its magic powers. He ran his fingers along the edge feeling the outline of the slightly embossed lettering, "With gratitude which can never be spoke of," he said aloud. "What does that mean? Thanks but don't tell anyone I thanked you?"

He turned it in his hand, and leant down, again placing it under the lamp, the Gold Eagle on the French flag, it looked official. He remembered Oli telling him about the ambush on the taxi. He thought out loud, "The blokes that took Warsabi contacted Gold Eagle over the radio didn't they, think Frankie, think. What's so special about this ring, it was what they were after, not Warsabi. The ring was the target. Then where is the bomber now? How does it link to the bombing, how does it tie in with the rape and murder in France? It's just a ring isn't it?"

He ran his fingers over the ornate front, the vivid flag inset into the gold, the eagle spread across all three colours, the sort of thing Napoleon would have had on one of those great big medals that adorned sashes across his uniform tunic. His finger rubbed over the eagle gently feeling its outline, what was its secret, what was its importance. Then as his finger caressed it he felt it move. Just ever so slightly, but it shifted. He wiggled it again, yes it was definitely loose.

"The eagle, Craig, the eagle is moving!" Frankie held it under the lamp and wiggled his finger over it. Lovan leant over his shoulder peering at it, watching intently. Frankie continued wiggling the face of the ring, suddenly it sprang up, the flag and eagle popped out, still stuck to the rubber of his glove.

"Well fuck me sideways!" Frankie exclaimed, inside the base beneath where the flag had been was something nestling on a very thin base of velvet.

A micro SD Card.

THE SHATTERED EAGLE

-FIFTYFIVE-
It Is Your Cross To Bear

Henri felt ill at ease, this was not the scenario he was anticipating for his next meeting with the Legion. Waiting outside the door he was flanked by two of Claude's bodyguards, whilst inside the meeting had proceeded without him. He had promised them results, said it would all be sorted, yet here he was about to be summoned into the boardroom, no longer apparently an equal, but a defendant in some kangaroo court.

He had been let down, it was now a case of taking control himself. Auguste Fredericks had been a great disappointment, his part was just foul up after foul up, the man he had seen and been so impressed by in Afghanistan, had proved to be nothing but a liability, at least he knew he could rely on his silence, that was something he was sure of. He had expected more, certainly not the pantomime that followed, but it was done now, it was a just a case of cleaning up, but alas, they couldn't even get that right.

No he would go and do it himself.

He was sitting in a soft chair in the reception area, he wondered how much longer they would keep him waiting, he imagined Michel in there, verbally assassinating him, denigrating his work and contribution to the cause.

The door opened and he was beckoned in by Claude.

"Henri, sorry to have kept you waiting, as you can imagine there was much for us to discuss before asking for your side of events. This has turned into a most embarrassing escapade, which still has the potential to explode in all our faces. Harold has offered to take over supervising the recovery of what you have so far been unable to obtain. But we have agreed that this duty should still be carried out by yourself. We are struggling to maintain the support of our friends in the UK, they are very robust in the assertion that all this should have been resolved far quicker than it has been. I cannot stress how perturbed we are at how this has all been conducted."

Henri knew that if Harold had offered to take over he had lost all support, he was his ally, no more than that - he was his friend - the one of the four he could rely upon, he had remained silent at their last meeting, but clearly now even Harold had run out of patience. Et tu Brute!

Claude continued, "We have agreed, and I have no need to explain why, that if this all goes wrong, if things do not get resolved, then you Henri will take responsibility, it is your cross to bear. I know your loyalty is not at question here, just perhaps your judgement. Do you understand what I am saying?"

Henri knew exactly what he was saying.

"Yes Claude I understand. But I am still sure that it will not come to that, I will be able to rectify matters. But yes you can be sure I would take sole responsibility if required, and will certainly ensure that any fall out falls on no one but myself. I can only thank you for allowing me to continue with this, and assure you I will not let you down."

Michel spoke up, as Henri knew he would, "A bit too late for that I'd say Henri, just make sure no further damage occurs. Already you have created chaos."

Henri looked to his friend Harold to rebut Michel on his behalf, show him some support, but he remained silent.

"Michel, I'm sure Henri is already aware of the failings of that particular episode," Claude said. "We are above such recriminations, Henri is after all still one of us, please respect that fact."

Still one of us! Indicating that this was by no means a permanent arrangement, that it was open to alteration and change. Henri nodded towards Claude as if thanking him for the vote of confidence, but realised that his statement was far more damning than anything Michel had said.

"Thank you Henri," Claude said, "That will be all."

Dismissed!

Like some servant who had just delivered breakfast! Henri left the room furious, although he tried not to show it. It was clear his days as part of the *Legion Secret de la Republique* were now numbered, and it was also clear that so would his days of living and breathing be numbered if he didn't sort this mess out. There was no way they would allow him to carry on with his life if he was implicated in this, just the risk of dragging them in was enough to ensure he would be sacrificed immediately.

As he left the building he strode towards his car, did he need to start checking under it prior to driving it anywhere? Was he safe sleeping at home? When or how would they come for him? Because he now knew they would at some point.

-FIFTYSIX-
A Big Problem Relating To An Eagle, A Tricolour, And A Gold Ring

"Hello JP it's good to see you again," Frankie declared as he shook Jean Paul's hand warmly. "Come, come into my office I have something to talk about."

JP looked well, he had obviously had some sun on his face since they had last met up, although Frankie could see signs of stress creeping into that normally calm visage, despite the Frenchman still playing the jovial nice guy.

"It's good to see you too Frankie, although I must confess I felt worse for wear after our last meeting, regardless of how much water I had consumed," he chuckled as he followed Frankie into his office, sitting on one of the soft chairs adjacent to the desk was Craig Lovan.

"You two have met haven't you?" Frankie said as they entered.

"Why yes, only briefly," Jean Paul said, shaking hands with Craig, who had risen from his chair.

"Good to see you again Mr Lovan."

"Likewise Monsieur Matrice," Lovan answered.

"Good, good," Frankie continued. "Because I want Craig to sit in with us."

"Sure, no problem." JP answered, Frankie looked at him, sitting there with that smile, that fucking horrible deceitful smile, still on his face. But he had to stay calm, he needed to find out what this was all about, and he was sure that shouting and hollering would have very little effect in ascertaining the answer to the burning question that would soon be leaving his own lips.

"You see JP, I do have a problem, it's one concerning truth and honesty. Friends sharing things with each other, it's good to share is it not JP?"

JP frowned, "It is good to share Frankie, but I'm at a bit of a loss, what is this about?"

"You see I have a dilemma a big dilemma relating to an eagle, a tricolour, and a gold ring, which you say you know fuck all about."

"Frankie, please, why are you speaking in such a manner?" JP replied, looking visibly hurt at this unexpected onslaught.

"Because Matrice, for the past two days this has been burning in my mind, like some toxic cancer, gnawing at my every thought, my waking hours dominated by one question, one question I need you to answer, just why the hell is my friend JP, the mate who I've allowed into my

THE SHATTERED EAGLE

house, who I've trusted more than my own people, who've I've shared everything on this case with, why has he been mugging me off? That's what's been keeping me awake, giving me bad dreams, making me feel sick every moment I think about it. So why JP, why have you been taking me for some fool?"

Lovan watched on, he appeared uncomfortable, but he was the only other person Frankie had brought into it, had included in what he had found out, he needed him there.

"But I do not follow?" JP again said.

"Time to stop this charade. Time to start telling Frankie the truth! The ring, the ring I asked you to explore for me, look into, investigate, call it what we will. The ring you said you had no idea about, couldn't help me with, but what's this? The ring that's on your fucking finger in this picture!"

He threw the blown up photo towards him, looking at it Jean Paul went very quiet, staring at the photo, at first the colour seemed to drain away from his face, then he gave a wry smile.

"Mr Lovan will you excuse us for one moment please, I need to speak to Frankie in confidence."

Lovan looked at Frankie, who nodded his head towards the door, the DI rose to feet saying nothing more as he exited than, "I'll be outside."

Once Lovan had closed the door, Jean Paul walked around the office, gesturing with his hands like he was an eager school teacher addressing a class of children. "Frankie, there is much we do not know in this world, much that has to be done in order to keep the world functioning, to maintain the status quo. You should understand this as a man who believes in right, a man who acts according to what is proper and correct. You are what people would describe as a forthright person, one who likes the truth, doesn't like unnecessary garnish. So I will speak accordingly. This does not concern you. This is way above your head, you are out of your league on this. You deserve some explanation, but forget the ring. Focus on your bomb, catch Warsabi, that should be your priority. Do not trouble yourself with something that does not concern you."

"Oh really. Just forget the ring, simple isn't it. Oh wow, what was that I was worrying about just a minute ago, oh shit I can't remember. Hmm that was easier than I thought. Oh wait! I do remember. What was that fucking ring doing on your finger!"

"I have already said this is none of your concern, out of respect for you I will say I do consider our friendship to be genuine, I have played no games with you. But there are far more important issues at stake, they are grave matters of state, and you as a servant of your country need to appreciate that. I will not apologise for serving my country, as you should now serve yours. I will leave now, we will not speak again Mr Howard, I can assure you of that."

JP went to leave the office, Frankie moved, blocking his way, clasping JP by his arm. JP swung around fixing

THE SHATTERED EAGLE

Frankie with an icy stare, none of the good humoured warmness visible, but Frankie wasn't backing down.

"Oh yes we will bloody speak again, you're not going anywhere. You can tell me here and now, or I'm arresting your garlic infested slimy French…"

The door to Frankie's office suddenly burst open, three men walked in.

"Isaac Crafton, MI5," a young immaculately dressed man held out an ID card in front of him. "We're taking Monsieur Matrice with us. You and Inspector Lovan are to stand down on the Northampton case, as from now. You are to hand over all evidence relating to the ring and any other matters connected to it. Once this is done all electronic information relating to the case is to be deleted."

As he spoke the other two men escorted Jean Paul from the office, Lovan watched on, as did Felix, Sylvia and Daggett, who were all in the open plan area outside.

"No you fucking don't!" Frankie shouted as he went to stop them. He was furious, this was his kingdom, no spotty teenage wanker from MI5 was walking out with Matrice, he still wanted answers, no needed answers, this was part of the Euston deal, and this was most definitely his investigation.

"Felix, stop them!"

Felix moved to block their path, Pete and Sylvia also backing him up. Lovan stood transfixed on the spot, just observing, watching a genuine standoff with MI5, no doubt thinking, 'what have I got tangled up in?'

"Please Mr Howard, we need to leave, move your Officers immediately!" Crafton instructed, his well-rounded vowels spoken with a calm authority that clearly demanded instant compliance, but not here, not in the Red House, not relating to this case.

"You stay where you are!" Frankie barked, "They're not going anywhere until I check who we have here."

Matrice spoke, his voice almost pleading, "Frankie you do not comprehend what is happening here, please don't make this any worse than what it already is."

"Mr Howard, Stand your people down, allow us to leave without the recourse to further action," Crafton again ordered.

"Further action, further fucking action! Get out of here!"

He pushed Crafton in the chest, he rocked back having to take a step to steady himself, the two other MI5 men moved towards him.

"You two better stop exactly where you are. Now listen, fuck off out of here!" he pointed at Matrice, who appeared to be watching on with an almost detached air, as if this didn't matter, he already knew the outcome. "You can have him, when, and only when I say you can, are we clear?"

"DCI Howard!" It was Crafton talking again, he appeared to have recovered his composure. "I said to stand down. I will not ask again."

Frankie went to speak, but was cut short.

THE SHATTERED EAGLE

"They said stand down Howard." The voice came from Chief Superintendent Gail Hopkiss as she entered the room, "And you will damn well stand down!"

The three ATU staff blocking the exit moved aside, Frankie could only look on gobsmacked as Crafton and his two henchmen immediately marched out with Captain Jean Paul Matrice.

Frankie turned to Hopkiss, he was enraged, what the hell had she just done? "That man is a major fucking suspect in my murder investigation and you've just ordered me to let him go!"

"No DCI Howard, I didn't order you to let him go, the Home Secretary has. And do not ever speak to me like that again, now in your office and close the door!"

Once inside she sat down, "Don't say it Adrian, it wasn't me, but they want that ring immediately. Where is it?"

Frankie bit his lip, he said nothing.

"I said where is it?"

"This is bullshit, total bullshit, Matrice has something to do with this, I have evidence of it."

"Adrian you have nothing, you have no idea. This has come straight from Number Ten, you need to play along on this. Now where is the ring?"

"Bollocks!" he slammed his fists down upon his desk, he was scarlet with rage.

"Tell me where the ring is, that is an order!" Hopkiss shouted.

Frankie knew it was no use arguing, he wasn't going to win this one, not now politicians had their grubby fingers all over it.

"Northampton, Inspector Lovan out there has it as evidence in his investigation, funnily enough into another three murders. But what the hell, twenty one dead people, what does that matter as long as the Prime Minister gets his way! Ma'am like I said Matrice is part of it, he knows what it's about, I need to speak to him." Frankie was now practically pleading with his superior, desperate for her to change her direction.

"Detective Chief Inspector, I frankly don't give a shit. Do not get involved with that ring, do you hear, for heaven's sake isn't the Euston bombing enough for you. We need results on that. Thames House is all over Matrice, it's not our fight. Now leave this office for a minute and send Inspector Lovan in."

THE SHATTERED EAGLE

-FIFTYSEVEN-
This Mr Lovan Is Your Last And Only Chance.

Once Chief Superintendent Hopkiss had departed with Lovan, Frankie opened his office drawer and pulled out his Police Federation diary, he opened it to his birthday, July the 17th, and there taped on the page was the Micro SD Card. He was sure that Lovan wouldn't mention it, but he also knew that it was that tiny micro-card which had caused all this chaos, and once they, whoever they were, realised it was no longer there, no longer hidden in the ring, both he and Lovan would be the people they came looking for.

He had of course plugged it into a computer, it was the first thing to do, but whatever it was, it was Password Protected, he had no idea what to do with it. He could just about send emails, navigate his way around *Facebook*, may be at a push work out how to access his home banking account, but hacking was way beyond his capabilities. If the Home Secretary was ordering him to stand back, then he sure as hell wasn't going to get authorisation for the boffins at GCHQ to sort out what was on that card.

He also had no intention of letting it go though, this was his investigation, but he would have to be careful now and so would Lovan. It wouldn't be long before whoever had replaced Auguste Fredericks came looking for them. Frankie thought how as a big part of the Anti-Terrorism Unit he always under threat, always on his guard. But what of Lovan? He didn't carry a side arm, he didn't spend his days taking on Republican dissidents, Islamic Extremists and animal loving people haters. He didn't check under his car when parked in certain areas, or have panic alarms in his bedroom. No, Craig was vulnerable as hell.

Up in Northampton two of the MI5 people escorted Lovan to the room with the safe, he handed over the ring in the evidence bag, and watched as they exited with it.

He immediately phoned Frankie, "They have the ring. Didn't take anything else, didn't ask any other questions, just took it and left, what's going on Frankie?"

"Craig, you need to be very careful, and I mean very careful, say nothing to no one, not even your team, head back towards here right away, I'll phone you as you're travelling, don't hang around, I mean it, get the hell out of there. Once they realise it's not in the ring they're going to be looking for it, and you're going to be their first call. We need to talk and work out our next steps."

Craig Lovan was an uncomplicated man, he didn't deal in grey areas or muddy his feet in the murky waters of 'Black Ops' or international terrorism. As he left the Police car-

THE SHATTERED EAGLE

park his mind was awash with the events of the past day. He had gone from heading up a murder investigation to fleeing from the very same people he was pursuing. It was madness, but he knew what they were capable of, he had seen it all too clearly with the slaying of George Morton and 'Rab the Cab' McKinnen. He needed to meet up with Frankie, get some kind of handle on what was occurring. MI5 in Northampton, it was ludicrous!

He pulled onto the M1 at Junction 15 and headed south towards London, it was busy, but it always was at that time of day.

He mulled everything over in his head, was he really in that much danger? Then he thought of Jim Bolton, battered senseless, the hole in his head, just because he may have had the ring, or more relevantly what was previously contained within it.

His phone rang, that would be Frankie, hopefully making some sense of this whole insane change of events. He pressed the *Bluetooth* button on his dashboard.

"Mr Lovan. I think you know what we require, and that you already appreciate the lengths we will go to get it."

The voice sounded robotic, distorted by some electronic device, a cross between Darth Vadar and a Dalek. But it wasn't the sound that had disturbed him so, had left him absolutely terrified, it was the fact he knew exactly what they wanted, and yes he was well aware of the lengths they would go to get it.

"Who is this?" he asked, though very much doubted he would get an answer to that particular question.

"This Mr Lovan is your last and only chance. I'm asking if you have what we want. Let's not even pretend we are ignorant here, I'm asking if you have the Micro Card. If you do, pull over onto the hard shoulder immediately. If you don't then we will assume Mr Howard has it. But be warned the only thing keeping you alive at this time is the fact we believe you may have what we want. I can assure you that failure to pull over will be taken only as one thing. You are of no use to us, just a hindrance, and you will be dealt with accordingly."

Lovan said nothing, he actually wanted to cry, his stomach was knotted, he felt hopeless, totally helpless. He accelerated, hanging the phone up. He was so scared, he was a Policeman sure, but not some automated super being. He breathed like other people, he had the same emotions, the same anxieties, and at this point a very big fear. He really genuinely wished he had the bloody card, because he knew for sure that he would have pulled over there and then and given them it.

The phone rang again, he didn't want to, but he answered it.

"Mr Lovan, we will not tell you again, if you have the item pull over immediately, any other action will be taken as a negative response."

The phone cut off. Lovan, pressed the green button on the *Bluetooth* controls on his dashboard, he needed to get Frankie, tell him of the call, warn him, but only static came through the speakers, he pushed it again, then again.

THE SHATTERED EAGLE

Nothing, he couldn't call out, and presumed he was unable to receive calls either.

He pressed his foot harder to the floor, as he moved to the outside lane. 90 mph, 95, mph, 100 mph. Just keep driving, keep going, stop at the next Services, ironically Newport Pagnall of all places, use a Pay Phone, talk to Frankie, this was his world, his domain, he'd have answers.

Craig Lovan hammered down the M1, adrenaline coursed through his veins, he pressed the Green button again, maybe he would have a signal back, but nothing, still just static…

Notice to Staff

It is with great sadness and regret that we need to report that Detective Inspector Craig Lovan of the Northamptonshire Police Force died whilst on duty at 17.55 on the 21st September. It is suspected his car suffered mechanical failure whilst travelling on the M1 Motorway, causing him to collide with a bridge just North of Milton Keynes.

At this time funeral arrangements have yet to be finalised, but we will inform all staff when this information becomes known. I'm sure you will join with me in offering my heartfelt condolences to Craig's wife and children, in what is a very difficult time for all of us.

The Commissioner
Northamptonshire Police Force.

THE SHATTERED EAGLE

-FIFTYEIGHT-
Never Use The S-Word Again, It Just Doesn't Suit You.

Once more it just went straight to voicemail, and once more he immediately hung up.

"Come on man answer your phone!" Frankie said out loud. Again he tried, then again and again, before reluctantly finally leaving a message, "Hey Craig, it's Frankie, for God's sake man answer your fucking phone in future. Look, give me a ring on my mobile as soon as you can, we need to sort out how we're going play this. Cheers."

Frankie put his phone back in his pocket, Lovan would call he was sure, he needed to stop worrying about him, the man was a Detective Inspector, not some four year old child, he was capable of looking out for himself. He hadn't discussed it with him, he didn't want to spook him unnecessarily, but once he got down to London he intended to find him somewhere safe, move his family there as well, he had seen what these bastards were capable of, and moral restraint wasn't one of those things.

He put Lovan to the back of his mind, at least for the time being and called for Sylvia, Daggett and Felix to come into his Office. Trooping in like naughty kids, they sat down before him, three of them squeezed into the two-seater settee, looking ill at ease and uncomfortable. Frankie said nothing at first, still thinking how to word everything, how to phrase what was basically a confession that he didn't trust them, well actually he had trusted Sylvia, but the other two could never know that. They were obviously expecting the worst, having not long ago seen him getting his wings clipped good and proper, and none of them broke the silence that was so awkwardly dominating his office. He knew they weren't sure what the deal was with Jean Paul Matrice, and he was well aware that they probably thought he was confiding in the horrible Frenchman and Lovan far more than he did them.

Finally Frankie spoke, "I need to talk properly with you. I need to explain a few things, hopefully un-muddy some pretty murky waters. With DeHavalland turning us over I've not been totally straight with you, I've left you out in the dark. I'm not going to go around the houses here, this doesn't sound nice, but it was because Jay told me at least one of you was rotten. I know, I know, but that's the reason."

Frankie couldn't work out if his team were hurt or angry, they had been through a lot together, and now he was actually saying what he was, it sounded far worse than he

THE SHATTERED EAGLE

thought it would. But they said nothing, just sitting there waiting for him to continue.

"I'm sorry, I really am, the whole thing's fucked up. I've deliberately not included you in any of the Northampton stuff, just kept you focused on the Euston case, which after all is what we're investigating. But in truth they're linked big time."

He then filled his team in on all he had excluded them from right up to Hopkiss and the spooks leaving earlier. Oli stealing a ring from Warsabi, Kate's kidnapping, the exchange, using Lovan to do what his team should have done at Newport Pagnall, Matrice wearing the ring in that photo, the whole lot. By the time he had finished the office was once more silent.

"So there you have it, you now know as much as I do. Look I really do feel shit over this, it's just I was lost, I really got thrown."

"Oh sod it Frankie," Felix rudely interrupted his awkward attempt at bridge building. "I can't listen to you apologising anymore, it's just not right, it's not natural, look it's now gone seven, you've kept us longer than you should have anyway, come on, come and buy us all a beer for God's sake, and never use the S-word again, it just doesn't suit you, you miserable old bastard!"

Three hours later they were still in the *Moon Under Water* sitting in a corner, surrounded by the ancient book spines and pictures of famous authors, it had been a good night, a cathartic air clearing exercise. Frankie had repeatedly tried to contact Lovan, but for some reason nothing. A pile of empty glasses and large plates of half eaten food in front of them bore witness as to how the evening had progressed. Pete was half asleep lying against a wall in the corner of the booth they were sitting within, occasionally he would snap out of his slumber to contribute a random sentence to a conversation, most of which related to something they had stopped discussing minutes earlier, before collapsing back again. Felix was a bit better, still every now and then lapsing into the unofficial language of total bollocks, but at least remaining conscious. Sylvia hadn't been drinking, she was supposed to be going out later with a couple of other friends, was driving, so she played the role of the responsible adult, but judging by the state of Daggett it was a role she hadn't played that well.

"Can I remind you all," Frankie announced, "that we all need to be up bright and early, there is now officially a shitload of shit that needs doing." He slurred as he spoke, "And tomorrow we will work very very hard to make up for this blatant dereliction of duty, you fuckers are a bad influence on me, very bad."

"I reckon I better get going," Felix said, before whispering, "I think we've still got our firearms, I know have."

He held his finger to his mouth, "Shhh, don't tell anyone!"

"Oh bollocks," Sylvia exclaimed, "You mean you didn't put it away before coming out on a bender, you can't go

THE SHATTERED EAGLE

back like that, give it to me and I'll log it back in, do either of you two have yours?" she asked Frankie and Daggett.

"I might have," Pete answered without even opening his eyes.

"And you Frankie?"

"No, course not, what do you take me for?"

"I know exactly what you are Guv' I was just trying to ascertain just how big a one you might be." She then addressed the other two, "Quick put them in my bag, under the table, be careful no one sees, I can't believe you two, I really can't, come on hurry up!"

She felt two heavy thuds in her bag as the two inebriated Policemen dropped loaded hand guns into her handbag. It was like working with idiots sometimes, taking guns out on the piss.

As they came outside the pub the night time fresh air hit Daggett hard, he tottered on the steps, with Felix and Frankie catching him before he could tumble down.

"We'll stick him in a taxi," Felix said. "Don't worry we'll make sure he's alright, we'll see you tomorrow Sylv!"

She gave them all a peck on the cheek before heading off towards the Red House, all too conscious she was walking around the West End of London with two loaded weapons in her handbag at ten o'clock at night.

Having walked about a hundred yards she turned around and saw the three of them still standing on the steps, illuminated by the entrance to the pub, not having moved,

Felix and Frankie struggling to keep Daggett standing upright. Geez, they were bloody useless, did she have to sort everything out, she turned and started to walk back. A black *Audi* suddenly screeched to a stop in front of the pub, she saw two silhouettes get out and move towards her three colleagues, oh Jesus, they had guns!

She immediately pulled one of the *Glocks* from her bag, before tossing the bag to the floor, the other gun still in it.

She dropped to one knee, drawing the weapon to the firing position, screaming, "Armed Police!"

She saw Frankie and Felix look around as she shouted, as one of the two men drew his weapon up, Sylvia instinctively fired a single shot hitting the assailant in the arm, he recoiled around, shocked and in pain, as the bullet shattered his humerus, the second man fired his gun, knocking Pete Daggett backwards, out of the grip of Frankie and Felix, onto the hard steps. He moved the gun in the direction of her DCI, she fired three times, all missing, then moved forward for a better shot. Frankie lunged forward at his attacker. People were scattering in all directions in the street, pandemonium had erupted, she couldn't see her friends and colleagues any more, nor could she see the attackers, people were running everywhere, she heard another shot, then suddenly the *Audi* drove off at speed.

Grabbing her hand bag from the floor she ran to the front of the pub.

"Armed Police, stay back!" she shouted at the crowd emerging from inside.

THE SHATTERED EAGLE

Then she saw Daggett on the floor, the trail of dark blood snaking from his head towards the pavement as it slowly moved over the steps. Felix and Frankie were bent over him, she ran over.

"I'm sorry Sylv'. There's nothing we can do." Felix was now sitting beside his deceased friend, Frankie the other side, both now stone cold sober.

"Quick, inside, move!" she shouted at her two superiors. "Quickly do it! Bring Pete, we need to get off the street, we're easy targets here, c'mon get him in!"

She yelled at the scores of drinkers blocking the doorway, "Get out of the way, move!"

Both Frankie and Felix, dragged Pete into the pub. Sylvia followed them in, just in time as more gunfire rained into the bar, shattering the glazed doorway, showering them with tiny shards of glass.

Sylvia crouched down by a fruit machine, her gun in one hand, the other waving frantically at screaming drinkers.

"Get down, get down!" she called to the terrified onlookers. She fished in her handbag and pulled out the other *Glock*, sliding it across the floor to Felix, who was crouched the other side of the doorway, with Frankie pulling Pete away from the entrance.

"Stay where we are?" Felix called to Sylvia, more a question than an instruction.

"Too right, I'm not moving anywhere, wait for the cavalry to come."

Neither of them could see where the shots had come from, but it was clear that going outside was only inviting danger. She had no idea whether their attackers were still out there, but she wasn't about to offer herself up as bait to find out. She was happy to follow her own advice, stay put, wait for help, and keep her head down.

Within three minutes the first Armed Response Vehicles had arrived, gunfire in London has a way of garnering a swift response. The heavily armed officers sealed off the street, taking control, containing the situation. Once established that the immediate area had been secured, the Ambulances were permitted on the scene.

Pete was dead, Frankie was kneeling over him, unable to do anything for his friend, who only days before he had considered capable of betraying them, but then he had trusted no one at that point, such was the magnitude of DeHavalland's treachery. Sylvia and Felix knelt beside him.

Frankie looked up, he appeared devastated, emotionally wrecked, "Are you both OK?"

"Yes Guv," Felix answered only just audible over all the chaos now occurring all around them.

"Good."

Paramedics were now taking over, asking for room to work, to attempt the impossible. The three of them stood up and wandered out in the cool air, Frankie had his arm around Sylvia, although he hadn't said any more, none of them had.

THE SHATTERED EAGLE

As the Ambulance took their now deceased friend off, Sylvia burst into tears in Frankie's arms, he stared out at the scene, the blood where Pete was killed, congealed where it ran down the steps, the trail where they had dragged him into the pub, the on-lookers, photographing the scene with mobile phones, a fine Officer had fallen in duty and they were photographing the aftermath to show their friends on the internet, souvenirs from their day in London. What sort of world did we live in, he thought, but he already knew the answer to that, he knew it all too well.

-FIFTYNINE-
Hackattack.org

Fran and the children were out walking across the fields to look at the horses and have a picnic by the pond at the bottom of the field. They had tried to persuade him to join them, but Gary fancied the idea of a little 'me-time', a chance for a bit of solitude and reflection. He had enjoyed a reasonable night's sleep, not even realising that the itch had given him a break, until waking up to see that his legs were free of fresh scratches and the backs of his hands devoid of blood or newly made scabs. Whilst his family traipsed over the freshly cut grass, the kids enjoying a game of hide and seek darting between the giant rolls of hay, expelling the pent up energy built up over the past few days, Gary was just lying on the sofa. Of course lying on anything other than your own bed was a big taboo in the Henderson household, but then neither Sheila nor Clive were there were they, he had considered taking his jeans and pants off, just to spite Sheila in her absence, but decided against it, too much explaining if Oli or Kate suddenly came down, to find him lying naked watching Jeremy Kyle, which was never a good look!

THE SHATTERED EAGLE

He wondered for a moment if his stress was at long last melting away, his mind had allowed him to actually think about a holiday, nothing extravagant, even in his fantasies his vacation expectations were grounded, but maybe a caravan in Devon or Cornwall, or perhaps even the South of France, when all this was over, with and normality returned, live a little. But then he reminded himself that they were only a week away from October, yeah perhaps next year, when that all-encompassing debt was nearer to being paid off. And here it comes, he thought, here comes the black cloud, once more his mind returning to familiar territory. He could feel his brow furrowing, the corners of his mouth turning down, and a sudden flash of an image in his mind, *that* image, the yellow dress, he sat up, shaking his head, 'get out, get out, leave me alone', he thought, but he knew that any respite was ever only going to be temporary. He walked over to the well-appointed kitchen and switched the kettle on, his mind clearing once more as the sunshine warmed his face through the open window. Then he heard the knock at the front door…

"Hello, wasn't expecting you, come in." Gary said, although Frankie had already brushed past him, striding into the hallway.

"Is Henderson at home?" Frankie asked, he appeared subdued, not really with it.

"No." Gary replied.

"What about Queen Boudicca?"

"No she's with Clive, both out for the day."

"Thank fuck for that."

Frankie strolled in making it plain that his shoes were definitely staying on his feet. There was something wrong, he was saying the words Frankie would, acting like Frankie would, but in no way was it all in the inimitable style of the curmudgeonly DCI.

"How are you Frankie?"

"Do you really want to know? Because to be honest I feel about as shit as I've ever felt in my life. I feel totally and utterly emotionally drained, and it isn't nice Gary, it isn't nice at all."

"What's happened, what's wrong?" Gary asked, perturbed to see Frankie so vulnerable, so, well so normal, just like everyone else in the world.

"Someone tried to kill me yesterday. Tried to kill all of us." His eyes were welling, Gary had never seen him like this, previously he had never appeared anything but in total control. Bullying, hectoring, charging in like some wild boar, yes, and as he had got to know him better, protecting, passionate, and even caring, but never ever so emotionally open.

"They've killed Pete."

"What!" Gary answered, gobsmacked by what he had just been told.

Frankie went silent for a few seconds, bowing his head, his eyes momentarily closing, before continuing. "Shot him dead. I was there, holding him whilst it happened. He died, and I couldn't do a shitting thing to help, just watching him, laying there. Dead Gary, he's dead!"

THE SHATTERED EAGLE

Gary stood there, should he hug him? 'Bloody hell, should I?' he asked himself. How do you comfort someone who is usually so strong? So commanding? Ah sod it, look at him, he's in bits.

Gary went in to give Frankie a hug.

"Whoa!" Frankie recoiled, taking a big step back, "You are joking aren't you. If you want to offer comfort and support put the kettle on, but please spare me the kissing and hugging, as well meaning as I'm sure it is!"

Gary felt embarrassed, he should have known, this was after all the hard-nosed bastard that had called him Weeping Beauty on their first meeting, but then he was also the man with very visible tears filling his eyes.

"What happened Frankie, when, where?"

He relayed the story of the slaying outside of *The Moon Under Water*, how Daggett had been worse for wear, Sylvia shooting one of the assailants, how they had another go afterwards, again opened fire on them in the pub. It was all so unbelievable, unreal, only Gary found nothing unbelievable or unreal anymore, it was all too real, and too scary, so bloody scary.

"Anyway I need you Gary," Frankie said wiping his eyes, "although let's get this clear right away, not in your give me a kiss and a cuddle sense. I need your help. You work with computers don't you?"

He had reverted back to type, no more moist eyes, public displaying of his inner feelings, Frankie was back in control.

"Well kind of, I'm no Berners-Lee, but I can get round a machine OK. Why?"

"Birnie-who?" Frankie asked.

"Berners-Lee."

"Never heard of him, still he's not here, you are. I need you to look at something for me. Can you open this up?"

He handed Gary the SD Card.

"I don't know. What's on it?" Gary asked.

"If I knew that I wouldn't be asking you to open it for me, would I. To be honest I haven't a clue what's on it, but a lot of people have died for it, a bloody good mate of mine included, and I want to ensure no more do."

Gary walked into Clive's study, and plugged the card into the port on the computer that was there. Immediately he could see it was password protected, but that wasn't necessary an insurmountable problem. Gary looked at the monitor for a minute. "Hmm, are you able to go away for a few minutes Frankie?"

"What?"

"Well this isn't what you'd call 100% legal."

"Don't worry about what's fucking legal, nor is what I'm asking you to do, why do you think I've travelled the best part of sixty miles instead of getting our people to do it. Just do what you've got to do, we're past the point of minor legalities by now, I want to know what's on it, what's so damn important it's worth killing for?"

Gary still felt awkward, his job was primarily to recover lost data, but every now and again the odd, 'private' job

THE SHATTERED EAGLE

would crop up. He typed into the address bar HAKKATTACK.ORG, a large pirates skull filled the screen, which mutated into a picture of 'V' from the movie 'V for Vendetta'.

He then typed in the word FREEDOOM, and a fresh page opened.

"This may take a while," Gary informed Frankie. "I'm pretty sure it's not going to be the name of someone's dog or their mother's maiden name."

He then typed some numbers into the space for the password of the unopened document. Words began to appear at lightning speed.

"Like I said Frankie you haven't seen this."

The words flashed by, thousands and thousands of them.

"What's it doing? Frankie asked.

"I've no idea," Gary responded, although he did know roughly, but thought by playing ignorant he would somehow help Frankie believe that this was an activity he had never dabbled in before.

Thirteen minutes later they both watched as the seemingly endless flash of words suddenly stopped. The letters ANNA*D*P were left in the box.

"Anna DuPont," Frankie muttered.

Gary pressed the return key and a 32 page Word Document opened, headed …

Secret Supérieur.
Retours d'Aigle d'Opération

-SIXTY-
Because He Found Out.

Less than half an hour after they had managed to open the document they were sitting around a coffee table discussing how best to deal with what they now knew. Although Frankie did have to question why he was talking to Oli and Gary, instead of just heading straight back to London, but then Gary had sorted it, broken into the locked doors that protected the *Word* document he was otherwise prohibited from seeing. Plus he was all too aware that MI5 would almost certainly come charging in if he tried to handle it through normal channels, Hopkiss too would no doubt block it, just as she would take great pleasure from pissing on his career from a great height should he not obey her every word, yet he couldn't leave it, he just couldn't, that 32 page document was the key to his investigation.

Oli had contributed little to the conversation, but Gary was full of ideas relating to leaking it here, there and everywhere, then acting on the fall out. 'Justice needs to be done', he had kept repeating, and if the law was unable to administer it, well then they would have to.

THE SHATTERED EAGLE

"Come on Gary, think," Frankie snapped, after once more the computer repair man made himself the expert in the room when it came to tackling international terrorism, "We're not fifteen year old anarchists, cyber terrorists or *Wiki*-fucking-*leakers*, I'm a serving Police Officer, you're a Dad – first and foremost that's what you are – who pisses around with computers, and Oli, well you're supposed to be a bloody Prison Officer, although to be honest a fucking great liability is a better description. If this came back to us we're buggered, plus it doesn't help us, and I mean *us*, not one bit, we'll still have bloody great targets painted on our backs, these people are seriously bad, it's got be resolved so you two Muppets can piss off back to Sesame Street at the end of this, and I can get in my motor without first having to push a mirror on a stick under it. And us acting as the great truth-sayers does very little to make that ideal scenario come about."

They had seen so much within the electronic document Gary had given them access to, but nothing that definitively solved the puzzle of why an eighteen year old kid from Somalia had planted a bomb on that train, nor more relevantly now, where he was now.

As the three of them sat there in silence there was a knock at the front door.

"That'll be the girls." Gary said as he went to answer it.

Frankie looked across to Oli, he was loathe to ask him for an opinion, his judgement had hardly proved to be spot-on with anything that had occurred of late, but thought he needed some back up, a bit of support, if for no other reason than to divert Gary from his obsession with world-wide media Armageddon.

"What do you reckon Oli?" he hesitantly asked.

"I don't know, I reckon…"

But Frankie never got to hear exactly what Oli reckoned, Gary had walked back into the room, he was pale and looked shocked, behind him stood Jean Paul Matrice, in his hand he held what appeared to be an automatic weapon, slung from a strap over his shoulder.

Frankie just stared, frozen to his chair.

"Hello Gentlemen, do excuse my intrusion." JP said, nodding to his gun as he spoke.

No one said anything in reply, Frankie remained seated, which was a pretty good thing to do as far as he was concerned, especially when confronted by someone carrying a *FAMAS* Assault Rifle. Oli was kneeling on the floor, where he had been leaning over the coffee table, and Gary slowly inched down into an armchair, Frankie's eyes were locked on JP, as he fumbled in his pocket, silently tapping his mobile phone.

"Well Frankie, I rather fear things have spiralled out of control since we last spoke. All you had to do was stick to your job. You had eighteen dead people, that should have been your concern, your raison d'être, but no, big Frankie Howard couldn't do that could he, couldn't stay concerned with matters he should have been worrying about. Of course not, it's not in his nature, he had to interfere, take what wasn't his, cause all sorts of grief for the people he knew and worked with."

THE SHATTERED EAGLE

Frankie raised his eyebrows, "I'm just a curious fucker I guess."

JP, gave the briefest of smiles, "No, just a fucker. Do you know the worst thing Frankie, we are on the same side, we have the same goals. Do you think I wanted to harm people who were basically good? Well do you? No of course not! I had no choice, I am preventing worse things from happening, bigger disasters than you can imagine. It's what you call collateral damage. You want to know what was on that SD Card, do you? Well I will tell you, what do we have to lose?"

"There's no need," Gary piped up, JP swung round to him, the gun now pointing at him instead of Frankie, Frankie could see that Gary had instantly regretted speaking. He said nothing for about ten seconds, but JP gestured for him to continue.

"Go on Mr Westlake, please tell me why is there no need?"

Gary was now speaking hesitantly, quietly, "We know what was on it, we've unlocked it. Yes Mr Matrice, we know."

JP kept the weapon pointing at Gary.

"Put the gun down." Oli said, "We're going to talk, all of us. I said put the gun down!"

Frankie was cringing, how would JP react to Oli's new found testicles suddenly appearing, but he saw him lower his weapon, clearly curious if nothing else.

"Obviously it's another game now, the rules have changed," Gary continued, Frankie was impressed with the courage of his two companions, although he was seriously questioning their wisdom.

"How do I know you have actually seen what you claim?" JP asked.

Frankie took a piece of paper from his pocket, "7th September, five years ago, Alaine DuPont commenced his education at the *Ecole de l'Afrique*. As did William Ngaroo, Yassar Salimi and Francois Ali. What sort of Education were they supposed to have JP? What sort of school trains kids how to plant bombs, set up IEDs, because I'm really keen to find out? Please tell me, tell me why they were apparently rescuing child soldiers from Africa, only to train them to become terrorists? Well?"

"It's not as simple as that, it's not…"

"Yes it is as simple as that, it's very fucking simple. We've seen it JP, we've seen it all. Training children, for crissake, to plant bombs in Syria, Egypt, Libya all over the shop. It's all listed on there you stupid bastard. How the hell did you think you'd get away with it? You even had the audacity to keep it recorded, a fully digitised record of it all!"

Frankie had risen to his feet, walking around, he shook his head continuing, "What happened JP, what made Warsabi murder Anna DuPont? Why did he come to London and blow one of our trains up, because my friend Gary here was on that train, hundreds of people were, and it doesn't fill me with joy to think somehow you were involved."

THE SHATTERED EAGLE

JP paused, considering his next sentence carefully, "A little while ago, I told you, that you didn't want to know the answers. I practically begged you to back off. But no you couldn't could you, you dragged others in. Do you really think they wanted to kill anyone? Inspector Lovan, you pushed him on, wouldn't let him stand back, no you dragged him along. Peter Daggett, they heard you telling him and the others everything in your office through their surveillance equipment, until then they were happy to let them carry on, but no, Frankie had to involve others didn't he.

"You want to know why Warsabi killed Anna. Because he found out. He found out that the people he trusted at his school, who he thought were looking out for him, caring for him, were in fact training him to die doing France's dirty work in some Foreign land. He found out the other three who joined the school with him, had been killed after carrying out their missions, because they were surplus to their requirements. It was a horrible brutal revenge. Why he planted the bomb on that train? Because they had taught him to, all he had to do was find someone willing to pay him enough to carry out what they had spent so much energy showing him. They created him.

"The ring, or more pertinently what was contained within, was their insurance policy, to keep those in power, for whom they acted, from betraying them, leaving them out to dry, as is still the case. That information on it, would bring down Governments, do you think your leaders were oblivious to what was happening? Really Frankie? Didn't you wonder why your Ministers authorised your Intelligence Service to come and fish me from your office? How in broad daylight one of your people was gunned down outside that awful pub? How they knew Warsabi was on that trip to hospital. They have eyes and ears everywhere!"

Frankie slammed his fist into the arm of the sofa he was standing by, "First of all JP, stop saying *they*, you mean *we*, you're part of all this shit, I don't know how deeply, but you're part of it alright. Secondly remember we have the card, we have the data, we now have your balls in our hands. And what's more we fully intend to use it. I don't give a damn about anyone that sanctioned all that, they're as guilty as you are. They deserve all they get. The minute those poor bastards died in that taxi, you were lost. Let alone killing people I care for, no JP this is over for you, and it's over for anyone connected with you."

JP stopped pacing the room, he still had the gun in his hand.

"And how do you plan to do that, finish me off, because the way I see it I have the gun, do I not?"

Gary held a mobile phone up, "I just press this button, it all goes to every news agency in the world, now tell me one of them wouldn't publish? Of course you can't, so sit down and start bloody talking!"

"From the beginning JP, from the beginning, we've got all the time in the world." Frankie added.

-SIXTYONE-
A Policeman From Brittany, Just Investigating A Murder Case?

Felix pressed his foot hard down onto the accelerator, switching on the lights and sirens of the unmarked Police car, he looked across to Sylvia who had unholstered her *Glock 17* pushing a magazine into the handle. The satnav said they still had ten minutes until they reached Mentmore, where they were due to meet up with Frankie, although that time would be reduced considerably, as they made their way around the by-pass that took them past Leighton Buzzard.

The muffled dialogue they were receiving from Frankie's pocket had alerted them that Captain Matrice was armed, and far from friendly, although they were only getting what Frankie was saying, everything else was just unintelligible mumbling, Felix strained to hear what others were saying, but it wasn't easy over the blaring sirens and the roar of the engine.

The screen in front of the windscreen had guided them around a roundabout and onto a winding B-road, which appeared to be made up of at least twenty seven different shades of tarmac where it had been patched up so many times over the preceding years. Sylvia let out a little gasp as the speeding *BMW* literally left the road as they flew over a large bump, traversing what was little more than a lane at close to eighty five miles per hour.

Through the speakers within the car they could hear Frankie, he was in trouble.

"Come on Felix, come on!" Sylvia urged her sergeant.

Felix saying nothing in reply, he was going as fast as he dare, in fact far too fast, the view ahead was limited by a combination of bends in the road, unkempt hedgerows, and the sudden blast of sunshine as they speeded in and out of the shadows. Sylvia had returned her firearm to its holster and had reached over to the back seat, unbuckling her seat belt and wrestling with the dark blue *Kevlar* vest as she slid it over her head, leaning forward in her seat, literally banging her head on the roof lining as they hit another bump in the road…

"You do understand that this conversation effectively signs the death warrants of all present, that you do not want to hear this. But then again it's already too late for all of us now anyway, I do believe our days are numbered, mine certainly are." JP gave an ironic laugh, although there no

THE SHATTERED EAGLE

mirth in it, "So you want the truth, well there is no truth in this, it's all lies and deceit, subterfuge and misdirection. You want to know what happened, then I will tell you, but you must understand we are now the damned, we may breathe, but we are effectively dead men. But that has been your choice, so I will honour your request. Henri DuPont worked for, and indeed still does, the French Intelligence Service. As you know his wife ran a charity called *Compassion Sans Frontieres*, it was a very worthy charity, working to give homes to children who had been involved in African conflicts, the war children that society had dispossessed. For Anna it was a genuine mission, her quest to make life better for those who had gone through so much, whilst still so young, it was her life."

He shuffled on the sofa, briefly closing his eyes, composing himself. Frankie considered rushing toward him, but thought otherwise, partly out of an overpowering survival instinct, in that it would very likely have entailed him being shot dead, and partly because he was rapt by what JP was telling him, keen to hear at last what it was all about.

JP opened his eyes again, "But Henri specialised in, how shall we say, protecting French interests over-seas. With the advent of the Arab Spring, France had a lot of interest that needed protecting, freedom and democracy were one thing, but we were financially bound to some of the old regimes, those interests needed maintaining, nurturing, new powers needed steering in the right direction. They were heady times, uprisings, civil wars, regime change.

Unfortunately these changes did not always go in the direction that the Republic, and her friends, wanted. Sometimes we needed to intervene, turn the tide of opinion towards calmer shores, discredit people, and maybe commit bad things in their name.

"This is where Henri utilised the assets that Anna had provided him with. Part of the charity's work was to educate these boys, hence *Ecole de l'Afrique*, here Henri arranged for sympathetic likeminded people to mould and train these boys, work on their beliefs, indoctrinate their minds, lead them to do what we needed them to. The three other boys Alaine was grouped with all were sent to carry out missions, or atrocities, depending on your point of view. One blew a train up in Egypt, another killed dozens of people in a market place in Libya, the third destroyed a Christian church in Syria, packed with worshippers. All the dead were innocents, but were deemed as being expendable, worth sacrificing. Needless to say these missions caused reverberations around the world, changed minds, and influenced opinions. Sadly these boys were not deemed trustworthy, they were considered liabilities, so it was decided that all loose ends should be tied up, no path left for people to follow to where these boys originated from, so all three were eliminated."

They could see at the top of the hill they were motoring up the sign for 'Mentmore'.

"You know which house it is?" Felix asked.

THE SHATTERED EAGLE

"Yeah, keep on, I'll show you when we get there." Sylvia replied.

As they entered the village Sylvia pointed out the Henderson's home, as Felix turned off the sirens.

"Right, here goes." Felix said...

JP walked around the room, apparently oblivious to the sirens which had appeared to be getting increasingly nearer before suddenly going silent, Frankie knew that Sylvia and Felix had arrived. Watching JP he could see he looked genuinely ashamed of what he was saying. But like some overburdened parishioner in a confessional he needed to carry on, and whilst he was carrying on he wasn't shooting anyone, and that had to be a good thing.

"Henri of course was not working alone, he was part of the *Legion Secret de la Republique* there were four of them, the only four people to have been awarded the ring. They were involved in much work of what could be perceived as being of a dubious nature, but feared betrayal, so recorded what they did, and each kept a copy. Henri on the card you now possess. Unfortunately Alaine DuPont realised what was happening, how he was being manipulated. He was always the most intelligent, yet also difficult of the boys, he was naturally bad, but also wilful and rebellious. Once he knew his three friends had died, he took his revenge on Henri, the way he knew would hurt him most, that being upon Anna. He then stole the jewellery from her bedroom, taking with him, unwittingly, the ring.

"We have since found out, that following that, he fled to North Africa. There he touted around his skills, doing some, for lack of a better term, freelance work, for whoever would pay him."

Frankie interrupted, "And how do you know that?"

"We've spoken to him of course. He was very reluctant to say too much, but eventually he opened up for us, quite literally actually. But unfortunately we hadn't found him in time to prevent him coming over here. He planted that awful bomb on that train, doing the work of al-Qaeda, for a huge reward. But that drew attention to him, we identified him before you did, our people nearly got him the next day. He ran scared, I presume he figured he was better in prison than in our sights, so he got himself arrested. It was all just a case of throwing money in the right direction after that, some of your countrymen are very easily influenced by large sums of money, ensuring we had people on our side that could help us.

"We didn't want to harm anybody, but the greater good made it necessary. We knew he had the ring, or at least did when he was arrested, so we thought we could bring Alaine home, and recover the information contained behind the eagle at the same time. But alas young Mr Allen here was a bit too nimble with his fingers. That's when it all got complicated. I think we all know the rest, do we not?"

"And what's your part in this JP? Just a Policeman from Brittany investigating a murder case?" Frankie scoffed. "What brought you into this, DuPont's money? What was it that turned you into a murderer? Someone who stands by and watches people he has worked with get killed?"

"Let's call it duty Frankie."

"No it's not fucking duty, you know that, your duty is to protect, your duty is uphold the law, not ride roughshod all over it. You're a disgrace man, and you're going down for it, you're doing big time JP!"

"Wait!" Oli interrupted. "You said only four people possess the rings, the members of the Legion of whatever it is, you have a ring, Frankie has a picture of you at the Presidents place, you must be one of them!"

Felix and Sylvia darted from the car, running around the side of the house, both had their weapons drawn, as they reached the end of the path they could see the patio doors open, could hear voices.

Felix drew his index finger to lips, Sylvia nodding in reply as they both moved towards the open doors in silence.

"Alas Oli, you still don't get it do you? Frankie does, I think he has since he saw the photograph of me with the ring, despite what he has just asked, either that or I underestimate you considerably Frankie. There is no Captain Matrice, just a man who has made some dreadful mistakes. I will take responsibility for everything, the blame, the shame and stigma of being a traitor to all he holds dear. I am now just a man who misses his wife terribly, a man who caused her death, a man who needs to make amends. Please forgive me for all I have done."

"Armed Police! Drop your weapon." Felix and Sylvia swung into the room where Matrice had his back to them, but he made no effort to turn, not even acknowledging the two officer's presence, his eyes fixed on Frankie's.

At that moment Frankie knew neither he nor any of the others were in danger, no more words were needed, he could see JP's eyes welling up, and knew all too well what was going to follow, even before JP had whispered, "Pardon mon ami."

JP pulled up the gun, Frankie sprang forward to grab it from him, shouting "No!"

Two bullets tore into the Frenchman's left leg, as he raised the weapon.

It was too late, Henri DuPont, who had nothing to live for, died instantly, the top of his skull was spread around the room with his brain raining down on the horrified on lookers, after he had discharged his *FAMAS* Assault Rifle into his own head.

THE SHATTERED EAGLE

-SIXTYTWO-
Funeral For A Friend.

Chief Superintendent Gail Hopkiss sat behind her huge mahogany desk, she pressed her intercom and said, "Send him in please."

Frankie entered the room wearing his dress uniform, his shoes were polished to a glass like shine, his hat was tucked under his arm, and Lilly-white gloves adorned each hand.

"Thank you Adrian for taking the time to see me, I appreciate it's a difficult time for you, and I am truly grateful for all you've done."

"Thank you Ma'am." Frankie replied.

"I wanted to talk to you before the ceremony, just to, how should I put it, clarify matters. Obviously there has been an awful lot of fall out over the past couple of days, and as the dust settles more and more innocent people are being covered in dirt, I would like to…"

"Can I stop you there Ma'am," Frankie interrupted. He leant over her desk, his hat resting between his hands, which were splayed over the desk top as he hissed, "I do hope you are not going to say what I think you are. I really do hope that. Because I think it's only fair to say had you not acted the way you did the other day Detective

Constable Peter Daggett would be enjoying a pint in the pub with me around now, and not being put in some fucking hole surrounded by…"

"DCI Howard! Can I remind you who you are talking to!"

"Oh I know who I am talking to, I know only too well, I'm talking to the woman who ordered me to allow Henri DuPont to leave my office when I could have questioned him. I'm talking to the bitch who allowed Pete Daggett to have a bullet pumped into his brain, and who would have been quite happy to have seen me, Hardacre, and Fernando blown out at the same time. How dare you call me here, on this day of all days, and try and weasel out of this. It's not happening, do you hear!"

Frankie cast a look that defied her to argue, challenged her to question what he was saying, but she said nothing.

He leaned back into the chair, picking a piece of lint from his hat, considering what to say next, before continuing his voice very calm, all matter of fact, "Now I will tell you what is happening. I'm walking out of this office now, and I'm going to bury my friend. You, you will not step a foot anywhere near that church, do you hear me. Now I'm not going to hang you out Gail, God knows I should, but I'm giving you this one chance, and this offer is just for today. Whilst I cry, which I'm sure I will, at the loss of my good friend, you will quit, you will phone up the Commissioner and you will resign. Make up any reason you like, but you better be gone when I walk in this building tomorrow. Are we clear Chief Superintendent?"

THE SHATTERED EAGLE

Hopkiss said nothing, just stared ahead.

"I said are we clear? Because you need to be sure that if you're still here, my God I will personally throw you out on your skinny horrible arse. Now one last time, are we clear?"

She whispered just one word. "Yes."

Adrian Howard had now worn his dress uniform on two occasions in the space of a week, he'd attended the funeral of Craig Lovan just two days earlier, a man he hardly knew, yet admired and liked immensely, and now he was carrying the coffin containing the body of Peter Daggett into All Saints Church, in his beloved Peckham. As they carried the Union Jack draped casket from the hearse he looked in front, Sylvia and Felix were also dressed as he was, he wondered how anyone managed to find a plain shirt in Felix's wardrobe, but then this definitely wasn't a Hawaiian shirt occasion.

There was a third funeral which Frankie hadn't attended, on the same day as Pete's, Henri DuPont was afforded no Military Honours or Grand Farewell, instead cremated at a small service, and his ashes sprinkled onto the sands of a beach close to the home he once shared with Anna. None of the three remaining members of the *Legion Secret de la Republique* attended the actual service. But Harold Latterdam, who had taken over the mission in England, killing Lovan and Pete, after they had decided Henri was not capable of doing it, watched through a pair of binoculars.

A tear flowed down his cheek, he was just pleased that Henri, in taking his own life had saved him the task of eliminating his old friend at Michel and Claude's behest. It had been nine days since the contents of '*Retours d'Aigle d'Opertation*' had been leaked to the world wide press. It had been reported as being the work of a French traitor, working alone for his own interests, Harold and his two cohorts were not even mentioned in any of the ridiculous conspiracy theories that circulated around the internet and corridors of Government buildings throughout Paris.

No one stood trial for the Euston Bombing, as without Abu Warsabi there was no culprit to put on trial. American Navy SEALS, during a raid on a noted al-Qaeda stronghold in the border region of Pakistan, discovered a host of paper work relating to the attack, including plans and details of money wired to a Swiss Account of one Abu Warsabi, but no survivors existed to ascertain any further information.

THE SHATTERED EAGLE

-EPILOGUE-
The Last Of The Loose Ends Get Tied Up.

Just outside Mogadishu was a dusty truck stop, it served mostly rice dishes and meat of dubious origins, disguised by a combination of fragrant spices and herbs. The old 1950's gas pumps were like relics from a museum, but still did an adequate job, even if they weren't entirely accurate, with any discrepancy always in the owners favour, but for such a service people needed to expect to pay a small premium. The heat was almost unbearable, even the flies were reluctant to buzz around the shit, preserving their energy until the dumpsters were opened around the back. The car park was almost empty but for a battered *Volkswagen* panel van parked out front.

The city shimmered in the distance, as Papa P looked out for possible business down the road, strewn either side with old tyres, piles of paper and assorted junk, which had been sorted through so many times it all truly served no useful purpose what so ever other than make the whole road look like a giant elongated landfill site.

He saw a spot emerging from the horizon, a shiny vehicle in the distance, glinting as it moved down the highway. Maybe it would be a minibus full of thirsty construction workers returning to one of the rural villages surrounding the city, a few freshly earned shillings in their pockets to spend on fizzy drinks and some food, he certainly needed the trade today, it had been almost dead, just a moped filling its tiny tank with gas, and a couple of truck drivers stopping off for some tea and a chat, besides that nothing.

The vehicle drew nearer it was travelling at speed, behind it dust in vast plumes, like it was towing a big storm. As it closed in he could see it was a *Toyota Land Cruiser*, silver or white, he ambled back into his dilapidated diner, it was either a westerner or warlord driving a vehicle like that, neither was likely to stop and buy any Nafaqo.

He pulled a bottle of *Fanta* from the rattling fridge, surely it would give up the ghost soon, it was practically held together with string and tin foil, the thing was nearly as old as he was, but he could ill afford to spend money on a new refrigerator, so he just hoped, as he did every day, that it would see him through until closing time. He popped the top off the bottle, and took a long hard swig from it, before emitting a loud belch, it was ice cold, just what he needed, that was probably his profit for the day he was drinking, but what the hell, man's got to live.

He saw the *Land Cruiser* slowing down, drawing to a halt, well maybe there would be some trade after all. It pulled up just past the pumps. Ha, ha, a tank that big, that's worth 100 mopeds! But then he saw the back door

THE SHATTERED EAGLE

swing open and a bundle of something rolled out onto the gravel floor, before the vehicle sped off, the door closing as it went. Papa P just stood and stared, hundreds of miles of highway to dump their trash on, and they go to the trouble of turning into his truck stop and dumping their shit.

He walked over to the bundle, a car like that may have generated some decent trash, they clearly had money. He looked down, it was the most hideous sight he had ever seen. It was a wretched thing indeed. A naked man, half covered by a blanket, skin torn and grazed from being deposited onto the gravel, devoid of any limbs at all, just short foul stumps, the hideous wounds still not healed, stitched together like the twisted ends of hotdogs. Papa P couldn't even think of him as a person, he was an 'it'. It gurgled, from a toothless mouth, unable to speak where its tongue had been removed, its face swollen and bruised almost making it impossible to tell whether it was in fact human at all.

"Oh Allah, oh my lord." Papa P said to himself.

The monstrosity was twitching on the floor, like a bloated slug in salt. Papa P, drew hard on his matchstick thin cigarette.

"What to do with you?" he said to the pitiful specimen at his feet, which just continued to twitch and wriggle, he was unable to tell if it was even looking back at him, due to the fact both eyes were just puffy bruises, swollen like two ripe mangos.

Yes what to do with it? It couldn't stay there, he had no intention of looking after it, tending to such wounds, he felt sick just looking at it, let alone bringing it into his house. He could call what masqueraded as the Police, but that would just bring trouble his way, they would just want paying to deal with it, and it wasn't going to cost him money, and even then they sure as hell wouldn't look after it. The thought of taking it to a hospital was ludicrous, there was no way he was driving that into the city, and once again it would only attract the attention of the Police, looking for bribes and pay offs.

No they weren't the sort of things a wise old owner of a truck stop eight miles out of Mogadishu would do.

He went round the back of his diner and wheeled the rusting dumpster around to where 'it' lay. He pushed the top open whilst holding the bottom of his filthy shirt over his mouth and nose, flies swarmed out, the stench was unbearable, decay and rot permeated from the open skip. The thing on the floor continued to jerk and twitch. Papa P, stood over it and gathered the corners of the blanket so that it was lying on the floor in a hammock like cocoon. He summoned all his strength and hoisted the bundle into the dumpster, he heard it fall into the putrid waste within, before he quickly shut the lid. He looked at dozens of fat maggots crawling along the lip where the door met the top.

Hmm, he felt kind of bad, but what else was he to do? They, those guys in the *Land Cruiser*, dumped it there, not

THE SHATTERED EAGLE

him, and if at some point in the future it was discovered, well they must have put it in there, not old Papa P.

Three days later, partially devoured alive by maggots Abu Warsabi already insane and mentally tortured beyond belief, squirming around in a pain no living soul could imagine, found his peace, for the hell he knew he was destined for was still infinitely preferable to one he was living in at that moment, the moment his wrecked and mutilated body finally let him go.

COLIN PAYNE

Also available in this series:

There's No Dignity In This
*

No Loose Ends
*

The Strange Tale Of The Missing Lord
*

Crash Dump
*

The Hunt For Amelia Clay

For more information please visit:
www.facebook.com/groups/theshatteredeagle
www.collers100g.wordpress.com

Made in the USA
Charleston, SC
16 September 2014